William McKendree Bryant

Life, Death and Immortality

with kindred essays

William McKendree Bryant

Life, Death and Immortality
with kindred essays

ISBN/EAN: 9783337397951

Printed in Europe, USA, Canada, Australia, Japan

Cover: Foto ©Andreas Hilbeck / pixelio.de

More available books at **www.hansebooks.com**

LIFE DEATH
AND IMMORTALITY

WITH KINDRED ESSAYS

BY

WILLIAM M. BRYANT, M. A., LL. D.

INSTRUCTOR IN PSYCHOLOGY AND ETHICS ST. LOUIS NORMAL
AND HIGH SCHOOL

New York

THE BAKER AND TAYLOR CO.

5 AND 7 EAST SIXTEENTH STREET

1898

PREFACE.

The essays comprised in this volume have developed one by one during a number of years past. It will be found that all of them are really upon one common theme—the religious aspect of human nature.

For the time being negative criticism of Christianity as based upon the "Sacred Writings," appears to have fairly exhausted its resources. And in doing so it has performed the very great service of preparing the way for further positive interpretation of the fundamental conceptions which constitute the core of the Christian doctrine as to man's nature and destiny. The studies here presented are offered as a contribution in the direction of such positive interpretation.

Four of the essays, it should be added, have previously been published in full—that on Buddhism and

Christianity, in the *Andover Review;* the second, the sixth, and the last, (as well as part of the first) in the *Unitarian Review*. The last essay has also been printed separately as a booklet.

CONTENTS.

ERRATA.

Of the misprints the following are those materially
affecting the sense :

Page 35, line 13 from above, omit *not.*

Page 124, line 2 from above, for *unit* read *unity.*

Page 208, last line (foot note), for 236 read 136.

Page 225, line 3 from below, for *lyrism* read *lyricism.*

Page 278, line 5 from below, for *resistance* read *existence.*

Page 337, line 5 from below, for *motive* read *nature.*

Page 402, line 5 from above, for *care* read *core.*

I.

LIFE, DEATH AND IMMORTALITY.[1]

[FROM THE STANDPOINT OF THE CONSERVATION OF ENERGY.]

1. *The Origin of Life.*

When it was suggested a number of years ago in one of the leading scientific assemblies of the world that the origin of life on the earth may have been due to the chance transmission through space of a primordial germ wrapped up in a meteorite, a discovery of real significance appeared to have been made. All the world was duly notified. And apparently all the world was expected to be duly content thereafter, as if nothing further was to be said concerning the previously much vexed question of the "Beginnings of Life."

The suggestion, as well as its ready acceptance by men of science, was indeed quite in keeping with an opinion more or less prevalent and which came to be formulated by the authors of "The Unseen Universe," to the effect that "it is not so much the right or privilege as the bounden duty of the men of science to put

---

[1] For a statement of the presuppositions of this essay the reader is referred to my volume: "*The World-Energy and its Self-Conservation.*"

back the direct interference of the Great First Cause —the unconditioned—as far as he possibly can in time."[1]

What the Great First Cause could possibly "interfere" with or in, outside of its own legitimate domain, or what possible efficiency "the man of science" can or could have to "put back" such interference in time in any degree, does not seem altogether evident on first glance to the non-"scientific" eye. Still less does it seem evident when one takes into account the full significance of the doctrine of the Conservation of Energy, upon which the man of science, with excellent reasons, lays so much stress.

In non-scientific ages, when people had not yet learned to really think, but only gave loose rein to their phantasy, they saw nothing contradictory in the supposition that any given portion of matter might wholly cease to exist, or that the non-existent might become solid reality. But now everyone knows how experimental science long since awakened men to critical habits of thinking, and how the mind, once awakened to this state, finds it utterly inconceivable that something should become nothing, or that nothing should become something. Form or mode of existence may here and there change—nay, *must* ceaselessly and everywhere change. But that

---

[1] First Edition, p. 131.

the total quantity of Energy should ever change is utterly unthinkable. It may indeed be *imagined*, for imagination is never troubled by a contradiction. But *thought* utterly and spontaneously repudiates contradiction. And the more clearly the contradiction is recognized as such, the more is it seen to be something absolutely and forever foreign to thought. The consistent alone can be received into the thinking consciousness and maintained there.

The "man of science" then is bound to recognize, and indeed is constantly insisting, that the total quantity of Energy is changeless. Nothing can be added to it ; nothing can be taken from it. And if this be true of the total quantity of Energy it must be true of each one of its modes. Each is a mode of the total Energy. Each is the total Energy in one of its modes. So that if in any given locality a given mode of Energy increases in degree, it must be through a corresponding decrease in degree of the same mode elsewhere. Doubtless locally the various modes of Energy are interchangeable. The disappearance of heat as heat at any given point must ever be the obverse of the coming into manifestation at the same point of an exactly equivalent amount of light, or of sound, or of electric tension, or of expansion of a mass of matter, or of all these combined. But as a whole the total Energy must, in its very nature as an unchanging total, preserve each of its modes undiminished, unchanged in its total compass as a mode of the total Energy.

But now assuming that the total Energy is forever the same, there is to be considered the further question : Can Energy be conceived scientific illy, can it really be *thought* as ever in any other state than that of total and complete activity? And the only answer which the really thinking mind can make to this would seem to be that Energy cannot exist otherwise than as active. Its activity is its existence. Were it partially inactive, it would be partially non-existent. And thus if it could ever for a moment cease its activity in whole or in part, then it would in that fact cease to exist in whole or in part. So that the total Energy as changeless cannot be conceived otherwise than as changelessly active.

That would seem to be the real meaning of the phrase : "Total quantity of Energy." And if so, then the Total Energy must be one and the same with the "Great First Cause," to the activity of which is due every phase of Reality. Whence it seems evident that the Great First Cause is a Power which in its changeless completeness is forever equal to itself in its activity, and hence also in the product of its activity. And if this is true, then it could not at some period "as far back in time" as "the man of science" can push it, have created a world and afterward left it to spin on of its own accord, without "interference," for an indefinite period following. Rather that same Great First Cause, whose creative activity was needful to give the world its existence at the "beginning," is not less needful, and perpetually needful, to maintain the world in its existence—as was long ago recognized and explicitly affirmed by Des Cartes. "In truth," he says, "it is perfectly clear and evident to all who will attentively consider the nature of duration, that the conservation of a substance, in each moment of its duration, requires the same power and act that would be necessary to create it, supposing it were not yet in existence ; so that it is manifestly a dictate of the natural light that conservation and creation differ merely in respect of our mode of thinking."[1]

Thus, whether we regard the phenomena of the world beyond us or the phenomena of the world within us, we are driven to recognize the fact that "each order of manifestations carries with it the irresistible implication of some power that manifests itself."[2] And ultimately these manifestations are nothing else than modes of activity of the Total Energy ; or, to use a phrase of Mr. Spencer's, they are "modes of manifestation of the Unknowable."[3] But we have

[1] *Meditations*, p. 48, trans. (5th Ed.) Edinburg.

[2] Herbert Spencer, *First Principles*, (N.Y. Ed.) p. 154.

[3] op. cit. p. 122.

already seen that the Total Energy must be perpetually and totally active ; so that the "Unknowable," as in a state of perpetual and absolute self-manifestation, may just as well be named the Progressively-Knowable to the finite mind—the progressive aspect belonging solely to the finite mind as advancing in power to comprehend the changeless Total Power. In other words, the Great First Cause is not merely a chronological first. It is the first, last, only and eternal Cause forever self-manifested in the total round of Creation as its infinitely adequate Effect. Cause and Effect are in truth but complementary aspects of the same Total. Cause cannot be where Effect is not ; and where effect is there and in that very fact is Cause, open, manifest, revealed as present, active, actual and knowable.

In short when one thinks, really *thinks* and does not merely follow the lead of his phantasy, concerning the Total Energy or Great First Cause, he cannot but see that, as applied to it, time has no meaning. For it there can be neither yesterday nor to-morrow, but only a changeless Now of absolute perfection. Within it every phase of change is perpetually present. If "here and now" there is a world in bloom, elsewhere and now there are worlds in the bud, and yet other worlds in the germinal state, and elsewhere still other worlds in fruitage, and again elsewhere worlds in decay. In the total round of the manifestations of the forever self-equal Energy, the full range of Integration is precisely balanced by the full range of Disintegration, as Mr. Spencer might phrase it; or if we use the symbols of Heraclitus, the Way Upward and the Way Downward are the unvarying reciprocals of the total, unchanging Process of Becoming.

In short if it be granted that the total Creative Process—that is, the entire range of activity involved in the conservation of Energy throughout space—is a process complete in itself and therefore absolutely unchanging, then all modes of existence must be perpetually represented in the total, ceaseless Result. So that, so far as appears, it would be just as well for the "man of science" to dispense with any further efforts to "put back" the activity of the Great First Cause in time, and, instead of this, to devote himself to lifting his own thought out of the forms of time into what Spinoza calls the "form of Eternity;" so far, at least, as to recognize the presence and activity of that Cause in every phase of reality.

And now to what does all this point respecting the "origin" of Life? Is it not precisely this: that Life itself is simply one of the necessary and hence perpetual factors in the total Process of the Universe? In other words, the truth appears to be that Life, as a necessary phase in the total process of creative Intelligence, must be *incessantly beginning* and therefore an *eternal fact*. Thus, as in any given locality, matter advances in this process "from the [comparatively] homogeneous to the [comparatively] heterogeneous," a stage of complexity must be reached in which the transition from the inorganic to the organic is just as "natural" as at another stage is the transition from the state of fusion to the crystalline state.

And so the exigencies of the case do not seem to call for the importation to our world of a primordial germ from the "void inane;" though it must be confessed that the conception of such wondrous voyage of Life from world to world is a very picturesque one—rivaling more than successfully the celebrated Trip to the Moon once made by a well-known Frenchman with his two or three companions.

It would seem indeed that "the man of science" should be the last to complain if the doctrine of the Conservation of Energy as unfolded in the general theory of Evolution is taken seriously and pressed to its logical—i. e. legitimate—conclusions. This, in truth, the man of science himself professes to do and not to complain of anyone else having done. And so, after having in one noted representative proposed the solution of the mystery of the origin of Life by the importation theory, he returned to First Principles in the person of another and declared that "matter" itself contains "the promise and potency of all terrestrial life." All the world, it would seem, should be astonished by so bold a solution of the problem. And for a little while a considerable part of the world was foolish enough to be not only astonished but duly alarmed and even angered.

And yet what does this latter solution signify but that scientific eyes recognize matter to be nothing else than a mode of Energy, a mode of the ultimate Substance which one may just as well frankly name the eternal, divinely rational, creative Power. In fact, the "man of science" himself is coming to recognize, along with the theologian, that all these later discussions concerning Energy are, in truth, but a widening and enriching of that conception which men have always held in one or another form, and which they have represented by some such term as "God." And so if it be said that matter contains the promise and potency of all terrestrial life, that can only mean, so far as it means anything, that matter is but one stage or phase of the total creative Process leading up, without the least break of continuity, from the relatively inert, space-filling modes of the divine Energy, through living units that are still predominantly physical, to a spontaneous, divinely gifted unit, capable of tracing out the main threads of the whole wondrous Process and of living that Process over again, at least in a dim way, in his own conscious existence.

The mystery of the Beginnings of Life, then, is no

greater intrinsically than the mystery which inheres
in the beginning of a crystal. The same totality of
Energy is required to explain the existence of the one
no less than to explain the existence of the other. In
the one case indeed the unit is "organic," while in
the other it is "inorganic." That is, the one performs certain functions requiring certain organs; and
the performance of these functions is itself a process
necessary to the existence of the organic unit. The
moment the process ceases that moment the unit
ceases to exist as an organic unit—a fact which, it
seems, Aristotle did not fail to notice. For he is reported to have remarked that a hand which has been
cut off has ceased from that moment to be a hand.
It performs no function ; there is no function performed in it. It is no longer an *organ* and is thus
essentially no longer in strict sense *organic*. It is
simply equivalent to so much inorganic matter, as its
dissolution or "decay" will speedily show. On the
other hand, while the crystal comes into existence
through a process, that process must be suspended if
the crystal is to be preserved. So that the crystalline
state is one of arrested process ; while the organic
state is one of continuous process. The crystal is
preserved by arrest of the process which formed it.
The organic unit is destroyed by stopping the process
through which it has come to be what it is.

2. *The Significance of Life.*

Thus we come to Mr. Spencer's definition of Life as the "continuous adjustment of inner relations to outer relations."[1]   It is not merely an adjustment ; it is a *continuous* adjustment.   And this already gives to the living unit the unique characteristic of self-movement, of which characteristic, as Mr. Spencer declares, "the lowest animal and the highest animal present no contrast more striking than that between the small self mobility of the one and the great self-mobility of the other."[2]

In short, if we begin with the highest organisms, and if while tracing the whole series backward, we note the steadily diminishing degree of self-mobility, we must expect to find at length an insensible transition from the unit having the least degree of self-mobility to a unit which is merely inert—which has no self-mobility at all ; and yet which *has* the *premonition* of self-mobility in its attraction for every other portion of matter.   So that the appearance of the simplest living unit on the surface of a planet on which organisms had not previously existed, must be but the next natural stage of advance in complexity beyond the ultimate limit of heterogeneity in inorganic matter as such ; just as the advance in the com-

---

[1] *First Principles*, p. 84.
[2] *Principles of Psychology*, opening sentence.

plexity of organisms from the lowest to the highest type is but a further manifestation of the same creative Energy, the continuous activity of which can alone be conceived as sufficient to account alike for the beginnings, the continuance, and the development of Life—whether on this planet or on another, from which latter Life might in vivid poetic fancy be conceived as finding transportation to this, *via* the meteoric line.

But Mr. Spencer's definition of Life presents us directly with the terms of a relation which it seems important to carefully consider. The terms are : "inner" and "outer." Let us try to discover as precisely as we may the relation here involved. And first, the merely physical, the merely space-filling phases of existence appear to be justly characterized as purely external. Any given mass of matter is said to have its outer and its inner parts. But the mass may be divided ; and thus parts that were before regarded as "inner" now appear as "outer." And this possibility has no limit whatever in thought. No particle of matter can be so small but that further division is conceived as possible. So that the "inner" parts of a given mass of matter must always be thought of as separable, as being side-by-side with one another, and hence as outside of one another. Hence however small the particles may be conceived to be in a given mass of matter, each particle is still "outer" or outside of every other particle, and thus in reality presents no phase that can be rightly regarded as "inner."

Thus, secondly, we come to enquire what must be the nature of that unit which can rightly be regarded as possessing the characteristic of internality. And here again we may borrow a clew from Mr. Spencer, though it is not so certain that he would approve of the use to which it is proposed here to apply it. The clew is to be found in the distinction which Mr. Spencer makes between the "objective" and the "subjective." The latter is the "world of consciousness." The former is the "world beyond consciousness," while both are "manifestations of the Unknowable."[1] Thus the physical is "objective" while mind is "subjective." Things are objective. Thought is subjective.

And now as we have just seen that things, in the sense of those facts which we know as the "physical" world, are characterized by externality to such a degree as that they present no phase to which the term "inner" can be rightly applied, it would seem that if the term "inner" is to find any point of application at all it must find it in the subjective or thought world. And this seems the more reasonable when we reflect that as a matter of fact the term "outer" is

---

[1] *First Principles*, p. 156. It is interesting to observe, by the way, how, even in Mr. Spencer's own phrase, the Unknowable, "manifests itself"—makes itself *known*.

as little applicable to thought as the correlative term "inner" is to things. For thought cannot be conceived as having dimensions in space. It can be conceived only as an activity which may indeed have reference to objects occupying space, but which cannot itself be bounded by or in space. Indeed thought has certain modes that have no reference to space or space-related objects. It may be directed upon mind itself in any of its modes ; and manifestly in such case its interests are essentially subjective or inner. It is a definite unit definitely related to itself ; that is, its activity is not directed upon some "outer" object, but is concentrated *within itself*. Self-relation—that is the essential characteristic of mind, and self-relation proves also to be of the very essence of internality. Mind is the "inner" then, and is thus the antithesis of matter as the "outer."

And yet it is important to note more explicitly that "outer" and "inner" are not merely antithetical terms, but rather that they are correlatives, and thus that either term in isolation must be wholly meaningless. The inner, if it is any phase of reality, must be the *inner of the outer*. The subjective is such only in immediate relation with the objective.

We will not stop here to consider what possible other meanings might attach to the terms subjective and objective (as that in the use of certain German thinkers, where subjective means "arbitrary" or "capricious ;" and objective means : universal, valid, true), but will proceed to follow out our newly found clew in its application to Life. As the inner is the subjective, then inner relations must be subjective relations. And as outer is objective, then outer relations must be objective relations. Whence it would seem that Life may be redefined as the continuous adjustment of subjective relations to objective relations. And if it be objected that this is inapplicable to vegetal life, it is to be answered that the terms subjective and objective, like the terms inner and outer, are of varying degree, and that wherever there is a living unit, there also is to be found as the central factor of such living unit the quality of internality or subjectivity. The more advanced the form of life the more manifest the characteristic of subjectivity is invariably found to be. Or, as Professor Huxley has said, "The lowest plant, or animalcule, feeds, grows and reproduces its kind. In addition, all animals manifest those transitory changes of form which we class under irritability and contractility ; and it is more than probable that, when the vegetable world is thoroughly explored, we shall find all plants in possession of the same powers, at one time or another of their existence."[1]

In other words the evolution of Life is the process

[1] Lecture on *The Physical Basis of Life.*

of the unfolding of intelligence in ever-increasingly adequate modes of conscious existence. And this is shown in the premonitional stage by what Darwin has described as the *Power of Movement in Plants,* and which Professor Gray has illustrated briefly in his little work entitled: "*How Plants Behave;*" while it is substantially affirmed, in respect of the more advanced order of life, in what is now a commonplace of science : that the measure of superiority in an animal organism is the degree of complexity of its nervous structure, which is of course in its turn the direct instrumentality of intelligence.

And this, manifestly, is in perfect keeping with what was before indicated ; namely, that the various phases of complexity in the inorganic world culminate in a state of matter, one further degree in the complexity of which must transform it into living matter ; must evolve, through increased complexity of relations in the external, objective or physical aspect of existence, the characteristic of the internal, subjective or psychical aspect of existence—the latter being destined, through unbroken continuity of the Process, to advance in adequacy until there arises a being of the highest possible type. And since intelligence is the mark of superiority (measured physically by the degree of complexity of the nervous system as instrumentality of intelligence), then the "continuous adjustment of inner relations to outer relations" must as a subjective process consist in the advance from the vaguest phase of subjectivity or conscious existence to the most complex and adequate phase—-from an amœba to a Shakespeare. And that contrast which Mr. Spencer finds the most striking of all as between the lowest animal and the highest animal—namely, the contrast in self-mobility —is in truth essentially a contrast involved in the advance from the living unit which is predominantly physical to the living unit which is predominantly psychical. So that the system of Evolution, as Mr. Spencer presents it, appears to be in its most important aspects just an elaborate description of the mode in which man is ever to "struggle upward out of nature into spirituality," as Hegel[1] had already expressed it. And these utterances but reaffirm, each in its own way, that man was "made of the dust of the earth"—"dust" being, let us repeat, nothing else than one essential mode of the divine Energy.

On the other hand the "outer" relations to which the inner relations are continuously adjusted in the process of life—what are they? The living, the conscious, the rational unit is unfolded through a continuous adjustment of the inner or subjective relations to those "outer" relations. Mind, the general type of intelligence, finds its realization in each indi-

---

[1] *Werke*, 2te Auflage, X², 120.

vidual thinking unit through this adjustment, as it takes place directly on the part of such unit, and also in a still wider sense as the adjustment takes place indirectly on the part of the whole race. So that there must be some characteristic in these "outer" relations which is after all quite like in nature to mind itself, since it is only by adjustment of itself to these outer relations that mind can become realized at all.

And now when examined more closely the whole range of the "outer" relations constitutes, as already pointed out, a system, or as Mr. Spencer names it, an "established order."[1]   But this system or established order may just as well be regarded—nay, cannot but be regarded—as the *Method* of the activity which the perfect Power or eternally self-conserved Energy must ever exhibit in changeless self-consistency.

It is evident then that what constitutes the sum of relations which to each individual created mind are "outer," can hardly be anything else than the manifestation, or utterance, or *outerance* of the perfect Power in its consciously-pursued method. For, as already intimated, the "outer" is in necessary relation with the "inner,"—is, in short, just the outer of the inner.   And when we consider these terms in respect of the total Energy, that which is "outer" to the finite mind proves to be nothing else than the ex-

---

[1] *First Principles*, p. 117.

pression or complex mode of manifestation of the infinitely manifold Thought of the divine Mind—of that ultimate Internality or Spontaneity which is referred to, often vaguely enough, as the "Great First Cause." It would seem then that this is the secret of the marvelous efficiency of these "outer relations" as stimulus and guidance for the individual created mind in its struggle upward out of nature into spirituality. At first indeed this struggle takes place blindly through vague instinct; and yet at length it proceeds consciously through realized reason. It is thus that the living unit of the higher order adjusts its inner relations to the outer relations in the midst of which its evolution takes place. And this unit characterized by realized reason becomes increasingly capable of tracing through these outer relations the evidences of a subjectivity precisely like its own in nature, though also immeasurably different from its own in the fact that it is absolutely perfect in realization. Even Mr. Spencer, with his insistent use of the term Unknowable as descriptive of the Ultimate Power, finds himself driven to a conclusion which would seem to be not far removed from that just reached. For in tracing the relation of the "faint states" to the "vivid states" of consciousness, he notes that states not self-produced, or, in other words, states not dependent upon one's own voluntary activity, are inevitably associated with those states which are so produced. Without voluntary activity I find myself experiencing states of consciousness which are like those following upon my own voluntary activity. And along with the former states there arise ''nascent thoughts of some energy akin to that which I used myself.''[1] In other words, I cannot in reality conceive of Cause without conceiving of it as ultimately a conscious Power. I cannot get rid of the conviction that body, or the resistant, is in all its forms merely the medium, or rather mode, of communication between initial force and initial force—between mind and mind.

In its fullest reality, then, life is a psychical process : a process which in its culmination consists of intellectual and moral activity. Always life is a constructive process. And, in this highest range which we are now considering, it is a constructive process in which intellectual and moral characteristics are the chief factors concerned. The fixed order of the World, which is in fact nothing else than the Method of the perfect Power, precisely that is the sum-total of ''outer relations'' to which the thinking unit must adjust all its inner life if it would truly live.

Rightly considered, then, this constructive process of Life, here regarded in its highest range of development as Life in its intellectual and moral aspects,

---

[1] *Principles of Psychology*, II. 475; cf. the whole chapter.

is but a phase, though it be also the highest phase, in the unbroken process of Evolution. The Total Energy, forever self-conserved, cannot but ceaselessly unfold, and forever present in its own unchanging Totality, every phase of this Process from the simplest to the most adequate phase possible. No factor can ever be wanting. The total change-producing Power is itself absolutely changeless; while within it, as phases of it, there must perpetually arise living units of each and every degree of complexity, from the simplest possible organism to that unit whose nature it is to advance out of the passive, dependent state of merely initial self-mobility to an ever-increasing degree of activity, of independence, of relatively great self mobility. And what in each unit begins as a self-mobility of the predominantly objective or physical type, changes more and more into a self-mobility of the subjective or psychical type.

Thus in such unit the continuous adjustment of inner relations to outer relations rises by degrees into a more and more explicit adjustment of the intellectual and moral powers of such unit to what he progressively discovers to be the fixed order of the world, the unalterable method of the Perfect Power— to the modes of the divine Thought as expressed in all forms of existence. It would seem, therefore, that Science, as the process by which man comes to comprehend one after another of the various phases of the fixed order of the world, is in its highest significance just one essential factor in the larger process by which man as the highest order of living units is ever, and with ever-increasing success, adjusting his inner or psychical relations to all "outer" or physical relations ; while still further factors in the same complex process are found in the steadily widening range of commerce and manufactures guided by Science, and in the means to the cultivation of the best qualities in the individual which the social world affords in ever-increasing degree of wise elaboration. And the further this process advances with each individual, the more evident must it become to him that the universal forms or modes of activity manifest in the objective world are after all precisely the universal forms or modes by which he is to guide his own inner or subjective activity if he would make any advance in the scale of being. Mr. Spencer declares that : "If there are any universal forms of the *non-ego*, these must establish corresponding universal forms in the *ego*."[1]   And why shall we not say more confidently that the universal forms or modes of the Total Energy, which become more and more evident to man as man advances in intelligence, are just those modes which are of necessity forever realized

---

[1] *Principles of Psychology*, II, 363.

in the Total Energy, and which man realizes stage by stage in his own life? for thus and thus only is the evolution of man in the highest sense to be accomplished. That is the highest term of the adjustment of inner relations to outer relations. That is the supreme significance of Life.

Let us dwell a moment longer on this point of increasing complexity of inner relations. We have already seen that advance in complexity of ''inner relations'' is essentially the same as advance in psychical qualities. Besides this it has also been seen that between the lowest animal and the highest animal there is a striking difference in the degree of self-mobility. It is true that self-mobility in Mr. Spencer's statement has direct reference to physical activity. But it is also true that the statement is followed up with an elaborate representation of the functions of the nervous system as an agency in the production of physical movements. But the nervous system is, let us repeat, the direct instrument of intelligence ; so much so that the grade of intelligence possessed by a given organism may be roughly measured by the extent and complexity of its nervous system. Nor is this a lesson offered to Mr. Spencer; rather it is a lesson to be learned from him. Essentially then, self-movement proves, on final analysis, to be the same thing as what may be otherwise called psychical or spontaneous power—simple spontaneity.

So that the extraordinary self-mobility of the mor؛ complex or higher animals, especially as represented in the highest example, man, proves to be of the utmost moment to man himself. For it is the logical outcome of an increasing complexity of those inner relations which constitute the living unit in the highest sense of the term. And the central factor in this complex of relations is just *self*-relation, under the transfigured form of self-consciousness. For self-mobility that is transfused with self-consciousness can be (here we seem definitely to part company with Mr. Spencer), nothing else than self-determination or Freedom. And the full significance of the conclusion just reached appears when it is recognized that self-determination is precisely the central characteristic of the Total Energy, the "established order" of whose activity can be nothing else than its own consciously pursued, absolutely self-consistent method of eternal Self realization. Whence it appears that Life, and most of all life as it unfolds in humanity is the process leading ever toward perfect existence

3. *Death.*

It has been seen that Life is a constructive process, or a phase of evolution. We have now to consider Death as the inversion of Life, or as a phase of dissolution. And first it is to be remarked that from the very definition of Life as a continuous adjustment of inner relations to outer relations, it is evident that in life itself there is involved a factor that is precisely the reverse of life. For a continuous adjustment implies a continuous need of adjustment which must arise out of a continuous undoing of the results of adjustment. Continuous integration implies continuous disintegration. And it is well worthy of note that in so far as these complementary processes are balanced in the same living unit there is continued freshness and vigor of life on the part of that unit. So that from this point of view, though death is in a certain sense the opposite of life, it is nevertheless also a normal factor in the total process of Life, and hence is after all not to be regarded as the mere inversion of life. In fact it is this ceaseless reconstitution of the individual living unit that makes possible and also perpetuates that extreme flexibility, that extraordinary self-mobility, by which the living units of higher order are specially characterized.

So long as life continues, then, death continues also as one of the necessary phases of life. Or, to quote again from Professor Huxley's lecture on the *Physical Basis of Life*: "Under whatever disguises it takes refuge, whether fungus or oak, worm or man, the living protoplasm not only ultimately dies and is resolved into its mineral and lifeless constituents, but is always dying, and, strange as the paradox may sound, could not live unless it died."

Only when disintegration becomes predominant is the process of life really inverted and thus presently brought to an end. And with the ending of life death must also have completed itself, and hence must also end. Death itself dies when life ceases. Equally, too, on the other hand, so long as life continues, death is present as a mode of transition from one to another phase of life. So that on this side death is nothing else than a mode of change in a living unit. As long as this phase is subordinated the living unit exhibits the characteristic of growth. When it exactly balances the constructive phase, the living unit just maintains its vigor unchanged. When it becomes predominant, disintegration of the living unit has set in.

And this is true of the living unit in its highest aspect as an intellectual and moral unit, no less than of the living unit in respect of its merely physical nature. Indeed the living unit cannot be of a "merely physical" nature. On the contrary, as we have already seen, it must, in the very fact of being a living unit, possess also in some degree a psychical nature. So that in reality what has been said respecting death already applies to all aspects of life, the psychical and the physical being but complementary aspects of every possible living unit.

Thus, as scientists are coming to recognize with perfect clearness, evolution looks both ways. There

may be degeneration as well as progression. For
death may be prolonged through many generations
by mere degradation of type, *or rather by degeneration of the realized forms pertaining to a given type.*
And thus, though evolution may be said to look both
ways, it is yet true that evolution in its *normal aspect* is still, as Mr. Spencer has defined it, a progressive unfolding of reality, including living forms, and
this always from the less to the more complex ; while
on the other hand degeneration is in reality an inversion of this normal process of evolution—a going
backward instead of forward, a mere retracing of
steps that had previously been taken toward the fulfillment of a given type.

In other words, evolution, whether regarded as
physical or as psychical, presupposes a definitely
fixed type or types some advance in the realization
of which must have been made before degeneration
could possibly occur. And hence if one holds to the
conception of the Conservation of Energy as in its
highest significance the continuous, perfect, changeless, absolutely self-conscious Process of Creation,
then there is after all nothing so very alarming, nor
even anything so very absurd, in the view that these
types are among the "pre-established," or rather the
eternally-established "harmonies." Nay, Mr. Spencer's own theory of evolution implies this, as he himself in the main concedes, while at the same time

giving it his own special interpretation.[1]   What, indeed, can the manifold types of existence be but just the special aspects of the faultless self-consistency of the divine Energy in its changeless self-conservation?

Even as commonly represented, the doctrine of the Conservation of Energy clearly implies this.   For if we may conclude from the relations of manifold "forces" to each other that they are in reality only so many modes of one all-inclusive Energy, then it seems equally legitimate to conclude concerning this all-inclusive Energy that it is the self-moved, spontaneous, creative Power which forever manifests itself in the infinitely manifold forms of specialized existence.   It is the total, unchanging Process of Self-differentiation in which integration and disintegration are forever exactly balanced.   That, doubtless, is the "ultimate equilibrium" which the Energy constituting the reality of the Universe does not "tend toward," as if that were an ideal unrealized, but rather the ultimate equilibrium, which is the more certainly "ultimate," because it is *forever maintained* in the changelessly complete self-manifestation of the Perfect Power.[2]

[1] *Principles of Psychology*, II, 195.

[2] There is surely nothing unwarrantable in regarding this inference as being no less truly within the range of the knowable than there is in regarding the inference that all "forces" are necessarily the complementary modes of the

Thus death in its normal aspect is necessarily involved in the very life of the Universe as a whole. It is the phase of dissolution necessarily involved in the perpetual Process of self-renewal. Is it not reasonable to regard this as the way in which the Universe is forever maintained in perfect maturity, and yet also in the freshness of a newly-unfolded creation?

And here let us again remind ourselves of the fact : That this total, self-conscious Process is the ultimate Type of every thinking unit ; the type, therefore, toward the fulfillment of which the unfolding of the intellectual and moral life of such unit must ever tend. Equally true is it that any mode of activity on the part of such unit that does not tend toward this fulfillment is abnormal—is death in the sense of self-dissolution. And because, as being infinite, the type is absolutely fixed, there can be no variation in the central law of its evolution. Doubtless individuals and races differ in degree as well as in mode of the realization of this Type ; but the ultimate Type itself, toward the realization of which in greater or less degree, all normal life is a struggle, is in its very nature something wholly unchangeable.

one truly persistent "Force" or Energy. On the other hand, it certainly *is* unwarrantable to infer, from the fact that relations are everywhere manifest *in* knowledge, that therefore one must accept the relativity *of* knowledge as the ultimate goal of thought.

But thus the individual thinking unit, struggling toward the fulfilment of this Type, must find his normal life a perpetually expanding one. Integration must ever predominate over disintegration. Complexity and specialization must be ever on the increase, and death as the form of change must thus ever be a subordinate factor.

Let us note then just what the disintegration will consist of in such normal life. In the first place, in such growing, expanding unit, there will be on the intellectual side a progressive discovery of the inadequacy of views that had previously been adopted as satisfactory ; while, secondly, in respect of the will it will be discovered that motives which had been unsuspectingly followed cannot be reconciled with higher interests. And again, sentiments which had been entertained and cultivated without doubt of their excellence, will prove incompatible with a well-balanced life. Such views must be modified ; such motives must be subordinated ; such sentiments must be purified. And thus the individual dies to one class of interests which he finds in their outcome to be narrow and unsatisfying, and yet in the very same process discovers that his life is expanding and becoming enriched through attainment to larger views and nobler motives and purer sentiments. It is thus that, along with Paul, all men sincerely devoted to right-living "die daily." Nay, in the communal life also, death is an essential factor. Society in all its phases is ever passing through Death into more adequate forms and modes of Life.

But the very fact that the individual thinking unit belongs to that type whose central characteristic is "self-mobility" of the highest order—that is, power to choose its own course and mode of activity—this very superiority of man's typical nature makes possible also an abnormal life on his part. At best such individual unit is but imperfectly developed intellectually, and hence he is liable to error. So also he is but imperfectly developed morally, and hence he may prefer a present good of a lower order to a deferred good of a higher order. In either case his development must be impeded ; and there can hardly fail in such case to result also the disintegration in greater or less degree of the intellectual and moral qualities he has already attained through the normal life he has hitherto led.

Thus, to use the ancient phrase in a modern way, "sin enters into the world, and death by sin." It is the irrational, self-contradictory deed that constitutes "sin." For "sin is the transgression of the law" in this sense : That the "law" is just the ideal or typical nature of all thinking units. It is therefore at once the divine nature, and also the true nature of man. And this divine nature, as constituting the "law" which man must obey in order to become in reality what he is in type or Ideal cannot be disregarded or "transgressed" by him without involving him in self-contradiction.   For the typical Self is the true Self of each and all such units.   And self-contradiction is the process of self-dissolution, of self-destruction.   It is the process of death abnormally developed into the *in*version of life because it is the *per*version of life.   Moral death is but another name for moral self-contradiction.   And this is the absolute justification of that seemingly strange saying : "The soul that sinneth, it shall die."   A life of sin is simply a prolonged death.

Thus death, especially moral death, is seen to be a process always more or less prolonged.   It is scarcely conceivable that the vitality of so complex and highly constituted a unit as the human soul could be quenched in a moment.   No single act of self-contradiction could do more than turn the tide of life backward.   Only a prolonged course of self-contradiction could even so much as threaten the utter dissolution of a living unit belonging to the highest type.   And this brings us to the question whether it is really conceivable that such utter dissolution can ever actually take place.

4.   *Immortality*.

It would seem then that the question whether if a man die he shall live again, may be given a more hopeful form.   And that form is : Whether in respect of man's essential nature as a thinking unit, death can ever be more than transition from one to another grade of Life—whether so complex a living unit as man can ever wholly die?

To this question the answer has in part been anticipated in the foregoing discussion of the nature of life and the significance of death. We have seen that Life is a constructive process. We have also seen that in the continuous adjustment of inner relations to outer relations which this process is otherwise described as being, there is necessarily implied the characteristic of spontaneity. Even at its lowest grade life is characterized by "self-mobility," and this quality increases in complexity and in positive significance with each higher grade in the scale of living units.

Indeed, it is this characteristic more than any other that measures the degree of advancement to which any living unit has attained. For the "inner" relations, as we have seen, are in truth the same as subjective or psychic relations. It is intelligence with its accompanying moral qualities that constitutes genuine internality. The inorganic world is the world of externality ; or, if one will, it is the world of Reality in its aspect of extent, while Intelligence in the range of its significance is the same world of Reality in its intensive aspect. So that in the advance from the inorganic, through the various degrees of the organic, to man as the highest organism there is a gradual transition from those aggregates of mere "matter" which are wholly destitute of self-mobility, through the automatic phases of self-mobility manifest in the lower organisms, to the unit in which consciousness has expanded into reason, and in which self-mobility has thus attained its highest type. This unit is indeed a bundle or complex of "inner relations" that has become unfolded into an organic whole, the dominant characteristic of which is *self*-relation. Such unit is self-conscious. It examines itself, criticises itself, condemns or approves itself, and thus shows itself to be its own measure. Mind alone can measure mind.

And now as to the nature of mind something also has already been ascertained. Chiefly it has been noted that this self-examining unit can discover no absolute limit to its own development. It can conceive of an infinite Mind, and can also conceive of itself as progressively unfolding its own powers to infinity. So that there can be no difference in kind between this self-examining unit and the perfect Mind of which it conceives. It is also true, as has been shown, that the perfect Mind can be no mere abstract Ideal which the self examining unit projects from its own phantasy ; but rather such perfect Mind can in truth be nothing else than the aspect of perfect self-consistency and therefore of perfect self-consciousness necessarily pertaining to the eternally self-conserved Energy. This indeed is characterized by internality or spontaneity in the highest degree ; and the universe in space can be nothing else than the perpetually complete utterance or *outerance* of that perfect Mind as the absolutely spontaneous, self-moved, all-inclusive ONE beyond which there is no reality whatever.

I trust that no apology need be offered for further strengthening this phase of the argument by references to what in such connection will doubtless prove to most readers an unexpected source. It is indeed not fairly certain that Mr. Spencer himself would repudiate the claim that such an inference as the one just arrived at can be legitimately drawn from his writings. And yet there are numerous passages which might be cited in justification of the claim. Nor can I help thinking that the real drift of his system is in this direction. For example, in discussing "the perception of resistance," he declares[1] that we can know nothing of any other order than the order of thought. And again[2] he says : "To frame a conception of force in the *non-ego* different from the conception we have of force in the *ego* is utterly beyond our power." And this statement, it seems to me, can have but one meaning, which is : that the inca-

---

[1]Op. cit. II, 233.　　[2]Op. cit. p. 239.

pacity we discover in ourselves to form such conception is due to the fact that the *non-ego* is only the outer mode of the ultimate *Ego*—the eternally self-conserved Energy—whose fundamental nature is repeated in the fundamental nature of each and every thinking unit throughout Creation.

But still further, the whole process of evolution as directly affecting man tends to confirm the same view. After referring to the structure of the eye before birth and pointing out the necessary implication thus presented of heredity with reference to the life after birth, he declares[1] it to obviously follow "that objective necessities of relation in space are represented by established nervous structures implying latent subjective necessities of nervous action ; that these last constitute pre-determined forms of thought produced by the moulding of Thought upon Things ; and that the impossibility of inverting them, implied by the inconceivableness of their negations, is a reason for accepting them as true, which immeasurably transcends in value any other reason that can be given." But "Things" are simply modes of the Total Energy. They can, in short, be nothing else than the outer expression of the fixed order, the method, the Thought of that "Persistent Force" or divine Energy to whose activity all reality owes its

____

[1] *Op. cit.*, II, 420.

being—in whose activity all reality inheres. Nay, our "reasoning itself can be trusted only on the assumption that absolute uniformities of Thought correspond to absolute uniformities of Things '"[1] And on the other hand, as we must insist, such "absolute uniformities of Things" can be nothing else than the perpetual manifestation of the "absolute uniformities" necessarily inhering in the Perfect Thought or self-conscious Method of the Total Energy. Whence it follows that the whole process of man's evolution is only a continuous adjustment of his inner or psychic relations to the "established order" of relations which the divine Thought exhibits in the whole range of man's environment—i. e., in the universe. Doubtless also one factor in the cause of the increasing complexity of psychic qualities exhibited by man is to be found, as Mr. Spencer claims, in the cumulative effects of inheritance. But this appears to me to include the phase of self-mobility in the sense of self-determination or power to choose a course of conduct either consistent with or contrary to the "established order" of the world, which is also, let it be repeated, the divine Type of every spiritual unit, and hence the divine Type of man. It is thus the evolution of man's freedom no less than the evolution of his intelligence. It is an inherited power-to-do no less than an inherited

------

[1] *Op. cit.*, II, 426.

power-to-think. The individual responds to the action of the environment—at first automatically, no doubt; and yet the *response* is a *reaction* which becomes more and more manifestly spontaneous or initiative until it becomes an explicit, conscious, intellectual and moral response to the appeal of the perfect Intelligence as manifested in the whole range of Creation. What else is Science than the eager response which man is ever making to the divine Thought, which is ever appealing to man through the outer forms or uttered modes of the perfect Mind? The more we insist upon the doctrine of Evolution the more are we bound to accept its legitimate and inevitable intimations. If man is what he is by descent, it must be borne in mind that he can inherit only what his real ancestry has been, and is, capable of transmitting. And that "ancestry" necessarily includes as its first indispensable term the great First Cause itself. Man as mind can descend only from that which itself is Mind. "The inconceivableness of the negation" of this, as we may well say in Mr. Spencer's phrase, "is a reason for accepting it as true, which immeasurably transcends any other reason that can be given." And Mr. Spencer cannot logically protest.

But now, to resume, if there can be but one type of mind, then the individual thinking unit, which may be said to constitute the extreme term of integration in the total process of Evolution, must, as already shown, be possessed of precisely the same typical nature as the perfect Mind itself. And in this identity of nature on the part of all conceivable minds there is implicit the answer to the question whether death can mean utter dissolution for man as a thinking unit. For on the one hand the identity in nature of all minds must mean that each thinking unit is in its typical nature infinite. The degree of its present realization may be ever so slight, yet because it belongs to the same type as every other mind and therefore to the same type as the perfect Mind, it may rightfully claim for itself the full import of its infinite ideal nature. Nay, it cannot divest itself of the full import of that nature, and hence it can neither escape the duties nor abrogate the privileges pertaining to that nature. Even in self-perversion it is exercising its inalienable privilege and power as an independent being.

At the same time it is to be noted that such ideal nature cannot be *his* even as an ideal or typical nature unless there also belong to him the full round of conditions for the ultimate fulfilment of that nature. But because his ideal or typical or true nature is infinite, and because he can accomplish its realization only by progressive, finite stages of development, then evidently man must by his very nature be destined to live without end. For in no less than infinite duration can he complete the realization of his own infinite nature.   If in every case Life is a constructive process, then for man whose life in its essential nature is of the highest type of self-mobility and whose typical nature is infinite, Life must signify nothing less and nothing else than an infinitely extended constructive process—a process of self-development, the full import of which is nothing less than this : that it constitutes the constructive realization in his own personality of the divine nature common to all thinking units.

On the positive side this would seem to be the answer to the question whether man is by nature immortal.   But on the negative side there remains the question whether by persistent self-contradiction man can ever actually accomplish his own utter extinction.   And here also in a measure we have already anticipated the answer.   For we have seen that death is in truth nothing else than the phase of transition from one to another degree of life.   In the life of the advancing individual death is present in due subordination as the elimination of factors no longer tending to increase the individual's vitality.   Whenever a factor ceases to be constructive and becomes obstructive, death as a necessary phase of life dissociates and removes such factor from the organism.

This is true even in the merely physical organism. And when we consider the intellectual and moral life then the spiritual organism with its vastly greater complexity, and especially with its immeasurably superior self-mobility, presents the aspect of death in still more perfect subordination as a phase pertaining to the total development of the individual. Here, as we have seen, death is simply the progressive, conscious, voluntary elimination of inadequate views, of lower motives, of less worthy sentiments, through the very process of the gradual clarifying and extending of knowledge, the strengthening of the will, and the centering of the affections on nobler objects.

On the other hand the individual may, through error or through deliberate choice, pursue lower instead of higher aims. Instead of following a course of activity consistent with man's typical nature, and which must therefore prove to be a constructive process for him, the individual may pursue a course of activity which contradicts man's typical nature, and which must therefore prove to be a destructive process for the one who pursues it.

But this is still a *process*. It is the inversion of the process of life. And it is not to be denied that the inverse process appears in general to be the swifter of the two. Disintegration is more rapid than integration. And if the process of death as the mere reversal of the process of life is the more rapid, then death as the utter extinction of life, not only for the individual but also for the race, would seem to be perpetually threatened.   Indeed it would seem fairly inexplicable that life should be maintained at all, especially in the moral sphere where there is constantly recurring hesitancy and frequent error in judgment, constant struggle and frequent failure as against the lower motives, constant division of the affections as between worthier and less worthy objects.

But though in general the phase of self-dissolution may appear to be more rapid than does the constructive aspect of life, yet the question may well be considered : Whether after all there is not a more or less radical difference in the *ratio* of the movement in the two cases.   Progress of the morally constituted individual means constant increase in complexity of realized power.   And such increase in complexity of realized power can only mean that with each stage of his advance the morally constituted individual possesses not only a wider range of view and a clearer comprehension of the right method of his own self-development, but that he has also increased facilities and means for accomplishing his self-development. So that his advance should be by a ratio which is itself constantly undergoing increase.

And this view appears more evidently to be the true one when we consider the multiplication of the aids to individual development through the combination of man with man, through that extension of the constructive process of life which we know as social life in the widest sense of the term. A single illustration must suffice. The invention of the steam engine was an exercise of intelligence with immediate reference to the emancipation of man from mere physical drudgery. Or, if one will, it was with direct reference to the more rapid accumulation of wealth. In either case there is increased means for the intellectual and moral advancement of individual men. In the one case there is increase in the proportion of time during which the individual may use his energies for the expansion of his own higher life. In the other case there is increased means for the enriching of the individual's life.

But the invention of the steam engine necessitates a vast expansion of intellectual life in another way. The makers of engines and the masters of engines must be men of trained intelligence and also of moral self-restraint. And this is only the beginning. For the steam engine opens the way for the fullest efficiency and hence for the utmost perfection in structure and in rapidity of use of the printing press. And this not merely nor mainly in the matter of mechanical perfection of the press as worked by the power of steam, but also and much more because of the rapid and extended diffusion of the products of the press. And again this opens a way to use information collected from day to day from all parts of the earth.

The steam printing press demands the telegraph, and the telegraph in turn gives to the daily publications of the press their widest value.

But this also ripens the demand for universal ability to read. The steam engine and the printing press and the telegraph and the railway lead inevitably to the primary school. And schools multiply the demand for books—for all the products of the press. It is thus that intelligence presses upon intelligence, ever stimulating intelligence, ever multiplying means and methods for its own further advancement.

Nor is this all. For this intellectual advance carries with it inevitably a corresponding moral advance. The very publicity given to any unusual deed of the individual is a strong stimulus to the doing of praise-worthy deeds, and an equally strong restraint as against deeds that are certain to be condemned. The newspaper is the daily register of the universal conscience, and thus the conscience of the individual is strengthened and constrained more and more to adapt itself to a rational course of conduct. And beyond this again the criticisms and comments of the press are as a rule uttered with a view to securing the approval of the general conscience. So that there is going forward a ceaseless process of the enlightenment and strengthening of individual consciences, the result of which in turn must inevitably be the gradual elevation of the average or general conscience. And this extends to all publications. One man writes a good book. Another man prints thousands of copies of it. Tens of thousands of other men are made better by reading the book. Thus each rational deed of each rationally disposed man connects him with all other rationally disposed men and makes him strong with all their added strength.

The reader can easily extend the illustration indefinitely and add others at will. Sufficient has been said to indicate the self-multiplying power of a reasonable life And this in turn emphasizes the reasonableness of the belief that the existence of a unit possessing this truly divine quality cannot be utterly destroyed by any other means at least than persistent self-contradiction. And one may well inquire whether, even so, the persistence in evil doing must not be continued to infinity before utter self-destruction could be actually completed.

But the immediate question we have now to consider is : Whether the process of self-annulment can, like the process of self-development, be self-accelerating and hence self-continuing? And in seeking the answer to this question it will be well not merely to recall the fact already noted : that disintegration is often observed to take place with greater rapidity than is the case with growth, but also to carefully consider what are the ultimate tendencies in the negative process.

Before proceeding with this particular question, however, it may be remarked that there is strong intimation of the truth in the generally recognized fact that the more complex the type the greater the interval between birth and maturity ; while on the other hand, maturity once gained, death as dissolution must in natural course inevitably follow at a period more or less remote as the period between birth and maturity is greater. The ephemera is born, attains maturity, and again by the inverse process reaches decrepitude and death, all within a day. Man as a physical being occupies many years in attaining maturity, while the process of his decline and dissolution also runs through many years. But in either case the type is finite. It is therefore certain to be fulfilled in natural course and as certain to undergo dissolution in the case of each individual embodiment of the type. In its very nature the physical unit cannot be immortal. Indeed the most dreadful of all imaginable conditions for such unit would be just the incapacity to die—as is vividly represented in the Greek legend of Tithonos, the human husband of the goddess Eos, who secured for him the boon of immortality, but thoughtlessly failed to include in her request that this should carry with it eternal youth. In short, no living being save one whose typical nature is infinite, could be immortal. And for such unit death as utter dissolution must be no less unnatural than immortality would be for the unit whose life is essentially physical. The type of the latter is finite. Such unit must therefore complete the period of its growth, must thus lose the gift of youth, and must inevitably fall into the feebleness of old age, culminating in complete disso·lution. On the other hand the being whose typical nature is infinite can never actually attain to maturity in the sense of complete fulfilment of its typical nature, and hence the period of its growth, the period of its youth, can never reach a natural termination.

And now we may return to the question whether for such unit the period of growth can ever reach an unnatural and utterly final termination. And the special form which this question has already taken for us is : What are the ultimate tendencies in the process of self-annulment on the part of a being whose real nature it is to be immortal? At the outset it is evident that if the process of disintegration should continue with even undiminished ratio it must speedily result in the utter dissolution of any finite unit ; and much more must this be the case if the ratio be increased. What then is the fact?

It has already been pointed out that for the individual as an intellectual and moral unit disintegration and growth alike result from a course of action which the individual himself chooses. Intellectual and moral growth results from a chosen course of conduct which is consistent with the ultimate ideal nature of all thinking units. Intellectual and moral disintegration results from a chosen course of conduct that is inconsistent with that ultimate ideal nature. But in either case the power actually exerted by the individual is the concrete result of what has been reasonable in his own life thus far. If that power is still reasonably used it must increase. If it be used unreasonably it must by that very fact be diminished. In the former case the capacity for further activity is increased and rendered more complex. In the latter case it is diminished and reduced in complexity.

It thus appears that with every self-contradictory act of the individual his total power to perform further acts of *any kind whatever* is thus far diminished. And this necessarily implies that his power to perform further self-contradictory acts is made less. Whence it is to be concluded that the further the individual proceeds in a self contradictory course of conduct the narrower becomes the reality of his life ; and not only so, but *the less also must his power become to further reduce that reality.*

So far then from there being an increase of ratio in the self-destroying tendency of a man considered as an intellectual and moral unit, it appears that in the very nature of the case the ratio necessarily diminishes with persistence in a self-contradictory course of conduct.

And the meaning of this can scarcely be mistaken. For though with progressive self-annulment the individual approximates toward what on first view seems but the necessarily logical result of such course— namely, his own actual utter dissolution and loss of identity—yet in this very process he becomes less and less capable of persistence in any definite course of action whatever; becomes less and less real as an independent, choice-making unit, and therefore becomes more and more dependent upon his environment. And as this environment is real, and as some phase of good must therefore constitute its nucleus and sustaining factor (for the good is the only ground of reality), then there is necessarily a residuum of influence for good in the environment, however low in grade the immediate environment may be. And that residuum of good must tend to prevent the individual from sinking below the grade of existence represented by his immediate environment.

And not only so, but the more dependent he comes to be upon this environment, that is, the further he has progressed in self-annulment, the more completely must the factor of good in his immediate environment prove to be the phase of power which he depends upon. And as he is thus at length seen to be dependent upon, and hence to be thus far under the influence of some phase of Reason, which is but another name for the Good, there must be a point in his progress toward self-annulment below which he cannot sink without exercising a definite power of choice in opposition to the phase of Reason which constitutes the core or central factor of reality in his environment. And yet the farther he has advanced in self-annulment the less is the actual power o choice he possesses to resist the influence which the rational element in his environment brings to bear upon him.

On the other hand the fact of his responding at all to that influence shows clearly that some shred of Good still exists within him answering to the exhaustless Good above and around him. Only in so far as he is good is he real. And only in so far as he is real can he perform any deed whatever, whether good or evil. The good alone is persistent. Evil cannot so much as bear the appearance of reality save through some phase of the Good being temporarily perverted. The ultimate divine Energy is in its very nature all-pervasive. Omnipotence cannot be withheld from it even in thought. So that no thinking unit, however degraded, can utterly escape from divine, restoring influence, save through utter annihilation. And this, as we have seen, cannot be accomplished save by persistence in self-contradictory deeds even after the individual's power has so far approximated

to nullity that further persistence in the same course
must thenceforward imply an increased exercise of
power to choose as against the restraining and re-
storative influences in his environment. And yet
with each additional self-contradictory deed his power
to choose must be still further reduced. Whence it
would seem that utter self-annulment must forever
remain impossible.

But habit—have we forgotten the fairly resistless
force of habit? What then is habit? To this it may
be answered that habit is definiteness of tendency toward a given course of conduct. It arises from repetition of like acts, is strengthened by such repetition,
and hence by such repetition is perpetuated. Doubtless it is also true that the cumulative effects of these
repetitions of like acts are inherited. But this again
presupposes only so much the more certainly that the
order of the environment is absolutely fixed. For
only so can habit, as one phase of the continuous adjustment of inner relations to outer relations, be preserved. Indeed habit in the higher sense constitutes
the concrete form of self-consistency. And this is itself
the highest term of that definiteness and consistency
of conscious life which originates from a prolonged
course of activity in unison with the established order
of the world. But were that order changeable, then
with each change the habit thus far developed must
tend to the destruction rather than to the preservation

of individuals possessing it. And the more matured the habit the more certain the destruction. Indeed the whole history of the evolution of life on the earth gives continuous illustration of this fact : that the more definitely an individual living unit is adjusted in its essential characteristics to one special set of conditions, only so much the more is it by that very fact doomed to perish when the conditions become radically changed. Nevertheless it is to be borne in mind that this change of conditions within a given locality is still but the manifestation of what in a wider range is the changeless order of the world or universe. And the higher forms of life give proof of their greater self-mobility and wider range of development by their continuous adjustment of themselves to the fixed relations of Energy as these relations are progressively unfolded in the advancing complexity of the local conditions of life. It is precisely this continuous conformity of the individual to the fixed relations of energy exhibited in his environment, that constitutes the essential condition of continuously expanding life on his part. And it is precisely this same steady conformity of the individual as a thinking unit to the rational order of the moral world that constitutes what are called "good habits ;" while a persistent course of activity in opposition to that order constitutes what are known as "bad habits."

The former course is self-constructive ; the latter, self-destructive.

And here etymology, though often a dangerous guide, may for once help us. Habit is from *habere*, to have. On the rational side then it means that the individual has certain definite, consistent, rational modes of activity ; that is, modes of activity by which the individual is more and more fully conformed to the fixed order of the moral world. On the irrational side it means that certain more or less gross, irrational desires *have the individual;* desires which, followed out, bring the individual into more and more pronounced collision with the fixed order of the moral world. This is the real demonic "possession." And this can have no other result than the individual's own undoing. Good habits then are modes of power, while bad habits are modes of weakness. They show, not what the man *is*, but what he is *not*. The bad habits are the ones we "fall" into. The good ones are attainable only through an upward and more or less prolonged struggle. Whence it appears that, after all, the question of habit falls within the larger question of the general development of the individual which we have already considered.

If now we summarize the results thus far reached respecting immortality, it would seem that on the positive side man's nature necessarily implies his immortality because of the highly complex constructive character of his essential or spiritual life, and also because his typical nature is infinite ; and that also on the negative side his immortality is fairly insured, because from his very nature as a being possessing the power to choose his own course of action, the tendency toward disintegration which is necessarily involved in the choice of an irrational course of conduct must rest upon itself and ultimately annul itself. And this annulment of the tendency toward disintegration on the part of the individual must ever take place before the annulment of the individual is effected ; and this because of his increased dependence upon the element of Good in the environment as he approaches nearer and nearer toward the final term of disintegration.

The individual thus remains as an indestructible unit whose central characteristic is: *Power to choose his own course of action*—the only restriction upon this power being that from his very nature the individual cannot so far misuse it as to bring about its utter destruction, so far as to effect the individual's own utter annihilation. But it is also to be observed that so far as he persists in choosing an evil course of action, the divine within him is changed inevitably into the demonic. The individual who refuses to advance through rational deeds toward Godhood chooses by that very fact to become or remain by so far an anti-divine power—a "devil." And, so long as this choice continues, by just so long must his anti-divine character continue, even though it be to eternity. He cannot attain annihilation, but he can choose the never-ending death of self-perversion. The persistent evil-doer transforms himself more and more into the moral deformity of diabolism and builds about and most of all within himself the hell of self-contradiction. Thus the law of everlasting punishment is rather the everlasting law of punishment, which, being interpreted, is : "*Whatsoever a man sows that shall he also reap.*"

One further remark suggested by etymology may be added. The word "individual" has come in course of history to be nearly equivalent to the word "person." Nevertheless it is in fact simply an exact translation, through the Latin, of the Greek word *atom*—"that which cannot be cut or divided." But the word "atom" became fixed in its significance during the period of Greek speculation as to the world in its *physical* aspects ; so that it serves very perfectly the needs of modern science for a term expressive of those smallest divisions of matter which occur in chemical reactions. On the other hand the word "individual" became fixed in its significance through the influence of Christianity, the latter holding up to view the spirituality of each human being and insisting upon his indivisible, inextinguishable nature, and his ultimate right to the complete fulfil ment of the infinite destiny involved in that nature. Thus the word "individual" is found in modern forms of speech as the name of the ultimate *social* unit or element.

Already with Democritus the term "atom" assumed a kind of transfigured significance. The atom was described by him as an eternal, independent, self-moving unit, which became aggregated with others into larger wholes rather by accident than otherwise ; these larger wholes in the nature of the case being always temporary. It would seem that in all this—unconsciously, doubtless—Democritus was but presenting, under a universalized image conceived as eternal, the fundamental characteristic of Greek life—Individualism. That was the quality which the Greeks so jealously guarded against all those influences tending toward tyranny that have come to be classed as Asiatic. And it is no wonder that, in the first great struggle for personal liberty, an extreme view should be arrived at as to what personal liberty really consists in. Thus the Individual in isolation, as a unit complete in himself, beautiful and worthy of eternal admiration, even though it be but in his outer form preserved in marble—that was their Ideal, which they still further transfigured into a multitude of gods, each also serenely perfect in his eternal isolation. It is true that a fatal defect lay at the heart of this conception ; and even the Greeks themselves at length became aware in greater or less degree that in spite of their divinity such gods are still finite gods, and therefore doomed to final overthrow.

On the other hand, in the Roman world the subordination of individual man to the law, as the expression of that larger personality consisting of the State, already constituted a stage in the process of educating man up to a rational conception of his universal and infinite nature. With Christianity this infinite nature was explicitly announced, and each man, each human being, was declared to be in his own person an *Individual*—an indivisible, imperishable unit. That was henceforth to be regarded as the one veritable "atom," the one genuine monad in all the universe, the changeless type of perfect Godhood unfolding through the ages in each and every human soul. And instead of saying that Christ "brought life and immortality to light," it might be more precisely descriptive of the fact to say that Christ brought life *as* immortality to light, in the sense that he was the first to show that life in its highest significance, life in its intellectual and moral phase, already involves the indestructibility, the immortality, of such living unit.

It is this view of immortality, shadowed forth more or less vaguely in the creeds of all races, that has become clarified and expanded in the minds of the more thoughtful, until at least the clew to its ultimate significance has been fairly attained. And the process of bringing this Ideal into fulfilment for each individual has become more and more apparent with each succeeding age. Not by isolation and self-deprivation, but by participation in the universal Life, through science, through all honest work, through the social organism in all its forms—only thus is the life of each to be rendered concrete, real, truly rational.

From having been abstractly idealized and figured in the form of the gods among the Greeks, man is now seen to have ever been little by little undergoing transfiguration into a richer, nobler life that proves him to be ever more and more worthy of recognition as himself "God manifest in the flesh."

5. *Resurrection. (A Corollary).*

If God were not manifest in the flesh—that is, in space-filling modes of existence—he would not be God. For, as ultimate, self-conserved Energy, God must be manifest in all modes of existence. In Him the subjective and the objective aspects of existence must be forever perfectly balanced. Thus Schopenhauer's epigram[1] —"No object without a subject is the final refutation of all materialism"—presents an essential truth, but a truth so expressed as to make it seem one-sided. It therefore requires the complementary form : "No subject without an object is the

---

[1] *Die Welt als Wille und Vorstellung.* I, 35.

final refutation of all mere idealism''—that is, of all idealism that assumes to dispense with a world in space. For mind, as we have already seen, is inner, subjective, spontaneous power, and can be conceived as in process of realization only through the medium of an outer, objective, passive instrument. Thought, to be real, must be manifest, must be expressed, must be embodied. The inner necessarily implies the outer ; the subjective is meaningless apart from the objective ; the spontaneous finds its complement in the passive ; power is powerless without instrumentality.[1]

Whence it follows that the more adequate and consistent thought is, by so much the more complex and extended, by so much the more perfectly adapted to the uses of thought, must the embodiment be. Advance of thought is inconceivable without a corresponding advance in the physical media of thought. Perfect Thought can only be conceived as perfectly expressed. And ''perfectly expressed'' means : absolutely *self*-expressed.

---

[1] Of course this is not to ignore the further and subtler meanings of the term ''objective.'' It is only the most immediate, rudimentary view that recognizes nothing as ''objective'' save that which appeals directly to the senses. Images formed in the mind and appealing directly to the imagination constitute the next higher sphere of objectivity ; while *relations* which present themselves to—more strictly speaking, *in*—reflective consciousness constitute the third and highest sphere. We apprehend the ''objects'' of the senses ; we contemplate the ''objects'' of the imagination ; we comprehend the ''objects'' of thought.

To this view, indeed, science is ever adding definite confirmation. In the field of comparative psychology there is no fact more clearly established than this : that advance of intelligence is invariably accompanied with a corresponding advance of mass and complexity of nervous organization. Nay, advance in complexity of structure, especially as corresponding with advance of intelligence, is true of the whole external form of embodiment. At the one extreme is the *amœba* with its *pseudopodia* which it thrusts out from time to time from its tiny undifferentiated mass. These serve alike as improvised organs of locomotion and of seizure, being withdrawn again into the mass when a particle of food is obtained. At the same time the food-atom sinks gradually into the mass of the little animal's body, which becomes folded gradually around the food, and thus constitutes for the moment a simple organ of digestion. At the other extreme is man with his complex structure, having specialized organs of locomotion and of seizure, as well as a jointed skeleton and a vastly elaborated muscular, respiratory, circulatory, digestive and, above all, nervous system, all serving to bring him into contact with his environment in endlessly varied ways. And from the one to the other of these extremes there are innumerable multitudes of organic forms, presenting in the whole range a fairly unbroken continuity of advance in complexity of structure corresponding to the advance in complexity of intelligence.

And here we may profitably refer again, however briefly, to the identity in type of all minds. As Mr. Spencer seems very clearly to recognize, and as he in one place[1] at least explicitly states: "There must be *some form of thought* exhibited alike in the very lowest and the very highest manifestations of intelligence." It is true that his statement is made while definitely looking backward from man to the lower animal organisms. And yet, logically, it is and can be none the less true when looking forward toward any and all possible grades of intelligence above man, as man is known upon the earth. As already so often insisted in this essay, there can be but one type of mind. There can be, and unquestionably are, endlessly varied grades of realization of that type. Doubtless there may be and are in reality not merely individual but also national "strains" or variants from the type. But such variants, persisted in, cannot fail to result in "arrested development." Persistent variance from the type means self-contradiction, means death. And it may be remarked by the way that the ever-widening process of intercommunication between individual and individual, between nation and nation, between race and race, has for its chief value the edu-

---

[1] *Principles of Psychology*, II, 298. See also p. 475, already referred to above, p. 20.

cation of humanity—the *leading-out* of minds from the dwarfing influence of merely local relations into the enlarging influence of genuinely universal relations.   It tends towards mutual inclusion, intellectually, of all men ; towards prolonged national growth, and hence towards the elimination of national death.

And now let us note some of the conclusions that appear to follow from what precedes.   In the first place, we are met by the truth which presents itself at every turn, that the ultimate Energy is to be regarded as just the Perfect Mind, and hence that as such it must be perfectly manifested or embodied. Nor is this anything else than the obverse of the statement that, regarded as space-filling Energy, its activity must be shown as the unfolding of a perfect method ; which again means nothing else than that the "Persistent Force" or Energy of the Universe is the one all-inclusive, self-unfolding Power conscious of itself in all its modes.   Secondly, it would seem that we may legitimately draw the conclusion that not only has there been a gradual increase in complexity of embodiment through the various advancing grades of intelligence from the *amœba* to man, but that as further stages are reached in the advance of mind there must still be a corresponding advance in the complexity of the instrumentalities through which mind is embodied and realized.

Nor is this without its confirmation in human history. Not merely is it that the sense-organs of man seem yet to be undergoing development in complexity and delicacy. But with every stage of intellectual progress man has shown his creative capacity by inventing new instrumentalities for the accomplishment of his constantly multiplying purposes. On the side of man's physical needs this is familiar enough. While man's merely natural physical organism was the only embodiment of man as struggling intelligence, he could do no more than creep, snail-footed, from place to place and must depend upon the spontaneous productions of the soil for his subsistence. Danger of starvation stimulated him to the discovery of implements of agriculture, as danger of being himself devoured stimulated him to the discovery of weapons or instruments of defense. And with growing intelligence these instrumentalities have been multiplied and increased in complexity and efficiency to an extent such that even here we have a fairly accurate measure of the enormous advance made by human intelligence since the first appearance upon the earth of a creature that could in any way be rightly called man.

But still more evidently has man's embodiment in respect of his intellectual needs become greatly extended, though here too the new instrumentalities constantly reach across and serve as means for satisfying his needs in the physical sphere, just as inventions on the latter side are themselves the expression of growing intelligence. The steam engine is an extension of man's hands. It is an added organ of seizure, of manipulation, of *manu*-facture. It is also an extension of his organs of locomotion, and at the same time a multiplication of his power of transportation. The telegraph system is a vast net-work of nerves, reaching out to every part of the earth's surface, and thus organically connecting each man's inner life with the lives of all other men. The printing press is the medium for the ever-renewed embodiment of all that is vital in human thought. The telescope, the microscope, and the 'spectroscope are but added organs of vision by which man is able to penetrate ever more and more deeply into the truths of nature.

These and endless other instrumentalities that man has shaped show how the embodiment of intelligence may be indefinitely extended, and also show how the extension of the embodiment follows inevitably from the extension of the intelligence itself. As man's comprehension of nature increases, so his power over nature grows. Knowledge of nature has displaced the fear of nature. The mystery of nature has given place to the ministration of nature. The overwhelming forces of nature have ceased to be worshiped, and instead have become the secure and efficient agencies of human will.

Is there any absolute limit to this process? That such should be the case can scarcely be believed. Mind is ever the same in its typical nature. Its modes of development cannot possibly contradict one another. The same general process of mental evolution must go forward in the same general course. The power of individual mind over the physical aspects of existence must ever be on the increase.

And death, as we have already seen, is but change or transition from one to another mode of life. Man as a thinking unit has for his normal, essential life the expansion and intensifying of his intellectual and moral powers. These powers, too, have constant relation to the external or physical aspects of existence. The more matured his powers become the greater is man's ascendency over the merely physical and external phases of reality. Man first adjusts himself to nature in the sense of tracing out the method of nature. And that, let us repeat, is the same as tracing out the manifestations of divine Thought in nature. On the other hand, however, in proportion as this tracing of the divine Thought is accomplished, man finds himself able to adjust nature to himself in the sense of controlling the forces of nature in such wise as to shape physical masses into instrumentalities, through which in turn those forces may be rendered efficient in the furthering of man's purposes in the present world.

Doubtless it is true, as Mr. Spencer urges, that man is just the logical culmination or highest product of nature. His powers, his tendencies, his passions, are what they are through that measureless process of evolution which we can dimly trace back through countless ages to an undifferentiated nebulous mass indefinitely diffused through a space far exceeding that marked out by the present limits of our solar system. But it is also true that, while we may thus trace back the process through which man has become what he is, to that aspect of existence in which (as the first law of motion practically asserts), there is no trace of self-mobility, yet through this same process which has such beginning there is seen to have developed a phase of existence in which self-mobility constitutes a definite, positive characteristic. Nay, this special quality had no sooner appeared in a given unit than it proved to be a characteristic marking off of such unit in a wholly new way from any preceding unit within the condensing nebulous mass. And the further this special quality became developed the more radically is it seen to have separated the unit possessing it from the inert forms of the inorganic world. For intelligence and self-mobility prove to be but different aspects of one and the same essential characteristic. The more definitely specialized intelligence comes to be, as intelligence, in like degree does the power of self-movement become more definite. Nor may the factor of heredity be disregarded or lightly esteemed. There seems no good reason to set aside the long-established though vague conception, which Mr. Spencer has more definitely formulated, that the accumulated experience of countless generations becomes organic in succeeding individuals; that the power to distinguish between objects that do not serve for food and those that do, between objects that are to be desired and those that are to be feared, becomes ever more precise; that the corresponding power of appropriate self-adjustment on the part of the unit thus affected must increase in precision and efficiency of exercise; and finally that out of such mere instinctive self-adjustment has arisen the phase of self-adjustment that comes from conscious calculation

Thus it appears that in its higher aspects self-movement, though in so large a degree organic through inheritance, is, after all, an *inherited power*, which the individual finds himself capable of *using independently in his own self-adjustment to his environment*. And thus the further the process of evolution extends the more significant does the power of self-movement become. So that one may well agree with Mr. Spencer in the statement that there is no contrast between the lowest and the highest organisms more striking than this. It is through this power, indeed, that man as the highest organism is able to

control with ever-increasing efficiency the very forces
of nature out of which he has arisen. It is thus that
he is enabled to make nature shield him against
nature. It is thus that with increase of intelligence
he proves to be an ever-expanding power, reaching
out through nature and moulding it into an ever-
increasingly complex embodiment of his intelligence.

And once more ; since nature presents itself as
nothing else than the outward form of an infinitely
complex and faultlessly rational process, faithful,
consistent and unwearying reaction upon which is
the indispensable primary condition of the development of human reason—since this is the undeniable
fact we are driven to recognize that the inner Substance and vital principle of Nature is actual and absolute Reason ; and that thus the arising of man out
of nature is in deepest truth the way of his descent
from the primal world-forming Reason. That is the
true "descent ot Man." And man's self-adjustment
to nature is but the elementary phase of the total process of his own self-unfolding, the highest term of
which consists in never-ending practical self-assim-
ilation to the likeness of the primal world-forming
Reason.   Primitive man—including the child of
modern man—is crude, unrealized as man. Hence
is he in that fact alienated from God. Civilization,
culture, religion—these constitute the way of his return to God.

It is to be noted, too, that man's increase of power over nature is manifest in another significant way. The extension of man's embodiment is an extension of his efficient energy without increase in the cumbrousness of the physical aspect of his own personality. In other words, extension of man's embodiment means simply extension of instrumentalities under his control—of instrumentalities that can be taken up and put down at pleasure.

Thus man's environment becomes gradually transformed into man's embodiment—into more and more perfectly specialized instrumentality, serving the purpose both of his self-manifestation and of his further growth as a living unit of the highest order ; as a living unit possessed of intelligence and self-mobility so matured and interfused as to make certain the unlimited extension of his existence.

But increase of intelligence means increase of power to apprehend and finally to comprehend in ever greater degree the "established order" of the universe. In other words it is increase of power to trace out and more and more adequately think the Thought of the Perfect Mind, as that is forever manifested in the Universe ; while increase of self-mobility is increase of power to adjust oneself to that order, to live in harmony with the law of Reason, which is the law of all genuine Reality. Intelligence is power to know the Truth. Self-mobility (or will) is power to live the Truth. And as these two aspects of living units expand into their fuller significance and rise into their maturer forms in man they constitute the vital characteristic which may well be named Freedom. For if Freedom has any meaning at all, it can be nothing else than this : *Conscious, glad conformity to Reason*—that is, to the "established order" of the world. And from this definition of Freedom it may be that Mr. Spencer himself would not seriously dissent ; though a hasty reading of his chapter on "The Will," can hardly fail to lead one to infer that we would dissent very emphatically. And yet that "freedom of the will" which he and others regard as impossible appears rather to be that immature, merely instinctive phase of will commonly known as wilfulness or caprice, which of course is self-contradictory and hence not free ; while in its proper significance the will is free or it is not *will* at all. For, as already indicated, each concrete will is an evolved power which in its very nature implies freedom. Indeed, as Hegel has remarked, "Will without freedom is an empty word." And if one recalls Locke's subtlety that the will, being a power, cannot be free though man as the agent possessing the power is free,[1] Hegel again furnishes an answer quite in keeping with the doctrine of evolution (for

[1] *Of the Human Understanding.* Book II, Ch. XXI, Sec. 19.

Hegel himself was a most thorough-going evolutionist), to the effect that "the difference between thought and will is merely that between the theoretical and the practical attitude [of mind]. Indeed there are not two powers. Rather the will is itself a special mode of thought. It is thought translating itself into practical forms of existence."[1]

Thus the conclusion to which the foregoing argument has led seems not only in accordance with the truth, but also to be the legitimate outcome of the doctrine of evolution as a whole, even as formulated by Mr. Spencer himself.

And now let us see what bearing all this may have upon the question of the "Resurrection." As commonly understood, the doctrine of the Resurrection ·has passed out of notice among thinking men, as a curious piece of symbolism belonging to an unenlightened age.

And yet the more carefully the symbols of earlier ages are examined, the more they are found each to involve some shred at least of truth. Is this symbol of the resurrection of the body an exceptional one? We have only to refer to what precedes to find an answer ; and, I cannot but think, the true answer. Mind is, as we have seen, no less unthinkable apart from its manifestation or embodiment than is the

---

[1] *Philosophie des Rechts.* S. 33. (3te Auflage).

latter apart from the former. Mind and matter are the two complementary, absolutely inseparable factors of the totality of Existence. And along with this we have also seen that death is but transition or change—that in such a being as man it is but transition from one to another phase of life. And finally we have seen how with every advance of intelligence there is necessarily a corresponding increase in extent and complexity of embodiment. Is it conceivable, then, that in the very progress of the modes of existence there should at length be reached a stage at which death should prove to be a sudden transition from a state of expanding embodiment to a state of literally no-embodiment for the mind? And what indeed could the latter state be but a "state" of utter annihilation—a complete severance of the individual from all relation to the modes of manifestation of the divine Thought?

If what is called the "future" life is really to be *Life*, it must be a continuance of the spiritual existence of man ; that is, a continuance of the exercise of those intellectual and moral powers (or rather modes of power), by which alone he can be conceived as immortal. And so far as these powers are realized in any given unit they imply a corresponding range of control over material forms of existence. Not, of course, that such unit can be conceived as having in any slightest degree a power to alter the laws of nature, to change the "established order" of the world ; but that through knowledge of those laws he may take advantage of them and by conforming to them may still secure the accomplishment of his own rational purposes through them. And those purposes can be essentially nothing else than the further expansion of those same intellectual and moral powers through a continued search after the Truth as exhibited in the infinitely varied forms of Reality, interfused with a like continuous effort to conform in all the modes of the individual life to the Truth thus discovered.

And as this implies the constant association of growing mind with growing mind it necessarily also implies the existence of appropriate and indispensable media of association—that is, some kind of embodiment. But also, as increase in intellectual and moral power means increased capacity to mould nature into the appropriate embodiment of the individual mind, so it would seem reasonable to conclude that through the whole range of existence of the individual thinking unit there must be a continuance of the same process which we now see to be going forward ; the process, namely, of extending the range of embodiment of such unit along with the expansion of its inner reality, and of rendering that embodiment more and more delicately and subtly adapted to the individual's needs. Does not the continuity of Life and its modes warrant us in drawing this inference from our observations and experiments in the only field where we can actually study the nature of mind and the modes of its advancement?

Thus far it would seem reasonable to draw a positive conclusion. The progress of individual minds each toward the fulfilment in itself of the one typical nature of all possible minds must be by a method as unalterable as is the type itself.

But if we attempt to picture to ourselves precisely what will be the form or series of forms of the embodiment that will suffice for the needs of a given thinking unit in its successive stages of advancement, then we find ourselves wholly at a loss. The general conditions of the Life after Death—and that can of course mean nothing else than the continued life of the individual thinking unit after the dissolution of the present form of embodiment—can be thought out, because those conditions join on to what we already know concerning the nature of the individual thinking unit. And we may also fairly conclude that, the more advanced the life of such unit becomes, the more extended and complex must its embodiment become also   But just for that reason it is wholly impossible to anticipate what the precise form of the embodiment may be at any given stage.

Nevertheless one further inference at least seems reasonable, though this is on the negative side.   It

is, that with the increased vitality of the individual
thinking unit there can scarcely fail to be less and
less dependence upon any one specific form of embodiment ; just as with the expansion of the life of
such unit it can hardly be doubted that increased
multiplicity and delicacy of forms must be demanded
to supply the widening range of instrumentality to a
power whose growth in extent and complexity has no
conceivable limit.

Finally, as everyone knows, "resurrection" means,
etymologically, a "rising-again." And this presents
an ultimate, transfigured meaning that is essential
and valid. It is this : With every sincere, consistent
effort, Man—he who thinks—rises out of a narrower
into a wider life ; rises from a less worthy into a
worthier existence ; rises out of his merely "natural"
or predominently physical range of interests into the
sphere of spiritual interests—interests which are, in
truth, to so highly endowed a unit, still more *natural*
than are the physical.

And so Resurrection proves to be a name for that
perpetual process through which, stage by stage, man
becomes in reality what he is in Ideal or Type. That
is, in its most vital significance, Resurrection is an
eternal factor in the life of Man the immortal. It is
the never-ending process of the transfiguration of
Man as the eternally begotten Son of God.

II.

ORIENTAL RELIGIONS.

Religion is a process. It is the mode of activity by which the individual spirit strives to bring itself into harmonious relation with the highest Power. It is the vital process of the spiritual evolution of man. It is primarily the concentration of the energies of the soul upon interests assumed to be of a permanent character. The objects of religion are "things eternal." These pertain to the inner life of man, and come at length to be sharply contrasted with "things temporal," with the changing phases of the outer world of space and time. Thus, religion in its essence stands in antithetical relation to all that is external and formal.

At the same time, religion can attain realization in the life of man only through the association of man with man. Man gathers some faint intimation of the Divine through his relation to the physical world about him, but most of all does man discover his relation to the Divine through his relation to his fellowman. But these relations are expressible only through external signs. Nay, the very process by which man discovers his true relation to the Divine, and unfolds that relation in his own life, must inevitably give proof of its vitality in outer signs or forms. And just so far as the life of the individual is bound up in the life of the community, by just so far must the forms expressive of the individual life be the forms expressive of the communal life.

But these outer forms are thus nothing else than the modes by which the inner expresses or manifests itself. So that in the progressive unfolding of religion, in the process of the spiritual evolution of man, there cannot fail to be a progressive modification of the outer forms in which this inner, vital evolution is made manifest. Forms are, as it were, something non-essential, in which, nevertheless, the inner, essential energy of the spirit gives proof of its truth and vitality. They are the indispensable modes, and yet the temporal, transitory modes, of what is true and eternal.

This spiritual evolution of man is, besides, the rendering explicit or real in man what was at first only implicit or possible for man. It is a work, too, which, with whatever of divine aids, man must ever perform for himself. And these divine aids are available to man precisely in the degree in which man is himself able to seize upon and independently make use of them. Hence, the beginnings of religion, like the beginnings of all things in the history of man, could not be other than vague and feeble. It is, then, by no means to be wondered at that the working out of his own salvation by man should necessarily involve a vast degree of fear and trembling on his part ; and this, especially, in the earlier stages of the process. For in those stages man can only vaguely surmise the true nature of the Divine, and can only grope about in the darkness for the method by which he can attain to a relation of harmony with the Divine.

It is this initial stage that is especially illustrated by the religions of the Orient—a fact proven beyond controversy by abundant documentary evidence now easily accessible. In what follows, an attempt is made to indicate the essential elements and fundamental phases of the development of the initial stage of religion.

In Oriental religions, everything is vague and implicit. No clear distinction is developed in them between the inner and the outer. The spiritual is still inextricably involved in the natural. Consciousness is not yet definitely unfolded into conscience.

It has just been seen that the outer expression must of necessity correspond to the inner spirit. Hence, vague conceptions can never find utterance in anything else than in forms correspondingly vague. But such vague forms rather hint at than express the spirit that blindly struggles up into them. They are, then, at best only signs, premonitions, *symbols* of what the yearning spirit vaguely feels, and yet is wholly unable to comprehend or clearly think.

This initial phase of the spiritual evolution of man has been called the "childhood of religion." It is, however, no less truly the religion of childhood. Nothing is clearly thought out by the child, the typical "primitive man." On the contrary, everything is to him wholly miraculous; that is, quite incomprehensible, and hence a perpetual occasion of wonder.

At first, doubtless, no clear distinction is made between the symbol and the thing or idea symbolized. On the contrary, the vague sense of a superhuman Power finds its expression in all the objects of the outer world. But most of all does this vague sense of the superhuman find its appropriate embodiment in just those phases of nature that are themselves most vague and intangible.

It is by no means strange, therefore, that primitive religions seem invariably to find their basis in the primal distinction which constitutes the condition of vision—the sense through which the individual receives so large a proportion of his impressions of the outer world. That distinction is the one between light and darkness. These opposite conditions of his life come and go, primitive man knows not how. He has, of course, not the slightest suspicion that light as illumination and darkness as obscurity are but states of his own mind. Whence he can but regard them as real existences, quite external to himself, and having power immeasurably superior to his own. The light comes, and brings him gladness; the darkness comes, and fills him with terror. He greets the coming of light with praise and thanksgiving. He shrinks from the darkness as from a gigantic power that had slain the kindly divinities, and would bring nothing but evil to man.

It is of no little significance, too, that the word "divine," found in so many modern languages, is traceable to the old Aryan root, *deva*, which meant "bright." The *devas*, the gods, were the "bright ones." And the most exalted worship of the men of the early world was offered to the sun, to the dawn, to the diffused, all pervading light of the sky. So, also, the lightning, and all forms of fire, were revered as "divine." Even the sky itself, visible by means of light, high above all, one and serene, was from the remotest times an object of worship.

At the same time, it is evident that all this is extremely vague and general. Or, in more technical phrase, thought itself, in its very nature, possesses the characteristic of universality. Hence, the simplest act of worship, as itself expressive of a thought, must have in it something universal. And yet, at this initial stage of worship, the object of reverence is apprehended only superficially and in very inadequate fashion. As thus seized, the universal nature of the object of worship is still abstract. The Truth, doubtless, is always infinitely concrete and real. But man, unable to comprehend the Truth in all its fulness, seizes from time to time upon some one simple, universal phase thereof and brings that into special prominence. Thus there is formed an abstract or inadequate view of the Truth.

Nevertheless, continued exercise of thought must have the effect of deepening and enriching man's consciousness of the Truth. And, as a matter of fact, we find that man began at a very early period to notice analogies between the outer light of the sun and the inner light of consciousness. Light came from without, but it also sprang up within. Thus already there was discovered a point of identity between the human and the "divine." The result was inevitable and far-reaching. The "divine" beings, the sources of light outside of man, the sun, the dawn, came at length to be looked upon as possessing the characteristics of consciousness and will. Hence, worship could not but become more definite; and prayer, the offering of the inner thought, must constitute an ever-increasing factor, and tend more and more to displace the outer factor of physical sacrifices.

This process involves another element also. It is this: Just as the rising sun brought gladness and relief from the terrors of the night, so the reappearance of the father of the family after his wanderings in pursuit of game or an enemy could not but bring a sense of illumination, and drive away the vague terrors and sense of defencelessness experienced during his absence. Whence, just as the attributes of humanity must inevitably be sooner or later assigned to the sources of outer light, so, on the other hand, the characteristics belonging to these sources of light cannot fail to be assigned, sooner or later, to the strong man whose presence brings security and whose absence causes gloom and dismay. Nor can the final departure of the strong man in death be thought of as anything more than a *departure*. However vague the form of the belief, the fact of the belief remains that in some way the strong man still lives and dwells, though now invisibly, in the midst of his people. And, just because of the indistinctness of view regarding the new mode of existence of the now invisible strong man, the imagination easily and inevitably represents him as having grown immeasurably in power for good or for evil. He is hence to be propitiated, worshipped. The dead man becomes a living God.

But this perpetual intermingling of human attributes, on the one hand, with the attributes of physical force, on the other, has also the effect of separating certain specially striking phases of force from their ordinary modes of manifestation, and of personifying them as gods in human form. Thus, while the sun was at first vaguely worshipped as a "divine" or luminous, joy-giving being, the light itself came at last to be spiritualized in human conception ; and this spiritualized light, conceived of as possessing a human form, comes at length to be worshipped as a god of *enlightenment* rather than as a god of mere physical illumination The most striking example of this is that of the old Aryan conception of the sun as the bringer of day gradually becoming transfigured into the conception of the god of intellectual clearness and moral elevation. It is in this sense that Apollo comes at last to be worshipped among the Greeks. And this worship formed the strongest element in all that was noblest in Greek life and character.

It is to be observed, however, that the first vague form of this transformation of the natural into the spiritual in the estimation of men is found in the wonder excited by the fact of *life* in general. Man can only interpret the facts of the world about him by referring those facts to his own consciousness, to his own personal experience. As his own movements are inseparable from his own life, so primitive man could not do otherwise than conclude spontaneously that whatever moves also possesses life. Nay, in his imperfect, uncritical view of himself and his limited world, he can neither suspect that movement is separate or separable from life in any respect ; nor can he suspect that life is anywhere different in kind from his own. If the sun, or the wind, or a cloud, or a river moves, it must do so because it chooses to move. And still more must a tree, or a bird, or a serpent seem not only a living being, but also a conscious, thinking being, possessed of a will. Is not the tree a creator of fruit? Does not the bird by its power of flight transfer itself at will to and from the invisible world? Has not the serpent power over life and death, as well as miraculous gift of movement?

Such, doubtless, is the clew to the otherwise strange fact that primitive man worshipped all objects of na- tvre indiscriminately, as embodying the mysterious, divine principle of motion. That principle he rightly interpreted as necessarily implying life and conscious- ness, though he failed to comprehend it in its truth as an evidence of the one living, conscious Energy that constitutes the unifying principle of the uni- verse as a whole. Here, too, is found the clew to the way in which the doctrine of transmigration grew into form. If life differs from life, not in kind, but only in form and degree ; and if the life manifested in a given form is still permanent as life, while the form in which it is manifest is evanescent—then a given unit of life may take on an indefinite series of forms running through all the grades which are in any way adaptable to life. Hence, a living unit that is now a man may, through former periods, have been an eagle, an antelope, a tiger, a fish, a serpent, a worm. Nor is there any hindrance to his becoming hereafter a god. The worm and the god are but opposite extremes in the at once upward-rising and downward-sinking scale of life.

This is the special characteristic of Oriental religions. Brahmanism rises to the figurative representation of a unifying principle of all things. Brahm is all. Hence, all is identified with Brahm. This is especially emphasized in the conception of the identification of man with Brahm through the Brahman, the deified man. But it also appears in germ in all primitive faiths in the worship paid to ancestors.

In Buddhism, also, transmigration is an essential thread. In this faith, which sets out with ignoring the idea of the existence of a God or gods in so far as worship is concerned, the culmination is reached in man himself becoming a god. That is, man reaches absolute perfection in an abstract universal existence by sinking into *Nirvana*—the indescribable state. To the western mind, indeed, this means non-existence; since whatever is real must manifest itself to the reason as possessing qualitative and quantitative differences or distinctions within itself. And the richer the reality, the more positive and multiform those distinctions must be. But the Real thus manifested is precisely what appeals and must ever appeal directly to reason, and is hence comprehensible and utterable. The absolutely unutterable is the absolutely non-existent.

The Oriental religions, then, present a confused representation, in which everything is divine, in which all is God; that is, the fundamental characteristic is *pantheism*.

But, as man cannot be content with mere passive awe and vague wonder in presence of physical *light*, so neither can he rest in the mere impression that there is something divine in the principle of *life*. His own spontaneous nature must impress itself upon the objects of his worship. His vague consciousness becomes enriched and invigorated and defined through centuries of spontaneous activity. And while, in the first vague universality of his consciousness, man was content passively to contemplate the divine in the objects of the surrounding world, he must, with an unfolding and deepening consciousness, be led at length to a more or less definite struggle to construct for himself his own expression of the universal and divine truth which he deeply felt and dimly saw in the world.

Thus arose monumental symbolism. It is, above all, in Egypt that this phase of the Oriental spirit is found in its culmination. It has often been said that the Pyramids are a proof of the overwhelming tyranny of the Egyptian kings, on the one hand, and of the abject submission of the Egyptian people, on the other. A truer view, however, must bring to light the fact that the faith in immortality symbolized in those huge monuments was the faith of the people no less than of the king ; and the nation doubtless toiled willingly to give monumental utterance to a sentiment pervading the inmost life of the whole people. Doubtless their toiling was *directly* an expression of simple obedience. But the king was the more willingly, the more spontaneously obeyed for the very reason that he commanded precisely that work the accomplishment of which was also implicitly demanded by the deepest convictions of the whole nation.

But the final, culminating symbol to which the Oriental consciousness gave rise, in its struggle at once to state and to answer its questionings concerning the nature of the Divine, and the relation of man to the Divine, was the *Sphinx*. One of the earliest of Egyptian symbols, it is incessantly repeated throughout the whole life of the Egyptian people. Even the huge Sphinx of Gizeh, constructed before the beginning of the Memphite dynasty, was at the outset dedicated explicitly to a divinity, and thus from the first possessed a deeply religious significance. It is remarkable, too, that it was dedicated to the rising sun, which to the Egyptians was ever a new-born God. This colossal image thus presents in itself the symbol of *light*, and hence joins on to the primitive phase of the worship of the inorganic in its sublimest form of illumination, as a life-giving divinity. But it was hewn out of a mass of live rock rising abruptly out of the plain. Hence in this rude but marvelous monument there is represented the rising of the inorganic, through the organic as mere animal, to man as the animal in whom the light of the spirit was at last to shine forth in its completeness as matured, self-conscious Reason.

Nevertheless, it is only in Greece, the dawnland of spiritual enlightenment, that this dumb symbol of the Orient.lives and speaks. There for the first time does it audibly utter its question. And yet no sooner does it find answer to its central question than it sinks back into dumbness and even into death. For man, the thinker, proves to be the solution of all riddles—man, the ever new-born son of God, whose undying nature assures him of an eternity in which to rise through all the degrees of realization of the divine nature within him. Hence, man is himself the explicit *utterance* of the ultimate problem of the world. He is also implicitly the final solution of all riddles, and thus the final dissolution of all symbols.

In the Orient, this culmination is vaguely yearned for ; in Greece, clearly prophesied ; in the modern and Christian world, realized. And yet Christianity

began in the Orient, and is now at length shining
back with its matured Light of Life into the Orient,
giving proof ever clearer that Religion is in truth
neither Oriental nor Occidental, nor external at all ;
but, rather, that it is something altogether internal
and spiritual ; that, as indicated at the outset of this
sketch, it is the one absolutely changeless method,
which every finite spirit must adopt and unfold into
genuine reality for itself as the vital process of spiritual evolution, if it would bring itself into genuine
harmony and living unity with the divine Father
of all.

III.

BUDDHISM AND CHRISTIANITY.

I.

The farther back we penetrate toward the beginnings of history the more strongly marked become the proofs that the narrators of events in those early times had little thought of representing events precisely as they occurred. Properly speaking there was no history, but only prophecy. And the prophet, far from entertaining the thought of making for future generations a faithful record of what was passing or had already passed, was only intent upon influencing as deeply as possible the people of his own time.

Hence he seized events in their main outlines and used them with perfect freedom as *plastic materials* out of which to construct a representation that should possess a certain artistic completeness, and thus prove specially impressive in the enforcement of some general doctrine which it seemed desirable the people should adopt. This was true in greater or less degree in all the countries of the ancient world ; in China, in India, in Greece, in Judæa.

Nor is this an evidence of cunning and knavery on the part of the prophetic narrators. On the contrary, it but proves that man had not yet awakened to a true sense of historic values. Thus the earliest "history" took the form of the myths in which the particular event is enlarged into a movement of universal significance ; while chronology drops out of sight altogether—or rather it wholly fails to appear—save in the form of sacred symbolic numbers.

This is the simple explanation—now well-nigh commonplace—of the fact that the history of early civilizations can be only partially made out through the most laborious and careful investigation of the fragmentary remains of the monuments and literatures which the peoples of the early world busied themselves in constructing.

Thus, by a new and wholly admirable development of analytical skill, entire cycles of richly unfolded literatures, which on first view are without date or any external mark of chronological order, have, by comparison of turns of expression and of phases of belief and thought developed in them, been brought into something approaching historical arrangement, from which the historical development of the peoples themselves may now be at least approximately traced.

This critical, comparative method, characteristic exclusively of the modern and Western mind, has been applied with special zeal and success within recent years in the investigation of Oriental literatures and religions. And, first of all, India has furnished

by far the most extensive as well as the most inviting
of the hitherto unexplored fields.

At the same time the critical spirit has fearlessly
cl imed the right to apply precisely the same methods
and the same tests that have here availed so much,
to the literature and religion not only of the ancient
Hebrews, but also of the Christians.

It has thus happened that wholly unrestrained
comparisons have been instituted between these religions, so revered in the West, and the leading faiths
of the "heathen" East Many, indeed, have been
the parallels already drawn between Buddhism and
Christianity ; and not seldom the conclusion arrived
at has been that the differences between these widely
desseminated faiths are differences of form rather
than of substance.

Not unfrequently, indeed, those who have most
zealously urged the importance of applying the comparative method to the study of religions, and who
have most confidently applied that method in such
studies, prove to have quite forgotten a caution of
Plato applicable to comparative studies generally.
One ought, he said, to be extremely careful in dealing with similarities, for they are "*most slippery
things.*" It is, in fact, altogether easy to find similarities between any two objects of attention above or
below the sun, provided one does not specially con-

cern himself regarding the depth or shallowness of import which the comparison unfolds.

It is certainly true—or rather a truism—that the Buddhist fa th failed to find permanent acceptance among the people of the same race as its founder, but spread irresistibly among an alien race, precisely as was the case with Christianity. And yet not "precisely" either ; since Buddhism became, and for centuries remained, the dominant faith in a large portion of India, while Christianity was from the first rejected by the Jews, not to mention the extreme differences of national conditions at the time of the origination of the two faiths respectively. Of course, also, a similarity so striking ought not to be disturbed by the further mention of the otherwise fairly noteworthy differences maniles between the Chinese, Tatars, Siamese, etc., among whom Buddhism has been more or less enthusiastically received, and the peoples of Europe and America, by whom Christianity has been accepted.

It is not, however, the purpose of the present paper to pursue this line of comparison, whatever possibilities of entertainment or even amusement it might be found to possess. We shall rather attempt to trace the chief conditions of the historical development of the two faiths respectively, and at the same time to present the fundamental conceptions by which each is characterized.

It must also be explicitly recognized at the outset that every genuine investigation is an appeal to REASON. Nothing can be admitted, therefore, that is not clear to the Reason—that does not, in fact, compel the assent of Reason. On the other hand, appeal to "miracle"—to something not comprehended—in proof of the divine origin of a faith, and you at once set aside Reason, which alone is capable of recognizing and verifying the divine elements which a faith may possess. All faiths are, in their origin, based on "miracles." Reason alone can discriminate between a true and a false miracle, between a divine and an undivine revelation.

If Christianity, then, is superior to Buddhism, it must give to the Reason convincing proof of its superiority. Reason seeks, and from its very nature must ever seek for what is highest and ultimate ; that is, for the concrete Totality of Truth. With nothing less than this can it ever be satisfied ; and to this it can only attain through an independent tracing out of the necessary and therefore rational order of relations in the world as a whole.

The final faith of the world, then, can be no other than that which presents to the Reason the clew at once to the fundamental principle of the world on the one hand and to the essential nature and final destiny of man on the other.

Does Buddhism present this clew? Does Christianity present it ? Which of these religions has advanced farthest toward the utterance of the final—which is also necessarily the primal—truth? This is the central question, to the investigation of which we have now to proceed.

II.

What were the chief conditions of the historical development of Buddhism? To this it is to be answered that Buddhism, taking its rise among the Hindus, was necessarily conditioned by the peculiar characteristics of that people. And what those characteristics were, thanks to the persistent energy and keen, critical insight of modern scholars, can now be briefly and confidently stated.

The Hindus are now well known to have been characterized from the earliest times by an activity and brilliancy of imagination even beyond that of any other primitive people. At the same time, that imaginative power, under the influence of the overwhelming nature-forces in the midst of which the development of the people took place, gradually unfolded into an uncontrolled fancy which never ceased to revel in the creation of grotesque, monstrous imagery. Reflection, careful testing, searching criticism, found no place , and the Hindu mind was at length overwhelmed with uncontrollable terror and despair in presence of monstrous beings which it had itself unconsciously called into phantasmal existence.

Thus grew up among the Hindus that fantastic theory of the world and of life at which the Western mind can never cease to wonder. At the same time the development of this theory is essentially connected with the attainment to supremacy on the part of the Brahman caste. The members of this caste alone, so they came at length to claim, were in possession of the key to the happiness of mankind, whether in this life or in the life to come. And this claim was for a long period almost universally admitted. Thus the Brahmans were enabled to develop a more and more elaborate ceremonial, and to enforce it with ever increasing complexity of requirements upon the hopelessly enthralled people.

The climax was fairly reached when, with a greatly overcrowded population, the caste system came to be firmly fixed and unresistingly accepted by the great mass of the population as the true system of relations between man and man. With the endless ceremonial and crushing terrorism of the Brahmanic faith, reinforced by the narrow, impassable limitations of the caste system, it could not be otherwise than that for a vast majority of the people life should be full of wretchedness and despair. And how much more as the conviction became everywhere settled that life ended only to begin anew, and perhaps in still more wretched guise! Even the good man, who through

long penance and multiplied lives of devotion came
at length to be admitted to the company of the gods,
could not prevent his hard-won virtues from there
crumbling away until, himself grown earthy and
heavy again, he must needs descend once more to the
lower sphere, albeit his return took place in the form
of a falling star !¹

From very early times, indeed, the conception of
transmigration became the fundamental tenet of the
Hindu creed. And thus the all-absorbing question
came to be : How can this seemingly ceaseless round
of birth and painful life and mocking death be
brought to an end? By penance and by scrupu-
lously minute observance of the Vedic ceremonial,
answered the Brahman. And millions of Hindus
helplessly, if not hopelessly, followed the injunction.

The steps of spiritual development on the part of
this people are, then : first, a specially lively imagination which, through its abnormal development,
led at length to belief in a wholly artificial relation
between man and the Divine Principle ; secondly, a
growing dread of that Principle, a dread having its
ground in endless mystification concerning the Principle ; and, thirdly, a consequent increasingly-abject
submission to the dictates of a class, the members of
which claimed to have exclusive knowledge upon

---

¹This quaint conception also makes its appearance, in
modified form, at the close of Plato's *Republic*.

these high themes along with power to determine the fate of the individual for good or ill.

Manifestly the tendency was ever toward a less and less sufferable condition ; and it is not to be wondered at that so far as the Hindu mind developed anything that can be dignified with the name philosophy, that philosophy should be distinctly tinged with this depressing character of the whole intellectual development of India. Hindu faith being pessimistic, Hindu philosophy is pessimistic as a matter of course. For the philosophy of a people is but the expression, in terms appealing to the reflective consciousness or reason, of what is already present, under forms appealing to the imagination, in its faith. But imagination, as we have already seen, is the predominant characteristic of Hindu thought. Hence the so-called Hindu philosophy never rises above imagination. Its best thoughts are still involved in imagery.

Nature, says their chief system, is fundamentally active. It therefore involves and is involved in change, and change is inseparable from pain. The soul, on the contrary, is changeless, altogether passive, and is connected with nature only by illusion. It is only through this illusion that the soul comes to be regarded as acting. Even "intellect" is a phase, not of the soul, but rather of nature or matter.

Now because the soul is thought to be inactive, and therefore not involved in change, which must ever infallibly bring pain, precisely for this reason is the soul assumed to be superior to nature. And still further : even this seeming connection of the soul with matter must be broken off in order to put an end to its seeming activity, and thus to bring about its deliverance from illusion and the fateful round of transmigration involved in this illusory existence.

But only by knowledge can illusion be done away with ; and. as we would expect, it is "by the study of principles" as unfolded in the Sankhya system, and thus alone, that true knowledge—and with it true deliverance—is said to be attainable.

Once in possession of this highest knowledge, however, says the author of the system, the truth for the individual is expressed in the formula : "Neither I am, nor is aught mine, nor do I exist ," or, as it has been otherwise rendered, "I am not, nothing is mine, and there is no ego" or thinking principle !'

Manifestly, then, the author of the system, so soon as he attempted to think of the soul as apart from matter[2] was able to think of it only in this purely

____

[1] *Sankhya Karika*, Verse 64. Colebrook translates : "So through study of principles, the conclusive, incontrovertible, one only knowledge is attained, that neither I am, nor is aught mine, nor do I exist." The second rendering is that of John Davies. See his *Hindu Philosophy*, (p. 46). London, Truebner & Co., 1881.

[2] And Kapila believed that the soul could only attain perfection through becoming "wholly separate from matter," and in this state the soul exists "without consciousness or sense of personality."

negative fashion,-that is, to imagine it as existing apart from all imaginable qualities or characteristics! It is nothing else than a blank denial of consciousness or personality side by side with the affirmation of the continued existence of the soul. The only escape from pain is through the loss of consciousness, and pain is regarded as unmixed evil. Hence the primal and only real problem of Hindu philosophy is : "How to obtain release from the three-fold kinds of pain ?"

Thus the only good toward which this strange system points is the empty abstraction of unconscious existence—an *impersonal personality*.

Now the Sankhya philosophy is a remarkable formulation of the implicit belief in and deep yearning for deliverance from the interminable round of the transmigration of the soul. And it is of special interest in the present connection, not merely from this fact, but also, and mainly, because, according to competent scholars, its development took place in the period just preceding that of the rise of Buddhism in India. Or it might be inferred from internal evidence, which is well-nigh the only evidence we possess, that the Sankhya philosophy and Buddhism both developed during the same period as outgrowths of the same tendencies, and were but different efforts put forth side by side from different standpoints with a view to meeting the most spiritual needs of the time.

Certain it is, at least, that at the foundation of both lies the same fundamental conception of the soul entangled in the meshes of interminable transmigration ; of life, with its constant recurrences of birth and death, as hopelessly full of misery ; while the one only way of escape from pain is assumed to be necessarily that of the complete suppression of consciousness. The philosophical system emphasized contemplation and knowledge as the way of final release. It therefore appealed to the few. Buddhism emphasized action, and especially action in behalf of others, as the means of attaining to Nirvana or eternal freedom from action. This appealed powerfully to human sympathy and identified in this strange way the interest of the individual in his fellow-men with his deepest interest in himself. Buddhism therefore appealed to the many.

Each was, then, in its own way, an utterance of the despair of the Hindu mind. At the same time each, it cannot fail to be noticed, involved the most glaring contradiction. The one declares that the only way of release from pain is knowledge ; and yet the release itself consists in the complete extinction of consciousness. The other no less unequivocally regards pain as inseparable from action, and complete cessation from action as the final goal ; and yet this very goal can only be attained *through action*.

Both, indeed, completely separate the theoretical from the practical ; and thus, in either case, the destiny of man proves to be nothing but the gradual canceling of all positive characteristics in his nature until he vanishes at length into something wholly unrecognizable, even wholly without the power of *self*-recognition—into a purely abstract existence which it seems well-nigh impossible to distinguish from non-existence.

Such, then, thus briefly indicated, is the fundamental characteristic of Buddhism. It is but one of many expressions of the spirit of a peculiar people under peculiar conditions of development.

III.

If now we turn to a consideration of the chief conditions determining the historical development of Christianity, we find ourselves in the midst of wholly different scenes, and confronted by a people of radically different convictions. We have seen that with the Hindus there was an abnormal development of imagination intensified by the overwhelming luxuriance of surrounding nature. When we turn to the Semitic race, we find among its more advanced divisions a special development of shrewd, practical judgment intensified by the barren simplicity of the outer world in the midst of which they found themselves at home. In the former case there was overwhelming tendency, both from internal nature and from external surroundings, toward endless mystification. In the latter case there was a powerful and likewise double tendency toward utmost clearness and simplicity.

Thus with the Semitic race in general, and with the People of Israel in particular, there came to be developed at an early period a deep sense of the supernatural character and essential unity of the Highest Power, as also of the complete subordination of nature to that Power.

Nay, rather, in presence of that Power, Nature was looked upon as mere means and instrument which of itself is mere nothingness. So intense, indeed, did this feeling of the Oneness and completeness and matchless might of the Supreme Power become, that men found full satisfaction in dwelling upon its glories, and sought for themselves only a long, prosperous life in the land which their God had given them. Far from exhausting their imagination in attempts to picture the conditions of a personal immortality for which, until late in their history as a people, they seem to have felt no need, their energies of mind and body were devoted to the enriching of the Present and to the enlargement of the visible Kingdom of God on the earth.

True, there always existed a strong reactionary

party who constantly, and at times more or less successfully, sought to restore the worship of the many gods of the old nature-religion. Progress, there as elsewhere indeed, could only be made through ceaseless struggle. And there, more than elsewhere (doubtless in part just because of this reactionary tendency), the steps of progress took the paradoxical form of reversion and restoration. The highest conception the zealous prophet could form of his God and of the divine requirements, that conception he boldly and sincerely announced as a long-neglected and forgotten command of Moses.

From this standpoint, indeed, what could be more natural or rational? Was not Moses the ideal lawgiver? And had he not provided his people with a perfect system of divinely appointed regulations for their guidance? Assuredly, if the code of laws known in the prophet's time fell short in anything, it could only be because the people in their waywardness had first neglected and then forgotten, until there remained but fragments of, the perfect law. It must, then, be the duty of the clear-eyed prophet to make good what he saw to be wanting, and at the same time to warn the people that as past humiliation had been caused by neglect of these requirements, so future misfortune could only be averted by their fulfillment.

Thus the innovator assumed with perfect good

faith the character of a restorer, and wrought his revolutions with the sincerest conviction that he was but bringing back the purity and perfection which his uncritical faith led him to attribute to the patri·archal age.

Nor is this a mere arbitrary conjecture, it having been elaborately proven in such learned works as those of Ewald and Kuenen, that the actual historical mode of development of the ''Mosaic Law,'' as now understood and received, was substantially that just indicated.[1]

But note, further, that from the time of the deliverance from Egypt the God of Israel came to be regarded especially in the light of a Redeemer. He would save his people, on the one hand from outward submission to the yoke of foreign kings, and on the other hand, from inward submission to the influence of foreign gods. This, indeed, is but a special phase of the general conception that man as a changeful, sinful being is perpetually in need of redemption, perpetually in need of being brought back to and rec·onciled with a changeless God.

The purpose of the party of progress received clear definition through the work of Moses; and from his time onward the struggle to elevate to a higher standard the conceptions which the people entertained

---

[1] Cf. also Canon Driver's *Introduction to the Literature of the Old Testament*, 5th Ed. 1894.

concerning their God was carried forward with ever-increasing zeal and consistency.

Not, however, until near the close of their career as a people had they come to conceive of their Divinity as a truly universal and spiritual Divinity. Rather had they thought of Him as exclusively their God, whose power was exerted solely in their behalf. Nor did they ever completely escape this narrowness of view. In truth, their national enthusiasm became the more intense, the farther removed the realization of their national ideal appeared to be.

It was precisely their incapacity to completely universalize their national ideal, at the same time that they were approximately universalizing their conception of their national God, which constituted the tragical element in the history of the People of Israel. The final result, indeed, could not be doubtful. The conception of a universal theocracy with its capital at Jerusalem, and with the Jews for its ruling class, must of necessity bring this proud people into irreconcilable hostility with the whole world. And precisely in the degree in which they were baffled in their purposes must the excitement among them intensify.

At the same time, this extreme anxiety concerning their political future could not but react powerfully upon their conceptions in the realm of religion. And so much the more as the state was looked upon as one phase merely of their religion. Thus the relation of man to the Divine came in this peculiar way to be the one all-absorbing theme in that period of eager hope and intense mental strain which followed the Roman occupancy of their country. A political savior was looked for with utmost longing ; and yet the need of a spiritual savior was felt no less deeply, at least on the part of the more thoughtful. The general view was, however, that both these needs must be met in the same person, who would in a special manner embody the Divine Principle, and with whose appearance the Theocracy, the genuine visible Kingdom of God on earth, would assume its completed form.

IV.

It was in the midst of this excitement and expectancy that Jesus of Nazareth made his appearance. No man ever broke more completely with the traditions of his own race and the convictions of his own time. And yet, like other and earlier prophets of the Hebrews, he was profoundly convinced that his mission was one of restoration rather than of innovation. He came, as he himself said, to fulfill, not to destroy—to turn divine purpose into human reality.

At the same time, his clear vision quickly penetrated through all forms and traditions, and recognized that the central demand of the time—nay, of

all time—was the establishment, not of a visible
Kingdom of God on the earth, but rather of a kingdom which should distinctly and finally reject all
pretense of external rule, and demand, instead, only
the homage of the soul. It was to be emphatically
the Kingdom of Truth, the Empire of the Spirit.
It was still to be a theocracy indeed, since God was
to be the sole ruler. Yet at the same time God was
expressly declared to be a Spirit to whom homage
must be rendered in spirit and in truth, rather than
in forms and ceremonies. The external and vanishing is set aside ; the internal, the spiritual and abiding, that alone is held fast to and prized as possessing any genuine worth.

Here, then, is the very focus of Christianity. The
local struggle of a particular and peculiar people is
universalized and transfigured into the eternally repeated struggle of the individual spirit to establish
within itself the Kingdom of God. For ideally this
kingdom is already within every spiritual being, and
only requires to be developed into consistent realization. What else, indeed, but the successive steps in
this endless process of realizing the Kingdom of God
within one can constitute the true significance of the
life and immortality which the teachings of Christ
have brought to light ?

Precisely here, indeed, lies the infinitely profound
significance of Christ's Messianic mission, to which

the Messianic idea underlying the whole history of the People of Israel naturally leads up. Every step in the genuine progress of man, every stage of his true spiritual development, is but so much accomplished toward the fulfillment of his divine Ideal. And when man's caprice, unfolding as it does in crime and sin, is understood in its proper significance as a wandering away from God, who is the eternal realized divine Ideal of man, then is it seen that the whole of human progress is but the total, ceaseless Messianic Movement that brings man back to God. Here, then, it becomes manifest that every *advance*, properly so called, is no less truly a *restoration*. Such is the ultimate conception of the restoration and fulfillment of the law—the divine Law of the Spirit, which constitutes the fundamental nature of the soul of man. _

Something fundamentally akin to this, indeed, had already been wrought out in another way by Greek philosophy. Aristotle in particular, through a thorough investigation of the doctrine of Causes and of the relation between Substance and its attributes, arrived at the clear conviction that the world or universe in all its phases necessarily presupposes an absolute, divine Spirit as origin and support. And he declared that whoever was the first to explicitly claim that Mind governs the world, "seemed like a

sober thinker in comparison with the talkers-at-ran-
dom of the earlier period."[1]

At the same time, the conviction of Aristotle was
arrived at by a complex, difficult method and set
forth in abstract, unfamiliar terms. As unfolded by
him, therefore, his conception of the fundamental
truth of the world could be intelligible only to the
few who would take the trouble to familiarize themselves with the special method and the special termi-
nology.

On the other hand, the Man of Galilee proclaimed
the same fundamental truth with a directness and
simplicity that appeal to all seriously minded people
regardless of technical acquirements. And still
further, it is to be noted that this infinitely clear
recognition of the spiritual nature of man, and hence
of the essential oneness of the human and the Divine
Nature, involving the immortality of man, awakened
within him the deepest yearning toward the oppressed
and despairful multitudes. Hence it was with
special zeal that he proclaimed his glad tidings to
the poor. These, too, must be taught to value
rightly their own destiny as immortal beings.

It is said, however, that the Buddha also manifested vast sympathy for the poor, and addressed his

---

[1] Metaphysics: Book I, Chap. III. The usual rendering
of this passage—"seemed like a sober man in the midst of
the drunken"—may be more picturesque, but it is non-Aris-
totelian both in form and in substance.

words of comfort especially to them. This, indeed, seems beyond question. And here we have a similarity of real interest and significance.

The difference, however, is not less significant. The Buddha shared in the superstition of his race. He belived, with them, in a fearful immortality of transmigration and measureless pain. His proclamation was that of a way of escape from this. And the escape was to consist in the final swoon of Nirvana from which the soul was never more to wake. This is assuredly the religion of *Pessimism*.

The Christ, on the contrary, proclaims the Beatitudes. This brief life, charged as it so often is with pain, is *not the All.* He who will deny himself of everything that is inconsistent with justice and mercy, and who will conform in his life to the law of the Spirit, is assured of an immortality of *ever-intensifying consciousness* involving not merely rest and freedom from pain, but also infinite—that is, free or self-consistent—activity, bringing the *deepest, richest, most positive enjoyment.* Assuredly this is the religion of *Optimism*.

Aristotle, in his philosophy, had transcended the religion of the Greeks, as Christ, in his prophetic, divinely human way, transcended the limits of all special, local forms of faith. Aristotle looked steadfastly beyond the fading forms of the Greek gods, and saw the necessary unity of the Divine Principle in one absolute, eternal Spirit. Christ looked within the human soul and saw there the image, the spiritual likeness, the ideal nature of the Divine. And his mission came to be summed up, as we have already intimated, in the struggle to awaken men to a clear consciousness of this divine ideal common to all, and also to arouse them to a determined effort toward its realization within themselves through the perfecting of their own lives.

And yet, with the intense political excitement among his own people, together with the complete preoccupancy of their minds with the ideal of a *political messiah*, it was but inevitable that they should give little heed to his words.

V.

Nor is it without deep significance that this religion found permanent acceptance first with the Greeks, among whom the foremost minds had already reflectively discovered the inner law of the spirit ; and secondly with the Romans who had for five centuries been unconsciously developing the external forms of that law.

It is true that with the Romans this process was a severe and even relentless one, as is illustrated by the story of Livy that after the expulsion of the kings the young nobles complained bitterly of the pitiless laws which could not be appealed to for sympathy or indulgence, and dealt with high and low alike. The growth of Roman law and the spread of Roman rule was, indeed, a leveling process. But it taught men, in however abstract and one-sided a fashion, the significant lesson that the same principles apply universally and alike to all men in their relations one with another.

Here, then, Christianity found its way prepared and its work already begun, though only from the outside. The old Roman *institutions* were, indeed, essentially pagan ; and Christianty could not fail of fierce opposition from the ruling class. For its success involved, and was felt at the time to involve, in important respects, a political as well as a religious revolution. Spite of all opposition, indeed, the revolution came. Old institutions were swept away, and new ones embodying the now victorious faith took shape.

After all, then, the purely spiritual theocracy which Christ proclaimed could not remain altogether indifferent to the visible and temporal kingdoms of the world. For the visible and temporal proves to be but the series of forms which the invisible and eternal assumes in its caseless round of activity. In proportion as man advances in the adequacy of his conceptions of the Divine and of his own relations to the Divine, in like degree must he find it necessary to reconstruct external forms and institutions, lest they shall come at length to contradict instead of giving proper utterance to his increasingly adequate conceptions.

It is a deeply significant fact, however, that the Roman *Law*, which had so long been maturing, remained. Though developed under pagan rule, it was found to be Christian law ; for it embodied the universal principles of the human spirit, and was thus the expression of Justice between man and man, regardless of time, or place, or race.

Thus, after the establishment of the Christian-Roman Empire upon a firm basis there occurs a period of special activity in the study, interpretation, and development of Roman law ; and a Christian emperor leads the way in securing a classification and reduction to manageable form of this sublime monument of the genius of the Roman people.

So, again, this Christianized Roman Empire, which finds the laws thus developed specially adapted to its wants and altogether adequate to its purposes, even serves in important respects as the model for the organization, on the side of *external authority*, of that mighty spiritual empire which also came to have its centre in Rome ; but which, on the side of *internal spiritual growth*, must ever find its centre and circumference in the soul of the devout seeker after Truth, be he ever so humble.

VI.

We have already noticed that in Buddhism there is developed complete separation between the active and the passive, between the theoretical and the practical. Our task further requires that we consider in what manner Christianity has dealt with these antithetical phases of life.

And first it is to be noted that during its earliest days, and for three centuries from the time of its founder, its votaries were constantly called upon to exercise the passive characteristic of endurance. Patience, submission, self-restraint—these are the specially lustrous virtues of the early Christians.

And yet this passivity is, after all, only one phase of a genuine and vigorous activity. "He that ruleth his own spirit is greater than he that taketh a city." Patience and submission, based on clear conviction of moral worth, mean *active self-conquest*; and the strength of character thus developed proves to be energy stored for further uses. And not only so, but no sooner does the individual become thoroughly permeated by the new spirit, with its passivity toward external opposition, than he enters aggressively upon the work of winning others to the same faith.

Practically, then the active and the passive can never be completely separated. And this proves true in the history of Buddhism also. But this fundamental distinction is to be emphasized here, namely : That the activity displayed by Buddhism has for its purpose the suppression of all positive characteristics, in order to the attainment of final and complete passivity. Buddhism, indeed, presents no clear conviction of genuine moral worth, for it *contains no clear conception of spirit or mind in its fundamental nature*. Hence it can only seek a negative release from pain through the ultimate suppression of all activity.

Christianity, on the contrary, with its clear grasp of the fundamental nature of the spirit, shows its period of relative passivity to be also a period of discipline and clearly defined evolution. Slowly and silently indeed, but also irresistibly, the new faith with its transforming power compelled the assent of reason, and became the dominant, formative principle in the lives of men throughout the Roman world. In a new and far profounder sense than had before been realized in this world, the passive phase of the lesson of submission and uncomplaining obedience was fairly learned, and men at length knew how to patiently "bear the cross."

But this was not the whole of the lesson. By slow degrees the maturing spirit gained power of wider vision into its external conditions, and of deeper penetration into its own inner nature. It could no longer remain predominantly passive, even externally. Suddenly, at length, toward the close of the eleventh

century, the voice of Peter the Hermit rings through
Europe. It is a new signal for Christianity. It is a
call to arms, though solely in behalf of the ideal element in the Christian faith. And Christian Europe
is ready for the call. Kings, princes, bishops, the
pope—all are moved. The people crowd together in
vast multitudes, listen breathlessly, then cry out
with a voice like the sea : "God wills it ! God wills
it !" And at once banners, robes, all things available
are torn into strips and sewn cross-wise on the shoul-
ders and breasts of the eager thousands who have
suddenly become fired with unquenchable zeal to
rescue the Holy Sepulchre from the hands of the infidels.

The cross thus ceases to be a mere symbol of submission and endurance, and becomes thenceforth a
symbol of aggression and conquest.

True, this significance of the symbol was at first
seized only superficially. And yet even this superficial
phase of its meaning was purely ideal ; a fact which
stamps the movement of the crusades as one of the
most significant in the whole history of the world.
Here, for the first time in the world's history, a
purely spiritual ideal seizes upon a whole group of
peoples and moves them to take part with an all-
absorbing enthusiasm in one grand common enter-
prise, which has for its exclusive purpose to honor

God and bring the souls of men into a closer union with Him.

Nor does the superficiality of that phase of the meaning seized by the earlier crusaders long escape notice. The conquest of Jerusalem and the Holy Sepulchre is hardly accomplished when the crusaders themselves begin to experience a somewhat uneasy feeling, as if the real purpose of the movement were after all not exactly accomplished. And when, later, Louis the Ninth of France (St. Louis of later times) begins making preparation to carry out an unreflecting vow of his early youth to go on a crusade to the Holy City, the most thoughtful, both among clergy and laity, endeavor to dissuade him from it. It is felt, if not clearly seen, that the best crusade the king could carry on would be a crusade negatively against wrong within his own dominions, and positively for the perfecting of the state. For the state is itself, in truth, but a means to the development of whatever is noble and worthy in man.

It was not, after all, a dead, but a living Saviour ; not a buried, but a risen Lord whom the true crusader must serve. Not for the possession of tombs, but for the possession of the living Spirit would he struggle.

Thus we are brought round again to the seemingly passive phase of symbolically bearing the cross through meekness and endurance, and find this to be, after all, the truer crusade. For, as we have seen, it proves to be, in truth, an active process, consisting of the genuinely aggressive movement of self-conquest.

Nevertheless, for the completion of this inward movement there was required also an outward one, consisting of the kindling of just such flame of universal enthusiasm as that which lighted the way to the great crusades, which fused all hearts into oneness of purpose, and at length awakened all minds into more or less clear consciousness that the Divine is, above all, to be honored through ceaseless struggle to refine and perfect the soul of man.

But organization—in short, the whole institutional world—is needful to the accomplishment of this end. Individual man can attain to the fullest realization of himself *as an individual* only through combination with his fellow-man. Here, indeed, lies the deep-reaching paradox of the Christian world. He alone can hope to be *free*, in any true sense, who *completely subordinates* himself to a highly complex social organism. He who loses his life finds it. Hence the crusading spirit finds its true permanent sphere of activity in the development of the world of institutions—the degree of the completeness of which world indicates, and also in great measure determines, the well-being of man.

Careful reflection, indeed, leads us to see that this paradox of Christianity is but the universal paradox of the world. Every phase of existence is antithetical. Everything is its own opposite. It is precisely because Christianity recognizes this duality, or rather infinite manifoldness, in every phase of unity, that it possesses so rich, so concrete a significance in the world's history. This it is, too, which brings it into such pronounced contrast with Buddhism and with all pantheistic forms of faith.

In further illustration of this, we have but to recall the estimate formed of pain in the different creeds of the world. The Hindu mind, including the Buddhistic development, as we have already observed, has invariably regarded pain as having objective reality. To live is to suffer. All change, all activity, of necessity involves pain, which is ever wholly evil. Hence life and activity are, above all things, to be shunned. The only substantial purpose of life and activity is to *escape from life and action.*

Christianity, on the contrary, subordinates pain absolutely ; and in doing so *transforms it into a good.* The law of the spirit is reason, self-consistency. Evil is unreason, the conflict of self with self. Or, more explicitly, error is the conflict of self with self in thought ; evil is the conflict of self with self in action; while pain is the conflict of self with self in feeling or emotion. But these three phases are inseparable from one another ; and error, evil, and pain are but different aspects of the same complex spiritual fact of self-contradiction ; just as truth, right and joy are but three different and yet at the same time complementary aspects of the one complex spiritual fact of self-harmony—the coalescing of the real with the ideal self.

Now this self-harmony, the symmetrical unfolding of the spirit in accordance with its essential nature or ideal as a thinking, acting, sentient energy, is the supreme demand of Christianity. "Be ye therefore perfect even as your Father which is in heaven is perfect." That is the way to escape pain. Do away with your negative, unreal self. Realize your true, positive self.

So far indeed from pain being an evil, it is essentially opposed to evil. It is assuredly inseparable from wrong-doing, but for that very reason it tends ever toward correcting the wrong-doing. Instead of being an evil it is rather a disguised divine messenger—a kind of fifth Evangel that has never ceased crying aloud to men since the foundation of the world, warning them of the ruin that must ever follow upon wrong doing, and thus urging the choice of the divine Way of Truth that leads to eternal Life. For the wrong-doer, through his evil deed,[1] lessens his power for action of *any kind*, and hence his power for

---

[1] Evil-doing, sin, is just the universal death-process. cf above, p. 24 fol.

wrong action.   Evil is therefore self-destructive, and hence has no true, abiding reality.

Were all action evil, then indeed Buddhism would be right, and non-existence must be the final goal of all things.   Only, the "blowing-out" (*Nirvana*) must have long since occurred, leaving no further possibility of controversy.   Or rather there never could have *been* anything else than mere *non-being*.

Here again, then, Christianity proves to be an optimistic religion, since it points to the Good as the self-consistent, and therefore possessed of unlimited power of development ; while it points with equal distinctness to the evil as, in its nature, self-destructive, and as therefore necessarily a vanishing phase.

VII.

But again ; the demand of Christianity for the perfection of the spirit is essentially a demand for a harmonious development between the theoretical and the practical—between thought and action.   On the one hand, man is to "prove all things," while on the other, he is to "hold fast that which is good."   He is to display *energy of reflection* as well as *energy in his deeds*.   In truth, his deeds themselves must be reasonable, and this of itself implies reflection at every turn.   Man's activity must be a *thinking* activity.   Indeed, thought is itself the characteri tic act of man; and, finally, is the defining factor of all real activity—of all *reality*. The theoretical and the practical are no less absolutely inseparable than are the active and the passive. There can be no truly concrete life otherwise than through the fused unity of these antithetical elements.

It was but inevitable, therefore, that Christianity, as the genuine Religion of the Spirit, should demand and constantly bring into service the best, that is to say, the *truest, most adequate* thought of the world. Note historically how early Plato and Aristotle are brought under requisition as furnishing a method for systematizing, for the speculative reason, the truths which Christianity presents in the first place under forms that appeal to the imagination.

The early Church Fathers, with their mystical interpretations of Christian conceptions, very naturally found in Alexandrine Platonism a congenial mode of exposition ; while the scholasticism of the Middle Ages could find nowhere else than in Aristotle an adequate method for dealing reflectively with the truths of the Spirit.

This movement, besides, led at length to an independent development of distinctively Christian philosophy. *St. Thomas Aquinas takes the place of Aristotle.* And yet this later development is so far one-sided as to exalt the intellect above the will—the theoretical above the practical—instead of recognizing that these are but co-ordinate phases of the *fundamental unity of the Spirit*.

The philosophy of Aquinas was, indeed, but the culmination or rendering explicit of what was involved in the dictum of St. Anselm ; "*I believe in order that I may know*."[1]   It lies upon the very surface of this dictum that faith is but one stage, and that a preliminary or elementary stage, of knowledge. A little evidence gives rise to belief, which is a vague, imperfect phase of knowledge.   Additional evidence, actively received, results in the deepening of knowledge.   And this process continued at length turns probability into certainty, timid belief into assumed confidence.

A little further consideration makes it apparent that there is also involved in the fundamental conception, common to Anselm and Aquinas, this significant truth : That a revelation to man implies that it is *understood by man*.   A revelation that is not in some measure understood is not yet revealed—is no *revelation* at all.   And it becomes more and more truly a revelation precisely in the degree in which it

------

[1] And thus transcends the relatively unthinking standpoint of Tertulian : "*Credo quia absurdum*." Even here, however, Tertulian expresses in hyperbole his boundless faith in the perfection of Reason as realized in the Divine on the one hand and his distrust on the other hand of Reason as imperfectly realized in man, as he is here and now. His words are hardly the self-stultification they are commonly assumed to be.

is more perfectly comprehended. It is, in short, as remarked at the outset of this paper, to the Reason —to the intelligence—and to that alone that a revelation ever is or can be given. It is the Reason and that alone which can decide, on final appeal, as to the merits of a proposed revelation. Man must first of all make searching proof of what is offered him, lest at length he find himself holding fast to that which is far else than good.

In perfect consistency with this truth, which is implied in the very nature of the Religion of the Spirit, the foundation of schools for the cultivation and development of thought has gone hand in hand with the advance of Christianity. Indeed, the Christian Church itself is essentially a vast school. Every pulpit is a professorial chair ; every minister is, in his own way, a teacher of Righteousness, appealing constantly to the understanding as well as to the imagination, struggling to enlighten men's minds, to increase their comprehension of the Divine Revelation and thus to render it a revelation in ever truer sense to each individual man. And precisely in the degree in which he does this *successfully* is he a *minister of divine things.*

Nay, Christianity in effect ascribes to the whole world the character of a school. "The law is a school-master, leading men to Christ." Not merely the formal law of outworn phases of religion, but rather the *universal law of the Spirit* as expressed in all human institutions (which give utterance more or less adequately to what is essentially rational and therefore right) this law, impressing itself more and more deeply upon the gradually unfolding spirit of man, must tend ever to awaken men to a deeper consciousness of the ideal perfection, the essential unity and universalty, of spirit or mind.

Still further: the world of nature, as contrasted with the world of man, proves also to have its laws, its manifestations of Reason. And as man becomes more clearly conscious of these laws he is driven onward, with ever-increasing rapidity, toward the recognition of a universal and divine Spirit as the necessary presupposition of nature and its laws.

Thus the Religion of the Spirit addresses itself to the spirit, and demands the fullest possible unfolding of the spirit. Truth, the perfect Revelation, is eternally present in all its completeness in the Universe; but it depends upon each individual whether he will unfold his power to comprehend it and thus make of it a revelation indeed and in truth to *him*. And this, clearly, involves the fullest development of the reflective power of the mind. It is only after the departure of the visible Messiah that the divine Spirit of Truth will be manifest to the individual in its fullness, and thus lead him into all truth. It is, in other words, only by transcending the sphere in which thought is wrapped in imagery, and is therefore finite, that the soul gains the mastery of Truth in its infinite nature, and thus becomes free indeed.

Christianity, then, has for its fundamental principle the spirituality of the Divine on the one hand and the spirituality of man on the other, with the necessary corollary of the essential oneness in nature or type of the human and the Divine. It is with perfectly logical consistency, therefore, that this religion demands a ceaseless struggle on the part of the individual for practical perfection—for the constant unfolding into reality of his own ultimate and essentially divine ideal—for the complete blending in his own life of the theoretical and the practical.

VIII.

The Christian faith thus proves to be at once the outgrowth and infinitely reverent expression of Reason itself. And as such it has ever received the most profoundly reverent treatment from those who have claimed most for Reason—from those who have claimed on the one hand that the essential, all-vivifying Truth of the universe is absolute Divine Reason eternally realized in all its fullness ; and on the other hand that human reason, to be reason at all, must be of the same nature as the Divine Reason, and hence must be infinitely perfectible.

To such minds there is, and can be, no dark, fateful

background of the absolutely "unknowable." There is, indeed, an infinite range of practically unfolded phases of the Divine Reason which the finite[1] mind can never hope to wholly master in *detail*, and yet of which there is no single phase which in its nature is absolutely beyond the power of the finite mind to comprehend.

Here the all-important thing to make and keep clear is the distinction just suggested between the impossibility of an exhaustive knowledge on our part of the world or universe in detail on the one hand, and the entire possibility, on the other hand, of arriving at a clear and absolutely certain knowledge of the world as a whole in its fundamental character, which character is that of a necessarily self-complete, self-active unity, whose phases of self-realization constitute the concrete sum of all that is possible in a perfectly rational world. In such world "what is actual is rational, and what is rational is actual." It is this infinitely active, vital Totality which constitutes the practically unfolded and yet forever unfolding phases of the Divine Reason; which process again is the eternal Revelation addressed to the finite spirit as itself at once a reflection and reproduction of the Divine Reason, and hence capable of comprehending the revelation.

[1] It is to be noted that "mind" can be finite only in the degree of realization of the one universal Ideal of Mind in the case of a given individual thinking unit.

It is not then that this revelation *comes to man*,
but rather that man, in his self-unfolding as a spiritual being, *comes to the revelation,* and in so doing
comes to *himself;* for he finds at the same time that
the truth of this revelation is involved in his own
ideal nature. The whole history of humanity in its
deepest significance, therefore, has been nothing else
than a feeling after, a half-blind search for, God;
who, after we have found Him, proves to have been,
all the while, "not far from every one of us."

It may be remarked by the way that the fatal point
of confusion in agnosticism is the failure to recognize
the distinction, just pointed out, between the world
as knowable in its fundamental principle, and yet as
also unknowable in the sense that no finite mind can,
in any finite time, ever attain to complete, exhaustive
knowledge of it in its infinite details. The latter is
the only "unknowable" world. And yet, it would
seem scarcely necessary to remark, this "unknowable"
is not the "world," but only a perpetually vanishing
phase thereof—vanishing more or less effectually and
rapidly in proportion to the vigor and wisdom and
consistency of the individual's own efforts toward
self-development in *power to know.*

It thus becomes evident (whatever the narrowness
and bigotry displayed betimes by certain classes of
the advocates of Christianity, moved as they are
rather by zeal than by knowledge) that the genuine

spirit of Christianity itself demands the freest, most perfect unfolding of the intelligence ; that it appeals constantly to the reflective consciousness or Reason, encouraging all earnest effort to comprehend and interpret into utmost clearness all phases of the infinite Revelation present in the world, physical and spiritual.

This, indeed, is the true reason why Christianity is, and since its advent into history has ever been, the fundamental faith of all the peoples of the world who have participated in the development of true science. The critical spirit, which demands that all things shall be "proven," rigidly tested, before they are accepted as "good," is nothing else than the perfectly healthy phase of skepticism which gives to modern science its keenly penetrating power. It is but the negative phase belonging essentially to all genuinely positive thought.

And what has been the record of Buddhism in this respect? The answer may be very briefly stated. Based on superstition, it has ever dealt in superstition and found its home among people dominated by superstition. The Chinese are classed as Buddhists But their reverence for Buddha does not in the least interfere with their building shrines to millions of native local divinities. Buddhism has not, in fact, displaced the ancient religions of any of the regions where it has found acceptance. It has not proven itself sufficiently vital to overthrow even the gross nature-worship of the rude Mongoloid races, much less to appeal successfully to the people of a higher culture—unless, indeed, that phase of the comparative study of religions which discovers similarities and discerns no differences should bring it into favor at last in enlightened Europe and America.

Christianity on its part is far less tolerant. It refuses to take its place beside other faiths. It demands absolute single-mindedness, uniformly declaring that no man can serve two masters. Wherever it has been thoroughly accepted, it has completely displaced the old nature-divinities and brought about the exclusive worship of one sole Divinity whom it ever declares to be a Spirit. Wherever the missionary of this faith goes, he carries with him the implements and methods of "secular" education as well, thus practically announcing with every step that Christianity can be received in its true spirit and significance no otherwise than by intelligence ; and the more truly and adequately received, in proportion as the intelligence is given a more thoroughly scientific —that is, more thoroughly rational—training. In short, where science has most deeply penetrated, there Christianity is seen to have already found the most thorough appreciation and most genuine acceptance.

IX.

At this stage of our investigation it will, doubtless, be well to consider certain objections to the line of argument here pursued, the objections being based mainly on the "New Buddhism" which has come to have a somewhat extended acceptance since the publication of "The Light of Asia." In this work Mr. Arnold seems to have adopted—unconsciously, no doubt—the spontaneous method of the ancient Hebrew prophets, in so far as he has freely used detached utterances of a noble, heroic character conspicuous in the early world, has gathered about that ideal personage as a nucleus many of the most beautiful characteristics of the sentiment of his own world, and through his own creative genius has brought into organic form, as the vital unity of these materials, a poetic representation of really marvelous beauty and power. One may well reverence and even love the admirable ideal he thus offers us.

On the other hand, however, it could not but be a most serious error to conceal from one's self the fact that, beautiful and noble as this ideal is, it falls far short of being an ultimate ideal. And still more, if it were proposed to take this poetic creation as a historical representation of the life and teachings of the Hindu prince Siddartha, one must protest on the ground that such acceptance necessarily involves the complete abandonment of those critical methods of investigation which so sharply distinguish the present from any former age.   Mr. Arnold writes as a modern ; could, of course, by no possibility write otherwise.   He is himself a conspicuous example of what an individual may become through the rich, highly complex culture of the modern world.   He finds in the ancient world a character specially adapted to serve as the central figure of an artistic creation.   He throws into his creative work all his brilliant power.   And this power itself is precisely the inheritance he has received from all the ages ; an inheritance, besides, which could have attained its high perfection and self-critical delicacy in no other way than through the vastly complex influences represented in a modern education, which again is the focus of all the institutions which give external form to the clarified Reason of the modern world.

Neither should it for a moment be forgotten that Mr. Arnold writes as a poet, not as a historian.   We might, indeed, as well take Milton's "Paradise Lost" as a historical document for Christianity as to accept "The Light of Asia" as a historical document for Buddhism.   And besides, let us repeat, whether he will or not, Mr. Arnold necessarily writes as a modern poet, not as an ancient one.   Hence "The Light of Asia" is not only a modern work, it also represents on the poetic side what is essentially the modern and

Western spirit under an antique and Oriental form.[1]
It is scarcely to be wondered at, then, that Buddhism,
viewed in this camera, should present so many startling analogies with the finest sentiment of Christianity! Indeed, one has but to make careful analysis of the poem to recognize that its real substance is
just Christianity itself; only that Christianity is here
stripped of its clearness and critical severity, leaving,
as the residuum, Christian sentiment in isolation
from its appropriate clarifying power of thought.
And sentiment, thus isolated, cannot but be in great
danger of passing over into mere sentimentality.

Doubtless strong natures will always be able easily
to preserve themselves from sentimentality, however much they may be moved and expanded by true
sentiment. But for weaker natures the danger cannot but be real and great. Even in its modernized
and most attractive form, then, Buddhism still presents this fundamental defect (already indicated on a
former page)—that it fails to seize the essential characteristics of spiritual being. It shows no clear recognition of the necessity of the development of reflective, critical thought as a necessary phase of a
genuine concrete will. Thus in its whole history we
find no scientific movements accompanying its devel-

---

[1] Since this essay was first published, Mr. Arnold has given
proof of what he could—and could not—do in dealing as a
poet with that greater theme: *The Light of the World.*

opment, no spontaneous growth of a system of thought as expressing an inner necessity of objective, logical utterance. All is vague. The face of Buddhism is turned steadfastly toward the *un*utterable—toward ''Nirvana,'' the meaning of which no one has yet been able to tell in terms of positive import. And as if the unspeakableness of Nirvana were not enough, the devout Buddhist vaguely strains his imagination toward a still more perfect state, which he names ''Para-Nirvana.'' The devout Buddhist also deprecates any criticism or pretense of analysis on the part of the uninitiated, and protests that only the true devotee can unfold the real meaning of this subtle faith whose essence escapes the grasp of the unsanctified intelligence. It is fortunate, therefore, that the genuine ''Esoteric Buddhism'' has at length been revealed to waiting humanity by one who stands within the sacred inclosure, and whose work has received the stamp of a third edition. On page 163 of this work (by Sinnett) the reader may find this luminous statement : ''And in some, to us inconceivable way, the state of Para-Nirvana is spoken of as immeasurably higher than that of Nirvana. I do not pretend, myself, to attach any meaning to the statement, but it may serve to show to what a very transcendental realm of thought the subject belongs.''[1] Whereat

---

[1] It must be confessed that this mode of view is paralleled in one of the foremost of modern philosophical works. Mr.

the profane mind is apt to marvel, and insensibly to become lost in admiration of that logic which is able to find, in the very fact that no meaning whatever can be gotten out of a phrase, perfectly satisfactory ground for concluding that the phrase is, therefore, infinitely full of meaning.

Now this very vagueness, this lack of precision in the body of the doctrine, this diffuse character of the light of Buddhism, is the chief secret of its easy adaptation to the modes of thought prevalent in Asiatic countries.   It has, no doubt, made "bloodless conquests," as is often claimed ; but there seems little difficulty in discerning that this is precisely because its mild light nowhere presents a sharp focus, nowhere a definite shadow, nowhere an image so clearly defined but that it yields on very slight pressure, and assumes a form to suit the imagination of the individual, whatever his habits of mind.   Hence it is that the peaceful spread of Buddhism has been almost wholly among the peoples of the Orient, where civil society, even in its most extended monarchies, still

———

Herbert Spencer (First Principles, p. 109,) after asking the question : "Is it not just possible that there is a mode of being as much transcending Intelligence and Will as these transcend mechanical motion ?" immediately adds : "It is true that we are totally unable to conceive any such higher mode of being.   But this is not a reason for questioning its existence ; it is rather the reverse." The inconceivable, it seems, is for that reason the actual.   One is tempted to suppose that the Unknowable is the only thing really worth knowing.

remains in the simple patriarchal stage. Thus not only does Buddhism itself exhibit the mildness of a very diffuse spirit; its spread has occurred among peoples who also present very little concentration of doctrine or thought in any form. The faiths of the Orient meet and mingle without shock or commotion of any kind, just as a number of different gaseous bodies easily become diffused through the same space and occupy it simultaneously without mutual disturbance. The more thoroughly nebulous the bodies in contact, the less must be the resistance offered by either, and such uneventful comminglings follow naturally, whether in the world of matter or in the world of mind.

But again, it is not so certain that the conquests of Buddhism were absolutely "bloodless." The sculptures at Sanchi (described and reproduced in photograph in Fergusson's "Tree and Serpent Worship") would seem to prove that in India, at least, either the progress or the defense of Buddhism involved extensive wars, and that battles were fought over the sacred relics—perhaps between rival sects of Buddhists. And this occurred too, let us note, precisely where Buddhism attained its most clearly defined historical development, and, therefore, where we would expect opposition to call forth the spirit of bitter rivalry and intolerance.

On the other hand, if, as has been objected, Christianity has given rise to endless wars, there are two manifest and valid reasons for the fact. The first is the precision and extreme complexity of the fundamental conceptions of that faith ; the complexity, on the one hand, rendering inevitable a wide divergence in the interpretation of doctrine, while on the other hand, the precision of those conceptions must render *peaceable* divergence impossible save within very narrow range. In such case, indeed, "it must needs be that offenses come," and it is equally inevitable that woes should be multiplied upon those by whom they come. Doubtless Christianity does in a literal sense bring a sword rather than peace. But this is because it insists with infinite emphasis that truth is absolutely unchanging, and that the individual must, therefore, adjust himself to the truth and not expect to adjust the truth to himself.

Note, however, as the *second* reason why wars have so prevailed in Christian lands, that the literal sword is, after all, introduced by the imperfectly Christianized man. Not because he is a Christian truly, but because he is a Christian only formally, and f ils to comprehend the deeper significance of the faith, does he become impatient and rush to battle. It is the imperfection of men that gives rise to one-sided interpretations of the truth, the end whereof is conflict ; and the conflict is and can be only the more relentless as, on the one hand, the individual fails to suspect his own one-sidedness, and as, on the other hand, the absolute necessity of understanding the truth *aright* is insisted upon.

With man's higher development, with his increasingly adequate comprehension of the gospel of peace, he learns at length that the sword which Christianity does in truth bring into the world in a new and special sense is the "Sword of the Spirit," the keen-pointed, keen-edged weapon of Reason, the first victory achieved with which is the victory over *self* on the part of the individual.

Again, Christianity has ever found its most congenial field in that part of the world where all has from the first tended toward concentration, toward increase of tension, toward multiplied complexity. So that not only has this faith constantly presented its highly complex doctrines in specially distinct forms ; it has also at every turn come in contact with a spirit already characterized by extreme tension and complexity.

From the very nature of the case, there'ore, antagonisms more or less violent were inevitable in the spread of Christianity ; and especially during the ages in which the peoples brought under its influence were yet rude and violent, and only very imperfectly imbued with the teachings of the new faith.

But it has been often suggested that what are regarded as the results of Christianity are really due to the innate spirit of the peoples classed as Christian. And in a very important sense this must be admitted to be true. The sublime ideal of Christianity could of course never be realized otherwise than through the actual spirit of a given particular people. And the spirit of that people must be of such type as to discern spontaneously that its true development can take place only as the working out into realized form of precisely the ideal which Christianity presents. So, too, the various divisions of such people will cling to the peculiar conception which they severally form of that ideal only the more tenaciously as they are the more firmly convinced that it is, in the final outcome, just their own Ideal. Thus the people of Europe and America, through their thorough adoption of and steadfast adhesion to Christianity, have given demonstrative practical proof that the real spirit of that faith is identical with the spirit of the highest enlightenment.

If attempts to christianize barbarous races have thus far in great measure failed, it seems but reasonable to recognize the fact that from the very nature of the human mind it is impossible that individuals should pass with a single bound from a very low to a very high stage of culture. The individual must of necessity pass through all the intermediate stages from the beginning onward, and must occupy a reasonable time in so doing. It is well that barbarous races should become civilized, just as it is well that a child should become a man. But it seems better in either case that time should be allowed for natural, healthy growth, rather than that attempts should be made to at once violently stretch the child into the dimensions of a man.

Christianity is, beyond question, an intolerant faith ; and most of all is it intolerant as against the ferocity of mere blind intolerance ; just as, in its character of the religion of Reason, it must ever repudiate the equally blind tolerance which, through mere complaisance, permits all opinions alike to pass unchallenged.

X.

Nor would we by any means ignore the supposed conflict between religion and science, of which so much is heard in recent times. This "conflict," indeed, is simply a misconception growing out of arrogance on the one side and timidity on the other. It is boldly assumed on the one hand, and admitted without due reflection on the other, that the Christian church is identical with the Christian religion. True, the church is the outward, organic form of which religion is the inward, vital substance. They are inseparable. At the same time, while the real substance, the ultimate truth, of the religion of the Spirit is unchanging, the church is manifestly but the external, the growing, *changing* form which the substance necessarily takes on through the activity of man.   And the adequacy of the form must depend upon the thoroughness of man's appreciation of the substance.   The more enlightened human intelligence becomes, the more adequate man's view of his own nature and of his relation to the divine nature, the more imperatively is there demanded a continuous revision and extension of the forms which give utterance to his view ; a necessity which, we have already seen, makes its appearance in the world of political institutions as well.   It is absurd to charge to a religion the revolting results of the bigotry of men who *mis*represent the religion, even while claiming to be its votaries.

And yet it has always proved specially difficult to see that a mode of utterance which has proved adequate to the expression of a given view of the truth is not therefore necessarily adequate to the expression of the *whole* truth.   Hence forms once established have ever been tenaciously adhered to ; and, not infrequently, to the hindrance of further advance in the comprehension of the truth.

Nevertheless, this dogmatic tendency is not exclusively hurtful.   Dogmatism, in truth, is just the conservative, as skepticism is the radical, element in human thought.   Both are necessary, for they are but complimentary phases of all rational activity.

Either becomes hurtful only when made to exclude the other. Give dogmatism the ascendency, and it reduces everything to mere dead forms. Give skepticism the ascendency, and it denies the existence of any fixed standard, and grows maudlin in the production of change merely for the sake of change. The doctrine of papal infallibility is the logical outcome of dogmatism; the Reign of Terror shows what mere skepticism is capable of accomplishing. But the true spirit of Christianity proves its completeness by demanding that these two opposites shall be constantly blended—fused into inseparable unity.

On approaching any phase of activity that may be proposed, but which for him remains as yet untried, the individual, if he is to exhibit the genuine spirit of Christianity, must first assume the skeptical or critical attitude and put to the proof the thing proposed. And yet this very process necessarily involves the conservative element, since the ''proving'' means nothing else than the critical reference of the thing undergoing trial to some standard already accepted as fixed. And once tried and found sufficient, the new fact or phase of activity comes to be dogmatically accepted and held fast among the things known to be good.

Such is the process constantly going forward in every genuinely free spirit. It is, in truth, the very soul of the thoroughly scientific spirit. So that once more the "conflict" is not between the Christian religion and science ; but between narrow, dogmatic theologians on the one side and equally narrow skeptical scientists on the other.

Note, too, that the theologian is sometimes flippantly skeptical in that he rejects without examination the richest results of science ; while the scientist is often no less narrowly dogmatic in that he assumes without proof that his is the only field in which "positive" results can be attained.

This, then, is the result of our investigation : That Buddhism, as based on superstition and finding acceptance only among people destitute of science and therefore wholly involved in superstition, can be perpetuated as a dominant faith only where, and so long as, scientific habits of thought fail to penetrate ; while Christianity, as the religion of Reason, and as therefore involving within itself the very soul of true scientific method, is not merely aided by but is also itself in reality a mighty aid to the advance of science, in the widest and most genuine significance of the term. It teaches man to value himself as a being possessed of infinite capabilities, and thus awakes within him an infinite longing to comprehend—that is, to know scientifically—his own nature, and also the world in the midst of which his own development must take place.

It thus, from its very constitution, shows itself to be

the predestined final Religion of the World. Its *forms*, as we have seen, may, and must, change ; but this only proves the exhaustless vigor of the inner substance—as the shedding of outworn leaves but proves the forest to be preparing for a larger growth.

IV.

CHRISTIANITY AND MOHAMMEDANISM.

The relations between Christianity and Mohammedanism have been of a nature quite unique in the
history of the world.   Both had their origin with the
Semitic race.   In the final outcome both have found
their strength mainly among non-Semitic peoples.
Each is in some degree a reaction upon and an extension of the Jewish religion.   Each aspires to the rank
of an exclusive world-religion.   They have struggled
with each other for mastery with fire and sword.
They have also done battle with the weapons alike of
prophecy and of logical deduction.   The antagonism
has been both external and internal, and in both respects it has been relentless.

It seems well worth while, then, to ask these two
questions, namely : What is the central element of
vitality in each ?   What is the ultimate promise of
growth in each ?

These are but the complementary aspects of one
and the same question—the deeply interesting question suggested by the history of these two religions.
The question is this : What religion answers best the
essential needs of the human soul ?   To this question

it is proposed in the present essay to seek a reasonable answer.

I.

And first as to their respective origins. Christianity in its immediate inception was but the culmination of that long period of inner struggle on the part of the People of Israel to discover the true nature of God and to learn the precise actual relationship between God and man. However much may be wanting in precise historical details, this much is fairly certain : That the inmost aspirations by which an entire nation had been guided for fifteen hundred years, found their logical culmination in the personality of the founder of the Christian Religion.

Leaving out of account all questions of the "miraculous"—a term which defies scientific definition, and which therefore must be omitted from any strictly historical investigation—it is evident that the personality of Jesus of Nazareth is a unique fact in the history of the world. And the explanation of this fact is to be found in the long struggle (to which reference has just been made), of the most intensely religious people the world has ever known.

Starting from the Mosaic conception of a national divinity, the People of Israel sought, with ever-growing earnestness, for a true knowledge of God. And however much and however often the body of the nation wandered from the essential aim, however far they misapprehended the essential character of that aim, yet the men of real genius which the nation from time to time produced were ever found bending all their energies to the better apprehension, and thus approximating ever toward the final solution, of the one great problem by which their minds were wholly and always occupied.

And yet, even in later times, these exceptional minds were never quite able to free themselves from the limitations of the traditional view in accordance with which the final theophany—the ultimate revelation of God to man—was to be in the character of a divine Ruler, who was to establish an ideal Theocracy with its capital at Jerusalem, and who was to make use of the Jews themselves as his favorite agents.   It was this ''Messianic hope'' that sustained the Jews in their latest and most crushing reverses. And yet the strain of mind due to the sense of irreconcilable contradiction between the promises of their God and their own actual state of humiliation at the time of the Roman conquest of Judæa became fairly insupportable.

God was to have come.   A Cæsar is here !   Jerusalem was to have been the capitol of the world.   A Roman legion desecrates the very courts of the Temple.   The enemies of Jehovah were to have been brought hither to answer for their offenses against the Chosen People. Those enemies have come of their own accord and with irresistible might to crush out the last remnant of the true believers and to flaunt insults in the face of the Most High ! Never was there such intimate intermingling of unconquerable hope with the deepest despair ! That the promise was sure they could not for a moment doubt. That its fulfilment was infinitely deferred who would dare to deny? No wonder that there should be wild outbreaks of fanaticism and multiplied cases of insanity !

And yet the problem was by no means an impossible one. It was only of a vastly deeper import than had yet been more than faintly dreamed of. But just this vague premonition it was that sustained hope in the midst of conditions that must otherwise have rendered all pretense of hope the veriest mockery.

Only he who had inherited the divinest qualities of his race could seize that deeper and deepest import of the great problem and find for it true answer. Only at the moment when excitement ran highest, only when all minds were turned with all-absorbing interest upon that problem could he have been stimulated to the fervor of inquiry needful even for him to seize and form the ultimate solution.

It was in this sense that he came "in the fullness of time." Devoting all his exceptional powers to the solution of the question in which the destinies of the whole human race are involved, he is indeed the Son of Man. Finding the solution of the question in the fact that God is the Father of every human being, he may well be looked upon as being himself preeminently the Son of God.

If now we turn to the origins of Mohammedanism we find here also a remarkable combination of circumstances. And these circumstances are very widely contrasted with that total sum of conditions which became focused into the germ of what the world has come to know as Christianity.

Unlike the People of Israel, the Arabs were of a serene and even joyous temperament. A race of rare vigor, cares nevertheless sat lightly upon them. And the great problem which so burned in the soul of the Jew scarcely stirred the thought of the free rover of the desert.

Distinguished by a wild grace of body and of mind these bold Ishmaelites were poets from birth. But instead of Davidic psalms their unwritten songs were the intermingling of soft strains of love with the fierce chanting of ideal deeds of battle done in the rescue of the loved one who had been ruthlessly borne away by a foe.[1]

Such appears to have been the well-nigh unvarying

---

[1] Cp. Emanuel Deutsch. *Literary Remains*, p. 452.

character of ancient Arabic literature, which was never written and which was "all in verse." Nay, "in the vast repertory of ante-Islamic poetry we hardly find a religious thought."[1]

Surely no greater contrast could well be conceived than that between the all-absorbing religious instinct of the worshipers of Jehovah and the care-free, sensuous spirit of the Arabs. With their high ideal working irresistibly, even in their early history, toward ever clearer utterance the Sons of Israel found life in the desert intolerable. Arid nature can never give birth to richly fruitful souls. Only in a "land flowing with milk and honey" can the highest grades of spiritual perfection be attained.

Renan has, indeed, urged that the abstractness of the desert was a primary condition for the unfolding of the sublime conception of monotheism. Doubtless, in a measure, this is true. But the truth of monotheism is an infinitely rich, concrete truth; while the very abstractness of the desert, though it might serve vaguely to suggest the conception of monotheism in its most rudimentary form, yet presents no stimulus to the further unfolding of such idea. On the contrary, as Hegel has remarked of the Arabs in respect of the origin of Islam : "Here the spirit is altogether rudimentary (*ein ganz einfacher*),

---

[1] Renan. *Studies of Religious History and Criticism.* N. Y. Ed., 1864, p. 238.

and the sense of the Formless is quite at home.   For in these deserts there is nothing which can be given clear definition."[1]   In short the desert is the condition within which the human spirit is forever debarred from advancing beyond the elementary aspects of its own development.

It is precisely this abstract character on the part of a people like the Arabs that for so many centuries could find full satisfaction in love of war and wars of love.   And it is precisely these two aspects of character—latent ferocity and sensuality—which, once brought into the service of a motive alike sublime and sensuously mystical, will bloom out swiftly into fiercest fanaticism.

Here, too, the waiting for a culmination extends through a period of fifteen hundred years ; though in this case the waiting was unconscious.   That is, it was destitute of any deep sense of contradiction and consequent necessity of struggle.

During all that stretch of time, indeed, this people remained free even from the disquieting element of historical premonitions.   Careless alike of the past and of the future, they lived in the present, never doubting that sufficient unto the day is the joy thereof.   And when at length they did awake to a consciousness of that sublime and mystical motive

---

[1] Werke, 3te Auflage.   IX, 433.

that was to send them like a whirlwind into the field of historical activity, it was yet from a foreign source that the stimulus was received.

It is beyond question that in the "Great Dispersion" many of the Jews had found a permanent home in the northern part of Arabia long before the birth of Mohammed. And wherever they went something of the influence of their faith must have been felt. This is so much the more probable, too, as they were the "people of a book," and were therefore looked up to as superiors by the untutored Arabs.

But it is also true that Christianity had been spreading Eastward as well as Westward during the six centuries preceding the rise of Islam. And always the adherents of this faith have been more or less actuated by the spirit of proselytism.

Could their presence have been wholly without effect? According to a Jew of great learning, as well as of brilliant powers of exposition, and whose premature death a few years since was a severe loss to scholarship in this field, "It has long been the fashion to ascribe whatever was 'good' in Mohammedanism to Christianity. We fear this theory is not compatible with the results of honest investigation. For of Arabian Christianity at the time of Mohammed, the less said, perhaps, the better."[1] Elsewhere the

---

[1] Emanuel Deutsch *Literary Remains*. p. 87.

same writer makes this claim : "But we think Islam neither more nor less than Judaism as adapted to Arabia—plus the apostleship of Jesus and Mohammed."[1]

These statements, when compared with those of other competent scholars, would seem to be a little tinged, though of course unconsciously, with the pride of race.   And yet, as Renan remarks, "possessing a law, a book, the depository of grand moral precepts and of an elevated religious poetry, Judaism had an incontestable superiority [to other religions of the ancient world], and it might have been foreseen that some day the world would become Jewish ; that is to say, would forsake the old mythology for monotheism."[2]   Further on, however, he adds :[3] "Hesitating between Judaism and Christianity, native superstitions and the remembrance of the old patriarchal faith, recoiling from the mythological elements which the Indo-European race had introduced into the heart of Christianity, Arabia wished to return to the religion of Abraham ; she founded Islamism."

Soberly examining this statement, one can scarcely fail to pronounce it misleading in so far as it attributes solely or even mainly to Aryan influence the mythological elements contained in that form of

[1] *Studies of Religious Hist.*, etc. p. 160.
[2] Op. cit. p. 64.
[3] Op. cit. p. 162.

Christianity known to the Arabs. Such elements appear to have been chiefly due rather to Semitic and Egyptian, or even to Abyssinian influences. But apart from this, which for the present purpose is merely incidental, Renan's statement contains a clew to the historical fact in the case as presented by the scholar who has doubtless done more than any one else—perhaps more than all others combined—to render Mohammedanism intelligible as an actual movement in the spiritual evolution of the human race. His investigations of the subject from original sources during many years of residence in Arabia[1] go to show that when Mohammed appeared something of a religious ferment had already long been in progress among the Arabians.

We have, indeed, only to bear in mind the actual movements of the time to see how much of inherent probability there is in the conception that strong infusion of both Jewish and Christian tenets into the simple faith of the Arabs must have taken place during the first six centuries of the Christian era. The destruction of Jerusalem, along with the extension of the Græco-Roman Empire to the East, must of themselves—to say nothing of voluntary propaganda— have resulted in an important transfusion of both

----

[1] A. Sprenger. *Das Leben und die Lehre des Mohammad, nach bisher groesstentheils unbenutzten Quellen bearbeitet.* 2te Ausgabe, 3 Bde. Berlin, 1869.

Jewish and Christian ideas into the minds of these children of the desert, however slow and indefinable the process might be.

But this is only one side of the process. The actual propagation of Jewish and Christian conceptions among people with such widely different habits of mind could take place only through those conceptions themselves becoming adapted to the minds having such peculiar habits and instincts.

Nor should the reaction to this action be overlooked. For evidently the very Jews and Christians themselves could not remain altogether uninfluenced by prolonged contact with mental processes so unlike their own.

Still further it is to be noted that the law of natural selection inheres in the spiritual no less than in the physical world. And according to this law it is evident that among both Jews and Christians those whose mental tendency was toward precise, scientific modes of investigation would inevitably be drawn westward into the countries where Greek and Roman influences were still preserved in their most vital form ; while those of a mystical, uncritical tendency would gravitate ever further into oriental lands where glowing phantasy was in no danger of coming into contact with the ice-bergs of reflective criticism.

Thus we might even easily anticipate, what Sprenger shows to be the historical fact in the case,

that there developed an "amphibious population
which occupied the intermediate region between the
denizens of the desert and those of the town ;" and
that among these there were "a number of monotheistic sects and brotherhoods which differed among
themselves more or less in respect of what they retained of Judaism or of Christianity."[1]

It is beyond question, then, that neither Judaism
nor Christianity presented itself in its pure form to
the Arabians. Though here too we ought not 'to
lose sight of the fact that the Jewish Scriptures were
the matured expression of a distinctly national spirit ;
while Christianity was a form of faith which, compared with the Jewish, was even yet not perfectly defined—which in its oriental development had, in
fact, exchanged primitive simplicity for extravagant
caricature—and which, nevertheless, everywhere
and finally assumed the attitude of a world-religion,
having no specific relation, save in point of historical
genesis, to any particular national spirit

And yet, precisely for this reason, Christianity
possessed a flexibility by which it became "all things
to all men ;" and this (as we have just seen), to the
extent of sinking, among the crude peoples of the
Orient, into a mere caricature of the original teachings of its Founder. So that, if we compare the

---

[1]Op. cit. I. 40.

Christianity of Arabia with the Christianity of the New Testament, and especially as developed in the modern spirit, it is no doubt true that "the less said of it [save in historical criticism], the better."

It is these caricatured forms of Christianity alone, indeed, of which the Arabs of the time of Mohammed could have had any knowledge whatever. But if we are to form a reasonable judgment of the possible or probable influence which such forms may have had upon the Arabs of the pre-Islamic period, we must compare the "Arabic Christianity" of that period with the still cruder and less adequate religion of the Arabs themselves, consisting chiefly, as it would seem, of various forms of nature-worship and perhaps also of hero-worship. When this comparison is made it appears by no means improbable that the Arabs may have received, even from such grotesque caricatures of Christianity as were known to them, a genuine and important stimulus toward the adoption of a monotheistic form of faith.

Nevertheless the actual information is extremely vague ; and hence the statement seems fairly justified that, as expressed by Emanuel Deutsch :[1] "We can but guess at the state of Arab belief and worship before Mohammed ;" though, as will be seen presently,

[1] Op. cit. p. 85.

Sprenger's investigations have thrown important lights upon the period otherwise so obscure.

Indeed Deutsch himself has some valuable information to give us respecting the pre-Islamic influence of Judaism upon the religious tendencies of the Arabs.   No doubt can reasonably be entertained, in fact, that this influence was much stronger than that exerted by Christianity.   The faith of the Jews was simpler, their superiority in point of learning secured the respect of the Arabs,[1] they appear to have spread more widely through the peninsula,[2] and, finally, there was clear consciousness of race kinship, which doubtless the Jews of the Dispersion did not fail to strengthen by making known the details of their common ancestry as set forth in their own sacred books.

Nay, as Deutsch insists, ''we cannot shut our eyes to the fact that Jews, 'worshippers of the invisible God of Abraham,' existed, though in small numbers in Arabia, at a very primitive period indeed.''[3] We are further assured by the same writer that ''the Talmud shows a rather unexpected familiarity with Arab manners and customs.''   And if we may follow the same learned author a step further, it is precisely

---

[1] ''The Jews, in fact, represented the culture of Arabia.'' Deutsch. Op. cit..   p. 91.

[2] Loc. cit.

[3] Op. cit..   p. 89.

in the Talmud we are to look for the source of Islam ; though we are not to take this as implying "that Mohammed knew it, or, for the matter of that, had ever heard its very name ; but it seems as if he had breathed from his childhood almost the air of contemporary Judaism, such Judaism as is found by us crystalized in the Talmud, the Targum, the Midrash."

If now we recur to the remark already quoted from Renan to the effect that Arabia hesitated between Judaism and Christianity, that at length she formed the wish to return to the religion of Abraham, and in this spiritual struggle she in fact founded Islamism, we may see that the two religions then existing which taught that there is but one God, really furnished each its own element towards the mental ferment leading up to the Koran and Islamism.

And that the element furnished by Christianity, however distorted the form in which it there appeared, and whether coming from Abyssinia or elsewhere, was really of much weight, especially in shaping and extending Mohammed's own personal convictions, is put beyond all reasonable doubt by Sprenger, partly in the first chapter of his Life of Mohammad,[1] in which he shows the evidences of Christian activity in the pre-Islamic period, and again in the eleventh chapter, which is devoted to

____

[1] Wherever quoting from Sprenger I have retained his spelling: "Mohammad."

the subject of "Christian influences upon Mohammad" himself, especially during the years 616–619.

But yet another fact is of special significance in
this connection as indicating that the ferment occa-
sioned by the gradual diffusion of both Jewish and
(pseudo)-Christian teachings proved the more readily
and at length the more thoroughly effective, because
in germ the conception of monotheism was already
present in the minds of the Arabs. This is shown,
for example, in an old legend made use of in the
Koran (37, 103). According to this legend, when
Abraham had prepared to sacrifice his son and the
latter had consented to be offered, both on the moment
determined to become Moslems. [1]

Now "the antiquity of this legend," as Sprenger
observes, "shows that submission to the occasionally
tyrannical and irrational will of Allah was at all
times among the Semites an important part of their
practical religion."[2] But, he adds immediately, "All
ideas are old, and the question arises, when did Islam
become the fundamental tone of religion and when
did its significance become so greatly extended? For

---

[1] "Islam is the verbal noun and Moslem the participle of
the root from which also the familiar word Salam, health,
peace, and Salem and Salym, sound, honorable, are derived. Islam, therefore, means: to render satisfaction to any
one, and indeed with deference. Hence it also means 'sub·
mission.'" Sprenger, I, 69.

[2] I. 70.

to Mohammad Islam meant, not merely submission to the will of Allah, but also faith in him."

What is here to be especially noticed is the fact that Islam, this "chief doctrine of Mohammad," was preached before his time ; though, as it seems, only with its more elementary religious meaning of submission to the will of the one God. In other words the leaven of the doctrine of monotheism had long been working in the minds of the Arabians; and, as has been mentioned above, that doctrine became a last the leading motive of their religion only because it had already from the first been present in their consciousness in germinal form.

It is this conception, then (which at this stage ought rather to be named "sentiment") of monotheism that pervades the mental atmosphere of Arabia at the moment when Mohammed appears. Not forty days only, but forty years, rather, he meditates in the wilderness on the problem of life which he everywhere hears talked of. And in the fulness of time this problem, for him and for his race, is raised in his mind to the highes. power. That is, it unfolds into its own answer: "There is no God but Allah, and Mohammed is his prophet."

There is, indeed, something peculiarly touching and appropriate in the legend which arose at a later period to the effect that in his early youth angels took out his heart, pressed from it the black drops of sin, filled it with the light of prophecy, and again replaced it.   Unlettered he no doubt was.   Ignorant he cannot reasonably be said to have been.   He was no dialectician.   He was an epileptic, a dreamer, a seer, a man of iron will, a born preacher of Fate, a proclaimer of the omnipotence of man through absolute submission to the will of Allah.

He might, nay must, listen intently to the words, now of the Jews, now of the Christians.   He must turn away at length from both, because both had mingled with the truth what seemed to him the grossest errors.   He must proclaim to his people the one God for whom their own hearts had long been unconsciously waiting.

And so he becomes thus far the prophet of his nation, the prophet whose words are to fuse them into that unity and intensity of purpose which will long render them irresistible to other peoples, and which will also irresistibly impel them to the conviction that the fate of the world is theirs to decide because they are the instruments of the will of the God of Fate.

But for the actual accomplishment of this an electrifying word was indispensable.   And Mohammed created that word.   In the spring of 622 (the year of the Hejrah), certain citizens of Medina came to Mecca to attend the ancient annual religious festival, which served to keep up a sense of unity among the various tribes.   The visitors made it the occasion

also to invite Mohammed to come to their city, his
own people having thus far for the most part treated
his mission with scorn.

On his part the prophet delivered to them a revelation[1] by which he announced that God had in
ancient times appointed the place of the temple at
Mecca as a residence for Abraham. To this the
prophet added the further declaration that Abraham
was the founder of the ancient worship at that place

Sprenger believes this to have been Mohammed's
own invention, pure and simple, no trace of it appearing in earlier tradition. On the other hand "most of
the other doctrines of Islam proceed from the *Zeitgeist.*" But "through this invention Mohammad
gave to Islam all that men need, all that separate;
religion from philosophy : [in short by this simple
stroke he gave to Islam] nationality, ceremonies,
historical reminiscences, mysteries, means to take
Heaven by force, means to mystify his own conscience and that of others. Through this arbitrary
creation Mohammad impressed upon Deism his own
human seal, and transformed it into Mohammadanism."[2]

---

[1] *Koran*, 22. 27-32.

[2] Op. Cit. II, 279. With this single exception, then, we
may agree with Renan in his declaration that "Mohammed is no more the founder of monotheism than of civilization and literature among the Arabs. The conclusion
from numberless facts noted for the first time by M. Caussin
de Perceval is that Mohammed only followed the religious

Summarily, then, the central factors in the origin of Islam may be stated as follows: (1) a certain simplicity of faith and of life on the part of the Arabs; with (2) an undercurrent of Fatalism tending toward a vague monotheism ; (3) an impulse from without, mainly from Christian and Jewish sources more or less intermingled and finding sudden entrance in greatly increased measure in the sixth century A. D.; and finally (4) that series of happy inspirations on the part of Mohammed, especially this one delivered to the men of Medina and which served as the electric touch which suddenly awakened these hitherto loosely related tribes into full national consciousness and brought them, vibrant with the sense of inextinguishable life, upon the arena of history.

II.

With such clew as to the origin of these faiths respectively, we have next to inquire what is the central conception of each.

As we have seen, Christianity and Judaism can scarcely have entered, even in their most abstract

---

movement of his time instead of leading it. Monotheism, the worship of Allah, the Supreme (Allah táala), seems to have been always the basis of Arab religion. The Semitic race never conceived of the government of the universe otherwise than as an absolute monarchy. Its theodicy has made no progress since the Book of Job ; the sublimities and the aberrations of polytheism have always been foreign to it." *Studies, etc* , p. 265. Further on we will find Sprenger emphasizing this point in another way.

form of monotheistic faiths, into the actual com-
position of Islamism. On the contrary it appears
that they but served to stimulate into actual life the
inherent tendency toward monotheism latent from the
first in the consciousness of the Arabs.[1] Once this
consciousness was awakened, the complexity, and especially the spirituality, of those faiths (now dimly
brought to their consciousness), proved incomprehensible and therefore wholly repellent to the untutored minds of the desert people. Hence those
elements were rejected by them as something wholly
foreign.[2]

Especially was this the case with the more deep-
reaching doctrines of Christianity. Above all, the
doctrine of the divine Sonship proved a stumbling-
block and rock of offense to Mohammed himself ;
and accordingly he did not fail to denounce it vig-
orously as insulting to Divinity. In the nineteenth
Sura of the Koran (parts of which, as Sprenger

[1] The truth is, doubtless, that this tendency is latent in
the consciousness of all primitive peoples Implicit or explicit, the conception of monotheism is a primal factor of
human intelligence. All monistic theories have their essential root in the fundamental, original unity of consciousness
itself. For further intimations on this point the reader is
referred to my *"Hegel's Educational Ideas,"* pp. 137 fol.,
("Language of Quantity").

[2] "Reduced to its essential points, Islamism adds nothing
to natural religion save the prophetic character of Mohammed, and a certain conception of Fatalism, which is less
an article of faith than a general turn of mind susceptible of
being directed to a purpose." Renan. *Studies, etc.* p. 282.

thinks, were composed for Naggaschy, the Christian King of Abyssinia, to whom certain of Mohammed's earlier followers had fled for protection from the Meccans), the Prophet gives his own version of the miraculous birth of Jesus, the Son of Mary. And to this version he adds the significant comment : "It is not worthy of Allah that he should have a child. Praise be to him (be it far from him)! When he has determined [to produce] anything he commands : Let it be ! and it is [but he does not beget]."[1] And further on : "Ye say: Rahman has begotten children. Ye have spoken a fearful word ! The very heavens should rend, the earth cleave asunder, the mountains crumble into fragments—because ye have ascribed children to Rahman. It is not fitting for Rahman that he should beget a child. Nay all [beings] in heaven and in earth bow before him as his servants. He comprises all and numbers all. On the Day of Judgment all will turn pale before his appearing."

Quite in keeping with this Mohammed does not fail to pronounce direst woes upon those who address their prayers to any other than Allah.

Very interesting in this connection is Sprenger's interpretation of the fact that in this Sura the name Rahman is used repeatedly in place of Allah. He

---

[1]Sprenger's Version. *Leben des Moh.* II, 182-193.

thinks this was done out of complaisance to the
Christians who were called Rahmanists, and toward
whom Mohammed was then favorably inclined. Indeed it would seem that at this period Mohammed
was quite mystified as to the significance of the
Christian doctrine, and especially in respect of the
doctrine of Grace with which the term Rahman was
closely associated in his mind. "If one would trans-
late Rahman," says Sprenger, "he must render it
through the phrase : 'Well-spring of Grace ;' for at
the time during which Mohammad preached Rahman
he brooded also over the idea that faith and happiness are the consequences of God's grace. The doctrine of Rahma, Grace, and of Rahman are indeed of
like origin. The concept which the pure Semites
had of the Essence of Divinity rendered impossible
for them the theory of redemption. But Christ remained the source of Grace—Rahman—and became
therefore the predeterminer of Fate."[1]

A few pages preceding the statement just quoted,
Sprenger intimates the ground of his interpretation,
as follows : "But that under Rahman was originally
meant the Son of Man appears likely, not indeed
from the spirit, but from undigested fragments of
those parts of the Koran in which Rahman is mentioned."[2]   And yet that by the expression : "Son of

----

[1] *Leben des Moh.* II. 205.
[2] Op. cit. II. 202.

Man," a meaning is conveyed quite foreign to that represented by it in countries now regarded as Christian, is evident from the nature of the case in general and from a reference elsewhere made by Sprenger in particular to the outer influences upon Mohammed's inspirations, and where he says : "We recognize in Rahman the demiurge (Christ) of the Jewish Christians."[1]

For a time Mohammed wavered, lured as he appears to have been by the vague phantasm to which the crude Oriental imagination had reduced the conception of the God-Man.   On the other hand, so soon as he became clear as to his own doctrine—so soon as he had once fairly put himself in touch with the *Zeitgeist*, i. e., with the real spirit of his own people—there was no longer any room for compromise with any other faith, no longer any hesitation on the Prophet's part.

"Would ye have any other worship than the worship of Allah? Before him bow, freely or of necessity, whatever is in heaven or on earth, and before his Judgment-seat must they at length appear." "This," says Sprenger, "is a precise expression of the doctrine of Mohammad and closes that doctrine against all other religions."   So that while at an earlier period of his career Mohammed was disposed

[1] II. 225.

to regard all the possessors of a written revelation as worthy of being counted Moslems,[1] his conviction became fixed at last that there is "no salvation outside of Mohammadanism,"[2] and hence that none but his own followers could be recognized as partakers of Islam ; that is, of the one "true worship of God."[3]

It appears, then, that while Islam, as the religion of the submission to the will of the one God, had been preached in Arabia long before the time of Mohammed, there was a definite advance in the doctrine as proclaimed by the Prophet. And the advance consisted in adding to the original idea of Submission, the new aspect of faith in Allah.

The doctrine was also clarified by the distinct rejection of all intermediate spirits. Thus it came about at length, as by a logical necessity, that to the untrained minds of the Arabs and the Arab prophet both Christianity and Judaism bore the appearance of being hopelessly polytheistic, and that hence these religions were at length vehemently put aside as corrupt and blasphemous.

At the same time Mohammed rendered Islam more tangible in two ways. The first was by adding to the doctrine of Islam his own personality. "There is no God but Allah, and Mohammed is his Prophet."

---

[1] Sprenger. I, 70.
[2] Op. cit. III, 500.
[3] Op. cit. 496.

Secondly he added to it the personality of the very people to whom he appealed.   For all true believers there was already prepared a Paradise of all delights that could stir the longings of such minds; while on the other hand the fire burned unquenchably for all who failed to accept his teachings.   Indeed it was the motive of fear even more than the motive of hope upon which Mohammed—rather instinctively than deliberately—relied as a means of converting men to active faith in his teaching.

Add to this his fine stroke of wisdom in proclaiming Abraham as the founder of the sacred rites at Mecca, and thus presenting the motive of national pride in a form inspired by religion, which religion was thus to be enforced by the sword, and we see what were the simple elements whose fusion constituted the fundamental principles of Islam as Mohammedanism in its initial form.   Evidently the very spinal cord of this principle is the *purest fanatical zeal.*

If now we turn to Christianity and inquire what constitutes its fundamental conception, the result reached is found to be one of vitally different character.

Jesus declared that He ''came not to destroy, but to fulfil.''   The trenchant clearness of this statement at once suggests inquiry as to the nature of the doctrines already developed by the Jews—the doctrines clearly intended as those to be fulfilled—and as to the precise interpretation which Jesus himself put upon those doctrines.

Through a long course of discipline the Jews had developed into clearness a strict doctrine of monotheism. Further than this their intensity of earnestness had so far clarified their convictions concerning the deeper significance of this doctrine that spiritual characteristics of the loftiest nature were at an early period already ascribed to their God.

It is true, there is here as elsewhere a manifest process of evolution. The earliest conception which the People of Israel formed of the Being who was for them the Supreme object of worship, was that of a national divinity who was at the same time a nature-divinity. Thus in a psalm[1] ascribed to David, and which Dr. Oort regards as in any case of a date earlier than the captivity, the national God is conceived as manifesting himself especially in the more striking forms of natural phenomena.

A portion is here quoted (from the rendering of Dr. Oort), as indicating the character of the whole :

" The snares of death were 'round me.
  Then I cried to Yahweh[2] in my distress,
  Yea, I cried aloud to my God,

---

[1] Psalm xviii, 1-17.
[2] Jehovah.

He heard my voice from his palace,
And my cry broke through to his ear.
Then the earth trembled and heaved,
The roots of the mountains shuddered,
And heaved because he was wroth.
Smoke rose up in his nostrils,
A consuming fire from his mouth,
Coals blazed forth from him.
He bowed the heavens and came down
With storm-clouds under his feet.
He rode on a thunder-cloud and flew,
And shot forth on the wings of the wind.
He veiled himself in a mantle of darkness,
And shrouded himself in dark waters and masses of cloud.
By the brightness before him his clouds were broken,
By hail and coals of fire.
And Yahweh thundered in the heavens,
The voice of the highest was heard.
He shot forth his arrows and scattered my foes,
Countless flashes of lightning to confound them.''[1]

Magnificent as is this representation of a Power imperfectly apprehended as personal, but also as exerting itself chiefly amid and through the most impressive aspects of natural forces, there is presented a still more sublime conception of a far more clearly apprehended Divinity in the following ''fragment of an ancient psalm of nature :''

''The heavens declare the glory of God,

---

[1] *Bible For Learners.* I, 124.

> The firmament heralds the work of his hands;
> Day upon day pours forth instruction,
> Night upon night bears witness."[1]

On the other hand the spiritual nature of Divinity comes more and more clearly into view with succeeding ages. The captivity was beyond doubt one of the most effective phases in the discipline of the "Chosen People." Their views of the world, of the majesty of Yahweh, their estimate of the intimate relations of individual man to God, are widened and deepened and clarified. It is perhaps from the time of Hezekiah that the following fine specimen comes to us :

> " Yahweh is our refuge and our strength,
> A help that fails not in time of trouble.
> Therefore we fear not, though the earth should swing,
> And the mountains tremble in the midst of the sea.
> Let the foaming waters roar;
> Let the mountains rock when the sea rages;
> Yet Yahweh of hosts is with us,
> Our fortress is Jacob's God.
> A rolling stream makes glad the city of God,
> That holy city where dwells the Most High.
> Yahweh is in her midst, she cannot be shaken;
> Yahweh shall help her at early dawn.
>   *   *   *   *   *   *   *
> Come and behold the deeds of Yahweh,
> Who fills the earth with amazement ;

---

[1] Psalm xix. See *Bible for Learners*. II, 314

Who makes war to cease throughout the world ;
Who breaks the bow, who shivers the lance, who burns the
     chariots ;
Be still, and acknowledge that I am Yahweh,
Exalted among the heathen, exalted in the earth !
Yahweh of hosts is with us,
Our fortress is Jacob's God."[1]

Again with the Second or Babylonish Isaiah the conception of the exclusive, absolute oneness of God is proclaimed with simple but most impressive dignity. The exiles[2] are brought face to face with the gods of the heathen. The prophet brings to his fellow-exiles the following assurance :

"Ye are my witnesses, saith Jahveh,
   And my servant whom I have chosen,
   That ye may observe it and believe me,
   And understand that *I* am he :
   Before me there was no God formed,
   And there shall be none after me.
   I, even I, am Jahveh,
   And beside me there is none that saveth."[3]

And again, still more emphatically :

"Thus saith Jahveh, Israel's king and redeemer, Jahveh of
     hosts :
   I am the first and the last,
   And beside me there is no god."[4]

[1]Psalm xlvi.   See *Bible for Learners*.   II. 282.
[2]Middle of Sixth Century, B. C.
[3]Isaiah xliii. 10 fol.   See Kuenen.   *The Religion of Israel.*
II, 126.
[4]Isaiah xliv, 6.

But also this prophet feels vividly and proclaims with confidence the personal sympathy which the worshiper of this sole, eternal Divinity may unhesitatingly expect from Him.

> " Why sayest thou, O, Jacob.
> And speakest thou, O, Israel,
> 'My way is hid from Jahveh,
> And my right passeth by my god ?'
> Knowest thou not, or hast thou not heard,
> That Jahveh is an everlasting god,
> The creator of the ends of the earth,
> Who fainteth not, neither is weary,
> Whose understanding is unsearchable ?
> He giveth power to the faint,
> And to the weak he sendeth great strength,
> Youths become faint and weary,
> And young men surely stumble,
> But they that wait for Jahveh shall renew their strength,
> And spread out their wings as eagles :
> They shall run and not become weary.
> They shall walk and faint not."[1]

And yet, though the return to Jerusalem kindles enthusiasm and is followed by the restoration and extension of the Law, it is but too evident that heathen influences work their way into the communities of the faithful.   Nay, it even comes to this, that foreign rulers persecute the most rigidly devout worshipers of Jahveh.

---

[1] Isa. xl, 27-31.   Kuenen. Op. cit. II, 127.

But this very persecution really serves to intensify their enthusiasm. And as the coming of the political Messiah seems further and further deferred, these eager minds. in their very desperation at this delay, turn more and more toward the spiritual aspect of their relation to God, and find in their own sins the explanation of the seeming failure of the divine promises.

Similarly, when they feel that they can claim to have rendered faithful service, they call confidently on their God for deliverance ; and when the false gods that have been introduced among them are driven out and the temple is once more cleansed,[1] they break forth in songs of rejoicing expressive of unbounded confidence in the saving grace of their God.

> "Give thanks unto Yahweh, for he is good,
>   His mercy endures forever!
>   *   *   *   *   *   *
>   It is better to trust in Yahweh than men,
>   Better in Yahweh than princes.
>   *   *   *   *   *   *
>   Blessed is he who comes in the name of Yahweh!
>   We greet them from Yahweh's house.
>   God Yahweh gives us light ;
>   Bind the festive offering with cords to the altar.
>   Thou art my God, I will praise thee!

---

[1] B. C. 164, the temple was restored to the worship of Jahveh, after three years of use for the worship of Jupiter.

> My God, I will sing thy glory!
> Praise Yahweh, for he is good,
> For his grace endures forever."[1]

The later part of their history is a long series of al-
ternations from hope to despair and from despair to
hope again. Through which process one may trace
the development and deepening into permanent form
of a peculiarly intense phase of feeling which in the
outcome shows itself plainly as completely *interfused*
hope and despair. Some indeed came to doubt God,
while the trust of others became the more passionate
as all outward signs of the fulfilment of the divine
promises seemed to fail.

Now it is precisely this passionate earnestness of
the Jews, blended with their elevated view of the
oneness and majesty of their God, that constitutes the
central element in the presupposition of Christianity.
Israel is "he who strives with God." Israel, in the
wider sense of the term, is the race which for thirteen
centuries strove with all its passionate energy to
possess itself of the divine Secret. And at length,
with perfectly logical consistency, all the noblest aspirations of this finely endowed people find their natural culmination in the Son of Man who teaches the
world that the fulfilment of all reasonable struggle to
find out God is to be discerned in this: *the divine*

[1] Psalm cxviii. *Bible for Learners.* II, 565.

Sonship of Man. "After this manner, therefore, pray ye : '*Our* Father, which art in Heaven!'"

The personality of the one infinite God, and its necessary corollary, the divine Sonship of Man—in other words the identity of man's nature with the nature of God—this is the core of the religion which Jesus taught the world. "God is a Spirit," and only beings of like spiritual nature *can* "worship Him in spirit and in truth."

Mohammed taught the religion of Force. Jesus taught the religion of Love. Islam is to be extended by means of the sword, and the terrors of eternal fire, and the allurement of a paradise for the senses. Christianity is to be propagated by persuasion, by assurance of eternal communion with God, by the stirring of the intelligence to recognize that this communion can be realized only through the progressive practical unfolding of the divine Ideal in the individual's own soul.

Or, the comparison may be presented in another form : Islamism, with its absolute submission to the will—that is, to the absolute Might—of Allah is the very religion of *Fate.* It presents no real stimulus to the higher nature of man. On the contrary, by its principle of Resignation to the ordering of the world in all its details (including every act of individual man) by the one changeless Power on the one hand ; and on the other by its constant emphasis upon not merely sensuous but also positively sensual delights as the reward of the faithful in the future life, Mohammedanism appears as a religion calculated above everything else to stimulate the sensuous nature of man and at the same time to lull into eternal sleep all the higher phases of his spiritual nature.

Marked indeed is the contrast to this presented by Christianity! With its clear insight into the identity of man's nature with the divine nature this religion announces once for all the spontaneous, creative quality of man's will and thus presents itself as in its very essence the religion of *Freedom*. So, too, by its emphasis upon the spirituality of man, and hence upon the spirituality of the life of the future world where (contrary to the ideal of Mohammed and his followers), there is "neither marrying nor giving in marriage," there is in Christianity ceaseless and ever-increasing stimulus toward the fullest and most careful cultivation of the whole spiritual nature of every individual. And in this there is involved the complete subordination of the sensuous nature, so that it shall without exception serve merely as instrument in the unfolding of the spiritual life.

It may be true, as Deutsch insists, that, "as far as Mohammed and the Koran are concerned, Fatalism is an utter and absolute invention;"[1] though even this cannot be accepted without modification. But the

---

[1] *Lit. Remains.* p. 129. cp. also p. 172.

whole course of the development of Islam, as well as the fundamental doctrines developed from the Koran by believers in it, render it impossible to accept the same scholar's implied denial of the "popular notion" that Fatalism is "the bane of Islam." Rather, as Sprenger intimates[1] at the outset of his consideration of the "doctrine of predestination," as an aspect of Mohammedanism, it is an undeniable fact of history that "most Moslems are Fatalists."

On the other hand it is no doubt true that the doctrine of predestination has found place also in the teachings of eminent Christians. And yet, however "similar" were the circumstances under which Augustine developed that doctrine, with those under which it took shape in Mohammed's mind,[2] the differences involved must not be overlooked. And these differences are especially important on the side of the possible or actual outcome of the interpretation put upon this doctrine by the Moslem on the one hand, and by the Christian on the other. And this interpretation takes shape practically ever as mere passive resignation to the will of Allah for the former; and, for the latter, as infinite spiritual striving.

Thus sensuality is the logical goal of the one faith, while the highest spiritual exaltation is the logical

---

[1] *Leben des Moh.* II, 300.
[2] Sprenger. II, 307.

goal of the other.   Such is the conclusion to which we are led by a study of the origins of these faiths respectively.

III.

We may now turn to the consideration of the relative capacity of Christianity and Mohammedanism to take up and assimilate "foreign" elements.   And this, rather than the fact of wide acceptance, as we cannot too strongly insist, is the real test of the "universality" of a religion.

The essential element, the fundamental principle of truth, in a religion constitutes its actual claim to be regarded as universal.   The more adequate the principle is to the ultimate needs of humanity, the more valid is its claim.   In this—the highest—sense a religion is neither more nor less universal because of the number of its adherents.   Hence it may be truly said that neither Buddhism nor Christianity nor Mohammedanism is either more or less universal to-day than when it was first promulgated.   Nor is Christianity any less universal than either of the others because its adherents are less numerous[1] than are those of the one or the other of those faiths.   Nay if *generality of acceptance* is to be counted as the test of the universality of a religion or a type of religions,

[1] That is, even allowing this to be the fact.

then it will have to be admitted that Monotheism itself is less ''universal'' than is polytheism.

On the other hand, according to the test indicated
above, it is evident that the most truly universal religion will be the one possessing greatest capacity to
take up and assimilate all essential elements in the
life of humanity.

With this preliminary remark let us trace the first
historical indications as to the capacity of Christianity and of Mohammedanism respectively, to re-
spond adequately to the demands of man's spiritual
nature.   And this may be best done by comparing
the most conspicuous personages succeeding the
Founder on either side.

For our present purpose we may allow all that has
been claimed as to the ''historical'' character of the
accounts we have of Mohammed's public life, and as
to the ''legendary'' character of the accounts upon
which we must depend for our knowledge of the life
of Jesus.   What is essential for us here is the fact
that however far legendary or historical (and it cannot reasonably be doubted that legend blends more or
less with history in both cases), the accounts that remain to us show the actual belief of the followers of
each of these characters respectively, and hence reflect in either case the nature of the teachings and of
the personal influence of the deceased leader.

.Compare, then, the narrative preserved for us in

the Fourth Gospel of the scene at the tomb of the
Master, together with its climax in the apparition of
the risen Master to Mary, and His comforting message
to his *"brethren"* saying: "I ascend unto my Father
and *your* Father, to my God and *your* God"—compare this with the mixed scene immediately after
Mohammed's death.   First Omar, that "terrible believer," as Renan[1] calls him, rushes out among the
people and threatens vengeance to any one who dares
to say that the Prophet could die.   But Abu-Bakr
came and said: "Ye people ! he that hath worshipped
Mohammad let him know that Mohammad is dead ;
but he that hath worshipped God, that the Lord
liveth and doth not die."[2]

Between these two representations the contrast is
striking and significant enough.   From the one we
may infer with perfect security, first that the doctrine
of the future life had been impressed with utmost
vividness upon the minds of the disciples of Jesus ;
secondly, that in the estimate of his followers he was
now not to be apprehended through the senses—that
in his transfigured existence he could not be touched
with the hands, that he could only be seen as a
luminous life, and hence only by the light of intelligence transfigured with love (as at Emmaus); and
thirdly, we may with equal security infer that the

[1] *Studies, etc.* p. 260.
[2] Lane-Poole.   *Speeches, etc. of Moh.*   Introduction, p. xlix.

conception had already become familiar that the disciples of Jesus—those everywhere and always who
heed his teachings—are the "brethren" of Jesus in
such sense that they, alike with him, could with perfect truth regard God as "the Father."

Thus the divine Sonship, in this universal and
eternal significance, is already at the point of emerging into explicit form in the newly unfolding "Christian consciousness." And with this conception
dawning in their minds the disciples turn from despair to hope, from grief to joy, from the uncertainties of earlier and more or less materialistic misappre-
hensions of the mission of their Master to the clearer
view of that perpetual and ever-enlarging spiritual
existence to which, now as never before, they recognize his teachings as having always steadily pointed.
It is the moment in which the Religion of "Israel"
—the religion of the genuine "striver after God"—
merges into its universal, eternal form.

In glaring contrast with this some of the followers
of Mohammed exhibit the ferocity of that zeal which
trusts in physical force, and in that alone, as the one
sure means of subduing doubt; while others manifest
complete resignation to the will of the all-ruling
Allah, who alone seems to live in this moment of
death.

But let us now enter more precisely into the comparison of these two religions respectively in so far as

they exhibit a capacity to take up and assimilate elements which on first view appear to be foreign to them.   And first let us, as already proposed, compare them in respect of the attitude which each has assumed toward science.

Here, too, the comparison will be the easier to make because each side presents a striking personage who may be looked upon as a thorough-going representative of the great movement in which he takes a leading part.

Omar has been called "the Simon Peter of Islam."[1] But such comparison is by no means deep-reaching. In fact it scarcely extends beyond the crudeness and impulsiveness of character in each of these two men. Much more significant are the points of likeness between Omar and St. Paul. They are alike positive and aggressive. At the outset each is conspicuous as a persecutor of the new faith. The conversion of each is sudden and dramatic. From the moment of conversion the zeal of each knows no bounds. Life itself is unreservedly devoted to the spread of the faith that had previously been hated. Nay, each becomes in a very important sense the second founder of the faith to which he has been won.

Mohammed had brought all Arabia to accept Islam. But after his death three-fourths of the peninsula fell

Lane-Poole. *The Speeches of Mohammed*. Introduction, p. xlix.

away, and evidently through the personal weakness
and faults which the Prophet himself had exhibited
in the latter part of his rule.[1]   His surviving friends
saved his religion from sinking into a merely local
sect, or even dissolving altogether.

Doubtless Abu-Bakr did much, but "the conquering principle of Islamism, the idea that the world
ought to become Moslem, is Omar's thought."[2]   Indeed Sprenger goes so far as to say that "Omar is the
actual founder of the Moslem power."[3]   And he further gives it as his estimate that "in every respect
Omar stands higher than the Prophet.   He is free
from the weaknesses and vagaries which stain the
character of the latter.   In short he was a man
full of virile earnestness and practical power."

"In more than one emergency it is Omar who de-
cides for the Prophet himself and secures him against
fatal mistakes.   And after Mohammed's death Omar
becomes the apostle to the gentiles—in his own terrible manner.   For "never did man believe so
fiercely."[4]   Even while the Prophet was living
Omar's ferocity of belief was but too often manifest.
Abu-Sofyan, hitherto an "unbeliever," is brought by
night through the camp before Mecca.   As they pass

<hr>

[1]Sprenger. Op. cit. III. Preface, p. v.
[2]Renan. *Studies*, etc. p. 249.
[3]Op. cit. III. Pref. p. v.
[4]Renan. *Studies*, etc., p. 249.

Omar's fire, Omar sees Abu-Sofyan and exclaims : "Praise be to God that the enemy of God has fallen into my hands without safe-conduct !" Hurrying to the tent of Mohammed, in hope of forestalling clemency, he pleads : "Allow me to cut off his head; for he has come without pledge of safety." And only by the intervention of Abbas, the Prophet's uncle, who declares that he himself has given his own guarantee of protection, is the life of this "enemy of God" saved.[1]

Evidently this chief apostle of Islam has never dreamed of the sacredness of human life as such. It is only a safe-conduct from one of his own faith that can restrain him from hewing off with his own hands the head of an "enemy of God" who has come within his reach. And yet in spite of this ferocity, (or shall we rather say: because of it?) "even during the life of the Prophet, Omar had been of greater service for the triumph of Islam, nay even for the purity of the doctrine, than had Mohammad himself."[2]

For such character science is simple, brief and absolute. His one argument is the sword; his one premiss, the Koran. And he knew the Koran ("by

____

[1] Sprenger, *Leben des Moh*. III. 317. Sprenger adds this interesting reflection: that "if the story be true the progenitor of the Abbaside Chalifs thus saves the life of the fore-father of the Omayids, and for thanks the latter usurps during a full century the rights of the former."

[2] Sprenger. III. Preface, p. v.

heart''—*not* by reflective intelligence) with an accuracy that doubtless no one but the Prophet could rival, unless it be Abu-Bakr.[1]

Surely with such an apostle to the gentiles all libraries, Alexandrine or other, are fore-doomed ! His dialectic is fiery and effective. Any book agreeing with the Koran must be useless. Any book not agreeing with the Koran must be pernicious. In either case it must be burned.

Could *a priori* reasoning (as commonly understood) be more perfectly or more exhaustively formulated ? Here is an original thinker. His science proves the absolute uselessness and even utter impossibility of all science—at least within the range of his sword or of his torch.

More ''absolute'' than this a religion could not possibly be. It has sprung into existence in absolute perfection. The Koran is simply a divinely given copy of the Original Book that is preserved forever, or rather which eternally *is*, in Heaven.[2] Its acceptance must therefore be absolute. And this means not only that those to whom this infinitely precious

---

[1] Op. cit., p. xl.   Sprenger relates (loc. cit., p. xxxvi) that when Omar brought Hischam to the Prophet to decide which of them repeated a certain passage of the Koran correctly, Mohammed, after hearing both, said they were *both* correct. The Koran had been sent to him from Heaven in seven different forms !

[2] If only such glimpse could have been pursued, what a revelation in germ lay there !

Book has been intrusted have the absolute right, or rather the absolute duty, to enforce with absolute authority this absolutely exclusive Faith; but it also, as a logical consequence of all this, means that Islam as proclaimed by Omar must absolutely ignore all psychological laws.   For by the very nature of mind the genuine spiritual acceptance of any doctrine is necessarily gradual.   And this is so for the reason that such genuine spiritual acceptance includes the intelligent comprehension of such doctrine—a result which can be achieved only through the gradual unfolding of the individual's own power of intelligence to comprehend the doctrine in question. In short, the Islamism of Omar is a direct practical denial of that law of necessary interrelation between Reason and Revelation already hinted at in another part of the present volume.[1]

And now, what of the Christianity of Paul? To many readers doubtless the first thing that will suggest itself is the fact that this "apostle of the gentiles" also wields a sword—though, as such apostle, his sword is the mystic sword of Reason. He is a man of aggressive energy who, under different circumstances, might easily have been a great military leader.

But his environment is altogether unfavorable to

[1] Cp. above, p. 127 fol.; also my volume: "*The World-Energy and Its Self-Conservation*," p. 225 f. l.

this. During the initial period of Christian development the learned professions offered the only available field for a young man of Jewish blood and faith
and who was moved by any really worthy ambition.
It was Jerusalem, too, that offered him both the
means of preparation for and opportunity to realize
his career. Elsewhere he must become "Hellenized;" that is, he must cease to be a Jew in the strict
(religious) sense of the term.

And yet Jerusalem itself could not wholly exclude
the liberalizing tendencies of the time. So that when
young Saul came up from Tarsus to perfect his education as a Pharisee, or member of the strict national
party, he had the good fortune to come under the in-
struction of the great Gamaliel, a man who was too
vigorous a thinker to allow himself to be confined
within the narrow limits of what was then looked
upon as the strictest orthodoxy.[1]

At the same time this surpassing the bounds of
orthodoxy could not have been anything approaching
a conscious criticism upon, but must rather have consisted simply in a profounder interpretation of its
fundamental tenets. Certain it is that Saul came out
of this school an uncompromising Pharisee. Whatever he may have acquired of Greek culture[2] did

---

[1] "His teacher, Gamaliel, was comparatively free from the
rabbinical abhorrence and contempt of heathen literature."
Schaff. *History of the Christian Church.* I. 289.

[2] Loc. cit.

not in the least disturb—or had not yet disturbed—his convictions as to the religion of his fathers.

And yet this very element of Greek culture, together with the fact of his Roman citizenship and all that this implied, must have produced in his active mind a ferment which, however unconscious for the time he may have been of the fact, could not fail to produce sooner or later on his part a more or less violent revulsion against the narrow, arbitrary formalism of the Jewish Law.

The serene gaiety of the Greek shines out alike in the rhythm of his art and in the subtle symmetry of his logic. The sedateness of the Roman appears everywhere in his administration of law—i. e., in the process of demonstrating the folly of resisting the organic might of the principle of Justice as embodied in the State. The infinite grace of the one, the overwhelming majesty of the other, these two agencies were working ceaselessly upon all minds, and most of all upon minds of a deeply earnest and active character.

Everywhere the results were plainly manifest. Everywhere, especially the Jews of the Dispersion, and even also the Palestinian Jews, were becoming "Hellenized." Even in Jerusalem this process did not fail to show itself.

Exceedingly interesting and important is the fact, too, that it was precisely these Hellenized Jews who formed a nucleus for the development of Christianity in its most vital form.   Nay, only three years after the death of Jesus a radical Hellenist is found among the seven deacons of the newly-founded church at Jerusalem.   This was Stephen, "a man full of faith and zeal, the forerunner of the Apostle Paul," who "boldly assailed the perverse and obstinate spirit of Judaism, and declared the approaching downfall of the Mosaic economy."[1]

Stephen's genius, energy and nobility of character could not fail of deeply impressing the young Pharisee recently graduated from the orthodox school ; and this the more since he himself already possessed within his own soul the leaven of Hellenism.   Nor was it in the least strange that the bold challenge thrown out against the mere legality of Mosaism by the free-thinking deacon of the newly-developed heretical sect should at first awaken in young Saul a horror and hatred all the more intense because in the same instant the personality of Stephen exercised upon him a genuine and powerful fascination.

Thus it must seem to him the supreme duty of the hour to suppress a movement so fraught with danger to the principle of nationality and orthodoxy to which he had but just dedicated his life.   The death of Stephen, by the usual means in such cases, could not but appear to Saul as beyond all question a thing

---

[1]Schaff, Op. cit. I, 249.

demanded by the very highest considerations. Should he hesitate he must at the very outset acknowledge himself to be faint-hearted and unworthy of the cause in which he had but just enlisted.

Can we doubt that the soul of Saul, in truth so deeply tender, must have reinforced itself with such considerations as the foregoing while he pursued the followers of the recently executed Jesus ; and while he stood by, outwardly calm, holding the garments of those who hurled the death-dealing stones upon the sinking form of Stephen? Nay, more ; can we doubt that, from the moment of this deeply tragic scene, there should be incessantly present, and with ever-increasing vividness to his mind, the upturned face of Stephen, transfigured in death, and that the last prayer of the dying man should day and night ring in his ears : ''Lord Jesus, receive my spirit ?''

Surely in the eager, earnest soul of this young Pharisee there are present the elements whose fusion must result in some memorable miracle ! Born a Jew, born to Roman citizenship, from his youth introduced to Hellenic culture, trained by the greatest of teachers in the recognized college of the national party, entered upon active duty as a conservative of the conservatives, consenting to the death of a man whose speech seems blasphemy, and yet whose dying look and word reveal him as a kindred spirit—with all this how could it be otherwise than that in the soul of Saul there should at length spring up a great light above the brightness of the sun—the clear light of Reason, by which for the moment he should be blinded, indeed, but by which also he should soon comprehend the great problem of Life in its essential features and thus be led to give his own life that he might bring all men to see, and henceforth to be guided by, the great Solution !

All this has come to us, indeed, in the form of a vision, an external appeal to the senses. The heavens opened and the Son of Man was seen. Distinct words also were heard : "Saul, Saul, why persecutest thou me ?" But none saw, none heard save Saul. *In no other soul were the factors present through whose combination such result could be produced.*

Doubtless the "vision" was confined to Saul, and doubtless also it was a "merely" subjective vision. But doubtless also the essential significance of the vision is the eternal fact that the Son of Man is no less truly the Son of God ; that the Son of God, in the universal significance of the term, includes every conscious unit in the eternal process of Creation ; and that there is "no other name given under Heaven or among men whereby we may be saved" but this of the eternal, universal Christ, which is the divine nature common to all spiritual units, and yet which can be realized in and for individual man in no other way than through the perpetual crucifixion of the flesh on the one hand and the perpetual resurrection of the spirit on the other.

That is the true Damascus vision. Thus Heaven opens. It is the clear recognition of the eternal Sonship as correlative with the eternal Fatherhood, the clear recognition of the spiritual as the vital, essential, eternal Truth in its own perfect realization.

The coexistence of a number of factors in the mind for a considerable period without any conscious combination of them taking place, and the subsequent sudden and seemingly spontaneous fusion of these elements into a new and, to the individual consciousness, more or less revolutionizing concept, is a fact which must be familiar to all who have a well-developed habit of introspection and observation.

Of course the character of those factors will depend primarily, in part upon the character of the mind in which they come to coexist, and in part upon the character of the environment ; just as the intensity and clearness of their fusion will depend upon the depth and earnestness of that mind. That is, given the mind of a Paul and given the conditions of his life, involving as they did the fundamental aspects of refined intellectual life (the Greek factor), of matured, organically unfolded life of the Will (the Roman factor), and the most intensely developed emotional life (the Jewish factor), and the product cannot fail to be the unfolding of a personality thus far unique in the history of the world.

The focusing of the wondrously complex environment of the then human world in the personality, first of Jesus, and secondly of Paul—that is the true miracle ushering in the period of genuine freedom, the millenium of divine Humanity. It is the culmination of the long process of Preparation, of the elementary aspect in the Education of Man. It is God manifesting Himself in the flesh to the degree of individual self-cousciousness; to the degree of infinite hope; to the degree of infinite renunciation; to the degree of unhesitating sacrifice of all that is merely selfish, and this for the sake of realizing the ideal of infinite selfhood; to the degree of joyously casting aside all that is merely sensuous and temporal because this is seen to be the condition of attaining that which is spiritual and eternal.

Compared with this any conceivable outward miracle is weak and meaningless. Nay, even at best the outward miracle, in the very nature of the case, can appeal only to the senses. It is only the inferred spiritual meaning that can be of real interest to man. Reason speaks to reason. The divine light of Revelation must spring up within the soul. Jesus as the God-Man who proclaims the eternal Christ-Ideal cannot be revealed to the eyes of sense. He can appeal to Paul, to you, to me, only in that vision in which the whole spiritual nature—intellect, sensibility and will—is focused ; only in that vision in which the identity in nature as between God and man is at once *seen* and *felt* and *willed*.

With Saul this miracle has taken place suddenly, overwhelmingly. He has seen God. He is blind to all else. Nay, he knows henceforth that the "all else" is *nothing*.—Fatal mistake, the devoting one's life to this *Nothing!*—Saul is dazed, bruised, benumbed. His world has in a moment turned to dust and vapor. With furious, feverish velocity he has come into collision with the divine World. He must gather himself as best he can from the wreck.

For days he shuts out the external light. It is intolerable. It renews the old contradiction of making him see as *reality* that which in truth is *nothing*. He would exercise his newly developed spiritual vision so that he may become well accustomed to this divine light of Reason that has sprung up with such dazzling splendor in his soul.

This fairly accomplished he finds himself utterly alien to this world that but now had seemed so thoroughly *his* world. He must for awhile betake himself to an unfamiliar world, to a world that is outwardly indifferent to him, so that he may without hindrance or confusion adjust himself to the newly-discovered divine World.

Thus for awhile he goes away into Arabia, into the

desert, into a world that is outwardly but a merely negative, abstract world, in order that there he may with the less interruption meditate upon this sudden revolution in his life ; that there he may study the Scriptures, may sound the depths of the Messianic Idea in its newly-revealed eternal import; may adjust himself to this divine World which but now he had believed to be undivine, but in which henceforth he was to find his life as endless approximation, through self-sacrifice, to Godhood ; that there he may learn to love that which hitherto had but called forth his hatred, and to hate, though still with infinite compassion, all that which thus far he had loved.

And now precisely where death unto life began, there the new life must put forth its first manifestation.   It is most likely that this will be at the risk of death ; but only at the risk of death in a sense that is now no longer dreadful.   For him henceforth death can have no other than a normal significance.   His whole soul is transfused with Love—that is, with absolute devotion to the divine Ideal as itself eternally realized in God, and at the same time to be progressively realized in the life of individual man.   For him, then, death can never mean aught else than transition from a less to a more adequate state of existence.   Nothing can put him to shame save his own unfaithfulness to the divine Ideal of Life, the essence of which is infinite Love to the eternal Father and to the Son as forever reborn in the ceaseless process of the human race.[1]   He will bear all things, brave all things that he may win men to the actual acceptance of this divine Ideal.

Mosaism had sunk into hopeless petrefaction.   As a faultless Pharisee Saul, literal sword in hand, would have constrained men to live contentedly within this life-destroying changelessness.   As a man keenly conscious of his own infirmities, but also wholly alive to the sublime possibilities inherent in the nature of man, this same Saul now yearns above everything else to persuade men by loving them, to convince men by reasoning with them, and thus to lead them to know with their understanding, with their hearts, with their whole souls the divinity of humanity, the boundless Love of God, the infinite dignity of Life as conformed to the Christ-Ideal.

Mocked, cursed, scourged, imprisoned, stoned, be-headed—from first to last not a moment's hesitancy in presence of a conceived duty, not even resentment save as against the hypocrisy of those who professed to be Christians and yet sought to destroy his work !

Through all this it is not to the present purpose to follow this Apostle of the Gentiles.   We have only to emphasize the contrast between the religion of Paul and that of Omar—the contrast between the religion

---

[1] That is, the race of spiritual or divinely constituted units throughout the entire universe.

of Ferocity and Force on the one hand, and that of Love and Persuasion on the other.   And to this end we have only to add a summarized view of the elements already present in the doctrine of Paul which must determine the attitude of Christianity, as represented by him, to the scientific interests of the race.

We have seen that Mohammed was constrained to reject both Judaism and Christianity and to restrict himself essentially to the narrow type of his own nationality, to that simple stage of spiritual development in which for centuries his own people had found contentment.   As we have seen, also, it was due to Omar that the religion of Islam was not merely extended to other peoples, but also that it was saved from sinking into an insignificant sect among the Arabs themselves.

But besides this we have seen that Omar was a typical Arab.   There is no evidence that he ever felt the influence of the Jewish and Christian elements which for a time promised to become real factors in Mohammed's own faith.   On the contrary Omar's mind was perfectly satisfied with the idea of absolute service to the one absolute, irresistible Allah.   And this service he could conceive of in no higher sense than that of a whirlwind of scimetars cutting down all opposition and exacting tribute from the conquered.

Omar was, then, let us repeat, a typical Arab,

And to this we may add : that as such his campaigns were really little else than nationalized raiding ex·peditions. Under Omar Mohammedanism resolves itself into a furious conquering *Will* from which all the higher aspects of intelligence and sentiment are excluded. That is, whatever we may say of the Koran, the Islamism of Omar is a religion of blind Fatalism whose rewards and whose penalties are alike materialistic and sensual.

Contrast with this, now, the central conceptions of Paul and his method of presenting those conceptions to the people he sought to convert. It is to be noted in the first place that the discipline which Paul himself had passed through was of a nature to develop into rich realization his remarkably endowed mind. Something of this has already been indicated. We have now to emphasize the essential points. He had learned the Greek language, and this was itself a rare training in the direction of clear and subtle judgment. He had, along with this, become acquainted with much of Greek literature ; and had thus become imbued with that fine breath of intellectual rhythm inhering in everything produced by the Greek mind.

It is the Greek spirit especially that sees things in due proportion. The Greek imagination was rational and the Greek reason was ever conspicuous for its fine discrimination between the consistent and vital and the fantastic and unreal. The Greek mind was full of gaiety.   But its gaiety was ever tempered with sobriety and moderation.

But Paul was also a Roman citizen.   He had passed his early youth in a province of the Empire sufficiently distant from Jerusalem to be free from the extreme rigidity of Mosaism, and at the same time to be constantly under the influence of Roman discipline.

Only a half-century before his time Pompeius had cleared the seas of pirates, and Roman legions had brought the wild mountain tribes of Cilicia into subjection to Roman law.   Tarsus, the capitol city of this province, was a Greek city noted for its commercial and also for its literary activity.   Thus as a native of this city, Paul was from the first under Hellenic influences while also he could not but receive a deep impression of that world-transforming process which in his own time the Roman power was but just completing.

That *naive* individualism which holds tribe in isolation from tribe, which knows no law beyond blood-relationship, and has no conception of God beyond that of a neighborhood divinity, all this world of capricious provincialism Rome in her harsh, compulsory way, had long been educating into wholesome respect for order based on rational method, for order based on law expressive of universal principle, for an order that transformed the mere dweller in the secluded mountain vale into a conscious citizen of the world. And if, by so doing, Rome was destroying his faith in his merely imaginary local divinities she was also, however unconsciously, preparing him for the acceptance of the message of Reason that was to come to him from the one actual God. Nay, this very unification of the world in the outward form of legal discipline was one of the essential threads of that very message of Reason which God was already delivering to man through Man. For it proved to be the process of rationalizing the practical man, the process of teaching human will this lesson: that the one way to genuine freedom is through obedience to the Law of Reason.

Of all this Arabia had remained serenely unconscious. Six hundred years after the time of Paul, Omar and his armies swept through Syria, through Persia, through Egypt, without the shadow of a dream as to the significance of what the theoretical reason of Greece and the practical reason of Rome had accomplished for the world. Blind worshipers of Fate, they will do their utmost to blot out once and forever the splendid products of the Greek Intellect alike with those of the Roman Will. Crude children of a natural desert, they would turn the world into a spiritual Sahara. And the one word of mitigation is: "They know not what they do."

On the other hand, Paul's fine mind is stimulated to utmost fervor of activity precisely through the assimilation of these elements.   He is a Jew, no doubt. But he is a Jew who has become both Hellenized and Romanized.   Let his education as a Pharisee be ever so rigid, he cannot remain a Jew in any other sense than that of race relationship.   He has taken up into his consciousness the elements that in due course must make of him a citizen of the world—a truly universal *man* who will count nothing that is genuinely human as alien to himself.

Recall now Paul's conversion—the moment of culmination in the fusion of all these elements in his spiritual life—and we see that his whole previous career has been a continuous, however unconscious, process of preparation for his work as the apostle of the nations, a process of preparation for his career as a proclaimer to all men, without reference to race, of the sublime doctrine that in the nature of the case there can really be but one "race," one type of spiritual beings, whether on this planet or any other ; nay that, as the one absolutely perfect Spirit, God Himself belongs to this "race ;" and that thus Man, as the created, progressively unfolding Spirit, is the Son of God who is the uncreated, eternally perfect, and therefore all-inclusive Spirit.

And now, let us repeat that in the Greek element we have, at the time of Paul, the world's highest achievement of intellect.   In Greek art and literature Imagination is realized, while in Greek science and philosophy Thought is given substantial objective form. Again, in the achievements of the Roman world the Will has become practically unfolded into a truly universal or rational method. And, finally, in the Jewish world the factor of Sentiment has been raised to its highest and truly rationalized power as worship of the One God—which worship, through the sublime personality of Jesus, has been transfigured into the spirit of divine Love, into the reciprocal relationship between man and God—infinite devotion of man to God, infinite compassion of God toward man.

The conversion of Paul, to repeat, then, was that divine moment in his life in which the Greek, the Roman and the Jewish factors, under the influence of the personality of Jesus, became fused in his mind into a product which must not only be regarded as absolutely unique, but also as up to that moment wholly unrealized in the history of the world. Jewish prophetic intensity, unbending Roman tenacity, midday Greek clearness, all these interfuse ; and the product is a character, a personality world-inclusive in its sympathy, world-conquering in its energy, and world-illumining in its brilliancy.

It is this all-sided completeness of the man that rendered Paul so thoroughly fitted to become the second Founder of Christianity. It is this that enabled him to discern and state with such marvelous terseness and simplicity, the truth of the Spirituality which Jesus had insisted upon as the essence of the highest religion.   It is this discernment of the genius of Christianity as the ultimate Religion of the Spirit, and hence as in its very nature demanding the fullest unfolding of every aspect of power inhering in the ideal, divinely constituted nature of man—it is this that proved so undeniably the superiority of Paul to the other disciples of Jesus.   Their tendency was rather toward reaction.   Left to them, it would seem that the sublime teachings of Jesus would at least have been in great danger of being overloaded with and obscured by mere formalism.   It is Paul, unquestionably, who alone sees this danger at all clearly and who accordingly exerts all his genius to show that form is deadly save so far as it is the organic structure unfolded through the infinitely vital functions of Spirit.

If, then, Omar saved Mohammedanism from sinking into a mere clannish sect among the Arabs, it also seems probable that Paul saved Christianity from being dwarfed into a narrow Jewish sect.   And further, if Omar's personal integrity secures to him the confidence and leadership of the simple-hearted people to which he belonged, so, on the other hand, Paul's unselfish devotion to the cause of Truth secures to him the unbounded love of clear-eyed people even though belonging to an alien race.

With Omar it is "Koran, tribute, or Sword." With
Paul it is the crucified and risen Christ.   By the side
of Omar's order[1] to burn the library of Alexandria,
place the splendid appeal to the Reason in Paul's
"*Epistle to the Romans!*"

Notice, too, the deeply significant point that Islam
secured readiest acceptance among those peoples who
were destitute at once of culture and of conviction.[2]
Syria was the crossing-point of all the great highways of the ancient world, and hence the region
where all the crude faiths of that period met and
mingled and dissolved by mutual cancellation.   Here
and in Egypt (which had been conquered and recon-
quered), there was no serious native opposition to
Islam.

On the other hand Paul, once he had entered upon
his great mission to the nations, appealed first of all
to the Greeks ; and this in the towns ; that is, in the
centers of intelligence.   It is significant, too, that his
appeals were made chiefly to the towns more or less
remote from the conspicuous centers of the ancient
world.   The latter had already sunk too deeply in

[1] I must remind the reader that the chief point here is :
What is characteristic of Omar as the representative of Islamism as a religion.   Whether as a matter of historical detail Omar ever really issued the particular order referred to
matters little.   It is true (or "historical"), in the deeper
sense of being in perfect keeping with his whole character
and career.

[2] Compare Essay on Buddhism and Christianity.   Present
vol., p. 236 fol.

corruption to regard in any serious way the lofty Ideal in behalf of which Paul appealed to them. Elsewhere, where corrupting influences had been less rife the people retained a fresher, more vigorous character.

But there is still another point of special significance. It is this : The way was already more or less prepared for Paul's work by the influence of Hellenized Jews. To these it was natural that Paul should make his first appeals. And at the beginning it was through them that he worked upon the Greeks. And yet by degrees he discovered that his appeals were responded to more readily and more perfectly by the "heathen" than by those of his own race. So that at length he comprehended and openly proclaimed his mission as being that of an "Apostle to the Gentiles"—that is, practically, he directed his efforts henceforth chiefly to the conversion of the Greeks, who, of all the peoples of that period, possessed the finest intellectual endowments, and who thus proved to be the one people capable of appreciating the subtle arguments and lofty sentiments which the genius of Paul could not stop short of presenting.

But besides this there was another subtle bond between Paul and his Greek hearers. It is nothing less than this : The Christian Ideal is in truth just the Greek Ideal transfigured. It was an old tradition of the Greeks that men—at least the men of their own race—were descendants of the gods. And this belief gave them a high sense of dignity and of the necessity of self-restraint. For he who felt himself to be a descendant of a God must also prove himself worthy of such ancestry. Hence came that charming rhythm of character represented by the fine word, *epieikeia*, and which Matthew Arnold fondly translates by the phrase : "sweet reasonableness."

And yet, though Paul occupied himself chiefly in attempts to convert the people of the Greek world, and though he found there the one field of genuine success, in spite of this it is still the fashion to assert that only the "poor" and enslaved responded to the early appeals made in the name of Christianity. Whereas, on the contrary, as Renan has well insisted,[1] the population of the Greek towns were people of intelligence and native refinement. The artisans of that period were very commonly artists, both in their feeling and in their work. And above all, among the slaves of that and later times were numbered people of all grades of refinement; among whom, in fact, were to be found such deeply learned and thoughtful minds as Epictetus.

While, therefore, it was mainly to the "poor," it was by no means to those who were poor in intellect, by no means to those who lacked power of discern-

---

[1] See his *St. Paul* (N. Y. Ed.) p. 259.

ment, that Paul addressed himself.   It was rather to the people of spiritual vigor and earnestness, people to whom, precisely because of their thoughtfulness, the old religions had already grown shadowy and unsatisfactory—it was to such people, we repeat, that the subtle arguments of Paul proved convincing, and to whom the noble character of Paul appeared as a revelation from a better world.

We set out with finding certain striking points of outward likeness between Omar and Paul.   And yet, even from such brief comparison as we have here instituted, what measureless contrast appears between them !   Everywhere Omar is seen wielding the iron rod of authority, while Paul addresses to men the winning words of Love.   The religion of Omar is the religion of sheer materialism and relentless Fate. That of Paul is the religion of the loftiest Idealism and hence of ever-expanding Freedom for man. Omar demands exclusive acceptance of the all-sufficient Koran.   Paul proclaims the splendor of the divine Life and illustrates his meaning from the literature of the world !   Clearly if Omar's religion meets with universal acceptance, the doom of science is sealed.   Only through the spread of the true Gospel of Peace, as proclaimed by Paul can the real scientific interests of humanity be secured against deadly materializing tendencies and inspired with the noblest aims.

IV.

But let us now indicate as briefly as possible the chief points of contact in the further historical development of these two religions.

We have already noticed the two factors which constituted the central threads, respectively, of the two great pre-Christian civilizations lying beyond Judaism ; namely: the Greek *Intellect* with its formulations of Truth in the fields of art, science and philosophy on the one hand, and, on the other, the Roman *Will* with its elaborate formulation of the method of Justice, first abstractly as Law, and secondly in concrete form as the administrative organization of the State.

We have now to add that it was in the assimilation of both these factors that Christianity gave final proof of its universality ; its adaptation to become the religion of the whole world ; and the more in proportion as the world should grow in genuine enlightenment.

The revision and re-enactment of Roman Law under the authority of Justinian, was the explicit, formal announcement that Christianity had found its own essential spirit substantially expressed on the side of the outer life of man in the legal forms created by the Roman people. It only remained for the Christian spirit to revivify those forms with its own transfigured conception of the divinity of humanity, and thus to show that what the Roman understanding had discovered to be the universal form of obligation of every man toward every other man, was in deepest truth the obligation which each man owes to himself as a divinely constituted being.

In other words, Christianity discovered the central secret of all institutional life to lie in that spiritual and divine nature of man by which all men are ideally equal.   For upon this view of the nature of man the duty I owe to my neighbor, to my fellow-citizen, is due to him on the ground of that universal ideal nature which is common to him and to me alike.   That is, my duty is to *man as man*, and therefore to *all* men, including myself.

Thus, any specific duty I owe to another is only a particular form of the demand which my own nature makes upon me to do honor to the Divine in the Human.   Hence, when I perform my duty to another, I also in that fact and in that far, realize my own right.

There is no reasonable sacrifice I can make that is not in truth for my own good.   From which it is evident that though all institutional forms appear to the untrained mind to be arbitrary, external powers which are ever encroaching upon the rights of the individual and restricting his liberty, yet through the maturing of reflection and the clearer recognition of

the fundamental nature of man the individual must at
length become aware that those same institutions are
but the appropriate, progressive expression of the
universal, divine nature of humanity, and hence that
they are indispensable means toward the realization
of that nature in his own individual life.

When I come to rightly understand Law, then, I
find it to be but the outer form of what in truth is an
essential, nay the inmost, demand of my own ultimate nature.

Such, indeed, is the essential significance of the
truly divine Law which Jesus announced: "Thou
shalt *love* thy neighbor as *thyself;*" and : "Do unto
others as you would have others do unto *you*."[1]

In the light of these simple, yet infinitely profound,
principles all institutions are seen to be but the organic expression of the divinely constituted human
spirit as it slowly unfolds itself into concrete realization in the course of the history of the world.

Jesus did, indeed, declare that his Kingdom is "not
of this world," but every syllable he uttered contributed to the perfect shaping of that Kingdom *for* this
world—that is, the rendering perfectly clear its ab-

---

[1] In this, as is well-known, Jesus but gave positive character to what was already current in negative form. "Hillel
impresses upon a Gentile, as the sum of the Law, What is
hateful to thyself do not to thy neighbor—an interpretation
of the Law which was at that time so generally current, that
we find it in both Jesus and Philo." Keim. *Jesus of
Nazara* (Trans.) I, 337.

solutely spiritual nature as the one vital principle whose functional activity must determine every aspect in the development of the structural form of any really rational world.

Thus it is in the very nature of the case that Christianity should claim as its own by absolute right whatever rational forms the human world has ever developed. The divine Sonship of man is the central principle of Christianity. So far as man's acts are reasonable they already pertain to the Kingdom of Truth ; and in just so far is the idea of the divine Sonship of man realized on the earth.

But not only had Christianity shown its assimilative, transfiguring power in respect of whatever is fundamental in external institutional forms ; it had also proven itself equally capable of assimilating and transfiguring the inner products of the most vigorous intellectual life. While Roman law was becoming infused with the Christian spirit, the foremost graduates of the Greek schools of Alexandria were finding the one worthy use for their dialectic in developing the fundamental conceptions of Christianity into explicit logical form.

Had Plato, with unaided human intellect, discovered those same truths which it had been supposed could come to man only through a miraculously given divine Revelation? The thought of it must have been like a breeze from the mountains.

At any rate the fundamental identity of conceptions was in many respects undeniable.

The conclusion finally reached was indeed that Plato must have had access to the Hebrew Scriptures. But however it might be explained the identity was the fundamental point.   Surely the method by which Plato confirmed to the Reason what Revelation had presented rather to the Imagination, could not but be itself a divine agency.   And so Christianity accepted fearlessly the fullest and freest activity of the intellect as a necessary factor in her own ultimate development.   So far from wishing to burn the Alexandrian library, Christianity sought only to spiritually consume and assimilate the best thought gathered in its volumes.

All this, indeed, could not but lead to grave dissension.   From Antioch, the Asiatic center, came Arius with his clear, but by no means profound, conception of the divine Sonship.   On the other hand it was the true Greek, Athanasius, who with his subtle dialectic, states this doctrine with marvelous depth and adequacy, and yet also in a form[1] that has proven

[1]Precisely in what form he stated the argument in support of the doctrine of the Trinity is not known.   "Under his name the Symbolum Quicunque, of much later [perhaps early part of ninth century], and probably of French, origin, has found universal acceptance in the Latin Church, and has maintained itself to this day in living use " Schaff. *History of the Christian Church*. New Ed., III, 891. Comp. also pp. 695 and 1034.

the despair of most theologians from that day to this.

Indeed for most of them (seeing their loss of dialectic skill), the only really frank word of justification
for its acceptance must be a desperate repetition of
the brave words of Tertullian : *Credo quia absurdum.*[1]

For the weal of Christianity, however much for the
woe of some of its individual votaries, the speculative
habit of mind became once for all at an early period
an organic phase of the Christian consciousness.   So
that for every truly thoughtful Christian the motto
must henceforth be, as Anselm afterward expressed it :
Credo ut intelligam; that is, Faith is but the first
step toward knowledge.

At length Islam too was offered to the Greeks—in
Omar's fashion.   But in the minds of the Greeks
Paul's message had already been in process of assimilation for six hundred years.   During that period not
only had the Christian faith become the accepted faith
of the whole Roman world; it had also given fullest
demonstration of its own genuine, vital universality—
a demonstration consisting in this : that everywhere
the most deeply earnest as well as most keenly critical
minds found in the Christ-Ideal that which proved
satisfying to the inmost needs of the human soul.

That is, Christianity had accomplished the intellectual and moral conquest of the Roman world.   Thus

------

[1] But compare above, p. 124. Note.

it was that when Omar's Gospel of Scimetars was proclaimed in the usual manner before the gates of Constantinople, all the energies of the Græco-Roman world were aroused in self-defense. And the result was like a whirlwind recoiling before a mountain wall.

The Arabs were never to take Constantinople. Not until eight hundred years later, when the Christianity of the Greeks had become a by-word and when the Arabs themselves had given way as the champions of Islam to a still wilder and more reckless race, was the Crescent to take the place of the Cross above the splendid temple of St. Sophia—a temple from that day forth no longer to be devoted to the service of *Divine Wisdom.*[1]

But Omar's plan for the conquest of Europe to the faith of Islam, included more than the assault upon Constantinople from the East. Another invasion was simultaneously made by the circuitous way of the Southern shores of the Mediterranean. In short the deliberate strategic purpose appears to have been to attack the Christian world at the same time both on its Eastern and on its Western frontier, and thus, by driving it in upon itself, to crush it out of existence.

Along with this it is a deeply significant fact that

[1] Unless Christendom should yet awake out of her sleep of shame, induced by wealth-and-power intoxication, as begins to seem dimly possible in these latter days.

no shadow of a thought of assimilating any of the institutional forms of the Græco-Roman world seems ever to have occurred, even for a moment, to the mind of a Moslem. Islam was already complete. Nothing but its corruption could follow the fusion with it of these foreign elements. Not to assimilate them, but to sweep them out of existence was the mission of Islam.

Thus the spiritual fate of the world depended upon the result of these furious invasions of Christian Europe by Mohammedan Asia.

What the final result was is sufficiently well known. In Africa the invasion was delayed for a half-century by the imperfectly Romanized and Christianized provinces. Then Spain, which from the earliest times was peopled by a mixed multitude, which had been subjected to conquest by the Carthagenians, and again by the Romans, and again by the Goths in the name of Rome, and again had been made the camping-ground of the Vandals on their leisurely way to Africa—Spain which had thus been harried for centuries and which had passed from the religion of the Druids to the worship of Moloch, and from the worship of Moloch to the worship of Jupiter, and from the worship of Jupiter to Arian Christianity, and again from the Arian to the Trinitarian form of the Christian faith—Spain with such a history could not for a moment be expected to offer successful resistance to the furious assaults of the Saracens.

From her geographical situation Spain had been the crossing-point of the great highways of the Western nations as Syria had been for the nations of the East. But against this last invasion in the interests of the supreme religion of Fanaticism, Christianized Spain was at length to react with amazing vigor and persistence. Nay, in this reaction Spain was herself to become the evangel of fanatical superstition in the name of the one absolute religion of Reason, the soul of that Christian orthodoxy whose cherished instrumentality was that of the Inquisition.

Through seven hundred years of struggle with Islam Spain became more than Mohammedan in her method of defending and propagating Christianity. And yet the seven-hundred-years battle of Spain with Islam is a phase of the world's history by no means to be despised. That long struggle was in fact necessary to confirm the results of the great battle of Tours.

It is the battle of Tours, indeed, that constitutes the chief focus of interest in the struggle between Christianity and Mohammedanism. It takes place in Gaul, that one of the modern countries which came soonest and most thoroughly under settled Roman discipline. It is here especially, also, that the Romans first took up the attitude of a civilizing power. Elsewhere, to the East, where civilization was already relatively matured, Rome could assume superiority only in a legal and administrative sense. Here in Gaul, on the other hand, she added to her task that of intellectual discipline.

It has been well said[1] that close upon the foot-steps of the Roman legionary followed the Greek school-master. And it is to be added that, following the Greek school-master, came at length the Christian missionary (himself, betimes, a well-trained Greek teacher), and proceeded unwearyingly in the task of fusing the spirit of Roman legality as expressive of regulated will, with the method of Greek intellectuality, in the fire of Christian sentiment raised to the intensity of divine Love.

Thus in Gaul, at the time of the Mohammedan invasion, the Roman, the Celt, and the Teuton had become elevated to the plane of universal manhood. And upon this basis they joined together as brethren in mutual defense of the infinite, divine Ideal which had become the clear representation of all that life could mean to them. For they already felt that in that Ideal there lies the perfect foreshadowing of every factor that goes to complete a human soul and thus to raise it to the rank of godhood.

And so, once more, the Christian world proved itself to possess in concrete realization so much of that

---

[1] By Mr. Freeman, if I remember rightly, though I cannot now give the exact reference.

divine Righteousness which is "like the great mountains" as sufficed to break the force of the plundering
whirlwind that had sprung up in the desert and
which threatened to sweep from the earth all elements of growth and thus to make the desert universal.

V.

And yet much has been said of the rich civilization
of the Mohammedans in Spain, of their refinement
and elegance of life, of their superiority in science
and philosophy.

This view is well expressed by Emanuel Deutch.[1]
"The Phoenicians," he says, "came to Europe as
traders ; the Jews as fugitives or captives ; the Arabs
entered it as conquerors. They inaugurated a reign
of science, of poetry, of learning, of culture, such as
had not been seen since the golden days of Hellas ; a
culture which has left its traces upon Europe to this
day, and which then shone, the only light in utter
darkness, over a people brilliant in chivalry and
song, full of noble courtesy and of simple piety. The
Jews furthered the work of Catholic human culture :
the Arabs inaugurated modern science. The day of
the fall of Granada was one of the saddest days in history."

---

[1] *Literary Remains.* p. 169.

Almost immediately preceding ·this statement the same author declares that : "The new-born Arabs, carrying everything before them, and appropriating to themselves the learning of all the peoples they conquered in the East and West, made Jewish literature what it now is, kaleidoscopic, cosmopolitan."

Just what peoples of any high degree of learning the Arabs ever succeeded in conquering, it might prove a little puzzling to discover. On the other hand it is not to be pretended that brilliant and valuable results were not achieved by both Jews and Mohammedans in Spain during the Moslem occupancy of that country.

But the essential question for us to consider at this point is that of the relation of the Mohammedan religion as such to the modern spirit of progress. And historical impartiality compels the conclusion that this religion as such has continued to be what it was from the first under Omar—that is, absolutely inimical to science, to freedom of thought in any form, to the whole essential organic process of institutional life by which alone the human Spirit can attain, or even approximate, maturity

Few facts, indeed, are more familiar in the history of philosophy than this : that in the realm of philosophy, properly speaking, the Semitic race has never shown that deeper originality consisting in the capacity to create a system —that is, in the power to

trace out in connected form the organic process inherent in, as the vital principle of, all true thought.
And the obverse side of this statement is : that the
Semitic race has also and equally proven deficient in
originative power in the field of science—that is, in
the power to trace out in connected form the organic
processes inherent in the world of things. And this
latter statement *is* the obverse side of the former because the process of things, in its ultimate significance, and as far as it goes, is one and the same with
the essential method of Thought.

No doubt the Semitic mind has accomplished great
things in the history of human intelligence. But its
achievements here have been in the field of poetry, of
prophecy, not in the field of speculative, or even in
that of experimental, inquiry.

It may be readily granted, indeed, that the defects
indicated have been due not so much to a lack of ca-
pability as to a lack of deep-reaching interest in such
modes of truth-seeking. As Sprenger has expressed
it with reference to one division of this race : "When
the Arabs reflect upon higher objects they think
clearly and logically, but they live within the day
and even the more gifted busy themselves very little
with such speculations."[1]

Granted that such is the explanation the fact can-

---

[1] *Leben und Lehre des Moh.* III. (Pref.) p. IX.

not reasonably be denied that "Philosophy has never
been more than an episode in the history of the Arab
spirit."[1]   Indeed, as M. Renan goes on to say, with
the Arabs the term philosophy does not signify "the
search for truth in general, but a sect, a particular
school, *Greek philosophy* and those who study it.
. . . . In so far as the Arabs have impressed a
national character upon their religious creations,
upon their poetry, upon their architecture, upon their
theological sects, in like degree have they shown
little originality in their attempt to continue Greek
philosophy.   We affirm, rather, that it is only by a
very deceiving ambiguity that the name, *Arab Philosophy*, is applied to a series of works undertaken by
way of reaction against Arabism, in those parts of the
Mussulman Empire furthest removed from the [Arab]
peninsula—Samarkand, Bokhara, Cordova, Morocco·
This philosophy is *written in Arabic*, because this
idiom had become the learned and sacred language of
all Mussulman countries ; that is all.   The true Arab
genius, characterized by the poetry of the Kasidas
and the eloquence of the Koran, was absolutely averse
(*antipathique*) to Greek philosophy.   Shut up, like
all Semitic peoples, in the narrow circle of lyrism and
prophetism, the inhabitants of the Arabic peninsula
have never possessed the least idea of that which can

____

[1] Renan.   *Averroes et. L'Averroisme.*   p. 89.

be called science or rationalism. It was when the Persian spirit (represented by the dynasty of the Abbasides), overbore the Arab spirit that Greek philosophy penetrated into Islam."[1]

Along with this it is interesting to note that more than two hundred years before the accession of the Abbasides the dying embers of Greek philosophy had been scattered through the East, and that this was caused by the order of Justinian closing the schools of Alexandria. As we have already seen, Christianity owed much to these schools during the period of their earlier vigor. Now in their decline it seemed that they threatened this religion with more or less grave danger.

It may be, too, that this danger was not altogether imaginary. For with the decline of originality there was inevitably an increase in arbitrary and fantastic interpretation of "authorities ;" and to close the schools was to protect the Church (in which the first great constructive period of thought had passed), from the danger of being led into the caricaturing of its doctrines through further following of a guide that once was altogether clear-eyed, but which at len.th had grown purblind.

Nevertheless, in their dispersion the members of these schools carried with them the works of their

---

[1]Op. Cit. p. 90. See also his *Studies* (cited above), p. 238.

predecessors, including those of Plato and Aristotle. Thus it happened that through translations these great thinkers came to be known to such philosophic minds as were to be found in the East.

At Bagdad,[1] especially, scientific studies greatly flourished for a time, under the encouragement of the Abbassides—that is, as we have seen, under a dynasty that was *Persian* in spirit.

It was in the tenth century that the influence of these studies began to be felt in Spain. The Chalif Hakem initiated a brilliant period of liberal studies there which, however, lasted but two centuries, and not without serious reactions and more or less prolonged interruptions.

Nevertheless in the reign of Hakem "liberalism" became the fashion—literally "the rage," as one might almost be justified in saying. Of all this M. Renan has given us a very seductive picture—a picture in which Andalusia appears as a charming paradise both without and within. "In this privileged corner of the world the taste for science and fine things had established, in the tenth century, a tolerance of which modern times can scarcely present us an example. Christians, Jews, Moslems spoke the same language, sang the same songs, participated in

[1]Compare Erdmann. *History of Philosophy* (Trans.), I, 360.

the same literary and scientific studies. All the barriers which hold men asunder had fallen down; all took part with one accord in the work of a common civilization. The mosques of Cordova, where students were counted by thousands, became the active centers of philosophic and scientific studies.'"[1]

And yet upon reflection one cannot but recognize the inexorable fact that all this is irreconcilable with the fundamental principle, alike of Mohammedanism, of Judaism and of Christianity.

As for Mohammedanism, its very conception of the Koran as a literal transcript of the one eternal Book preserved in heaven and containing all truth, was absolutely irreconcilable, not only with speculative inquiries of any kind whatever, but also with any other form of faith whatever. On the other hand the Christian consciousness was by no means as yet so clearly defined but that the spirit of complaisance might easily obscure the radical differences between the two faiths.

If extreme distance reduces a star to a mere abstract point of light, so a candle-flame may be brought so near as to dazzle and cause the loss of all sense of proportion. It was needful for the purposes of accurate definition that those faiths should be held well asunder. True Christian tolerance is not one

---

[1] *Averroes et L'Averroisme.*   p. 4.

and the same either with blindness or with indifference as to error.   The falling down of ''all barriers that hold men asunder'' is far from being necessarily an evidence of either intellectual or moral progress on the part of the human race.

In fact it was not to be forgotten that Christianity and Mohammedanism had offered themselves to men, each as claiming to be an adequate and therefore final interpretation of the world and of man.   Mere good fellowship, the sinking all differences in simple Edenic placidity of agreeable feeling will never bring the world to perfection.   Differences, and most of all the deep-lying differences, must be felt and seen, nay, they must also be *willed*, even though in this process the world quiver to its center with pain.

It is precisely this necessity that constitutes the germ and ground of existence of all fanaticism. There are, in fact, countless degrees and kinds of fanaticism. Happy he whose '' fanaticism '' proves to be but the fiery conviction of essential Truth, and therefore of abiding Actuality !

No doubt, as M. Renan remarks, ''religious fanaticism was the fatal cause which, with the Moslems, smothered the finest germs of intellectual development ;''[1] just as it is religious fanaticism which in the Christian world has sought more or less persistently

----

[1] Op. cit. p. 4.

to crush out all freedom of thought, especially as applied to questions of the origin, nature, and course of historical development of the Christian religion itself.

But no less is it the fanaticism of "liberalism" to chant a *Te Diabolum* over an age or a coterie that has lost all reverence for sacred things, and to whom therefore no sacred things exist—as M. Renan himself seems in some danger of doing in his reference to " the blasphemy of the Three Impostors,"[1] or as Dr. Draper has done only too unmistakably in his triumphant " demonstration " that Heaven vanished quite away upon the making known of the Copernican theory of the Solar System.[2]

It may be that here, too, " *Réfuter c'est faire connaitre*,"[3] to refute is to publish. For if Heaven has " vanished " before the discoveries of science, it has " vanished " only as the poor, limited, local object of the more or less grossly sensuous imagination, and in so doing has expanded into infinitely rich reality for the essentially spiritual nature of man.

[1] Op. cit. p. 292 fol.
[2] *Intellectual Development of Europe*, Vol. II, Ch. viii, concluding part, on "Progress of Man from the Anthropocentric Ideas to the Discovery of His True Position and Insignificance in the Universe." Evidently human intelligence is just significant enough to comprehend the infinite significance of the Universe—and thus to know its own utter insignificance! A miraculous "finite," truly, which is driven to the recognition of its own utter and hopeless finitude through the positive discovery and clear comprehension of the true and actual Infinite!
[3] Renan, *Averroes*, p. 281.

Indeed, in our hunting down of superstition we are in danger of falling into a still worse superstition—that of dreading antagonisms and of exalting "liberalism" until all differences, all substantial, specific characteristics are set aside, leaving us a world utterly empty and desolate. Such "liberalism," if given full scope in science, would cancel all distinctions between Chemistry and Geology, between Geology and Physics, between Physics and Astronomy, between the physical and the moral sciences ; that is, it would make an end of science and blot out all trace of "Intellectual Development," in Europe or elsewhere.

This, essentially, was the danger that threatened at Cordova during the reign of Hakem II.—a danger to which "religious fanaticism" shortly put an end. Such would seem to have been the historical fact rather than that smothering of "the finest germs of intellectual development" which M. Renan fancies to have been the fact.

And not only so, but, on the Christian side also, "religious fanaticism" proved in a very important sense to be a saving clause rather than a destroying element. In the twelfth and thirteenth centuries, after the crusades had brought the East and the West face to face in a relation beginning in the mere ferocity of religious fanaticism and culminating in mutual admiration—military, scientific, social, and even religious—it seemed that the people of Europe had "arrived by all ways at the idea of comparative religions, that is to say, at indifference and materialism."[1]

Now it is precisely this abstract, negative result of "indifference and materialism" toward which philosophy as pursued by Mohammedans, has ever infallibly tended. Their crude, dry monotheism could not but culminate in what Sprenger aptly calls the soul-killing (*Geist-tödtende*) doctrine of Predestination.

So frankly do they accept this doctrine, indeed, that they ' seldom hesitate to admit the consequences of their premises, and hence most of them ascribe sin to God."[2]

Surely if anything could "smother the finest germs of intellectual development," it must be precisely this "soul-killing" doctrine that the soul's question, alike with the answer thereto. is but the manifestation of an arbitrary, all-decreeing Will which thus must prove to be simply a blind, resistless Destiny !

[1] Renan, *Averroes*, p. 282.

[2] *Leben und Lehre des Moh*, II, 306. And on the following page he adds: "Wir finden schon früh Spuren des Prädestinationsglaubens in Koran. Das Schicksal jedes Menschen ist nicht nur vorher bestimmt, sondern es ist auch schriftlich vorhanden; und das Leben verhält sich zu dieser Schrift wie ein Schauspiel zum Text des Dichters. Allein diese Lehre erscheint in Mohammad's Inspirationen, als etwas Unorganisches, Aeusseres, und es wird daher ebenso oft behauptet, dass Engel die Thaten des Menschen aufzeichnen, aber erst nachdem sie geschehen sind. Wo immer Mohammad seine eigenen Empfindungen ausdrückt, erkennt er, besonders in der frühesten Periode, die Freiheit des menschlichen Willens an."

Thus, however true Hegel's assertion may be that "Man is a born metaphysician," and that only animals are free from speculative difficulties, it is also evident that in men who seriously accept a faith like that of Islam the speculative instinct itself, rather than the "finest germs of intellectual development," must inevitably be stifled, and that hopelessly.

Indeed, if such men ever come to make use of philosophy at all, it must be for the infinitely paradoxical purpose of destroying philosophy. And this proves to have been the historical fact in the intellectual career of Islam. For a time Greek philosophy seems to be taken up with enthusiasm into the very life of this religion. And yet in the outcome it is found that this philosophic movement, as we have already seen, is primarily a reaction against the religion of Islam itself, while in a secondary sense it is a process of forging weapons against the intellectual aggressiveness of Christianity.[1] We repeat that Arab philosophy is so only in name. In spirit it is Persian. And now when we consider that Mohammedanism established itself as a religious movement only by deliberately restricting itself to the narrow limits of the Arab spirit, we cannot be in the least surprised that the attempt not merely to engraft philosophy upon an anti-philosophic faith, but also to do this in the spirit

---

[1] Erdmann. Op. Cit., I, 359-60.

of an alien and conquered people, should find itself opposed by the fiercest "religious fanaticism."

Even Averroës (1120-1198), the chief of Mohammedan Philosophers, lived a more or less precarious life—sometimes in official position, sometimes in disgrace, and again practicing medicine. Everywhere he "busied himself with philosophy, and thereby brought upon himself the hatred and persecution of his countrymen."[1]

Under such conditions the fate of philosophy cannot be doubtful. Finding no response in the surrounding world it must turn upon and consume itself.

This result was reached by the Mohammedans of the East more than a century earlier than by those of the West. Employed as a teacher at Bagdad during the last decade of the eleventh century, the philosopher Algazel became disgusted with philosophy and wrote "*A Refutation of the Philosophers.*"

On the other hand while Islam recoiled from philosophy as something wholly irreconcilable with itself as the religion of unquestioning—that is, unthinking—submission to the will of Allah, yet in the face of the "Religion of Reason," as Hegel has well named Christianity, Islam was in a measure compelled to make use of philosophy.

Christianity, on the contrary, had from the first, as

---

[1] Erdman. Op. Cit., I, 369.

we have seen, made use of Greek philosophy for the
two-fold reason that (1) the form of that philosophy
was found to be precisely the instrument needed for
the further unfolding of the new doctrines into that
clear and adequate expression which alone could
prove satisfying to thought; and that (2) in their
inmost spirit the highest speculations of the Greek
mind were essentially one with the central doctrines
of the Christian religion.

It is extremely interesting to note, too, that while
the Mohammedans were drawn toward Aristotle, the
earlier Christians were chiefly influenced by Plato.
The dry formalism of the one, with his elaborate
treatment of the physical sciences, with much plaus-
ibility could be interpreted so as seemingly to harmo-
nize with the rigid materialistic monotheism of Islam;
just as the more mystical speculations of the other,
with their insistent and inspiring emphasis upon the
questions of the nature and destiny of the human
soul, might easily appear to early Christians as but
another version, addressed to the higher intelligence,
of the richly complex, wholly spiritual doctrine of a
triune personal God with whom each individual soul
stands in infinitely intimate relationship.

It is true that the early Christians did not wholly
neglect Aristotle. But it is not a little significant that
with them "the Aristotelian philosophy was studied

more by heretics than by Orthodox Christians."[1] Not until more than a thousand years had been expended in maturing the Christian spirit could that spirit so far comprehend its own deepest significance on the one hand, and the truly organic and profoundly spiritual import of Aristotle's teachings on the other, to recognize for a second time in the history of Christianity the essential inner unity as between the Christ-Ideal of Divine Love, and the Greek Ideal of absolute devotion to truth as the eternal Divine Order of the World.

It is precisely this radical difference in the relation to philosophy which these two religions assumed respectively that constitutes the secret of the extreme differences of results achieved in the one case from those achieved in the other. In its struggle with Christianity Islam must withdraw more and more into its simple doctrine of the absolute oneness of Allah as Will. And this, reflectively formulated, must be seen to exclude absolutely all other wills.

Even in the Koran this ultimate inference is already foreshadowed, as the following will sufficiently illustrate: "These revelations are a reminder, and whoever wills, strikes upon a way leading to his Lord. But ye cannot will unless Allah wills, for Allah is knowing and wise. He leads whom he will into

---

[1] Ueberweg. *History of Philosophy*, I, 403.

his grace, but for the unrighteous he has prepared a fearful punishment.''[1] If none can will save as Allah wills, then Allah alone wills, and Allah alone is Will.

Christianity had made the divine nature of man and his consequent immortality its central doctrine. On the other hand in its very emphasizing of the exclusive divinity of Allah, Islam, and philosophy in the service of Islam, was driven logically to deny the immortality of the human soul.

Christianity had at first found specially to its liking the poetically idealistic philosophy of Plato. Now, after more than a thousand years of accumulated vitality, all the vigor of the Christian spirit was required to redeem the more rigidly systematic Aristotle from the wreck of materialism to which he had been reduced by his Mohammedan commentators.

It is true that Aristotle was first made known to the Christian world of the Middle Ages through these same Mohammedan commentators. But this is much the same as to say that while the crusaders were making their prolonged and finally unsuccessful attempt to permanently rescue the empty tomb of the historical Christ from the possession of the Mohammedans, the Arabic versions of the great Greek thinker were invading Europe and producing, for the

---

[1] From Sprenger's Revision of Sura, LXXVI. 29-31. *Leben und Lehre des Moh*, II, 36.

time, the hope-destroying impression that all the universe is but a tomb in which every human being, each in his turn, will be buried, never to wake again.

This materialistic tendency percolates like a subtle poison through the convictions of the period. At Padua, at Paris, in the great universities, the writings of Averroës came to be eagerly studied, so that his interpretations of Aristotle were at length accepted as final.

This is not the place to discuss the question whether, as Renan thinks, Aristotle expressed himself obscurely as to the individuality and immortality of the human soul.[1] Allowing this opinion to stand as representing the fact, it is evident that Aristotle's own presentation of the question admits of an affirmative as well as of a negative interpretation. And it is also evident that the interpretation will be the one or the other according to the attitude of mind with which the investigator approaches the text.

With the Mohammedan thinkers the materialistic tendencies so far predominate that the only consistent result possible for them in philosophy was pantheism pure and simple. As Allah is the one will by which all things in the universe subsist, so there can be but one Intellect of which every particular intelligence is but a passing manifestation. The human mind, like

---

[1] *Averroes.* p. 124.

the flower, the star, the cloud, is but an emanation from the one eternal Reality, into which cloud, star, flower, mind, all alike must at length be reabsorbed.

What could lead so directly or so irretrievably to absolute indifferentism as this enervating, materialistic identification of man with the fleeting forms of nature? This is, indeed, but the inevitable outgrowth of what, from the first, constituted the true germ of Islamism. Since the Will of Allah is all, since your individual existence and mine, is each but for a moment, what matters it whether we have the same belief any more than whether we have the same outward complexion?

M. Renan looks upon "the facility with which the comparison of religions"—leading to "indifferentism and materialism"[1]—"offers itself to the spirit of the Moslems," as itself "a thing surprising."[2] To the present writer nothing could be more surprising than just this opinion.

The saying of the Sufis is the one natural form of confession for this faith: "When there is no more of *me* or *thee*, what then will signify the caaba of the Moslem, or the synagogue of the Jew, or the convent of the Christian?"

If that is the result to be attained, then the world may very well dispense with the "comparison of re-

---

[1] Compare apove. p. 232.
[2] *Averroes*, p. 293.

ligions!"[1] And still more may such comparison (the "comparison" in which only similarities are noted), be dispensed with when it is remembered that the doctrine of "indifferentism and materialism" thus attained has always been welcomed with a fairly feverish delight by gross minds, as justifying beyond cavil the fullest indulgence of sensuality, even in its most brutalizing forms. It was precisely this liberty of license which in the Middle Ages found *its* confession of faith in "the blasphemy of the *Three Impostors*," and which, let us repeat, represented the outgrowth of that "materialistic skepticism" developing, as M. Renan himself says, "out of the study of the Arabs and cloaking itself with the name of Averroes."[2]

Against all this it was necessary that there should be a determined and persistent revolt if the results promised at the Battle of Tours were ever to be realized. There was once more to be practically considered, and now once for all decided, the question whether Europe was to be Mohammedan or Christian —whether it was to sink into "indifferentism and

---

[1] I need hardly say that to me the "comparison of Religions," properly speaking, is not merely the noting of points of likeness—a process which may very well lead to "indifferentism and materialism"—but also the equally careful noting of fundamental differences. Doubtless the latter alone must lead to "religious fanaticism." The blending of the two can alone lead to enlightened judgment

[2] *Averroes.* p. 292.

materialism,'' or to rise into an ever-increasing vigor of hopeful spirituality.

Surely it is not strange that the ''religious fanaticism'' of the Christian world should assert itself to the uttermost degree at the reappearance of the old question in this new and subtle form. For the new tendency was indeed like a veritable ''Satan lurking at the bottom of the heart of the century.''

And now let us remind ourselves again that there are all degrees of ''religious fanaticism,'' from that of mere blind ferocity—like that of Omar—to that of joyous, reasoning, all-energizing devotion to Truth— like that of Paul. The latter is that transfigured form of fanaticism which is named *Enthusiasm*, and which, being interpreted, means : *The sense of God within one.*

VI.

The influence of ''Arab philosophy'' proved, indeed, to be relatively short-lived, while the ''religious fanaticism'' of Christian Europe was but the superficial manifestation of a profound undercurrent of genuine rationality. We have seen in the personality of Paul the initial point of the fusion of the three fundamental factors of the world's history. We have also noted the first step in the wider development of this process in the fact that in the West the Greek schoolmaster followed closely upon the Roman legionary, and that the Christian missionary followed closely in the path of the Greek schoolmaster.

We have now to add that the work of Charlemagne was essentially the bringing of these earlier, spontaneous, and thus far in great measure isolated, factors into organic union. As Roman Emperor, this great man seems to have appreciated to the full both his opportunities and his responsibilities. With his armies he compelled the obedience of Europe, not to his own mere arbitrary will, but to the laws as the systematic expression of the matured universal (rational) will of the world. But, as he clearly saw, this work could be but temporary in its results unless the undisciplined people he was bringing under control could be brought to recognize the essential validity of the laws he was enforcing, unless they could be brought to see that their own true freedom depended upon their own voluntary obedience to Law as but the outer form of an inner demand of their own nature.

But this could be brought about only by the intellectual discipline of these peoples. Hence Charlemagne devoted his energies no less to the establishment of schools within the empire than to the organization and management of that splendid police system by which he enforced order within his realm and maintained it securely against dangers from without. Nay, without this external order and security the schools could do nothing toward developing that inner spiritual order and security as a means toward which those schools were established.

But even so the Empire would still be hopelessly materialistic unless the genuine religion of spirituality should become the religion of the people of the Empire.   Europe must become Christian.   It must learn to love as God loves.   To become Christian it must be educated.   It must learn to think as God thinks.   To become educated it must be subdued.   It must learn to will as God wills.

Unquestionably Charlemagne was a practical believer in compulsory education.   But the lesson of which he taught Western Europe the rudiments is the lesson of what might be called absolute psychology. It is the central lesson of Christianity—the infinitely significant lesson that the essential nature of God is also the essential nature of man, and that therefore the true destiny of man, of every individual man, is to "live unto God" an endless and endlessly expanding life.   It is the infinitely inspiring lesson that so far from being lost by reabsorption into the one eternal Essence, he is rather, by endless progression, to absorb the Divine into himself.   More correctly, he is to unfold the divine potential of his true nature into ever increasing divine reality.

Occupied with a purpose so comprehensive and profound, Charlemagne could not be indifferent toward

Islam. As a matter of fact, he undertook no less than seven expeditions against the Saracens in Spain. And yet his best defense of Europe against Mohammedanism was his establishment of educational facilities by which Europe became trained into such power of clear discrimination as enabled her to discern the infinite superiority of Christianity as the religion of Spirituality and Freedom over Islam as the religion of Materialism and Fatalism.

Now it is this Christian rationalism, to which Charlemagne gave so powerful an impulse, and which went on increasing through the work of such men as Erigena, Anselm, Abelard, Hugo of St. Victor, and Peter Lombard, that constituted, as was said above, the deep undercurrent of what, on its surface, bore the character of mere "religious fanaticism" on the part of Christianity as against Mohammedanism.

And this is the more manifest when we note the fact that the anti-Arabic movement proved its wisdom, not so much by personally persecuting those Christian teachers who had imbibed the taint of the materialistic tendency, as by gradually gaining control of the schools and teaching there a truer, freer, more Christian philosophy.

For a time, indeed, the study of Aristotle was prohibited in the schools. But with the development of direct translations of his works it came about that the study of those works was not only permitted, but actually prescribed.   For now it began to be discovered that the genuine Aristotle afforded the one really adequate guide to the method required in the development of the highest Christian philosophy.

The *theology* of the Christian world (formulated in the third and fourth centuries), is Platonic in its structure.   It is at once scientific and mystical.   The *philosophy* of the Christian world (formulated in the thirteenth century), is Aristotelian in its method.   It is scientific even to the degree of being fearlessly speculative or rational.

Nevertheless in the use of Aristotle as a guide to method and a stimulus to thought, Christian philosophy remains none the less Christian.   On the contrary, in their use of the method of the great thinker, the schoolmen of the Middle Ages interpret his teachings in such way as to transfigure them out of the mere narrow worldly-wisdom, in which alone the Arabs had felt at home with him, into the fullest measure of that ideal sphere which constitutes his highest claim to be the guide of those who feel the need of seeking after truth by means of the specu· lative reason.

It might, in fact, be said that the schoolmen of the Middle Ages converted Aristotle to Christianity as well as converted him to the uses of Christianity, were it not far nearer the truth to say that when they relieved him of Mohammedan disguises they discovered him to be already Christian at heart.

And here we have the clew to the vastly different results attained in the two cases through the avenues of philosophy. The Moslem "lives within the day," and troubles himself very little as to the invisible and intangible. By word and by example the Prophet taught his followers to expect a sensual paradise.

Thus, in proportion as his followers came to really reflect upon these teachings, the only conclusion they could consistently reach was, that as the sensuous perishes so the paradise for the believer is—really *is*, only here and now—coarsely sensual, if he would have it so, refined and intellectual if so he prefers, but in any case temporal and vanishing. Individuality is literally a mere dream, naught else than a passing shadow. Hence what signifies difference of creed? What object in considering the relative merits of different theories save so far as it may afford a pleasing pastime? "Great is Allah!" exclaimed a serene Moslem. "Behold that Frank furiously walking about when he might just as well be sitting down!"

"Indifferentism and materialism" are the inevitable culmination of the Mohammedan faith. There is no other logical outcome for it but intellectual stagnation and moral corruption. Its field of activity is within the range of things tangible. Hence in periods of peace its vitality consumes itself, and only in war blooms again into vigorous life.   For then the grand national raid is astir, and the motive of ''booty and beauty'' sets the sensualist imagination aflame. Islam lives on destruction and must die with the establishment of the rule of Reason over the earth.

On the other hand the Christian lives for the future.   And *to* him that future is the infinite sum of possibilities *for* him. It is the organic form of an infinitely rich ideal. And through the meager sum of Reality constituting his actual Present, he has caught an inspiring glimpse of that ideal as being his own infinite ideal nature to be progressively realized by him through an endless and unweariedly active existence. And for the actual performance of this infinite task boundless courage unfolds within him through the recognition on his part that precisely the same ideal is also the ideal nature of Divinity forever realized through his perfect activity in the *eternal Now*.   Nay, the eagerness of the Christian in this work grows perpetually since every step of progress he makes only reveals to him more clearly that thus he is becoming more l ke the Perfect One in reality as he is forever identical with that One in ideal nature.   Where knowledge fails, faith's guesses lead.

And so, too, this at length dawns upon him: that by forgetting the present and living for the future he is steadily unfolding for himself and within himself an ever richer Present that is never to become past.

For he is fulfilling Divinity in himself and thus emerging out of Time into Eternity.

By word and by example the Founder of Christianity taught his followers that the sensuous is worthy the attention of man only in so far as it serves as a means to the spiritual. To the unreflecting consciousness this is a shocking paradox. And yet in that very fact it stimulates reflection and tends to awaken the merely sensuous consciousness into anxious inquiry concerning itself ; and the furth r reflection progresses the more infinitely significant does difference of creed appear and the more infinitely perilous is error of judgment, falsity of theory, seen to be.

Thus Christianity, instead of finding its culmination in "indifferentism and materialism," exhibits, by its own inherent dialectic, perpetual increase of self-criticizing carefulness and thorough-going spirituality. Instead of intellectual stagnation and moral corruption as the logical outcome there is intellectual eagerness and moral austerity.

The activity of the Christian world is within the range of things "invisible and eternal." Science, art, philosophy—the tracing of the evidences of the creative Thought even in things insensate; the seizure of the rhythm of the world as of the pulsations of the heart of Deity; the comprehension of the unity and method of the world as of the process of the Divine Will—these, and above all as they are given the form of living reality in the slowly maturing world of human institutions, constitute increasingly the objects of interest in the Christian world.

Hence in periods of war the Christian spirit droops as from inherent contradiction, while in periods of peace it unfolds into richest realization. For its votaries the splendor of its Ideal remains undimmed and all energies are bent toward its speediest fulfillment. Christianity dies through the wasting of human energies in mere outward conflict. Its life will be fulfilled through the establishment of the rule of Reason over the earth.

Institutional life is, indeed, the necessary medium for the extension of that rule. On the one hand Mohammedanism is in its very nature antagonistic to all true institutional life. Christianity, on the other hand, is by its nature the guiding principle in the full and free development of that life. For institutions are but the outer, organic form which all rational communal life assumes, and must ever assume. And in its inmost nature Christianity is, let us repeat, the very "Religion of Reason" itself.

It is true that to the full significance of institutional life the Christian consciousness itself is even yet by no means perfectly awakened. We have caught a glimpse of Charlemagne expending all the energies of his "terrible will" in enforcing upon Western Europe the mere rudiments of this lesson.

What he accomplished in this direction was never wholly forgotten, and yet, three hundred years after his death it seemed that Europe was in danger of relapsing into a forgetfulness of its true spiritual aim, and hence in danger of becoming broken up into local groups pursuing increasingly materialistic purposes, the result of which must be an ever-growing hostility one toward another. All which could end only in mere savage anarchy.

And not only so, but, as we have seen, the poison of Moslem "indifferentism and materialism" was already preparing in its subtlest form under the smiling skies of Andalusia and would presently pass into the schools of Europe, thence to be carried into the life-blood of Christendom. What antidote would suffice to neutralize this poison?

VII.

The antidote, indeed, had also long been preparing. It was to consist in a quickened and enlightened conscience on the part of the people of Europe. But the result could be brought about only by the reawakening of the Christian consciousness to the one great Ideal of Life, constituting the essential element of unity for all Christian peoples. And to be effective for the unification and inspiration of the people of that period this Ideal must at first present itself in the form of an outward symbol serving as a motive alike for all. It must appeal to the whole Christian world as one common purpose. And because it must take an external form its objective point must be beyond the limits of the Christian world.

Quite unconsciously the people of Europe had long been bringing this symbolical motive into matured form. This was no other than the conviction, at length wide-spread and profound, that on the one hand not only were all Christians disgraced by the fact that the Holy Land—the sacred place of the birth, the life, the sufferings, the death, the sepulture, the resurrection of the Man who was God—should be in possession of scoffing unbelievers; but that also, on the other hand, every Christian was in some sense actually guilty of sin in so far as he consented to the countenance of that possession.

So universal a conviction could have no other than a divine origin. It is the "will of God." Such is the universal assumption.

The conviction is fairly Mohammedan in its simplicity. But nothing could be further from Mohammedanism than the ideal character of the motive, even in its most external form. The thought that consciously stirs in men's minds is : that of a purely unselfish deed—of a deed done in honor of God and of Him alone.

Thus the third 'great reaction of Europe against Asia is formulated and set in actual movement.

And now let us note, however briefly and inadequately, the central characteristic of this Reaction.

It was at the close of the eleventh century that the fading Ideal of Christianity was fairly recalled to vividness in men's minds in the form just indicated. That form, as we have seen, was exceedingly simple and abstract. But for that very reason it was the more easily seized by the multitude and the better suited to awaken unreflecting fanatical zeal.

The tomb of Christ must be rescued from "infidels." And yet conflict with those who in the abstract were infidels, was also contact with those who in the concrete were human beings. The abstract infidel was a "devil." The concrete human being was, after all, a man, a neighbor, nay, even a brother, who had indeed gone sadly astray, but who could no longer be looked upon as a mere monster. Evidently the first estimate of the case in this respect must be amended.

And the tomb of Christ? Even if its identification were beyond all question, it is still precisely the spot from which Christ is *absent*. As the crusader looked

---

'The first was the mythico-historical one (of Troy) in defense of social life (the institutions of the Family); the second was in affirmation of political institutions (the State, based on universal principles of Right formulated in Law). It was begun in the Persian Wars and completed in the conquests of Rome.

within this tomb a voice must inevitably whisper to him : "He is not *here*, but *risen*."

So also looking into his own soul the crusader could not but feel more or less keenly that there, too, Christ had died out—that in very truth "He is not *here*, but *risen*." Thus the humiliating discovery could not be long delayed that the sordid purposes having in reality so great a part in leading him to the Holy Land to rescue what now he began to feel was only the empty outer tomb of Christ, were but the dust and ashes filling the otherwise empty tomb of Christ in his own heart.

To find the *living* Christ he must look *upward*, must forget the selfish aims that isolate him from the Ideal, the Universal, the Divine Man, and, by self-forgetful combination with his fellows, seek to dis· cover and make use of the instrumentalities that will bring him into vital oneness with the living Christ.

Those instrumentalities, indeed, are none other than the institutions of the human world—the Family, the State, the Church, together with the school as growing out of all these.   It is the latter which serves as an instrument to clarify the minds of men as to the ideal nature of the other institutions severally, and also as an instrumentality for the enlightenment of the individual man himself as to his own nature and true destiny.   Standing at the brink of the universal Tomb of the world the crusader has caught a glimpse of the universal Life ot the world.   Life does not end in death, in a handful of dust on the floor of the tomb, in the nothingness of a mere point in space. It "ends" rather in resurrection, in a world-filling expansion of spiritual energy.   Clearly. then, the crusader cannot but feel that precisely here in this Tomb is the very reverse of all that his soul has most deeply yearned to find.

Hence there is but one thing left for him to do. He must go back to Europe where alone on this planet the souls of men as yet even approximate to fitness for becoming the dwelling place of the living Christ in his "Second Coming," but where also the souls of men seem in utmost danger of becoming the tomb of Christ crucified a second time.   For a counter-crusade of a subtle and deadly character is organizing to invade the Christian world.   Nay. the invasion has already begun.   Islamism has put aside its ferocity for the time and has assumed a seductive form.   It is persuading the half-educated mind of Europe that there is but one "active Intellect," as there is but one persistent Will.   The belief is spreading that only benighted minds believe in the immortality of the individual human soul.   Hence infidel passions, infidel habits, infidel indifferentism, infidel materialism—all these are even now swarming within the very heart of Europe.

To such poison nothing else will serve as antidote

but the vigorous development of human institutions through the Energy of men inspired by the Christ-Ideal.   And above all at such crises the schools must become the defenders and promoters of this spirit in forms appealing to human reason.   The doctrines of Christianity nust be restated with reference to the new danger, while at the same time the irrational character of the new "enlightenment" must be exposed.

In the outcome, in fact, the subtlest forms of the poison will find their perfect antidote in the teachings of Albertus Magnus and of Thomas Aquinas.

In their first forms the crusades were to all outward appearance little else than grand continental raids.   Attacking Mohammedanism by Mohammedan methods, Christendom was baffled and thrown back upon herself.   Attacking Christianity with the weapons of reason, Mohammedanism proves its own inherent incapacity and shrinks back to die of inanition beneath the smiling, "liberalizing," Andalusian sky.

Thus, however abstract and fantastic the immediate form of the Ideal which led to the crusades, yet in due course the crusading spirit became transformed and even transfigured into a means of raising the Christian consciousness of Europe to the point of an ideal unity of interests which were truly spiritual.

Doubtless Europe continued to be filled with conflicts—above all which raged most conspicuously, the

conflict between the absolutist claims of emperors on
the one side, and the no less absolutist claims of popes
on the other.　The attempt of Henry III of the Empire to establish an absolute monarchy, in the service
of which the Church should be reduced to a mere political engine, was followed at no distant day by the
reaction under Hildebrand, bringing the Church into
a state of healthy vigor, guaranteeing Europe thereafter against any further danger from imperial abso-
lutism.　So that when, long after, we hear the brilliant but scoffing Frederick II exclaim : "Happy
Saladin who has no Pope !" we are prepared to re-
spond : Happy Europe, which has not lacked a Pope
to withstand the deadly materializing tendencies of
unrestricted imperial power !

Superficially regarded, these conflicts are a measureless scandal to the Christian world.　And yet in
truth the outer conflicts unfailingly provoked an inner conflict of mind with mind.　That is, discussion
was called forth and attempt made to prove the *reasonableness* of either party to the conflict.　But this in
turn could not fail to aid greatly in deepening and
rationalizing the consciousness of Christendom as to
its true Ideal, and thus in redeeming Europe from
the "indifferentism and materialism" which threatened to overwhelm it.

Thus was the still new Western world rendered increasingly faithful to its truer self as the proper agent

for the gradual unfolding of the Kingdom of God in the hearts of men—increasingly conscious, too, that this could be accomplished in no other way than by means of those institutions through which alone the communal life of man can be rendered truly organic, and which thus constitute also the instrumentality through which alone the life of individual man can be matured.

Nor can this latter point be too strongly emphasized. In the light of Christianity it is precisely the individual human being who is immortal, and who by that fact is of infinite significance. Institutions are but the outer forms assumed by what is universal in man. They constitute the organism of the human spirit, *as far as this is here and now already realized.*

Hence they are of value in just so far, and only just so far, as they serve as instrumentalities in the unfolding into reality of the universal Ideal of *Man* in individual *men.* It is for this reason that institutions are ever proving useful and also ever proving hurtful. So long as they are fresh and flexible—that is, truly organic—they are conducive to life. So soon as they become hardened into rigid forms—so soon as they cease to be organic—they prove to be repressive of life. They are the skin of the Serpent of Thought which must be cast from time to time in order that "civilization" may not become blind and venomous; in order that the genuine spiritual life of a people may not be stifled, but that instead it may be allowed the full range of natural conditions for its perfect development.

Such are the conclusions at which we arrive through a critical comparison of Christianity and Mohammedanism. Only by sacrificing its character of genuine universality can Christianity make concessions to the faith of Islam. Only through its own dissolution can Islam approximate Christianity. As forms of religion they are wholly irreconcilable. Vital education must destroy the faith of the individual Moslem in his creed; and the only logical culmination of this process must be his conversion to the "Religion of Reason" as founded by Jesus of Nazareth, as formulated by Paul of Tarsus, as elaborated by the science, the art, the literature, the philosophy, the institutions of all succeeding ages.

V.

THE NATURAL HISTORY OF CHURCH ORGANIZATION.

A half-century ago a great German philosopher, looking through spectacles that had come to have a decided Prussian tint, beheld the Church dissolving in America as a consequence of the separation between Church and State.

To day there is also a ''new'' America. But now it is an overwhelming tendency toward centralization that has seized upon all forms of communal life, and which, on first view, seems to threaten the total suppression of independence in the individual life. Nor is this without its seeming justification. There can be no reasonable doubt that organization is the one only condition favorable either to the development of power or to its effective employment. But neither can there be any reasonable doubt that ''organization'' may become mechanical, and thus result at length in the extinction of the most essential of all the qualities constituting an organism—the quality of life itself.

Historically, indeed, this has been the actual result in only too many instances. Among these none are more conspicuous than those presented in the course of the development of the Christian Church. As everyone knows, Christianity first struggled into form as an organization in irreconcilable conflict with the established religion of the Roman Empire. But success in this struggle was no sooner assured than Christianity itself became the established religion of the same Empire. Nor was this "establishment" of the Church a merely formal aspect of its development. At that time no one, of whatever party, doubted for a moment that the only normal relation between Church and State was that of completely fused, organic union. Thus far, the organization of the Christian Church was based mainly upon the model of the Jewish Church, that is, upon the idea of Theocracy. As yet, however, the political aspect was wanting. And this was now to be supplied in the union of the Christian Church with the Roman State.

But this union could be effected only through mutual concessions. The Church had conquered the Empire by converting the people of the Empire to the Christian faith. The Empire surrendered to the Church, that it might possess the strength of the Church. The Church was now in turn to surrender to the Empire, that it might possess the marvelously efficient organization of the Empire. The Empire became Christian in its creed. The Church became imperial in its outer forms of life. And why not? Could anything be more manifest than that this same marvelously efficient organization was a "fore-ordained" instrumentality for the complete establishment of the kingdom of God on the earth? Evidently, in such case,

> "To doubt would be disloyalty;
> To falter would be sin."

Nevertheless two centers quickly developed as rivals in ecclesiastical authority—Rome and Constantinople. The Roman and the Greek spirit once more contended for the empire of the World. The question now was: Which should determine in detail the ultimate form into which the Christian world was to be moulded? And, however little it was understood to be the case at that time, the answer to this question must depend upon the answer to the further question : Which of the two, Roman or Greek, was already the more vitally related, or possessed the gifts for becoming the more vitally related, to the spirit of the peoples that were then just budding into national life?

To this question the answer assumed two widely contrasted forms. Externally these forms were as follows :

First, at Constantinople the imperial authority was directly present in the person of the Emperor. Thus at that point ecclesiastical authority was completely overshadowed. The Greek ecclesiastic was therefore first of all a theologian. He could not aspire to be

also a politician.   As a Greek he had but one world
of activity, and that world was the world of thought,
of speculation.   He might advise.   He might justify
authority.   He could never exercise authority.   He
might mould the inner world of thought, but not the
outer world of affairs.

At Rome, on the contrary, the Christian Bishop
successfully rivaled the imperial representative, and
soon became a practically independent authority. The
Greek genius of Athanasius might be required to
formulate the doctrine of the Trinity; it required the
Latin genius of Augustine not only to give to that
doctrine its final touch of precision, but also and especially was this Latin genius required to incorporate
into a finished system the entire body of Christian
doctrine thus far speculatively developed, and to give
to that system the legal aspect of dogma to be enforced sooner or later, if need be, by secular power.
It was this finished, imperial character which made it
possible for the Church of Rome to take the initiative
in giving a distinctively Christian trend to the new
states that gradually grew into form amid the chaos
of the Roman imperial world, and to exercise within
them an ever-increasing influence.

The *second* outer form assumed by the answer to the
question whether Greek or Latin Christianity possessed the gifts for becoming vitally related to the
spirit of these new peoples, is to be found in the atti-

tude which the Greeks and the Latins assumed respectively as Christians toward art. To the Greeks there remained the splendid traditions of classic art. But its forms belonged irrevocably to the now abhorred religion of polytheism. Nay, it proved that in the service of this religion the Greeks had really exhausted their capabilities in the field of art. Nor did they dare attempt to use, for the art purposes of the new faith, the typical forms which the genius of their race had thus produced. Or, if a few timid attempts were made to this end the quickness and completeness with which this class of representations was abandoned only proves the more clearly how wholly alien such representations were felt to be to the new themes.

On the other hand the case was radically different with the Romans. In their earlier history they had not been an art-loving people. So that whatever capabilities of art they might possess still remained latent. At the same time the new faith in its complex, abstract form could not be seized by the imagination. And yet for the multitude its themes must somehow be represented to the eye. Especially was this the case, not only for the later Romans who had become more and more accustomed to magnificent pageants and who were growing less than ever capable of abstract thinking ; but also and still more was it the case with the rude minds of the barbarian peoples in whom lay the destinies of Europe and of the world.   If the pictorial form was not the only one that could appeal effectively to these untutored minds it was at least the form that could appeal to them in such way as would most ennoble sentiment and yet tend least to crystalline fixity of superstitious conceptions respecting the new faith.

Thus as the authority of the Roman Bishop grew it became possible for him to extend the ceremonial of worship and enrich it with the most varied and imposing characteristics.   Carved images, too, were multiplied without number, while the walls of churches were covered with ever freer and more life-like representations of the sacred personages of the growing faith.   Nowhere in the history of the world has there been more striking illustration of the fact that in its highest significance art is nothing else than religion struggling to express itself in forms of beauty.

That in these two respects the widely contrasted aims and methods of the Greek and Latin divisions of the Church are to be considered as in reality the specific forms in which were expressed their widely contrasted views concerning the ·'Procession of the Spirit,'' can only be hinted at here   What we must especially notice at present is the fact that the Latin Church proved itself to be a veritable Teacher ''sent from God'' to the newly appearing nations.   Its organization assumed a character of vital plasticity serving wondrously the needs of the newly developing type of spiritual life.

The Greek Church, on the other hand, submitted passively to being moulded into an instrument of imperial power. The Roman Church rapidly developed into a practically independent power that soon proved itself capable of well-nigh world-wide dominion. Its finely vibrant life was an aspect of the Spirit proceeding from humanity as the Son.

But it is not to be forgotten that the organic form which the Western or Roman Church assumed was the definite outgrowth of the Italian spirit. Its imposing ceremonial, its magnificent pageantry, were direct products of that restless fancy, that buoyant vivacity which in the Italian came at length to replace the taciturnity, the abstract sobriety of mind of the Early Romans. Thus it is that Roman Christianity is neither more nor less than that particular form which the Christian Religion assumed when adopted by one specially endowed people. The epithet, "Roman Catholic," is indeed a direct contradiction in terms. And with perfectly logical consistency the use of the epithet has always been resented by the Church of Rome; though this resentment is based upon the untenable ground that the Church, having its central authority at Rome is simply and exclusively the Catholic. i. e., universal Christian Church.

On the contrary, as we have just seen, the church

having its center at Rome, whether we view it from the side of its imperial organization or from the side of its magnificent ceremonial, is unquestionably local, distinctively Roman-Italian.   It has, indeed, with all its one-sidedness, its non-universality or non-catholicity, proven itself to be the form of Christianity native to the Latin races.   And this is shown still further by the very fact that no other form of Christianity has ever been able successfully to compete with it among those peoples; just as, on the other hand, the fixed, finished, inflexible character of that form, especially among those peoples, shows them to be as a whole, still characterized chiefly by the imaginative, non-reflective phase of mind ; and thus to be ever satisfied with an external, spectacular presentation of the truth.   Indeed what is distinctively called the Catholic Religion to-day is, on its ceremonial side, in great measure an outgrowth of, and in turn most ef-fectively appeals to, the art sentiment of the Christian world.   It is the reduction of the Beauty of Holiness to the sensuous, imaginative form.   It is and can be a satisfying faith to those and only those whose mental habit "is to accept the world as they find it," and to whom therefore the world presents no speculative problems.

And this is precisely the reason why the Italian form of Christianity proves to be fatally lacking for the Teutonic nations.   For from the earliest times those nations have been characterized by their individualism—their high estimate of the rights and duties of each individual member of the nation. The very core of this characteristic, as need hardly be said, is the sense of intellectual freedom with its healthy, robust vein of skepticism that would prove all things in order to be the more sure in the outcome of holding fast to that which is good, and to that alone. And the more mature the Teuton became in this character of individualism, only by so much the more did he become aware of the utter inadequacy of Italian Christianity to his needs.

Thus it was that the Reformation, in deepest reality, proved to be nothing less or else than the spontaneous unfolding of a new form in which to organically express the Christian faith as it appealed to a newly developed phase of human intelligence. Here the spectacular fell into abeyance. Nay, in the reaction against the spectacular form it was but inevitable that an extreme view should be reached to the effect that this form was mere delusion, a pleasure to the eye at the expense of the soul's real interests. Thus, if the Italian was charmed and satisfied with a splendid ceremonial that seemed to him to realize the utmost Beauty of Holiness. the Teuton came to feel that nothing was worthy of his effort or even of his attention save the inner, vital essence. The Power of Godliness alone could avail.

To the Italian the Reformation was as the coming of Antichrist. To the Teuton it was the beginning of the overthrow of Antichrist. Doubtless also to non-Christians it seemed the first sure sign of the disintegration of Christianity itself. And yet in truth, as has now long been evident, the great movement of the Reformation was but the bringing into realization that deeper truth of Christianity which had previously been shadowed forth only in symbols.

This splendid symbolism still remained, indeed, because the phase of intelligence to which it appealed, and by which also it was produced, still remained. But also and equally the newly developed forms were necessary. For now there had come to something like maturity a new phase of intelligence which saw in Christianity a deeper aspect of truth than symbolism can ever hope to express. And so the unfolding of a new form of the Christian Religion only gave proof that it possessed not less but greater vitality and wealth of significance than had hitherto been at all suspected.

In short what is specifically called the Reformation is but one specially conspicuous stage of a process that has been going on ever since the beginning of the religious consciousness of man. That process is but the progressive multiplication of forms through which to express and in which to realize the steadily unfolding, infinitely varied spiritual nature of man. This might, indeed, on first sight seem to be contradicted by the fact that multitudes of pagan religions have faded away when brought into contact with the religion that has found its surest acceptance among the people of greatest intellectual vigor.   A further examination, however, shows that while this religion has proven itself to be in its universal character the true Light of the World, in the focus of which indeed no false religion can fail to be dissolved ; yet this Light, itself, shining through the endlessly varied media of human intelligence, has not failed and cannot fail to flame out in ever new splendors of color, progressively revealing the exhaustless wealth of its divine significance.   In other words, just because of this wealth of significance it must the more certainly appeal to various types of mind in correspondingly various ways.   And the result of this can be nothing else than the multiplication of outer forms expressive of the varying modes of apprehending the central truth which the Christian religion presents.

It is true that this involves a vast amount of caricature, none the less gross because unintentional. But it is nevertheless needful that the child—including the immature man—be permitted to make the mistakes of childhood in order that by the exercise of his own slight powers those powers may become matured and the child thus devolop into actual manhood.

Nay this is the central, divine secret of Christianity

itself, that it declares the infinite significance of the *individual*, and demands therefore that above all things the individual shall himself put forth every effort to unfold into richest maturity the divine nature within him. Man, the thinking unit, perpetually arising and unfolding in the eternal process of Creation, that is the ultimate truth of "God manifest in the flesh." That is the highest term of the "eternally-begotten Son." That is the central conception of Christianity in its truly Catholic or universal form.

But in the very nature of things this divine truth could not be seized in its full significance at the first moment of its presentation to man. Rather in the process of comprehending it, even after its specific announcement, human intelligence must needs pass through the stages of childhood and youth before it could arrive at maturity. And the stage of childhood was the stage of symbolism—Italian Christianity— while the age of its youth was the age of dawning reflection—the Christianity of the Reformation period. In the former stage the maturity or self-dependence of the individual was not expected. He must submit unreservedly to authoritative guidance. In the latter he was brought to claim maturity as his right, but was practically debarred from making the claim good. Nor is this phase of the Reformation even yet passed, though at the present day rapidly passing.

Let us note now summarily, first, that the Christian religion is distinguished from all others by the fact that it announces the infinite significance of each individual human being ; and second, that Luther simply formulated the legitimate corollary from this that individual man has absolute right to the full, free exercise of his powers as the necessary condition to his own attainment to maturity.   And let us also note at the same time the fact that while Christianity for the first three centuries of its existence was per-force a non-established religion. nevertheless the existence of a religious organization otherwise than as a phase of a political organization, was as yet evidently regarded as something wholly abnormal.

Doubtless as claiming to be the world-religion, Christianity could not at the outset consistently ally itself with any other than the world-empire.   But there was no hesitancy concerning this alliance when the moment for its consummation arrived.   And thenceforth the "establishment" of Christianity as the State religion in countries not acknowledging the imperial authority, was still regarded as but the progressive unfolding into reality of the ideal World-empire as a Christian dominion.   If the political organization was unable independently to realize the conquest of the world, the Church believed in its own power to make that conquest an accomplished fact.

Thus from having been co-operative powers, the Church and the Empire came to be antagonistic powers. And we have now to note that if the genius of Hildebrand constructed an impassable barrier to the fulfillment of the ambitious schemes that had been formed and in part realized by Henry III, so the growing individualism of the Teutonic peoples still further kept in check the absolutist tendencies of the imperial authority, and at length also drew the line of ultimate limitation to the fulfillment of the Papal dreams of absolute dominion.

Not in that exclusive fashion was the principle of Autocracy to be realized. Rather it was to be realized in the truly catholic or universal spirit of Christianity which demands that the principle of autocracy shall be unfolded in the form of self rule on the part and in the very life of each individual human soul.

Such is the true Christian ideal. And it was this deeper phase of Christianity which Luther definitely announced in the Declaration of Religious Independence which he formulated. And thus it was that Luther proved to be the genuine representative of the true spirit of individualism which first came to maturity in the Teutonic world.

But again it is not to be forgotten that, the more richly significant the ideal, only so much the more certainly must its complete realization be long delayed. The differentiation of the Christian church is necessarily involved in the differentiation or unfolding of the principle of individualism which underlies

the very existence of that church.   At first, however,
this fact was by no means clearly recognized by the
reformers.   It was only when forced to do so that
they accepted this as a logical consequence of their
protests against arbitrary rule.

It is significant, too, that the individualism which
they looked upon as the vital one was not personal,
but political.   Each *state* might determine its own
form of worship.   And this really meant that each
ruler of a state might decide the form of worship for
all individuals under his authority.   Thus far the
principle of autocracy was specialized.   And because
the autocrat or ruler would probably represent the
spirit of at least a majority of his subjects, the true
spirit of autocracy was thus specialized to a greater
degree than would at first sight appear.   Nevertheless it is not to be overlooked that the "autocracy"
of the subject in such case must be not genuine, but
merely on sufferance—a change of rulers rendering
possible a complete reversal of forms of worship.

Indeed there was anxious solicitude for the restraint
of the individual member.   Left to himself he must
follow his own unchecked fancies and soon wander
into ruinous heresies of thought and deed.   And it
was not for a moment doubted that the authority of
the state was required as at least a supplementary restraining power.   Nor can there be any reasonable
doubt that this is true ; though as yet there was by

no means a clear understanding as to the proper line of distinction between the political and the religious authority as a restraining power.

It is true that this differentiation of function had already reached an advanced stage. The State was especially watchful against heresies of deed, as the Church was especially sensitive in respect of heresies of thought. But that these two functions should still be joined under the ultimate authority of the ruler of the State there had arisen no shadow of doubt. Rather the separate existence of Church and State was without hesitation assumed to involve an extremely perilous relation between Church and State.

And so the ideal of Henry III reappeared. The Church as the established religion of the State and as thus dependent upon the State for its support, was already subordinated to the will of the ruler of the State. Hence it could be used by him as simply a part of the political machinery at his disposal and through which he might accomplish his own purposes. And from the English Henry VIII to the German Bismarck how many conspicuous examples does history furnish to show that the possession of this power presents a temptation too great to be resisted ! The extent to which the Church of England especially has been put to use as a political engine is sufficiently well-known.[1]

In fact, it was largely the reaction against the English Church as a political engine that determined the precise character of the American commonwealth. For that reaction was the reaffirmation of the principle of individualism or autocracy in its ultimate significance.   And this reaction could with least hindrance and delay be developed into its positive form in a country remaining to be peopled by a civilized race.

This appears the more significant, too, the farther one looks back along the stream of events that led to the settling of America by refugees from Europe. From the Saxon Heptarchy through the Norman Conquest and the Wars of the Roses, to the American Revolution, there is one continuous process of natural selection.   And "American" is rather the name of a peculiar type of mental and moral development than the name of a resident of a particular country. Doubtless in this sense Americans were born before Columbus sailed across the Atlantic ; but each was thus "a man without a country."   Only since the "Treaty of Paris" have the increasing millions of such souls known precisely whither they should go

---

[1] The extreme logical outcome of all this is of course to be seen in its greatest fullness of practical illustration in the case of the Greek Church in Russia, reduced, since the time of Peter the Great, to absolute subordination to the State

in search of what in deepest sense is their true native land.   And no matter at what particular spot on the surface of this planet he may have first seen the light, unless a man belong essentially to that type he is not an American, but an alien to all that gives significance to the name.

The true autocrat is the self-ruled man, and that is the typical American.   Self-ruled, and therefore is he the direct opposite of the lawless man, the anarchist, who will have no rule—who will least of all rule himself.

And so it is in America that the Christian Ideal has for the first time in the history of the world been given explicit utterance in its ultimate significance through the social organism.   Here is the true monarchy—not the rule of one man, for that must vary with each succeeding reign, nay with the successive caprices of each individual ruler—but rather the rule of the one unalterable Principle of Freedom, involving identity of nature and therefore equality of rights for all the Brotherhood of Man.   The true "monarchy" is based upon the legitimate kingship, not of one man, nor of some men, but of all men.

So well indeed was this Ideal understood by the founders of the American Union that the functions of the religious organization were by them completely differentiated from those of the political organization. The church was no longer to be considered as an institution of such doubtful validity that its perpetuity could be insured only on condition of guaranteeing its support by the State. At the same time its sacredness was so far recognized as, by its complete separation from the State, to at least negatively secure its freedom from perversion to other than its legitimate functions. Not because the American people are indifferent to religion is the name of Divinity omitted from their Constitution, but because the entire spirit of the people, as voiced in that document, is pervaded by the profoundest faith in the divine governance of the world and in the divine destiny of man as the genuine Son of God.

Thus, for the first time since the first three centuries of its existence, could the Christian religion assume without artificial hindrance a form consonant with the Spirit in which it was received by its votaries. If a group of Christians differed as to the proper mode of worship, or as to the precise form of Christian doctrine—that is, if there proved to be a well-marked difference in their mode of apprehending the fundamental truths of Christianity—nothing more was needed to reduce the antagonism to its lowest terms than to separate into distinct congregations and develop in each group what seemed to it the legitimate mode of embodying those truths.

Discussions, often angry, sometimes unseemly, no doubt resulted. But it is also true that these discussions had the inestimable value of concentrating attention upon what were believed to be fundamental questions.   And this was the one sure way of discovering at length where lay trivialities and where lay the essentials of truth.

Meanwhile it is not to be much wondered at that Hegel, with all his marvelous powers of dialectic, should still be so far a victim to the bias of his time and immediate surroundings as to mistake this process of differentiation for a process of disintegration. Sects were at that time multiplying so rapidly as that dissolution might well be thought to have fairly set in.

But this very freedom of division proved to be the means of its own cancellation.   Differences which at first seemed vital proved under the light of discussion and mature deliberation to be but incidental and transitory.   The homogeneity of sentiment that constitutes the deep-lying basis of the American Brotherhood, also proved to be a check to ecclesiastical division.   With no established church political sentiment served rather to allay than to intensify religious strife—a fact not less significant than novel in the history of humanity.   And if the resistance of Northern and Southern divisions of many of the denominations seems to contradict this, still even here there is rather confirmation than contradiction.   For with the vanishing of slavery there vanished also the only real ground of both political and religious division. And that division even as a sentiment is now being rapidly succeeded by both political and religious fraternity.

But this tendency toward unity—has that no natural limit short of the actual merging of all denominations into one United Church of America? Let us attempt to find a reasonable answer to this question.

To say that man is a progressive being is as much as to say that man is an imperfect being. And imperfect as he is it would seem that the only security against fatal one-sidedness in his development, is to give free play to his tendency to inquiry and experimentation. There are opposite tendencies that balance one another in the human world no less than in the inorganic. What at one time seemed mere antagonism between the principle of local and that of central government, is now recognized by all thoughtful Americans North and South, as being only a reciprocal relation. Local government is but the mode through which a general government becomes realized in its richest significance. The general government is the focal power through which local government is rendered perfectly secure and vital.

And now comes the claim, repeated again and again, that by analogy the religious organization of the people should be extended and unified on the same grand scale.   Economy of power, increase of efficiency; these are the complementary aspects of the gain that is thought to be necessarily involved in the merging of all (Protestant) denominations in a United Church of America.[1] Thus the Christian Ideal which is given its ultimate political form in America would unfold in the same land into its ultimate mode of religious development.   Protestantism, after resolutely separating itself from the tyrannies of the Old World, would thus at length unfold into the fully rounded form of Freedom in the New World.

The vision is an attractive one.   And doubtless what renders it attractive is just the undeniable germ of truth which the vision involves.   But for all that, doubts still force themselves to the surface when one thinks of the form which the vision assumes.

That germ of truth consists in the fact that there is strength in union.   But while this may be beyond doubt as a general proposition, it is equally true that there are modes of union and degrees of unification the result of which must inevitably be a reduction rather than an increase of strength.   It is the "glittering generality" that is alluring—so alluring often as to cause forgetfulness of irreconcilable differences.

---

[1]Of course the Catholic Church could not be thought of as entering into a scheme like this, since it could logically consider no other union than that which would take the form of the complete submission of all Protestant denominations to and the complete merging of them in the one "Catholic" Church.

Arguments from analogy are no doubt indispensable and highly serviceable. But it is equally true that they are never wholly safe arguments. In them similarities are emphasized and differences slurred over. And the captivating scheme of a "United Church in the United States," appears fatally defective on just this ground. For the religious life of man presents characteristics fundamentally different from those of his political life. It is true that the religious life and the political life are but different aspects of the same life. But that is far from lessening the importance of the fact that they *are different* aspects, and that they must therefore demand correspondingly different means and methods for their development.

Political freedom is secured by the organic union of man with man. Religious freedom is secured by the organic union of man with God. True, there can be no doubt that these are still but different aspects of the same truth. Doubtless man can be organically united with man only through the divine in man. And doubtless man can be organically united with God only through the co-operation of man with man in the struggle to unfold into reality the divine nature which is implicit in every human being. But there remains a specific functional difference to which there must ever pertain a corresponding difference of structure.

In each case, too, there is both a positive and a negative aspect to the process of unification. Negatively the process of political unification has for its purpose first of all to protect man from man in respect of physical violence. On the other hand religious unification has for its negative purpose to protect individual man from himself in respect of error in thought and desire. The State is an indispensable institution whose chief negative function is to restrain men from violent deeds—deeds that are contrary to reason. The Church is an indispensable institution whose chief negative function is to restrain men from violent opinions—opinions that are contrary to reason. Again, political unification has for its positive purpose to provide man with such means to the full realization of that phase of his freedom which is expressed in his deeds, as in the nature of the case he cannot as an individual provide for himself. And religious unification has for its positive purpose to provide the individual with such means to the full realization of that phase of his freedom which is unfolded in his thought and sentiment, as he cannot in the nature of the case as an individual provide for himself.

Restraint from what is irrational, aid toward what is rational—these are the complementary phases of the function, both of State and of Church. But it is to be observed that on the one side the restraint and the aid are alike primarily *physical;* while on the other side the restraint and the aid are alike *spiritual.*

Doubtless both the State and the Church have educational functions to perform. But with the State, Education—the symmetrical unfolding of the intel·lectual and moral powers of the individual—must ever be a means ; while with the Church it must ever be an end. Preservation of society as a whole is the supreme aim of political organization. Preservation and normal growth of the individual is the supreme aim of religious organization. And, let us repeat, these contrasted functions are none the less to be regarded as fundamentally distinct because they also merge into one another and prove to be but complementary phases of the larger functions of human society as a whole.

And now, having thus briefly indicated the essential difference between the State and the Church, both in function and in final aim, we may next proceed to inquire : What are the natural limits of organized religious union ? Or, in other words : What constitutes a church as a truly organic unit ?

The clew to a reasonable answer to this question may be found in the fact already indicated that individualism in its richest significance is the central conception of the Christian faith. And it is but a logical inference from this that the supreme aim of a Christian Church should be : the securing for its individual members such conditions, negative and positive, as will most conduce to the symmetrical development of each as an individual. And here the most vital and permanent interests of the individual are those directly concerned. If the State has especially to secure the individual in his temporal interests, the Church has especially to provide means for the increased security of the individual in his eternal interests. The intellectual and moral state of the individual—the orthodoxy of his belief and the morality of his conduct—these especially, nay these exclusively, it is the mission of the Church to cherish into fullest vitality. For the unfolding of these into living reality constitutes that process which is known as genuine spiritual regeneration.

This accomplished, all else follows. In the degree that reasonable belief and right conduct are matured in the individual, in like degree must he prove himself to be an exemplary man and a faithful citizen. That is, the more richly unfolded he becomes as an individual the more richly developed his social life proves to be, and vice versa.

It would seem, then, that the Church is an organization which, more specifically, has for its supreme office, first, the formulation of the beliefs that men should adopt with reference to the intrinsic and absolutely permanent phases of their own nature and destiny; secondly, the providing a system of principles for the guidance of men in their conduct, and thirdly, the furnishing practical aid toward the individual's self-realization in both these respects. To show men what is the ultimate Ideal of man, and to guide them as individuals toward the fulfilment of that Ideal—that is the mission of the Church.

Thus there are seen to be two special phases of the organic unfolding of a religious body which would seem to determine from within the body itself the limits of its own healthy expansion. The church is, in fact, a human institution progressively developing toward completeness as an embodiment of man's pro-gressively expanding conception of a divine Truth which in itself is unchanging. And for this reason it is inevitable that with widely varying mental habits—as for example those already cited of the Romance peoples on the one hand and of the Teutonic peoples on the other—there should arise specific differences of organic form. And, according to the vigor and individualism shown in the mental constitution of a people, by so much the more must varieties develop within the limits of the species. And just this characteristic we have seen to belong especially to the Teutonic peoples.

Here as elsewhere specific difference of functional activity or vital process must result in corresponding specific difference of organic form. In the religious world it unfolds itself as a process of differentiation, resulting in multiplication of specifically different and hence independent or mutually exclusive organizations.

On the other hand the true reciprocal of this process is to be found, as already intimated, in absolutely free discussion, which constitutes the more definite phase of the process of natural selection in this sphere, and through which no opinions other than those that possess some germ of truth can long survive. It is thus that the multiplication of sects is kept within natural or rational limits.

It is next to be noted that the tendency toward heterogeneity is on the one hand a mark of relative immaturity. The multiplication of varieties in church organization is based upon multiform modes of comprehending one and the same truth. But it is equally important to note that the individual can neither arrive at, nor even so much as take the first step toward, maturity as an individual otherwise than by the exercise of his own mental powers—otherwise than by exerting those powers for the specific purpose of comprehending that Truth. If therefore the supreme mission of the church is to be fulfilled, it must include this very phase of development. The multiplication of sects is one necessary phase in the unrestricted organic development of the church.

On the other hand with increasing maturity of mental power, men discover the one-sidedness of their opinions and recognize the extent to which apparently contradictory opinions are in reality only complementary ones.   Thus there is brought about a return toward uniformity.   But this "return" is none the less an advance.   And the uniformity reached is found to be vitally different from that which existed primarily.   The initial uniformity in church organization was implicit only.   It had its ground, not in thought, but rather in lack of thought.   The uniformity arrived at in later times is explicit, though it can of course, in the very nature of the case, never be more than approximate.   It has its ground in the very process of the development of thought.   And thus at every stage it presents increasingly rich variety, i. e., multiplied evidences of maturing vigor. The first is the uniformity of a vacuum.   The second is the unison of a world rich in harmonious, vitalized forms.   With uniformity of inner substance or vital principle there is multiformity of vital characteristics and therefore also multiformity of outer modes of manifestation or embodiment.

It thus appears evident that religious organization is no exception to the general law that real advance is from the homogeneous to the heterogeneous; although the heterogeneity in any given instance is nothing else than the necessary outcome of that process which consists in differentiation, in specialization.   In other words it is the outcome of that process which consists in the unfolding into its full significance and realized form of that one primordial principle or elementary Truth which underlies and gives vitality to the whole movement.

Nor should it be forgotten that this fulfilment or realization of the fundamental principle of Christianity, is something that takes place progressively, and that this progressive development occurs by no means uniformly over the world. The ultimate Ideal of Christianity—that the typical nature of man is one with the divine Nature—is indeed something in itself absolute and unchanging. But on, the other hand it is inconceivable that when this Ideal was first announced it should have been at all adequately comprehended even by the few whose minds were best prepared to receive it and appreciate its sublime import ; while it cannot reasonably be regarded as anything strange that to the many such announcements should seem a mere vagary either foolish or blasphemous. Nay, even after centuries of mental and moral development the ultimate significance of this Ideal is yet but very imperfectly apprehended by the average Christian ; while to many it is still a stumbling-block or a mere absurdity. So that the more closely the progress thus far made is examined only by so much the more meagre does it seem to be in comparison with the boundless range of the still unfulfilled phases of possible development.

Meanwhile there is one thing at least that has become fairly evident to many minds and is rapidly becoming evident to many more. And that is that this divine Ideal which it is the peculiar merit of Christianity to have clearly presented to and to have persistently urged upon the attention of humanity, necessarily involves the right and duty of each human being to unfold for himself in his own life this divine nature common to all. And in this growing conviction there is necessarily implied a further one—namely : that, as each individual is thus essentially an independent unit, having his own special characteristics and placed as he is in the midst of an environment never precisely the same as that of any other individual, it must follow that the very Ideal of man which the Christian faith primarily presents in such absolute uniformity, must nevertheless involve endless multiformity in the very process of its realization by and in individual men. And so, once more, it appears that wherever Protestantism develops it proves, and must ever prove, to be but the manifestation of that inner, vital principle of Christianity—the principle of divine Individualism. And as men become increasingly aware of its true import there must ever in like degree be developed a demand for increasingly manifold modes of outer manifestation or embodiment of that principle.

In other words, Protestantism is in its very nature

the perpetual protest of reason against any and every attempt to confine it solely to one single set of formulas. The spirit of man, infinite in its nature, refuses to be checked in its development by being permanently encased in one and the same mould. Nay, in the final outcome it utterly refuses to be "moulded" at all. It claims to have the inalienable right of unrestricted *growth* in accordance with the divine type to which it belongs. And this the more as it learns that thus alone can it maintain itself as a truly living unit.

It is not for the Church to "mould" a soul, as if it were some plastic, inorganic substance Rather it is for the Church to cultivate and train the individual soul as the most complex and delicate of all organic units—keeping ever in view the soul's own typical nature.

And if this be indeed the mission of the Church, then assuredly its outer forms and formulas must be ever maintained in a state of organic mobility. For they are but the outer modes of the inner spiritual vitality of the Church itself. And with the unfolding of that inner life the outer form must be ever in process of modification, so as to maintain continued adjustment to that life. Permanent incrustation can have no other effect than the death of the organic unit thus enclosed.

And here we have to note another specific difference between political and religious life as expressed or developed in a community. It is this : States never interfuse. Their boundaries are sharply defined in space. In religious organization, on the contrary, space boundaries are indifferent. Here indeed the boundaries are qualitative rather than quantitative. They are to be found not in space but in difference of mental habit. No two states can coexist within the same space-limits. And because of this mutual exclusion the natural barriers presented in the forms of the earth's surface have ever been found to be an essential factor in determining the boundaries of nations. On the other hand, with the specific differences of mental habit certain to be possessed by the various inhabitants of a given region, especially as the region becomes densely populated, and still more if the people are characterized by vigorous individualism, it is evident that since the function of a church is to embody the specific convictions of its members in clearly defined forms, there must inevitably arise many and various church organizations within the same territory. Indeed many parishes must practically coincide, while not infrequently members of several differently organized parishes will be found under the same roof.

It would thus seem that the natural limits of a religious organization do not consist of lines drawn in space, but rather that those limits are to be found in certain characteristic habits and tendencies of mind, the outer form of which must consist of correspondingly different creeds and ceremonial. So that no one form can possibly suffice for the spiritual needs of Christendom.

And this brings us to repeat that the existence of these specific differences of mental habit is a manifestation of mental and moral vigor. It reveals a healthy state of spiritual development. And hence any tendency to repress this free unfolding of the individual mind—involving as this tendency does its own corrective, namely perfect freedom of mutual criticism—is in its very nature reactionary rather than progressive, and so far as it has practical effect can only result in hindrance to the spread of vital Christianity. For vital Christianity, let it be remembered, places infinite emphasis upon the divine nature of the individual and hence insists upon the right and duty of the individual to unfold into reality this divine nature in his own life, and to do this with the utmost energy and rapidity as being the one legitimate purpose of his existence.

And if this seems to present the egoistic aspect too prominently, we have only to note that egoism and altruism are in truth not conflicting modes, but rather complementary phases of the one true mode prescribed by Christianity itself for the realization of the highest ideal of humanity. "He that loseth his life,'' in its capricious, narrowly egoistic aspects, and does so for the sake of the typical Man, for the sake of the divine nature in all men, he it is who finds his life in its truest significance. A reasonable altruism is the one only means of attaining the highest egoistic results.

It is worth observing, too, that the gradual enlargement of the individual's own life through the free play of his own powers, stimulated as they must ever be to the fullest and most healthful activity through unrestrained criticism of individual by individual, must tend ever to secure to the virtue of tolerance a more and more rational character. It is true that just as there are yet many men who persuade themselves that a man's faithfulness as a citizen is to be measured by his recklessness as a partisan, so there are still to be found those who persuade themselves that a man's faithfulness as a Christian is to be measured by the recklessness of his adherence to some denominational *credo*. But the ''independents'' in both the political and the religious world are steadily increasing in number, and with continued freedom of discussion must continue so to increase. And if this absolute freedom of discussion is a necessary phase in the education of a self-governing people politically, so it is none the less a necessary phase in the religious education of man. Thus only can the essentially Christian principle of Individualism be unfolded into concrete reality—a result that could hardly fail to be indefinitely delayed by the merging of all denominations into one with the inevitable consequence of smothering freedom of inquiry and discussion in respect of religious themes.

We have said that the Church is a human institution expressive of human convictions respecting a divine principle. It seems needful to add that the Church is made up of human beings with human passions, and that for this reason were the Church once fairly established in America as a single organization with "maximum efficiency," there must then be overwhelming temptation to use its vast power for the purposes of determining political results. The Church must once more become ambitious of ruling the State. Even now it is a sufficiently conspicuous fact that some of the stronger denominations have put forth efforts, and not without result, in that direction. And in this field what begins in more or less timid suggestion would be only too likely to advance toward confident and even arrogant dictation.

Nay, in such case, "political" methods must enter more and more into the very life of the Church itself. In other words corrupting influences must play a larger part in proportion as the prize of power becomes more luring to ambitious men. As it is, the American State has nothing to fear and much to hope for from the influence of the Church as exercised in its own legitimate field. As it would be, with a single gigantic Church organization, the State must be ever on the defensive against the Church. And this must tend inevitably toward reversion to an "established" Church under control of the State. Strange attitude for America while England is struggling toward disestablishment!

It appears then that the plea of maximum efficiency is a delusive one so far as it is to be gained by the union of churches. Increase of efficiency as regards external authority might indeed be attained for a time. But this could be only at the expense of that efficiency that comes from perfect soundness of inner life. And the genuineness of this latter efficiency can be proven in no other way than by the Church directing all its powers with perfect "singleness of heart" to one end. And that end is the awakening of men to, and the convincing them of, the truth as regards their own natures, with their consequent conversion from the way of Death to the way of Life.

As a final word it may be added that Christianity has long since proved itself to be possessed of inextinguishable vitality by refusing to be limited to denominational rolls of membership. The Phariseeism that insists upon the restriction of the name Christian to those who are within the "Church" is constantly put to shame by the noble Christian lives of many

who fiud it impossible to make profitable use of the
ceremonial of existing churches.

Doubtless such lives would be still better had they
the advantage of a form of church organization adapted to their needs and based upon a creed consisting
of the fundamental principles of Christianity trans-
lated out of mediæval symbolism into the clearer and
more adequate forms of modern intelligence. For
man is helped by association with man.   And this is
no less true of his religious nature than in respect of
any other phase of his essential life. Meanwhile,
the sincere soul, striving honestly to fulfil its destiny—to such soul the name of Christian cannot be
Christianly denied.   And it is not impossible that yet
new denominations may be required for the help of
such seekers after the divine life.

VI.

THE HERESY OF NON-PROGRESSIVE OR-
THODOXY.

Revelation involves two factors. The one factor is a receptive mind. The other factor is a mind giving utterance to itself. The degree in which the revelation is realized as such will depend not merely upon the completeness with which the communicating mind utters itself, but also upon the capacity of the receiving mind.

The perfect Mind must of course give to itself unceasing, perfect utterance. But only the perfect Mind can perfectly comprehend its own perfect utterance. For this reason an absolutely perfect revelation is possible only in the sense of the eternal self-communication of the perfect mind to the perfect mind.

For any finite mind the divine revelation can never be perfect ; though for the normal finite mind that revelation must be progressive, must be a continuous approximation towards perfection.

But now, since individual conscious units are forever arising in the eternal process of creation, that special phase of revelation which consists in the unfolding of an individual consciousness as a power to comprehend the truth is manifestly an abiding factor, ever present in that eternal process. The changing, the progressive, the struggling conscious unit, which has been named "individual" because indivisible, that unit is still only a more richly endowed pulsation within the self-sufficing conscious Unit that forever works and moves all, while yet itself is resting in moveless, eternal calm. It is this perfect activity in perfect rest that constitutes the self-conservation of the ultimate Energy, the infinite self-renewal of the eternal "I AM."

The phrase "primitive revelation" is thus seen to have two eternally valid meanings. On the one hand, it is the truth in its unchanging totality, forever present in all its details to the Divine Consciousness. On the other hand, the primitive revelation is just that primary phase of truth which appeals to and is received by any and every individual consciousness in the initial stage of its development.

In this sense "primitive," so far as it refers to time at all, merely indicates "the year one" of each individual's life-history so far as he is a self-conscious being. In this respect, the Oriental method of chronology is the true one. For, in the genuine kingship of humanity, a new empire, destined to infinite expansion, is established with the birth of each new soul; and the life and reign of that royal unit begins with the initial elementary modes of its intelligence, just as if no such royal units had previously existed.

Thus to the individual created conscious unit it is *as if* the divine revelation were made solely through time, on special occasions, for the special benefit of such created conscious unit. And yet, in reality, the manifestation of the perfect Mind recognized in any given case by the created mind is new to such created mind, because the latter is new to the manifestation. The truth (that is, the particular phase of truth) which I learn to-day seems to *me* so new that, for the moment, I spontaneously assume it to be an absolutely new development. And for this reason I go abroad proclaiming it until I am met with the calm assurance that the same phase of truth had been known by others before me before I was born, before the tongue I speak had yet become a living mode of expression ; nay, that *Truth* is eternal, and that hence no phase of it can be "new," save to the consciousness newly awakened to receive such phase.

The accumulated experience of the race of man does, indeed, serve to lighten the difficulty of the individual's development. But it does not and cannot relieve him from the necessity of passing through every single stage of that development. In other words, the individual mind can become realized as such in no other way than through the exercise of his own powers. Or, again, since man is divine in nature, he is a self-unfolding unit. His independence is measured by the degree in which he has attained to realization of the divine nature in his own present concrete life. And no single phase of that realization can be attained by any individual save through that individual's own efforts. All the universe may help him, but only on condition that he accept and independently make use of that help.

It need hardly be added that this is true of every phase of man's nature,—that only by the reasonable exercise of his own powers, whether of body or of will or of intelligence, can those powers increase. Whence it is evident that ready-made opinions cannot make us really wiser ; any more than ready-made spectacles can make us skilful opticians. Only as one *thinks* the truth can the truth become really one's own. Only by progressively knowing the truth, in the sense of thoroughly assimilating it. can one unfold the divine nature within him, and thus become a self-poised, genuinely free being

"Ready-made opinions" may, it is true, be safely adopted by the individual in the elementary stages of his development. Nay. doubtless it is exceedingly unsafe, not to say altogether suicidal, for the individual to reject the opinions of his time and race. It can, indeed, be nothing else than the mark of immaturity and lack of wisdom to reject those opinions

without being able to give clear proof of their inadequacy or of their erroneous character.

At the same time it would be none the less a mark
of immaturity and lack of wisdom to overlook the
fact that those opinions are themselves no more than
the slowly, and at the best but partially, matured
fruit of human inquiry. All discoveries are made
progressively. The magnet was discovered centuries
ago, and it is yet far from being fully discovered.
Newton discovered the law of gravity. It had been
known long before his time ; and, nevertheless, it yet
remains to be perfectly unfolded. The magnet, like
any other given physical centre of energy, is but a
focus of relations, the total sum of which relations
comprises the whole physical universe. In that universe (or, rather, aspect of *the* universe) Truth is forever present, so far as expressed or expressible, in
physical relations. In this round of relations there
is presented one fundamental phase of the eternally
perfect revelation.

On the other hand, man's consciousness of that
phase of revelation can unfold by only such slow degrees as his sense of scientific wonder grows and
urges him on to careful scientific investigation. Thus
only can he become aware of the abiding Truth thus
unfolded. But precisely in the degree in which his
investigations have been consistently carried forward,
precisely in the degree in which science has become

a reality in this world of ours, in just that degree has man really become aware of the abiding Truth unfolded in physical relations.   Precisely thus, too, has he come to be emancipated from superstitious fear, from the slavish worship of natural phenomena, so that at last he stands erect, self-assured, and (at least relatively) free.

Similarly, that immeasurably more adequate aspect of the Truth which pertains specifically to the nature of the conscious unit is also forever present in perfection in the universe as a whole.   Its fundamental phases were doubtless felt in some measure, however vaguely, by "primitive man," using the phrase now in the sense of the earliest living units on this earth that could rightly be called minds.   By degrees these fundamental phases were more definitely recognized, and at length became formulated with greater or less approximation to accuracy and adequacy by the finest minds of various peoples in succeeding ages—by Confucius, by Buddha, by Zoroaster ; with far greater clearness by Moses, and, first of all, with perfect precision and adequacy by the Son of Man. Indeed, the further investigation proceeds— the more searching it becomes—only so much the more manifest is it that, while Confucianism and Buddhism and Zoroastrianism and Mosaism were each and all local, tentative formulations of the truth concerning man's spiritual nature, the formulation called Christian is essentially faultless as indicating the ultimate Truth concerning the nature of man and his relation to the supreme creative Energy.

But even that formulation, precise and adequate as it is in principle, does not profess to do more than give the clew to the genuine eternal life of man. And by this clew the eternal life of man is nothing else than the progressively unfolding concrete life of each individual man in accordance with the one eternal type of all conceivable spiritual units. "Eternal life" is, in reality, nothing else for the individual than the ceaseless, progressive moulding, or rather unfolding, of his present life into the "form of eternity."

We are now prepared to say that "Progressive Orthodoxy" is nothing else than the ceaseless deepening and enlarging and clarifying of human opinion respecting the eternal Type to which every individual —that is, indivisible or immortal—spiritual unit must conform if it is ever to rise above a merely phantasmal existence. So that, concretely, Progressive Orthodoxy may be again defined as the continuous unfolding of man's knowledge of the Truth in its spiritual aspect, whereby man brings into ever-increasing realization within his own life that divine self-consistency which constitutes true freedom.

At best, indeed, no human formulation of the divine message to man can be more than a dim intimation of what that message is in its full wealth of significance. All Bibles contain some such formulation. And, if the Christian Bible is the best of all Bibles, it is because it presents, in consistent form, the central thread of that message—the veritable clew which, faithfully followed, must lead to endlessly progressive realization of eternal life.

But that clew is still only a clew. Of itself it does nothing and is nothing. Only when a human soul seizes upon it, examines it, learns its use, and *uses* it persistently and intelligently and honestly, only then is it of any value whatever. It is a map, not a country. It is not life. It is merely a guide to true living.

And I am to accept it "just as it is." There is, indeed, nothing else that I so much desire to do. I want, above all, to know its true, its full import. I want to know all that it *is*. And yet its significance becomes richer with each new examination. *Becomes?* Does this guide, after all, change, then, and with each fresh glance I give it? What *is* it, then? And how can I ever hope to know it, to receive it, "just as it is?"

Nay, but this is mere casuistry. The guide does not change. It is a perfectly definite principle. What I have before me is a finite formula, suggesting the infinite import of that principle. And, since the guide does not change, for that reason the change is in *me*. My mind expands. A thought new to me takes shape and reality in my consciousness. A fresh impulse arises in my life with each additional honest effort I make to find for myself the whole truth contained in the formula.

Shall I, then, content myself with mere repetition of the formula? Or will it be reasonable for me to add to the formula an explicit, progressive statement of the various phases of truth which I am progressively discovering to be implicitly contained in the formula?

Newton formulated the Laws of Falling Bodies—including their ultimate generalization in the Law of Gravity—with such precision that every variation from his formulæ appears to have no other result than the introduction of obscurity or even of actual error. The Newtonian formulæ seem to be faultless, and hence permanent. And yet, taken literally (and so much the more when taken separately), these formulæ are mere abstractions. They serve no further purpose than, on the one hand, to indicate vaguely the rich sum of relations existing in the physical aspect of the world, and, on the other hand, to intimate the course of study through which one may hope to become increasingly aware of the beautiful phases of truth exhibited in those relations.

So the Son of Man gave concise formulation to the fundamental laws of all spiritual being. These laws,.

necessarily, are abstract statements.   But they serve to indicate the infinitely rich sum of relations existing in the spiritual aspect of the world, and also to make plain the never-ending course of training by which one may hope to become more and more clearly aware of, and in ever fuller degree to realize in his own life, the infinitely varied and surpassingly beautiful phases of Truth forever unfolded in those relations.

Doubtless any attempt to replace those formulæ could result in nothing else than the introduction of obscurity and error.   For the original Christian formulæ prove under every test to be faultless, and hence permanent.   But to suppose that any one may become a mature Christian through mere repetition of those formulæ, however devout and persistent the repetition might be, is no more reasonable than to suppose that one can become an accomplished physicist by simple repetition of the Newtonian formulæ.

Each formulation of a genuine mode of the divine Energy is so far a truth.   But it is none the less a grave error to assume that such formulation is an exhaustive statement of the truth.   For this would, in reality, be assuming that one comprehends at first glance the full significance of a given fact or formula.

Untruth creeps into human speech while human thought lies idle.   And few of such untruths are more pernicious than the frequent thoughtless declaration that "first impressions are best impressions." One need only call his thought into active wakefulness to recognize that first impressions are commonly the shallowest, poorest, least trustworthy impressions. In the very nature of the case, they can be no more than merely initiatory, rudimentary. They may remain uncorrected, undisturbed ; but that can be only because no actual examination of the subject is ever undertaken. It is thus that we may, and often do, become *familiar* with objects, facts, persons, while yet remaining in utter ignorance of them. Nay, we may even mistake familiarity for knowledge, and thus unwittingly make sure of our ignorance remaining the more impenetrable. A first impression may indeed be accurate enough, true enough, so far as it extends. But, even so, as "first impression" it can scarcely extend below the surface, can scarcely be other than superficial. The more complex the case, the more superficial the impression. To remain content with such impressions is to accept unconsciously the limitations of mind in its merely rudimentary stages of development. It is to confine one's self to a merely mythical interpretation of the facts of the world. It is, in short, to repudiate science in all its phases : for science is a process of criticism, of verification.

Now, theology is a science. Or, rather, it may properly be said to be the culmination of all science.

In its fullest sense, science is the study of phenomena, of manifestation, of revelation. And through this study man is led inevitably to inquire concerning that which is manifested or revealed. When the latter phase of study has so far advanced that that which is manifested is recognized, however dimly, as a process of self-manifestation, then theology, or the science of God, has entered upon its realization. And, the further this process of critical investigation extends, the more matured does the science of divine things become.

Passing over pre-Christian theologies with the remark that they are nothing else than the initial stages of theology as a whole, of which Christian theology is but the culmination, we have to note that Christian theology itself exhibits a sufficiently marked process of development. Its basis consists of the recorded utterances of Christ. And we are assured on excellent authority that these recorded utterances constitute no more than a very brief series of typical sayings, collected out of the vastly richer whole of his actual utterances. And doubtless also they illustrate the law of the "survival of the fittest."

The assertion, indeed, that, if all he said and did had been fully recorded, "the world itself could not contain the books that should be written," is often cited as an example of hyperbole. And if the assertion is to be taken literally, or "just as it is,"—that is, in its most superficial meaning,—doubtless it cannot be put to better use than that of an example of extravagant rhetorical figure. But, on the other hand, there is a sense in which hyperbole vanishes, and the statement is "literally" true, though with a vastly deeper meaning. It is this : the statements of Christ contain implicitly the whole truth as regards the divine nature, on the one hand, and human nature, on the other, together with the essential relation of these. each to each. And to set forth all this *fully* would be no less than to re-create the whole universe.

But the universe is in actual and perpetual process of recreation. And the self-unfolding of each individual conscious unit is an essential factor of this process. Let us repeat, too, that such unit is of precisely the same type or nature as that of the divine unit, or Person. One ought, besides, to dwell upon this identity in nature as between man and God so far as to apprehend clearly what is implied in this identity.

In the present connection this implication is as follows : If my nature is really infinite, then, because I have as yet realized that nature only in mere rudimentary degree, and because I can at best further realize it only stage by stage or progressively, then am I truly an individual ; that is, an indivisible, indestructible unit. For, if an infinite nature is really mine, then all the conditions for its perfect realization are also mine. And one necessary condition for the perfect fulfilment of an infinite nature on my part must be endless persistence as one and the same unit. For in no less than endless duration can I, a finite being, unfold into reality an infinite ideal. If death, in the sense of utter cessation of my identity as a conscious unit, could occur, then my nature would prove to be not infinite, but finite.

It thus appears that whoever entertains a rational belief in immortality for the individual must also believe in the individual's unlimited progress in the knowledge of God as revealed or realized in the physical aspect of creation, on the one hand, and in its spiritual aspect on the other. And, since this progress in the knowledge of God is nothing else than a progressive clarifying and enlarging of man's opinion respecting God as manifested or revealed in both natural and spiritual phenomena, then "Orthodoxy," as human opinion upon this all-inclusive theme, must in its very nature be progressive.

Only a living, growing faith is really orthodox. It is such faith that is ceaselessly, progressively, "swallowed up in sight." It is such faith that *now*, to-day, sees through a glass darkly; but which will *then*, to-morrow, see God with truer vision and, relatively, face to face. It is such faith that goes on *unto* perfection in its special, particular phases, and thus ceaselessly *toward* perfection in its ultimate, universal, divine fulness.[1]

The antinomy of "Orthodoxy" has ever been this: the finitude of the symbol, on the one hand, and the infinitude of the symbolized significance, on the other. The Bible is the infinitely significant—that is, infinitely *suggestive*—"Word of God." Nevertheless, we are to take the words of the Bible, and, above all, the few recorded words of Christ, "just as they are."

And strange things, indeed, have been compassed in the attempt to follow this rule. When Jesus said: "If a man keep my word, he shall never see death," the people who heard took the words "just as they are," and exclaimed indignantly, "Now we know that thou hast a devil." When Jesus said: "The bread which I will give is my flesh, for the life of the world," those present took the words "just as they are," and therefore "strove with one another, saying, How can this man give us his flesh to eat?" And, when Jesus repeated: "Except ye eat the flesh

---

[1] It seems hardly necessary to mention that shallow form of "progressive spirit" which indulges itself in mere change, in the mere substitution of one fancy for another, and complacently regards itself, as for that reason, far in advance of those who have found the clew to fundamental principles, and are content to develop patiently in their own minds a deeper apprehension of all that those principles imply. And yet, now and then, the wildest vagaries of a Tolstoi are claimed to prove the greatness (instead of the painful weakness) of such a mind.

of the Son of Man, and drink his blood, ye have not life in yourselves," many, even of his disciples, taking his words, "just as they are," grew impatient, declared it to be a "hard saying" which no sane man could tolerate, and hence "went back and walked no more with him." It was of no avail that Jesus attempted to show them the higher truth to which he would awaken them by the use of such startling symbolism. In reality, as it proved, the twelve alone had progressed far enough to see beyond the mere ordinary use of the words, and hence to apprehend, at least in some degree, the value of the interpretation in higher terms which Jesus immediately gave of his first statement.

Even to-day there is persistent insistance that these *"words"* shall be "taken just as they are." And with what result? What but this? That the words, in reality so significant, so full of suggestion, are reduced to and accepted as a mere fetish, on the one hand, and, on the other, are declared to belong to fetishism merely, whence they are scornfully thrust aside without so much as a moment's serious examination. The reduction of "the Word" to the uses of a gross magic could hardly fail to find its antithesis in a mocking skepticism. Thus, on the one hand, we see a devout "Christian" opening at random to a text for guidance in case of doubt (like a good pagan casting a glance into the sky to note what bird flies by, and in what direction), and trusting implicitly to that as a special divine intimation.   On the other hand, we now and then see some one just sufficiently awakened out of the same dogmatic stupor to fly to the other extreme, and in wholly unsuspecting confi·dence that *he* at least comprehends the case with perfect clearness, assume it an indispensable and also indubitable mark of his own superior intelligence to look upon the whole collection of texts as nothing else than the outgrowth of superstition, unworthy a moment's notice on the part of a truly wise man.

Such in character is the contradiction that must continue to present itself in practical life so long as the antinomy of Flesh and Spirit, of symbolizing Word and symbolized Significance, fails of explicit reconciliation in theology.   And Progressive Orthodoxy is just that reconciliation.   It is the recognition with steadily increasing explicitness that the Word is ever dual in meaning, unless it be quite meaningless. "In the beginning was the *Logos*."   But *Logos* is at once intelligence and a symbol of Intelligence. Looked at in one way, it is the divine Reason, or God.   Looked at in another way, it is the manifestation of the divine Reason in the total and infinitely varied forms of Reality.   It is neither the one nor the other exclusively, for it is both in perfect interfusion and absolute perfection.   The divine Reason manifests *itself* in the infinitely varied forms and modes of

Reality.   It is thus that the *Logos* becomes flesh and dwells among us.

And, because "Orthodoxy" has tended always towards insistence upon some one set of forms as the sole, exclusive manifestation or revelation of divine Reason to man, the phrase, "Progressive Orthodoxy," is needed, even though it should be only temporarily, to emphasize the fact that special forms are in their very nature nothing more than the embodiment of special phases of the Truth ; and also that, to the individual intelligence, even the significance of these special forms can become known only gradually, through the progressive unfolding of that individual's power to apprehend the Truth and apply it in his own life.

The schools of Christendom in general, then, and the theological schools of Christendom in particular, are in truth nothing else than the media for the progressive awakening of men to a clearer consciousness of the infinitely rich truth symbolized in the original Christian teachings, and progressively unfolded into ever-increasing accuracy and adequacy of expression through succeeding centuries.   And not only are the schools of Christendom the media for leading the minds of a given generation to a clearer apprehension of the truth already discovered ; they are, of right, equally the media for extending and deepening that same process of discovery—media, that is, for the fuller, richer interpretation of the elementary symbols to which Christ gave shape, and to which he gave shape no less for the stimulus than for the guidance of human intelligence. Evidently, then, to apply such schools to the enforcement of mere dogmatic formulæ as such is the deadliest of perversions, the transformation of Orthodoxy into the most ruinous of heresies.

It is a dying faith that wraps itself in the winding-sheet of mere forms and emblems, and resents all efforts to stimulate it into increased life and activity. And whoever insists upon an Orthodoxy from which progress is excluded, by that very fact convicts himself of heresy in a form that drives out all real ground of hope in immortality. For, as we have seen, immortality can really mean nothing else than this : a never-ending renewal, enriching, unfolding of the divine Life in the individual soul. And, it need hardly be added, this must include the unceasing growth of intelligence on the part of each individual soul, involving continuous revision and extension of forms of expression, so that these forms may be ever adequate to the actual utterance of the steadily growing mind.

It can be mentioned here, only incidentally, that in such revision and extension of forms the individual cannot escape, even if it were desirable that he should escape, the corrective and stimulating influence of other minds. Indeed, the school, in its best sense, is the ideal community, whose chief energies are combined to raise this corrective, stimulating influence of mind upon mind to the highest degree of actual efficiency.

In the foregoing argument there is implicit the following important corollary ; From the fact that immortality means unending progression towards absolute perfection, the conclusion follows inevitably that for the individual soul "probation"—that is, the possibility of error, with its necessary reciprocal, the possibility of recovery from error—can never be wholly ended, but that, on the contrary, it must continuously be transferred to ever more advanced grades of the soul's life. The possibility of choosing the "lower" instead of the "higher" can never be eliminated from the finite mind. On the other hand, with the normally advancing soul, any phase of the lower, which at any moment would constitute a real "temptation," must prove to be of a less and less ignoble character. After the dissonance of actual self-contradiction has ceased to have any attraction, there may still be the choice of a less rather than of a more richly rhythmic duty—as if one were to content himself with a life of mere melody when he reasonably might (and therefore ought to) add to his experience an ever fuller range of harmony.

Let us note, finally, that not only is the "future"

life an extension essentially of the present life, but, also, that the future life is not really *life* until it ceases to be future and becomes present. Man lives in a *progressive Now*, as God lives in the *eternal Now*. It is thus and thus only that man attains, or can attain, to ever richer degrees of the Life Divine.

VII.

MIRACLES.

As intelligence my nature demands that I shall
know the world. As will my nature demands that I
shall control the world. As feeling my nature demands that I shall enjoy the world. But the "world"
—what is it ?

That is my question ; and equally, as would seem,
the answer must be my answer. No answer coming
from without can satisfy any question coming up
from within. A question—*every* question—presupposes alienation, in one or another degree, between myself and the world. Were I wholly at one
with the world, there could be for me absolutely no
question. And thus, in real truth, every question is
itself an imperative demand of my whole being that I
shall make myself at one with the world. This, too,
I must accomplish either by adjusting the world to
myself, or by adjusting myself to the world.

Ultimately, then, the core of every question I can
ask is just this : What *is* the world ? For, what the
world is that, in the outcome, must I also be. Somehow the world and I must be at one. The question

is my question and the answer must be my answer. The answer will not come to me of itself, and, as I find at every turn, the world will not come to me with the answer. Rather must I take the initiative, go to the world, fuse myself with the world, the world with myself. Thus and thus only can I hope to attain true and sufficient answer to my question.

Fuse myself with the world—that does not mean that I shall stand outside the world as a mere looker-on, and so get my answer. Far enough from that! Moreover, as intelligence merely I cannot hope for such true answer as my whole nature compels me to seek. I must wield the world to know the world; and to wield it I must will it.

Doubtless the world comes to me with stimuli, myriad-fold in number, variety, and quality. But these stimuli serve only to excite my curiosity, only to awaken the questioning mood within me—*never* to answer my questions. My answer must consist simply in my own interpretation of these stimuli.

But also when I attempt to will, or wield, the world it refuses to be willed or wielded. I put forth my Energy as will that I may shape the world and fuse it with my will. Could I succeed in that then the answer to my question would be this : The world is but the expression of my will, of myself. In going to the world I have come to myself, then. And there is doubtless a glimmer of truth in that.

Yet not so simple is the answer !   I do *not* succeed; or, at most, my success is only superficial and even illusory.   The world *out there* resists my efforts to fuse it with myself.   Resists?   Why, then, I have already found answer.   The world is *resistance*   And further, through experiment I find that the world yields, or seems to yield, more to my will when I exert my will in special ways.   And the more I experiment the more I discover that there is absolute uniformity in the resistances and yieldings of the world to my will.   Examining the processes unfolding in my own mind, processes consisting of my own efforts to wield the world, I discover that when those processes are most "intelligent" the world "yields" most readily and most completely to my will ; and when least intelligent its resistance is most stubborn.

And so the world as resistance to my will is energy, as I am energy ; and as compelling intelligent or systematic action on my part before it will "yield" or prove responsive to my activity it proves to be an energy whose activities are uniform, regulated—an energy, in fact, which can be comprehended only as a concretely unfolded *system*.   Nor can I discover any phase of this system that appears defective.   Rather, the more I experiment upon it and examine into it the more am I impressed with its greatness and perfection *as a system*.

Attempting to adapt the world to my will I find the

world resisting my effort. Thus my intelligence is stimulated to the point of devising new modes of exerting my energy as will. And when I have devised such modes as make me the seeming master of the world, I discover that I have reduced my activities to a system which but reproduces thus far the system of the World as Energy. I dreamed of mastering the world—of making it one with myself. I have really been mastering myself by making myself one with the world.

And the further I advance in this experimentation the more evident becomes to me the fact that the world as Energy is absolutely universal; it is all-inclusive; it is literally the *Universe*—the *All* turned into *One*. Thus it proves to be universal Energy constituting a concretely unfolded and all-inclusive System—a System, therefore, which cannot be moved from without, but can be moved only from within. It is of necessity self-moved, self-active, and hence self-regulating. But a self-active, self-regulating Energy cannot be conceived save as conscious of its own activity and of the System or method of its activity. And a self-conscious unit of Energy can be conceived no otherwise than as *Mind*.

Observation and experiment, then, force me to this conclusion: The world is resistance; the world is energy; the world is self-regulating Energy; the world is Mind. As the one all-inclusive System, it

is infinite, self-unfolding Mind.   It is infinitely active
and hence infinitely productive.   Looked at as a System, its activity appears as an absolute process of
Evolution.   Looked at as Mind its activity appears
as a process of absolute self-realization.   Looked at
as the all-inclusive, infinitely live. self conscious ONE,
its activity appears as the self-manifestation of the
one eternally perfect Person.

And so I attain a glimpse of "the high and lofty
One who inhabiteth Eternity," who is "without
variableness or shadow of turning," and with whom
therefore "a thousand years are as one day and one
day as a thousand years."   And this brings me to
notice that the infinite creative process, consisting of
the self-manifestation of the eternally perfect Person
cannot but be perfectly regulated in every phase and
degree throughout its whole extent.   It is nothing
less than the perfect reign of perfect Law.   It is the
perfect Law of the absolute, inherent *necessity* of self-
consistency which constitutes the essence of perfect
freedom on the part of perfect mind.

But I too am mind.   Nor can I conceive of more
than one type of mind   As mind, then, I am already
one in type with the perfect Mind.   Were I as mind
less than perfect in type, I could never know myself
as being imperfect in realization.   Were not I as
mind infinite in nature, I could never know myself
as finite in attainment.   A finite being can never

know itself as finite. Limit—finitude—exists only for that being which sees beyond the limit, beyond finitude.

The world is Mind. I am mind. Potentially, ideally, therefore, I am already one with the world. That, in truth. is the reason why every question I ask presupposes practical alienation between myself and the world; for otherwise no question could arise as a mode of my consciousness. And so also I find in this the explanation of the fact that every question I ask is in truth an absolute demand of my whole being that I shall make myself at one with the world. And, as I now recognize, this reconciliation of myself with the world can come about not by adjusting the world to myself but by adjusting myself to the world. I can know the world only by thinking the thought of the world. I can control the world only by willing the Will of the World. I can enjoy the world only as feeling—only as reproducing in myself—the actual rhythm of the world.

II.

In such world what can be the real meaning of the word "miracle?"

Words, as I have come to notice, are just the outer aspects of ideas. My present question, then, is this : What, exactly, is the idea which has assumed organic form in the word "Miracle?" In its rudimentary form, indeed, the answer to this question is already a simple and familiar one. The word "miracle" expresses the idea of something exciting wonder. But also I discover that to many minds it has come to mean : "That which is out of the ordinary course of things, and even that which contradicts the ordinary course of things." In which case a miracle is nothing less than a positive interruption of the great World process itself. It is a "suspension of the laws of Nature," brought about by the divine Author of Nature who condescends to give to man such transcendent proof that mind alone is essential and that thus nature itself is only incidental, both in use and in significance.

A wonder indeed were such things actually to be ! And so long as I "think" only in images ; so long, that is, as imagination takes precedence of critical investigation in my consciousness, there appears no contradiction in such assumption. On the other hand, when I subordinate imagination to reflection and really *think* what is involved in such assumption, the case appears radically different. For I find it quite impossible to represent the great World-process in forms of the thinking consciousness otherwise than as absolutely continuous in its perfect wholeness and self-consistency ; impossible deliberately to entertain as rational the assumption that the divine Author of the world should suspend either the laws of nature or any other aspect of the great World-process in which his own eternally perfect, and hence unchanging, inner Life is ceaselessly expressed. To say that the miracle is *out there* in the form of an interruption of the great world-order—that attracts my imagination, but repels my reason. I may *dream* it ; I can never *think* i . When reason awakes, the dream of imagination, so far as it conflicts with reason, cannot but fade away.

Nevertheless the miracle exists. I can no more deny that than I can accept as true the statement that its existence takes the form of an actual interruption of the perfect and absolutely changeless process which constitutes the outer aspect of the self-unfolding of the one eternally self-equal Mind. And so I am driven to search within my own imperfectly unfolded and slowly unfolding mind ; it must be there that I shall be able to locate the miracle and to find its right explanation. Indeed it now occurs to me again that, in strict truth, the essence of the miracle is *wonder;* and I can conceive wonder as existing only in just such imperfectly developed mind as mine.

For wonder is only a more developed form of surprise ; and surprise again is an uneasy state of consciousness, to which I am more or less rudely awakened by some unexpected stimulus or shock seemingly coming from without. In reality it consists partly of the sudden awareness that the world is not as I had hitherto assumed it to be ; partly of the fear lest now it may prove to be what I would wish it not to be ; and partly, in such case, of the determination—blind in itself—to bring it back to full agreement with my own inadequate preconception of its true nature.

The relation between myself and the world has changed. And if the relation has changed one of the related terms must have changed. The change, seemingly sudden, altogether unexpected, has excited my surprise, and surprise has grown into wonder. At first I assume without question that the change is *there*, in the world beyond me It is that seeming fact which excites my wonder. It is that which constitutes the miracle. And, now that I reflect upon it, this is itself a wonder. For, if it were in the nature of the world to change, such change could in no way be the occasion of surprise, of wonder, on my part. And so I am led to reflect again that in truth the deepest presupposition of my own nature is that the world in its inmost nature is unchanging. Nay, I also feel that somehow I too am unchanging. The world and I are the two terms of a relation. The relation changes ; yet neither of the terms is changeable. And this is a greater wonder still.

But also I have already seen that in type, in kind, I as mind am one with the perfect Mind ; for only one type of mind is at all conceivable, viz., in the sense of being really *thinkable*. On the other hand, while the perfect Mind is wholly and eternally self-realized I as mind am so imperfectly realized as scarcely to apprehend myself as progressively undergoing self-realization. Feeling myself to be unchanging in type, I fail to recognize myself as changing in degree of fulfilment of that type on my own part. Perhaps that is the real reason why I assume that the change must be in the world and not in me. But also feeling (however dimly), that the world must be unchanging in its nature, I am surprised at the seeming fact of change in the world, and so I declare such seeming change "miraculous." And yet sooner or later I am compelled to recognize that my preconception of the relation between myself and the world is full of error. I learn of the universal laws, as expressing the unchanging nature, of the great World-process. In doing so I come to recognize those laws as modes of the thought of the perfect Mind. By as much as I comprehend them I develop them in my own consciousness, and thus prove them to be modes of the thought native to myself as mind. Thus I adjust my thought to the thought of the perfect Mind. Or rather, responding to the stimulus I receive through contact with the great World-process, I develop my own thought ; and in so doing discover my thought to be in essence one with the thought of the perfect Mind. Considering which, I cannot but wonder and say to myself : This is the first miracle of mind.

Following such clew I adjust my will to the Will of the perfect Mind. Or rather, responding to the stimulus I receive through contact with the great World-process, I develop my own will ; and in so doing discover my will to be in essence one with the will of the perfect Mind. Considering which I am again brought to wonder, and say to myself : This is the second miracle of mind.

And again, in my self-adjustment to the thought and to the will of the perfect Mind, I find myself unfolding within myself as mind a boundless sense of unison, of rhythm, the perfect degree of which I cannot but recognize as absolutely and forever realized in and for the perfect Mind. So that in this way also I cannot but see that my mind is in essence one with the perfect Mind Considering which, I am still further brought to wonder, and to say to myself : This is the third miracle of Mind. And yet, clearly, these three miracles are but mutually complementary aspects of one and the same inward change.

The seeming miracle of change in a world essentially changeless is found to have its truth in the real miracle of change within myself as a mind ; and such real miracle is possible only because I am at once perfect and hence changeless in type, and also imperfect and hence changeable in respect of the degree of my own self-realization in accordance with that type.

The relation between the world and myself changes. The world does not change. It is I that change. Striving to make the world one with myself I succeed only in making myself one with the world. The world is perfect. It is the expression of the perfect Mind. I can know the world only by thinking the thought of the world. I can control the world only by willing the Will of the World. I can enjoy the world only as I reproduce in myself the actual eternal rhythm of the world. I can *be* at all only as I make myself one with the world of infinite *Reality*.

The miracle is not external ; it is internal. It is not beyond me ; it is within me. When first awakened to the error of my presupposition as to the world and my relation to the world, I was startled. surprised, alarmed, resentful. As I come to comprehend with increasing clearness and precision and adequacy the world and myself and the true relation between my-self and the world, surprise blossoms into wonder. and wonder grows into love, and love ripens into ador-ation. For through patient, careful investigation I discover that the true miracle consists in the actual self-unfolding of the individual mind into ever greater degrees of realized likeness with the perfect Mind.[1]

---

[1] And doubtless here is the clew to the real truth involved in the doctrine of the "Emanation" of the human soul from

And this is actually brought about through willing response of the individual mind to the infinitely manifold stimulation forever brought to bear upon it by the perfect Mind through its own faultlessly self-consistent self activity.

III.

And yet we must not lose sight of the fact that great and unquestionable historical miracles have actually been wrought. What can we say of them? For answer, let us examine three typical instances.

1. First of all, for our present purpose, there is that great national miracle of which Joan of Arc is the personal focus. How are we to understand that? France is in political death-agony. No one thinks or speaks of aught else than the national peril and the cruel, brutal foe. In the peasant's hut as well as in the palace, fear grips the heart of old and young alike. But there is one heart in France that feels the pulsings of the Eternal Heart. A shepherd girl has

God and of its "reabsorption" in God. "Emanate" from God it no doubt does; but by a perfectly rational and hence in the outcome perfectly comprehensible process. On the other hand, its "reabsorption" can properly mean no more than the progressive self-unfolding into reality on its part of the primal divine likeness—of its inherent typical nature as mind which at first, for it, is no more than a potentiality, though it be truly an infinite potentiality. It is the process of "identification" of the individual soul with the eternal Mind, but in such way as to ceaselessly intensify, instead of cancelling, its individuality.

heard, and hearing has believed, that God is good
and true and infinitely able to save his worshipers
from wrong. And God is unchanging. To her there
can be no interruption of the great world-order. The
King and France have forgotten. If only the King
and France could be awakened from this dream of
fear they too would know, and knowing would take
courage and sweep the enemies of the true worshipers of God completely from the land.

No shadow of question clouds this infinitely clear
vision. If only the awakening would come! It *will*
come, but *when* will it come? She watches her
flock, keeping it from the wolves of the wood. God
watches His flock, keeping it from the wolves of the
world. Yet the wolves are savage and threatening.
When will King and people awake—when will the
flock of the divine pasture seek the one true shelter?

Day after day passes. The danger deepens. Can
it be? God whispers in her soul a startling message.
"*You* are my under-shepherd. Of all the souls in
France you alone have felt the real pulsings of the
Heart of Truth. Go to the King; go to the people;
wake them out of their sleep of fear; bring them to
know again that God is unchanging and that they
who trust in his unchanging nature are invincible."

Poor, quivering, fateful maiden soul! It has been
caught in the flame of divinely transcendent duty,
and in that flame its earthly life must be consumed.

What will father think? What will mother say? Will the neighbors mock? Will the priest believe? Whatever else betide she must obey the divine command and save the flock of God's pasture from being devoured by the savage wolves.

Nor had the science of the fifteenth century a word to say that could tend toward the dissipation of such vision. Rather the habit of mind of that time was such as tended to the ready acceptance and wholly literal interpretation of the message. The only doubt is as to the genuineness of the vision in this particular case ; not as to the origin and nature of the vision in itself. To-day, with our habits of reflection and critical psychological analysis, the claim to having experienced such vision and received such message, would be set down to the credit of hallucination ; and if the individual persisted in the claim we could only feel bound, sorrowfully, gently, but firmly to consign the claimant to a secure place in the asylum for the insane.

On the contrary the uncritical habit of mind of that day made the acceptance of the vision a logical necessity, and the map of Europe was shaped accordingly. And as for the tragic soul of the shepherd maiden, her inner life became a consuming flame ; so that her life was the immediate form of the light of the world, guided by which France was redeemed from national ruin ; while her outward life was already consumed in the great deed of her inspired heroism. And the flame of the otherwise impotent rage of the English Fenris Wolf but made this fact apparent to all the world.

A miracle truly ! And we must now add that an age of crude, uncritical faith is just the indispensable pre-condition of every such miracle. And further, the instinctively assumed, wholly unanalyzed underlying principle in every such case, is that of the absolute changelessness and trustworthiness of the essential, divine World order. Men may change, but God is in deepest truth "without variableness or shadow of turning." In short, the miracle of which the Maid of Orleans is the focal personage, is not only a real miracle ; it is also wholly to be explained upon psychological grounds. And precisely upon these grounds it is self-evident that the more highly civilized, the more thoroughly enlightened, the world becomes, the more manifestly impossible must the recurrence of such miracle prove to be. Instead of these we now have the telegraph, and the dynamite gun, and the electric engine, and the printing-press with its search-light corollary, the newspaper, all expressions and instrumental forms of the progressive miracle of history which consists in the self-unfolding of the human mind through its subjugation of brute force to right reason on the one hand, and through its own self-adaptation to the modes of the eternally perfect Mind on the other.

2. But we have now to consider other typical forms of what we may call the miracles of faith—miracles of which we have the most circumstantial account in a book which has for centurie, been held in such reverence by the Christian world that any attempt at interpretation of its contents through critical analysis is still sure to be met with more or less vehement protest. The book is a revelation—*the* Revelation to man of God's purpose in the world and of God's will as toward the members of the human race. The very earnestness with which this is insisted upon often causes the fact to be wholly overlooked that a revelation, as elsewhere urged in this volume,[1] can really be such only so far as it is understood or comprehended. So that in reality the subjective aspect of any possible revelation—that is, its more or less intelligent acceptance—is the necessary reciprocal of the objective aspect—that is, of its occurrence at all as revelation. No doubt, as the expression of the perfect Mind, the great world-process is an infinite, eternal self-revelation. That is, the perfect Mind cannot but perfectly comprehend its own perfect expression. And even so the subjective and the objective aspects cannot but sustain to one another the re-

---

[1] Cf. above, p. 124 fol., and variously elsewhere. Also my *World-Energy and its Self-Conservation*, p 229 fol.

lation of absolute reciprocals. Whence I cannot do otherwise than conclude that the total world-process can really be a revelation to me only in so far as I reproduce in my own mind the modes of consciousness which that process expresses.

Besides, if that process really constitutes the perfect expression of the perfect Mind, then it must be infinite in extent and in complexity, and hence I cannot possibly attain full, exhaustive knowledge of it in less than infinite duration. And further, after freely admitting that the Bible is the great central Book of the world in point of real ethical and religious import, the fact cannot be put aside that it bears unmistakable marks of race-peculiarities, and that it is limited to the symbolism of a special phase and grade of civilization. Taken in its external form, therefore, it is the expression of the imperfect thought of what in this particular world of ours may very well be symbolized as the slowly developing Son, rather than described as the full expression of the perfect Thought of the eternally developed Father. It is true, indeed. that precisely in this Book the Son first appears as clearly knowing himself as Son ; and so, for the first time in the history of this world, as articulately and joyously calling God by the love-warm name of Father.[1]

[1]See below, close of essay, for further intimation of the significance of the divine Sonship.

In fact, it is just this infinitely vital relationship as between the individual human soul and the absolute, divine, eternal Spirit, symbolized in the reciprocal terms : Son and Father, which constitutes the inmost secret of the Bible and makes of it the one gravitative, luminous, thermal, magnetic centre of all the finest literary constellations of the world.   Its aim is neither to excite nor to satisfy our interest in death-involved matter ; but to awaken us to the comprehension of the ultimate worth of life-evolving Mind   Its writers—at least those of the later period—have no care for the external and vanishing, but only for the internal and abiding.   They are not concerned with the perishing body of man, but only with man as a growing, expanding, imperishable soul.[1]

Now it is precisely to the life of the soul as outwardly expressed in the body that the most vitally significant of the miracles recorded in the Bible refer.   Of these, two stand out as having transcendent interest, and are specially adapted to our present purpose. They are : the raising of Lazarus and the resurrection of Christ.   The former represents the power of the Christ in renewing the lives of others.   The latter demonstrates the power of the Son to subordinate death to life, first in his own person, and afterward in the life of the race.

[1] This reservation must of course be made : that the early Hebrews appear to have had no definite doctrine of or positive belief in a life after death.

In dealing with these we are first to again remind ourselves of the general oriental character of the symbolism of the Bible ; of the race-quality marking its specific thought ; and of the highly poetic but wholly uncritical habit of mind constituting the definite and very positive limitation not only of the writers to whom the record as it has come down to us is due, but of the entire race of which those minds were specially worthy representatives. In the second place we are again to recall the fact that in strict truth it is simply impossible to conceive, in the sense of really thinking, any change in the great World-order, whether in the form of the suspension of the laws of nature or in the reversal of the laws of mind. If in the great struggle for possession of the promised land of truth, I reach betimes a turning point at which the threatening twilight of despair is suddenly replaced by the noonday sun of confidence, I may seem indeed to myself to have won the special favor of the Ruler of the world, who has thus been brought to stay the universal course of things that I might, without interruption, bring my battle to perfectly successful issue. Yet when I review the case with care and reflect upon its real motive, I cannot but see that such seeming suspension of the universal World-process for the sake of insuring unbroken continuity in the fulfilment of my individual plans, cannot be regarded as actually taking place. On the contrary, I am driven to recognize that the only really thinkable explanation I can find for such seeming contradiction is this : That the inner process of my mind has been of such nature that with the actual solution of the given problem the sense of relief and triumph, has been so vivid, so intense, that the sudden inner illumination could not but project itself into the form of an external miracle consisting in the actual prolongation and positive brightening of the outer day. A miracle has actually occurred, but it has taken place within my own mind, and it is only by a sort of divine illusion that this inner transformation has appeared as taking place in the form of a suspension of the workings of the actual outer world of Nature. In short, I am driven to conclude that the miracle is essentially psychical and only in appearance physical. The further I examine into the matter the clearer it becomes to me that the outer world of nature is the realm of absolutely unvarying law, of unequivocal necessity, while in mind alone there is manifest the infinitely more complex law of self-activity, of literally free self-definition. And where mind as individual is imperfect in attainment and hence is limited to cumulative self-development through time, there and there alone can there be transition from one to another state of consciousness, there and there alone can there be possibility of the appearance of change in the great World-order.

And yet, being mind, the individual may be said to be by his own inmost nature predestined to attain at length to such degree of critical, reflective consciousness as to recognize that the absolute self-consistency and self-sufficiency of the perfect Mind cannot but necessitate the absolute changelessness of the actual World-order, since the latter is nothing else than the spontaneously produced expression of that Mind. In which case the individual mind cannot but be assured beyond all peradventure that every appearance of change in the total World-process is nothing else than the simple illusion by which the individual mind itself unconsciously projects into the outer world of nature its own spontaneously imaged form of a more or less radical transition which in reality has taken place in the inner world of the growing individual mind alone. With the divine instinct of its own inherent changelessness *as mind* the individual mind at first unsuspectingly assumes that change is possible only in the world which seemingly exists *there*, external to mind. It feels, however vaguely, that the inward and spiritual is the eternal; that the outward and material alone can change and perish. At a later stage it awakes to the deeper consciousness in which it sees that the "outer" is after all only the outer of the "inner ;" that in fact the outer world of nature exists and can exist only as the least adequate form of the outward expression of

the inner, spontaneous, infinitely self-sufficing and
eternally self-unfolding perfect Mind.   And the
awaking to this fact consists in seeing that "matter"
is but the illusory form of Energy which, both in its
total quantity and in its ultimate modes of manifestation, is absolutely unchanging.

And now if we remember that the oriental mind is
characteristically unreflecting, and hence that whatever processes take place within it are by it never
critically observed as such, but are only unconsciously
unfolded in the form of vivid imagery which, in the
very fact of being produced, is necessarily projected
into the world of outer phenomena and implicitly believed in as constituting part of its reality—if we remember this we may find therein a valid clew to the
reasonable interpretation of those miracles which the
Christian world has always, and rightly, looked upon
as having a positive and vital import as foreshadowing
the real nature and destiny of man.

How then shall we understand the account of the
raising of Lazarus? What else is it than a specially
striking phase in the drama of the human soul?
"Lord, if thou hadst been here my brother had not
died."—"Jesus wept."—"Lazarus, come forth!"—
Soul speaks; soul responds; and life triumphs over
death! Surely there is a subtler chemistry in that
than the mere reversal of molecular relations in a
human body already in process of decay! And even

when we add to this the calling back of the departed soul and its reunion with the body now revivified, this still is only an external relation. A body restored to life is still a body ; and as such is still subject to disease and predestined to a second dissolution. Whence the resurrection, taken in this literal sense —that is, in its lowest terms—must necessarily involve whatever agonies a second death entails.

Nay, in truth, it is in no wise a convincing argument in proof of immortality. Rather, in essence, it is precisely the same argument *against* immortality as that drawn in Plato's *Phædo* from the analogy of the weaver and the succession of coats worn out and cast aside by him, though he too comes at last to dissolution. Let it be proven beyond all controversy that immortality necessitates reincarnation, yet the fact of reincarnation could never suffice as ground for faith in immortality. If the soul is immortal it must be so from its own inmost nature as self-centered, spontaneous, self-moving ; and this characteristic can in no way be strengthened by any quality inhering in matter ; for matter is characteristically external, each particle having its center in another, and, in fact in *all* others, being essentially inert and moved only by impressed forces.

While, therefore, the vivid dramatic representation of the raising of Lazarus may serve as a means to strengthen the faith and stimulate the hope and increase the present comfort of unreflecting minds, it can have for reflecting minds no such values unless it can be found to involve another and more subtly spiritual meaning than that commonly assumed. In fact, the story must be interpreted in the light of other central doctrines of the Christian world.

One of the profoundest, and hence to most minds one of the "obscurest" of these doctrines is that of "original sin." "All men are born in sin." "Man is by nature evil." Not indeed because he is evil is he immortal; and yet were he not immortal he could not be evil. Not because man sins is he divine in nature; and yet were he not divine in nature he could do no sin. "Original sin," the primal evil in man, consists in the negative fact of the infinite discrepancy between the fundamental Type or divine Ideal, which it belongs to man as mind to fulfil, and the infinitesimal degree of that Type realized in and for the individual at any given moment, and above all at the moment of birth.

Out of this state of "original sin" it is the true destiny of every human soul to be redeemed. And, it may be added, failure (which involves refusal), to make use of the proper means to this redemption, such failure inevitably resulting in "arrested development," is precisely and in its very nature the "unpardonable sin."

Again, "original sin" is "transmitted," only in the

sense that at birth the individual mind is what it is only through heredity.[1] But also it is simply negative (1) in the sense that the inherited tendencies of the individual mind, by the very fact that they are inherited, are present at first only in germ and involve endless contradictions because derived through an indefinite multiplicity of lines of inheritance, and (2) in the sense that, as being rudimental, the whole character of the individual awaits unification and completion through its own positive activity as an individual. But the inherited qualities of the individual are *predispositions* to act in this and in that particular way—in ways indeed which are mutually contradictory, and above all in ways contradicting the fundamental Ideal or typical Nature which it is his true destiny to fulfil, and toward the fulfilment of which the deepest element in his heredity—his divine instinct due to his descent as mind from the perfect Mind—also predisposes him. He is predestined to act sanely. He is predestined to act insanely. He is predestined to act divinely. He is predestined to act satanically. He has predispositions toward the angelic life and predispositions toward the

---

[1] That the sin of the first, or any other, parents should be transmitted, *as sin*, as specific, positive offense, is certainly a doctrine worthy of Pascal's description (*Pensees*, Article IV, ii), as "a mystery utterly foreign to our reflective consciousness—*le mystère le plus eloigné de notre connoissance.*" In respect of heredity, compare below, Essay on "Christian Ethics as Compared with the Ethics of Other Religions."

merely brutish life. Such chaos of contradictory predispositions is infinitely evil. And yet it is only as these are merged in him that he can even be conceived as emerging into individualized, conscious existence. And so the individual is not only predestined to this chaos of evil ; it is absolutely inevitable that he should be so predestined if he is to exist as an individual at all.

Nevertheless, the very fact of his existence as an individualized conscious unit necessarily involves a *sense* of this contradiction, and this is a spur to remedial thought and action. That is, not only is it his destiny to suffer the pangs of this chaos ; it is also his destiny to enter at once upon a struggle having for its fundamental purpose the turning of the chaos into cosmos. It is precisely this struggle, duly regulated, that constitutes the process of his *redemption*. And because the struggle is primarily the individual's own struggle, it necessarily involves the individual's own *choice* as to time, as to means, as to method of the struggle.

Evidently, then, man is not only predestined to act ; he is also predestined to choose the time, the means and the method of his own action. But choice is nothing else than self-definition of the mind as will ; that is, choice is just the initial form of self-determination or Freedom. So that, strange as it may seem, it is but the literal truth to say that man is predestined to be free.

But again, his freedom may assume the negative form ; so that the acts he chooses may only fulfil the less adequate—i. e., the bruteward tending—predispositions of his nature. Nay, he may even choose to fulfil the perverted or demonic predispositions. In which case he only chooses to prolong and intensify the primal chaos of his being ; and that is the same as refusing to realize the cosmos, to which his highest or divine predispositions urge him. And, let us repeat, it is this setting up and emphasizing of self-contradiction—of "rebellion against the higher law" of his own nature—as the permanent state of the individual: it is this which constitutes the really "unpardonable sin." From which it becomes evident that the soul that sins dies in the fact of sinning ; and "the wages of sin is death," precisely because "sin is a transgression of the law" of mind as Mind.[1] This, indeed, would seem to be the most direct and reasonable interpretation of the statement attributed to Christ[2] that "whosoever shall speak against the Holy Spirit, it shall not be forgiven him ;" especially when taken in connection with that other declaration also reported of Jesus[3] that the Paraclete,

---

[1]Cf. above, p. 31 fol.   [2]*Matthew*, XII, 32.

[3]**Fourth Gospel, XV, 26.**

proceeding from the Father, is none other than the
"Spirit of Truth."

And now, through the lens of the fundamental doctrine thus briefly indicated, we may look for a more
vital meaning than the one usually assumed as being
involved in the story of the raising of Lazarus. In
seeking for this more vital meaning it will be well to
notice in the first place that the household of Bethany
where Jesus was so especially at home, consisted of
three strongly contrasted personalities. Of the two
sisters one was so intently occupied with present
domestic duties as to preclude any very elaborate consideration of a world beyond. It may even be suspected that her method of housekeeping was not far
removed from that peculiarly solemn kind which so
cleans the windows that instead of polarizing the light
of paradise and filling the atmosphere of every room
with the glow and prismatic beauties of the heavenly
radiance, only produces such tension in the glass as
stops out all the warmer undulations and lets in those
alone beneath which all things assume a spectral,
sepulchre-anticipating hue. Far removed from this
the other sister was characteristically enthusiastic,
mystical, devotedly religious. Her chief anxieties
were directed toward learning the secret of the leaven
of that bread which cometh down from above, and in
becoming rightly trained for such housekeeping as
will be of most avail in the mansion she had come to

look forward to as being prepared for her in the
Father's House. Quite different from either of these
appears to have been the brother. A healthy, kindly,
cheerful mind, we may safely assume that he went
about his work from day to day with no sense of
present burden or of haunting questions concerning
the future life.

Upon such nature the visits of Jesus would for long
be without appreciable effect. No doubt his kindly
nature, never yet stirred deeply, would experience a
vague degree of added warmth in presence of the
mildly grave, intensely earnest, personality of Jesus.
Yet the Master's words, which were as sunbeams to
Mary, were to Lazarus no more than far-off music
scarcely perceived.

How long did this seeming passivity continue?
We know nothing of the details. We can only infer
that with each new visit the distant music grew more
distinct—came nearer. More and more, too, Mary's
words must have awakened within him the same
vague sense of rhythm. The elements were gathering within him for the repetition of the world's first
great miracle—the awaking of a human soul to the
consciousness of its own true destiny. And while
they were only gathering he could not in the nature
of the case be in the least aware of what was in progress.

At length the fusion came. Just how it came we

can only dimly guess. All we know is that some sudden, terrifying change had come over Lazarus— a change that seemed to involve his death. The most probable conjecture would seem to be that of his sudden awakening to the full significance of life—so sudden and overwhelming as to produce a state of trance with rigidity and seeming lifelessness of body —and that when he awoke, Jesus, who had been called, was there to comfort him and to complete his waking into actual newness of genuinely spiritual life.

With him the primal chaos had been so diffuse that half his life had already passed before the inherent contradictions of that chaos developed sufficient tension to produce within him any really deep sense of insufficiency or need of transformation on his part. And when the shock of consciousness did come it was with such force as to seem fairly annihilating. Living so long without true life, he must indeed be killed that he might be made alive. In short, his appears to have been one of those cases in which the actual inner conscious process of individual redemption takes place with such suddenness and completeness as well nigh to threaten the sense of personal continuity. Awaking, conviction, conversion appear to take place all in the same instant; and the transformation which usually takes place so slowly as to occupy a life-time here assumes so violent and impetuous a character as to suggest the simultaneous annihilation and creation of a world. Whence all men look on in amazement, and say one to another: "Can this be the same man we have known hitherto?" while he himself is also dazed in his own self-recognition. He is alive; but his life to-day gives the color of death to all his past life. Out of such death-in-life he was awakened by the truly divine personality of the Master. In these last moments he has been brought to the clear consciousness of the real truth and blessedness of the actual spiritual life in which true immortality inheres. And in every word he has heard the divine command: "Loose him and let him go;" and in every movement of his soul he feels the grave-cloths of mere dead custom and formality bursting asunder and leaving him free to live the life of genuine, practical reason and thus to develop an evergrowing rhythmic relation to the eternal Father of all.

What Lazarus did thereafter we do not know—need not know. He had doubtless always been a kindly soul; he must thereafter have been a noble soul; a great soul he was not in the sense of being fitted to do the great deeds of the world. But what is of most significance to us here is this: That, looked at in the way just indicated, the "raising of Lazarus from the dead" assumes a meaning universal and richly practical as being essentially typical of the process of re-

demption which is indispensable to the really matured life of every human soul. On the other hand,
the question whether the miracle of the literal restoration to physical life of a man who had been some
days dead, so that decay had already become far advanced—such question is in truth of as little real religious moment to the reflective consciousness as is
the question whether mere water was ever directly
turned to wine. And as for scientific significance,
such question, on the face of it, has none whatever,
being self-contradictory in its very form.

Nevertheless, to the unreflecting consciousness,
which sees all things as in a vision and cannot
recognize the truth except in the form of imagery,
the pictorial form is undeniably helpful and even
altogether indispensable. Let not him who has
grown beyond the need of the elementary media of
the world's education scorn these media as being of
no further use at all. The immature ye have always
with you. Let the worthiest and most efficient
means to their advancement beyond immaturity be
preserved and rightly valued. Nay,' the beauty of
the image as apprehended by the higher sensuous
consciousness itself is only enhanced as the image
becomes increasingly transparent to reason which is
but the more deeply discerning and more widely
comprehending mode of mind. So that so far from
any one, in the course of truly rational self-develop-

ment, ever getting "beyond" the image in the sense of reaching a stage of advancement where the image ceases to interest and charm him, his higher cultivation only reveals a subtler value in the image than he had hitherto suspected, and thus makes of it a richer means to his enjoyment and further growth. Though here, too, it is not to be overlooked that the real miracle is that primal, essential miracle consisting in the inner process of the mind's own self-unfolding, the first step in which consists in awaking to the consciousness of "original sin" as consisting in that chaos of contradictory tendencies inborn in every member of the race.

And now let us turn to that great central miracle of all history—the miracle of Christ's own resurrection. The rapid culmination of the career of Jesus was but the outward expression of his rapidly self-unfolding inner consciousness. His whole doctrine focused in the conception of the absolute unity of the human and the divine nature. First of all he feels this in his own personality, and through that personality in its every mode and every degree he strives to bring his disciples, and, through them, all the world to the same state and same degree of consciousness as that to which he has himself attained. "I and my Father are one." "He that hath seen me hath seen the Father." "In that day you shall know that I am in the Father, and ye in me, and I in you."

"It is your Father's good will to give you the Kingdom." It is this central conception of the unity of
the human spirit with the divine spirit, which was
afterward so wonderfully summarized by Paul in the
declaration : "All things are yours, and ye are
Christ's, and Christ is God's."[1]

As the end approached the consciousness of the
Master rapidly intensified. And this intensifying
consciousness involved a deepening sense of contradiction between what had been accomplished and
what he had hoped for ; so that on more than one
occasion grief at seeming failure threatened wholly
to overwhelm him. Yet in reality this grief was
only the measure of the clearness of the vision with
which he saw the infinitely rich, divine Ideal of
positive spiritual Life which each and every human
soul must realize in and for itself in order that the
abstract typical oneness of man with God may be
fulfilled or rendered truly concrete and vital.

It was in this way that, in those last conferences
between himself and his disciples, conferences match-
lessly epitomized, if not also idealized, in the Fourth
Gospel—it was in this way that Jesus was led to
dwell wholly upon the future and to see with redoubled clearness the absolutely spiritual nature and
also the world-wide, time-filling extent of his mission

----

[1] I *Corinthians*, III, **23**.

to mankind. And as he faced with this steadier gaze
the eternal import of his message to human souls the
last shadow of temporal Messiahship faded utterly
away and every sentence uttered by him seemed only
intended to prepare his disciples for that culminating
affirmation: "My kingdom is not of this world:
if My kingdom were of this world, then would·my
servants fight * * * [rather] to this end am I
come into the world, that I should bear witness unto
the truth."

Clear beyond all question as to the true import of
his mission, he could not but see unmistakably his
own approaching death. Refusing to lead an insur-
rection against the Roman power, his own people
would turn the edge of the irony of fate against him
by causing him to die under the charge of stirring up
sedition. And yet the sense of the unity and universality and eternity of the type to which all minds as
minds belong lifted him above all fear and all equiv-
ocation, and bore him onward without the slightest
hesitation to the end

It was this truth which he so profoundly felt, and
which he so vividly figured to himself and to his disciples under the form of his own oneness with the
Father and of their oneness with him. And yet this
truth presented a still deeper and wider meaning than
could be adequately indicated even through such imagery. Hence such deeply significant mystical expres-

sions as that given in his reported and, as can hardly
be doubted, idealized direct communing with the
Father :[1] "O, Father, glorify thou me with thine
own self with the glory which I had with thee before
the world was." Being one with God he could not
be less than eternal in his existence. And that he
did not confine this mystically apprehended universality and eternity of existence to himself is put beyond all question by the expression just preceding,
to the effect that "this is life eternal, that they should
know thee the only true God, and him whom thou
didst send, even Jesus Christ." Clearly the assumption here is that the "eternal life" is the perfect life,
and pertains to each and all according to the degree
of actual rational self-development attained.

It was quite in this mood, too, that he said to his
disciples : "I came out from the Father, and am
come into the world ; again I leave the world and go
unto the Father." In fact there were two phases of
his existence—his eternal existence with the Father,
and his temporal existence with men. But also such
announcement could not be comprehended in any
adequate degree by the disciples, and so could not
but awake within them deepest sorrow and anxiety.
And recognizing this he adds the assurance : "In my
Father's house are many mansions ; if it were not so

[1] *Fourth Gospel*, XVII, 5 fol.

I would have told you ; for I go to prepare a place for you.   And if I go and prepare a place for you, I come again, and will receive you unto myself ; that where I am there ye may be also '' The eternal aspect of life is theirs no less than his.   Nay, more, he assures them that he will not leave them desolate. He will intercede with the Father so that another Comforter shall be given them.   And that Comforter, Helper, ''Paraclete,'' shall be nothing less than the Spirit of Truth, who, when he is come, will ''guide them into all the truth.''

The outlook widens, then!   He is going away for their good !   ''It is expedient for you that I go away ; for if I go not away, the Comforter will not come unto you ; but if I go, I will send him unto you.'' What a vista is opening out before them, could they but understand !   It is in truth nothing less than the whole history of the world.   The universal, eternal Spirit of Truth can really be present to the individual consciousness only in proportion as outer sensuous forms dissolve and fade from view.   The science of the world is possible only in so far as the things of the world become transparent and reduced to the rank of mere media—media revealing to the deeper vision of Reason the universal, vital relations which give to outward things their reality and concrete significance.

And yet, doubtless, to the man Jesus also, the outlook was rather a mystic vision than a positively reasoned representation in clear detail, of the actual process by which the Spirit of Truth was to enter into the present concrete process of human development and prove to be the efficient Comforter, Advocate, Helper, Paraclete, of all struggling, erring, despairing, hoping individual human souls. Indeed his own assurances waver, and cross each other, and yet blend, like the prophetic dissolving view they really constituted. He has but just promised them the Comforter, whose coming depends upon his own departure and hence renders that departure expedient for them. And now, almost in the same breath, he assures them : "A little while. and ye behold me no more ; and again a little while, and ye shall see me." The Comforter is necessary to them. But the Comforter will not come while the Master himself remains visibly present in their midst. Yet his absence is not to be permanent nor even much prolonged. "Again a little while and ye shall see me." After all, though the Comforter will not come while the Master remains present to their senses, yet as the actual Spirit of Truth it will not depart when he returns in his truly universal and glorified form. The dissolving of his outward form from the time and space to which thus far their consciousness had been mainly limited, will give occasion for the unfolding of those higher modes of mind through which they will be able to recognize his spiritual and far more truly real Presence.

Such would seem to be the real clew to the actual meaning of the story of the resurrection of the Christ as formulated and related by his disciples. Wrought up to the most intense degree of mingled hope and fear concerning the Master's fate and their own destiny, wholly occupied with the mystic sayings in which he had latterly so much addressed them, and which at the best they could comprehend only in their least adequate import, the disciples, dazed and helpless, could only await the unfolding of events.

Stunned by his actual tragic death, they could only cower in fear and gather in secret places to comfort one another and stimulate hope through repetition of his words and recalling his wondrous personality. Dwelling in timid expectation upon those of the Master's words which most vividly expressed his love for them, they could not but center all their thoughts upon his promise of return, and all their hopes upon its literal and speediest fulfilment. And, utterly uncritical in habit of mind as they were, they could see no real contradiction in the thought that he would bodily revive and once more live and dwell among them. Nay, they could not clearly conceive of his being still alive save in the actual form of his bodily presence. Despairing in his absence, hoping for the renewal of his sensuously real presence,

they were in just such state of expectancy as by mutual excitation actually to bring themselves to see
what above all else in all the world they most desired
to see.

The first to experience the vision of the risen Lord
is the deeply emotional, mystically minded Mary,
who had already beheld two angels in the tomb and
heard them speak. Then he appears to the assembled disciples while they are mutually encouraging one another to expect his reappearance. A
third time, according to the fourth Gospel, while
some of the disciples were engaged in fishing, he appeared to them. Going back to the occupation from
which he had called them to a higher mission, it is
not strange that the memory of him should recur so
vividly in their excited minds as to amount to an apparition—the act recorded as being now performed by
him in their presence being precisely the same as
they had so often seen him perform before.

Specially striking and suggestive, on the other
hand, is the account of the journey of Cleopas and
his companion (two otherwise unknown disciples),
to Emmaus. These the risen Christ joined on the
way, but remained unknown to them, and even
made as if he knew nothing of the sad events concerning which they were communing with one
another by the way. In fact, it was only through
his breaking bread and blessing it at the meal at

Emmaus that their eyes were opened to know him. And in that same instant he vanished out of their sight. The more deeply spiritual manner involved in his exposition of the whole of the Scriptures, beginning from Moses and the prophets, they had failed utterly to recognize. Only in the simple, sensuous fact of breaking bread did they discover the likeness. And in that moment the apparition vanished—a moment the psychological significance of which is marvelously (however unconsciously), symbolized in Rembrandt's "Supper at Emmaus," where the joy of recognition is suddenly eclipsed by their amazement at the blinding light which remains in place of the Master's vanished form.[1]

According to Luke, who alone gives this story circumstantially, these two disciples returned at once to Jerusalem, where they found the eleven, with others, assembled. By their testimony these two added to the general rejoicing at the evidence thus far received of the actual return to life on the part of Jesus. And even while they were rejoicing another apparition of the Master occurred to them. And though this was what they desired, yet none the less it terrified them. And their terror was only allayed by proofs of his real bodily presence—proofs by which they were satisfied that they had not "seen a spirit," as at first they feared. Following which the apparition led them to another place, where again it "parted from them," or disappeared.

Both Matthew and Mark, however, relate that even then these apparitions were by no means accepted by all as actual appearances of the risen Lord. And assuredly we may easily see at the present day that these psychological conditions were such as to render the apparitions easily explicable as simple psychological phenomena. In which case we are left free to regard the miracle of Christ's bodily resurrection as thus far a purely subjective miracle ; that is, as having taken place only in the highly wrought imaginations of some (not all) of his disciples.

But thus we are the more bound to seek for a deeper and better meaning as involved in the hope and the belief of the Church, then and now, concerning this great Mystery. For there can be no reasonable doubt that there is vital truth in Paul's declaration that "if Christ hath not been raised, your faith is vain ; ye are yet in your sins." And, further : "if in this life only we have hoped in Christ, we are of all men most pitiable."[1]

And now in our search for this better interpretation let us begin with that wondrous, dazzling Light which the limitations of painting suggested to the genius of the painter as the one way of representing

[1] *I Corinthians*, XV, 19.

to the eye on cauvas the miraculous disappearance of
the just now visible bodily form of the risen Master,
and also the transfiguring effect produced in the
minds of the two disciples by the assurance that he
still lived. It is a flash in the gloom ; it is the dawn
of spiritual day, even while the outer corporeal
personal presence is vanishing into the night of dissolution and indistinguishable, irreclaimable dispcr-
sion amid the elements. It is the first stage in the
fulfilment of the Master's promise that on his departure from their midst the Comforter, in the form of
the living Spirit of Truth, would come to them. The
"natural body," consisting of the outward form of
their Lord, now present only to the yearning phantasy, was already dying and dissolving into the
"spiritual body"[1] that was to be. The qualities of
divine personality, so conspicuous in the living
Jesus, now that he had died, were for the first time
beginning to be clearly manifest in their truly universal character to the sorrowing disciples. More,
directly, the immediate indispensable condition of
their clear apprehension of the ideal character constituting the deeper truth of the Personality of Christ
was just the disappearance of the individual, sen-

---

[1] *I Corinthians*, XV, 42-44. The analogy of the seed dying
into the life of the plant is of course only an analogy, and
evidently so intended by Paul. Yet with him the inference
is still left in mystical form—in marvelously beautiful and
suggestive poetic imagery—not to be otherwise understood.

suously apprehended form in and through which that ideal character had just become clearly manifest to men.

Doubtless any given type is at first most easily seized in one particular form. But the permanent holding fast of such single form produces the tacit conviction that the type is really present in that form alone. In other words, through such restricted view of the universal type as manifest in just the one form only, the type itself appears not merely *in*, but also only *as* that one particular form. Whence it is evident that if we restrict our view of the universal type of divine-human Personality to the one man Jesus we lose, or rather we fail ever to possess ourselves of, the real truth of the universal, eternal Christ. The individual, historical, human Christ is held in the imagination as a fixed, relatively lifeless image pertaining to a far, and increasingly, distant *past*. And this prevents us from developing the richer, deeper consciousness of the infinite, universal, divine and hence eternal Christ who is absolutely one with the Father—the all in all of the ceaseless, living *Present*. We will not allow the sensuously apprehended Master to take his departure from us ; and so we make it impossible that the Spirit of Truth should unfold into living reality in our higher or thinking consciousness, and thus deprive ourselves of the real presence of the Paraclete—the measureless comfort of knowing the truth in its universal and infinitely richer forms.

And yet he himself declared in his own mystical way : "If ye loved me, ye would have rejoiced because I go unto the Father ; for the Father is greater than I."[1] Not distinguishing between the particular form and the universal substance, we check in its earlier, rudimentary stage the great miracle of the new birth—which is also the resurrection—of the universal Christ within ourselves ; and by precisely so much do we fail of realizing that "hope of glory" of which the actual practical unfolding of the true Christ-nature within the individual soul is the indispensable condition. Faithless in our faith we bury the image of his crucified temporal presence in the tomb of our phantasy, and will not hear the voice of the Angel of Truth bidding us look up with the Eyes of Reason and behold, as the real truth figured in the story of the physical resurrection of Jesus, the eternal Presence of the universal Christ in humanity, assuring eternal life, endlessly deepening in wealth of import, to every individual soul really conforming to the divine Law of Reason inherent in each and all alike.

And here we come upon the truth vaguely shadowed forth in that world-old doctrine of the "transmigration of souls." The universal Christ, the eternal Christ, one in essence with the Father, that is

---

[1] Fourth Gospel. XIV, 28.

the infinite type of Personality. And that type is
forever reunfolded, and in ceaseless process of unfolding, in individual minds, in self-conscious, spiritual units. So that the actual arising of each and
every unit of this type is the "reincarnation" of the
universal Christ. And the progressive unfolding of
more and more complex forms as expressive of the expanding wealth of continuously developing individual spiritual life—when individualized consciousness has really been once attained—that is the truth
of the transmigration of the individual soul. Nay,
doubtless such "transmigration" necessarily involves,
in its own degree, "reincarnation" also.

If physiological chemistry is to be trusted, the individual human soul, in the course of an exceptionally prolonged earthly life, already passes through
a dozen "reincarnations." And doubtless also in the
course of its further progress it will continue such
"reincarnations," though always in strictly logical
consistency with its own needs as a mind or conscious
unit of energy developing in accordance with—or
degenerating in contradiction to—the fundamental,
unchanging and unchangeable law of Mind.[1] In
other words, it will rise in the angelic scale or sink

---

[1] Indeed it may be said that even degeneracy still illustrates law That sin entails death—spiritual death (cf.
above, p. 31 fol.)—is but the negative aspect of the law of
mind. And he who breaks that law only breaks himself on the
wheel of the law of lawlessness.

in the scale demonic, precisely according as it con-
forms to or defies, the essential, eternal Christ-ideal.

But there is a further phase in the miracle of the
resurrection of the Christ. Had the man Jesus undertaken the Messianic task in the sense expected of
him by the people of his own race, he might possibly
for a time have led his nation to greater or less victory and temporary independence; though in that
period it can scarcely be conceived that such line of
effort should at last have ended otherwise than dis-
astrously for leader and people alike. Happily for
the history of this world Jesus chose to accept the
then existing political situation and to urge that the
first great need was the establishment of the Kingdom of Truth in the earth. The greatest epoch in
the world's history was already entered upon when a
man had arisen divine enough in thought to see and
formulate, and divine enough in character to un-
flinchingly declare, and in his own conduct to illustrate the doctrine: "Seek ye *first* the Kingdom of
Heaven and its righteousness, and all these things
shall be added unto you." For such personage, distinguishing with perfect clearness between the inner,
permanent Reality, and the outer, passing show of
things, the minimum of food, and raiment and shel-
tered resting-place suffices. Nay, in contrast with
the eternal Kingdom of Truth, the kingdoms and
empires and robes of state of this world, alike with

the individual garments and hovels of the most abject slaves, are but forms of the mere phantasmal
"here and now." Social organization and individual
organism—these are but the momentary outer phases
which the divinely constituted, undying spirit of humanity assumes in its own progressive self-unfolding
throughout the ages. Only, the richer the degree of
actual inward spiritual quality developed in individual human lives, the subtler and more complex
must both the outward individual organism and the
outward social organization become.

In other words, the universal, eternal Chri-t, the
infinite, divine Ideal, realized once for all in the absolute, personal Creator in his character of Redeemer
—this universal Christ which for every such world as
ours throughout the whole of infinite space and infinite duration, is at the outset only a latent form, an
unsuspected possibility—everywhere this universal.
eternal Christ works, not merely through but in and
for the growing individual and national and racial
consciousness ; so that particular personages and
special state constitutions unfold, and serve their
purpose, and outwardly disappear, at once preparing
the way, and making room, for higher forms in any
given particular world.

And what is this but a glimpse of the truly universal Christ eternally in process of "becoming," of
evolution, of "transmigration," as the real historical

Christ—as the actual, eternally-begotten Son of God? Not less than this can the real resurrection of the Christ signify. And this includes his "second coming,"—includes it as the perpetual reappearance of the infinite, divine Type in the form of individual immortal souls new-born in perishing outward bodies ; and also in the more cumbrous and wholly perishing forms of those institutions which embody the spirit of an age and serve as media for the education of the self-centered yet universally related and imperishable conscious individuals constituting the actual race of the Sons of God.

Such, then, is the great, eternal, all-inclusive Miracle of the Resurrection of Christ. And as for the individual human body—including the body of the Son of Man—that is sacred only to the uses of the human soul; when it ceases to be organic to those uses it becomes itself a sepulchre. To be progressively redeemed out of this, and out of all other cramping, material limitations, into the genuine freedom of ever-increasing fulness of rational self-consciousness and genuine spiritual life—that is the true resurrection of the individual human soul—a resurrection that can be completed only through endless individual existence.

Jesus is the central figure of the world because he taught mankind the divine secret of genuine spiritual life as the central truth of the world. And in truest sense the miracle of his resurrection is to be seen in the spiritual resurrection of the world. Bringing life as immortality to light, in the sense of declaring the ideal oneness of the human spirit with the divine Spirit, and thus indicating that immortality pertains to the human soul from its very nature, he proved not only his own immortality, but proved also that above all others he was himself the Christ—the "Anointed One"—because his mission transcends all other missions. Nay, in declaring the identity in nature as between God and man Jesus made practical affirmation of the infinitude of man as mind, and thus opened the way for the demand on the part of man that ultimately for him there shall be no insoluble mysteries, no hopeless wonders, no reason-defying miracles ; but that rather, in the course of his endless and endlessly intensifying individual existence, he shall be actually guided by the Spirit of Truth into all the truth. Only thus can be realized the good will of the Father to give to the Sons of God the Kingdom. Only thus can rational confirmation be found for those triumphant words : "All things are yours, and ye are Christ's; and Christ is God's."

NOTE (omitted by oversight from p. 359): A sermon of rare beauty and suggestiveness was preached, now some years since, by the Rev. R. A. Holland, S. T. D., of St. Louis, on the theme, "*By the Way*," and interpreting the appearance of Christ to the two disciples at Emmaus. It is greatly to be wished that this and other like utterances of his may yet be rendered generally available in book form.

VIII.

CHRISTIAN ETHICS AS CONTRASTED WITH THE ETHICS OF OTHER RELIGIONS.

It may be assumed as an axiom that Ethics is possible only to a thinking being. Ethics is the science of the principles which are directly involved in moral action, involved to such degree and in such sense as that they determine action as moral. Only a being capable of reflecting upon the nature and end of his own conduct is capable of conduct involving the quality of morality. That conduct alone is moral which tends toward enriching the life of the conscious being performing the actions constituting the conduct. And this must be understood as meaning that the conduct is of such nature as to enrich the life of the individual in his character as a conscious being, as a mind. All conduct is original, self-determining exercise of power. No one ever speaks of the conduct of an animal, but only of the conduct of a man. Conduct is normal or moral in so far as it results in the unfolding of the entire individual conscious unit of energy, in accordance with the ultimate type of such conscious unit. To which we may add that only a thinking being is capable of developing any science whatever, which implies, of course, that only such being can develop a Science of Ethics.

But also it is important to notice that the very unfolding of science by such being is itself nothing else than one aspect in the total process of the self-unfolding of such being. And by as much as the typical or ultimate nature of the thinking being is complex, by just so much must the actual evolution of individuals comprised within the type be complex and prolonged.

In fact, this evolutional process is nothing else than the process known as History. And this again must really be understood as including the whole essential process of biological history as leading up to man physiological, as well as the sociological history of man as the process of unfolding the life of man psychical, of man as a thinking, feeling, willing being.

The purpose of the present essay is to present in one connected view the fundamental aspects and stages of this evolutional process in so far as it consists in the unfolding of an adequate conception of the nature and basis of moral obligation. Of course the essay, with its deliberately chosen limitations, can be no more than the merest sketch. But the ''mere sketch'' has, or may have, the value of bringing to light fundamental principles which to most minds are likely to be obscured through excess of illustration in more elaborate treatises.

The process will be traced through three essential stages : (1) The first will be that in which consciousness had as yet attained maturity only in its sensuous aspect. In this stage, accordingly, the highest intellectual products are those presented in the form of imagery. (2) The second stage will be that in which reflection has so far unfolded as that imagery has ceased to be in itself of leading interest, but also in which thought has not been able wholly to free itself from imagery. It is the stage of the "abstract understanding." (3) The third stage will be that in which the reflective consciousness has completely mastered imagery, or is in the clearly apprehended way of doing so, and in which it grasps the concrete infinitude and self-containing Totality of the World. It is the stage of Reason, properly speaking.

No doubt imagination, understanding and reason are fundamental modes of mind as mind. No doubt, too, they were all present and must have been present from the first in the actual evolution of mind in the history of this or any other world. But also there can be no doubt that in its evolution mind attained maturity first of all in its character as imaging power ; that a longer period was required for it to become explicit as a power to seize relations, while still the relations seized were of limited range and involved in tangible, sensuously apprehended facts. Finally, it was only as the outcome of a still more extended disciplinary course, including those already named, that the unfolding mind of man attained the power to comprehend that total complex of relations which binds all into one—a complex which thus constitutes the essence of the actual, total, concrete Universe.

I.

The first stage—that is, the stage in which imagination is the maturest phase of intelligence as yet unfolded—presents itself to our view as that period of history known as the age of Primitive Man. It is the period of "ancient history," properly speaking. In its simplest degree also it is the stage of transition out of mere animalhood into manhood, and thus suggests the whole process of organic evolution as its logical presupposition.

One remark must be made in this connection, however, by way of caution. The theory of evolution, as ordinarily presented, breaks down in its attempt to account for the development of man. In fact, so far as this theory assumes to account for more complex forms of life by tracing their lineage, through less and less complex forms, back through time to the protoplasmic or germinal aspect of matter at the bottom of the primal sea, it really reduces the whole evolutional process to a mere elaboration of relations of physical energy ; in which case it breaks down altogether. For such vastly complex and faultlessly consistent process as that which, beginning in the mechanical and chemical reactions of a nebulous mass, has unswervingly pursued its course, through primitive cell, and multicellular unfoldings, to the realization of endlessly varied organic forms including the human organism itself, with its manifold and successively appearing inner indications of relationship to all the essential types of the animal kingdom—such vastly complex and faultlessly consistent process involves of necessity a further factor than the self-styled evolutionist is ever willing wholly to admit. The process is one whole process. As such it is but the concretely realized form of one whole method. And yet method is really inconceivable save as consisting of thought self-defined. But thought defining itself—that is nothing else than self-conscious energy or mind realizing itself through its own self-differentiation.

Clearly, then, not only is mind the culmination of the whole process of Evolution ; Mind is also the necessary presupposition of that process. Whence man as organism may indeed be the complex focus of the whole process of organic evolution ; but even so he is not derived *from* the lower organisms, but only *through* them. Thus, even as animal, man derives his being from the primal Energy or Mind, without which self-conscious primal Energy the evolutional process cannot be really *thought* at all, however easy it may be to *imagine* the process as taking place otherwise. How much more, then, is it impossible to really think the origin of man as mind to have its explanation in mere physical forces which are themselves inexplicable save as the simpler forms of the expression of Mind !

Doubtless it is true that individual man is what he is at birth solely through the process of "heredity." But the supreme factor in his heredity is just that which the primal Mind itself constitutes   From that Mind, and from that alone, man not only derives his whole being, but above all inherits his *essential nature as man.*[1]

[1] The following is from my volume, "*The World-Energy and Its Self-Conservation,*" p. 295, published in 1890: " Evidently, then, the descent of man from successively lower and lower orders of animals, which themselves constitute a minutely graded series of thought-forms, and even of thought-functions, is, after all, nothing else than his ascent or evolution in the scale of godhood. And always it is to be remembered that the descent of man cannot possibly have been from animals, merely as animals, merely as physical or material, or brute natures (allowing that such 'natures' are thinkable). On the contrary, every step, every factor in this ascending scale of his evolution is possible for man only because each step and each factor is expressive simply of the method by which Man the Son, is born of God the Father. Just as Life can come only from the living, though it may be through units which are in themselves not living; so Man the thinker can come only from God the Thinker, though it may be through a marvelous series of complex, more or less conscious forms, which in and of themselves cannot be said to think."

At birth each individual is what he is through heredity. What further inferences may we draw from this? It is that he is predetermined or "predestined" toward manifold courses of action. But we must not forget that, above all, his heredity connects him vitally, in type, with the primitive, eternally creative Mind. So that if he is predestined to feel the pangs of hunger and to put forth effort to satisfy that sense of contradiction in his outer, animal life, he is not less predestined to experience the uneasiness of wonder and so to put forth efforts of intelligence to the end of satisfying this sense of contradiction in his inner psychic life. Man is foreordained to live. He is foreordained to act outwardly. But he is not less surely foreordained to act inwardly. He is foreordained to think, to define himself in consciousness and thus to regulate himself in action. Or, as we may just as well express it, man is *predestined to be free.*

Thus at birth man is a complex of qualities all which are due to heredity. But his inheritance is through diverging and vastly multifarious lines. He inherits from all his ancestors, vicious and saintly alike. And all these inherited tendencies constitute in sum the whole of his instinctive nature.

As instinctive, therefore, he is a measureless aggregate of mutually opposing tendencies. Or, to use a figure, he is a bundle of contradictions, and as such

is beyond human calculation. In him there shine
alternately, and even simultaneously, the life-inviting
light of Paradise and the life-withering fires of the
Inferno   By birth, by instinct, man is at once
coward and hero ; at once faithful and treasonable ;
at once brute and angel ; at once a devil and a god.

Thus the great central problem of human life is
this : How to reconcile these inborn contradictions.
And it is just the divine instinct of reason within him
—the essential, unifying element in his nature as a
thinking being, due to his descent from the primal
Mind—this it is which makes certain the arising of
that problem in his consciousness and also prompts
him irresistibly to efforts toward its solution. It is
the problem of the Education of man. To unify
and reconcile these innate contradictory tendencies,
and in unifying them to transfigure the lower by
bringing them into full subordination to the higher
—that is the central task of civilization and the central purpose in human history.

It is due to the workings of the divine instinct of
reason within man that man came at first, and comes
forever, to recognize the workings of Divinity in the
great world beyond man. It is through this instinct
that man has ever discerned, however dimly, the oneness of the human with the divine nature, But because
at first reason was only an instinct in man and, from its
subtle, highly complex character, could not be other-

wise than slow in developing into clearness and adequacy of positive power as reason, man could only
grope and guess in his earlier efforts to find solution
of this great central problem of his own existence.

Meanwhile imagination, as the simpler mode of
mind, grew into relative maturity and thus proved to
be that productive mode of mind through which for
the time man could best satisfy the instinctive demand of his rudimentary reason for some expression
of his conviction that the powers superior to men are
still like men. Thus in the nature of the case, it was
but inevitable that the gods should be imaged and
that they should be imaged in the form of men. The
divine instinct of reason in man could not fail to assume that the highest image of the gods must ever be
the human form.[1]

Thus in the phantasy of primitive man the divine
world came to be a copy of the human world. Natural elements were, indeed, intermingled; but the
human aspect never failed to be predominant. The
natural elements tended to confuse the human, and
did in greater or less degree give rise to a confused
estimate of Personality. On the other hand the sense

---

[1] Xenophanes (or whoever else), in saying that if lions had
been sculptors they would have represented the gods in the
likeness of lions, failed to notice that only thinking beings
could be sculptors, and that thus if lions had been sculptors
they would have been more than lions—they would have
been thinking beings; i. e., *men.*

of personality could not be altogether obscured or turned aside.

Nevertheless, just as the endlessly manifold in-stinctive tendencies in man remained for ages, throughout the lives of all individuals, mainly an un-reconciled multiplicity ;[1] so, in the earlier representa-tions which were made of the divine world multi-plicity and contradictoriness of powers were taken as a matter of course and without so much as a suspicion that such representation itself was at all contradictory. There were political gods, and gods of commerce, and domestic gods ; gods of refinement and gods of ferocity, gods of truth and gods of falsehood, gods pure and gods impure.

Such confusions in the represented divine world did, indeed, but reflect confusions in the actual hu-man consciousness. Yet such was the only divine world known to man. And so long as men's wor-ship was addressed to such divinities—divinities mu-tually antagonistic and even essentially capricious—religion could afford no real ground of certitude and could therefore be no other than a *Religion of Fear*.

It follows also that so long as the world of the higher powers appears to man as a world of caprice, there could be no definite standard of moral obliga-tion, and the Ethics of each tribe and even of each

---

[1] And such must ever be the case in the earlier years of each individual.

individual would be always variable and at any moment be high or low according to the character of the god who chanced to be the immediate object of worship.

II.

But also it could not fail that the divine instinct of reason in man should at length rise in revolt against such self-contradictory representation of the divine world. For though this ideal representation was really modeled upon the actually existing human world, yet in the immediate consciousness of men the existing human world seemed rather a reflection of the ideally represented divine world. And because the divine instinct of reason worked most effectually in the minds of some—who by that fact were the "best" minds of the race—and because the accepted ideal representations of the divine world were due to just these minds, it did come about that the actual human world, which at first served as stimulus toward those representations, was more and more reconstituted with the view of bringing it into more complete conformity with the ideal divine world. Though the gods were formed in the likeness of men, yet men never so much as dreamed that this was the way the gods had come to be. The god in man saw God beyond man with so clear and transfiguring an intuition as to leave no room for doubt as to the reality and boundless superiority of the divine world. To man the gods were real·and the will of the gods must be the true law of the life of man who dimly felt himself to bear the likeness of sonship to one or another of the far-off gods.

, Nevertheless the more earnestly men sought to make real the will of the gods in the lives of men the more must the divine instinct of reason in the human soul be shocked into questioning mood concerning the gods through the contradictions unfolding in actual human life ; for human life itself is just the attempt to realize the mutually contradictory wills of the many gods. Where is the limit of the one god's province? Where the limit of the province of another? The divine world—ought not that to be a world of harmony? The gods must meet in council, then. But who knows the decisions of the councils of the gods? Who knows what the divine Will is? There must be a chief god, to whose will the wills of the other gods are at last subordinate. But a god subordinated—is that a god at all?

Thus, step by step, men could not but be led to feel the contradictoriness of that ideal representation of the divine world in which that world appeared as consisting in a multiplicity of gods, and to see at length that somehow the world must be swayed by a single, resistless Might. Toward this goal all primitive religions have manifested an inherent tendency.

It was the Greeks, with their fine native sense of Beauty, so finely cultivated, in whose religion the sense of the necessity of unison, of self-consistency within the world of the gods, grew into that beautiful image of the Republic of the gods with Zeus at the head and Destiny over all, uniting all into One ; though this One was still only an imaged One whose unity was at best external, and which thus possessed no power really to renovate the human world. In fact, with the Greeks as a race, religious interpretation always assumed the art form, and within this form sculpture determined the character of all. It is the plastic form in which the outward shape must be absolutely clear and exact in definition. It presupposes a multiplicity of gods and necessarily dissolves and vanishes with the development of consciousness that there are no gods, but only God. It grew in might through contemplation of the gods. It could not see God and live. It was in this form of religious interpretation, too, that the Greek genius as such exhausted itself. And doubtless the conquest of Greece by Rome deprived the world of nothing in possession of which the world would have been the better.

It was another race that first broke quite away from definite imagery as direct representation of the divine world, and thus came to behold the world as subject to one measureless, resistless Power. To the Semitic race, indeed, the art form of religious representation never developed beyond the rudimentary stage. It was the present living God who appeared to them in the storm-cloud and in the lightning, and whose voice was the thunder, though also God was in the "still small voice" of the inner conscience or divine instinct of man himself ; and this sufficed. And so far as the art-instinct of this race developed in the form of poetry as giving definition to religious senti‑ment, the poetry was still pictorial, discriptive, though descriptive of the might and the goodness of Divinity in the world beyond man, or of the yearn‑ings within the soul of man toward God.

Such was the case with the Hebrews, and this clew led up to the unfolding of a still more adequate and clearly defined conception of God and of man's rela‑tion to God as the one perfect Mind. We have now to notice the most conspicuous example of the tran‑sition form of faith between the earlier polytheistic rel'gions and this modern and highest monotheistic view. This example of the intermediate degrees of the religious consciousness presents itself in the form of the Mohammedan religion, which is essentially the highest term of the spontaneous native Arabian faith.

(True, this religion assumed positive form at a rela‑tively late period in history, and was the outgrowth of the spirit of a people practically isolated from the other peoples of the world. It was the religion itself in its fully developed character that brought the

Arabs into actual relation with other peoples and thus introduced them upon the stage of the world's history. On the other hand their earlier religion was polytheistic and gradually became merged into precisely that form of monotheism which serves as the best, because simplest, logical example of the transition stage in the development of religious consciousness. Of course Mohammedanism no more grew out of the Greek faith than the Christian faith has developed from the Mohammedan. And yet, what specially characterized the Greek faith and is most conspicuously unfolded in that faith—viz., its polytheism—was in essence the same with the earlier Arabian faith ; just as what specially characterizes and is most conspicuously unfolded in Mohammedanism—viz., its monotheism—is the central element in the Christian faith. Christianity presents itself as an enriched monotheism which has its root in the abstract monotheism of the Hebrew faith ; and this in turn is the direct resultant of a struggle, centuries long, through which that devoted people clarified its own consciousness and freed itself from the contradictions of what was at first a crude polytheistic religion. It is only to bring into sharper contrast the fundamental stages of this evolutionary process that the Greek religion is taken as a conspicuous example of polytheism on the one hand, and that Mohammedanism is selected as

the most conspicuous example of strict abstract monotheism on the other).

After this explanatory note we may proceed to indicate the characteristic limitations of the latter type
of faith as furnishing a basis for ethical doctrine.

And the first thing we have to notice is the fact
that this type of religion has always developed with
a people who have not as yet advanced beyond the
stage of the "abstract understanding." They view
the events of the world more or less distinctly under the
form of cause and effect. But as yet they are unable to
seize the causal relation otherwise than externally.
The cause is something by itself and quite apart from
the effect, which likewise exists for itself and quite
apart from the cause. So also with them the process
of causation can actually take place only in time, the
cause appearing first and the effect after. If God is
the cause of the existence of the world, then God
must first have existed by himself and must afterward have brought the world into existence ; though
now the world, having been brought into existence,
no longer requires the activity of the creative Power
and hence exists as something over against that
Power.

But also that Power created the world as he chose.
By an act of the same power the Creator could anni-
hilate the world. Doubtless in his own good time he
will do so and create another world as he may then

choose. His ways are not man's ways and are past man's finding out. The divine instinct of reason in man bows before such Power in a worship which consists of absolute submission and self-surrender as reason. The ruling Power of the world is conceived as an arbitrary Will which wills what it will, and which therefore no reason can hope ever to fathom. The world, including man, is precisely what Allah wills it to be. If it should prove different to-morrow, it will be because Allah would have the difference arise. No one knows the will of Allah, or can know, save he to whom Allah wills to reveal his will. It is even futile and irreverent to seek to know.

It is precisely this fatalistic attitude of mind, which has so often and in such various forms been manifest in the history of the race, and to which Goethe gave utterance in the following lines:

> "The highest might
> Of science quite
> Is from the world concealed!
> But whosoe'er
> Expends no care
> To him it is revealed."[1]

---

[1] The English is by C. Kegan Paul. The German is as follows:

> Die hohe Kraft
> Der Wissenschaft,
> Der ganzen Welt verborgen!
> Und wer nicht denkt,
> Dem wird sie geschenkt,
> Er hat sie ohne sorgen.

Mr. F. H. Bradley makes good use of this quotation as

It need hardly be said that logically such faith condemns all research and renders science wholly impossible. And if individual Mohammedans have nevertheless dealt in science and more or less contributed to science, it is because the divine instinct of reason was so exceptionally strong within them as to cause them to bid defiance to the necessary implications of their faith.

But also—and this is what specially interests us here—in forbidding science and rendering revelation altogether arbitrary such abstract monotheism hope-

---

against Hedonism, which is only another reason-paralyzing form of fatalism. See his essay: "Pleasure for Pleasure's Sake." *Ethical Studies*, p. 80.

Meanwhile the special connection in which Goethe introduces the lines above quoted is not without its hint. The scene is that of the "Witch's Kitchen." After wild banterings between Mephistopheles and the witches, the former calls for wine, which is really to be a potion working the transformation of Faust. The witches make extravagantly ceremonious preparation, including a reading from a huge volume. First in which there is a pretense of mystic numbers, ending with:

> "And nine is one,
> And ten is none.
> That is the witches one-times-one."

With all which mummery Faust is greatly disgusted. On the other hand Mephistopheles is charmed, and in mock solemnity assures Faust that a "perfect contradiction still is mystery-crammed for wise and fools alike;" adding that "for the most part when men hear but words they believe there must be somewhat in them to stir up thought." Upon which the witch reads on as above: "The highest might," etc. That is, Goethe, in these words, quotes what he deems the sentiment of bedlam. It is of a piece with the witch's multiplication table, and as such would seem well worth considering by those who fancy that the incomprehensible, the unutterable, the Unknowable, is so far superior to definite, explicitly unfolded thought.

lessly obscures the standard of right doing and opens the way to the grossest license in point of conduct. For in all his deeds, whether of tender kindliness and noble purity or of brutal cruelty and brutish licentiousness the individual Mohammedan devoutly believes himself to be but the instrument of Allah's Will and can therefore neither esteem himself for his worthy deeds nor condemn himself for deeds unworthy.

Such faith, indeed, cannot pause with conceiving all inferior gods as merged and cancelled in the might of one resistless Will ; it is also driven onward to the point of regarding man himself as nothing else than simple medium of one Will in whose presence all are as nothing. And thus the clew to the fundamental identity as between the divine nature and the nature of man which appeared in polytheism seems hopelessly lost in the abstract monotheism which merges all reality in the one measureless Might and so leaves no room whatever for the unfolding of human personality.

And this, too, involves a corresponding reduction in the estimate put upon the dignity of man, including the moral quality of human character. In fact the ethics of Mohammedanism is lower in its demands upon the votaries of that faith than was the ethics of the religion of Apollo in its demands upon

the Greeks. The Turk of to-day is but the practical
exemplification of the empty ethics involved in the
all-annulling faith of a simple, undifferentiated monotheism. Self regulated ambition—above all, ambition toward sustained intellectual and moral self-
unfolding and refinement—must forever remain impossible to the actual votary of such faith. He acts
only from impulse. All his impulses are alike divine
to him. Hence he neither acquires nor seeks to
acquire the subtler, nobler qualities of mind which
constitute the tendencies to worthier forms of action.
Rather, all his impulses remain of the coarser sort
and become more brutal through unrestrained indulgence.

To which, as we must again remind ourselves,
there are doubtless many individual exceptions. But,
as we must also repeat, this is only because the primal
divine instinct of reason is strong enough in such
cases to annul the actual tendencies which the faith
itself necessarily involves.

Logically, the Mohammedan—-that is, the votary
of any abstract monotheistic faith—can only renounce
his reason[1] and submit himself unresistingly to the
one absolute Will as the mere instrument of that
Will. Such religion can be nothing else than on one
side the Religion of Fate, and on the other side the

[1] Cp. Above, pp. 189 and 211.

Religion of Resignation, the inevitable tendency of which is to empty ethics of all positive import. And if the votaries of modern monistic doctrines in Europe and America are in practice immeasurably superior to the crude ethics which in strict consistency must follow from such rudimentary forms of faith it is because they owe their education and entire nurture to a race whose whole spiritual life is the expression, the concrete outer form, of an infinitely richer degree of the religious tendencies inherent in the human soul.

III.

To indicate the central characteristics of the Christian religion as itself presenting in concrete form this richer degree of the religious and ethical tendencies of the human soul is the direct purpose of the remaining portion of the present essay.

And first we have to notice that the fundamental conception of Christianity is that the world—i. e., the universe—is nothing else than the outward manifestation of one eternal, infinite, absolute Personality. In this it is contrasted with all the polytheistic religions, the fundamental conception of which is that of a multiplicity of divinities, which are personal, indeed, but each of which had a beginning in time and is limited in space and in power; no one of which, therefore, is eternal, infinite and absolute.

Again, Christianity is contrasted with all simply monistic faiths in that, as we have seen. all such faiths are logically bound to deny to the ultimate, supreme Power the personal characteristics of actual intellectual self-consciousness as well as that of feeling, especially feeling in the form of personal sympathy. For such faiths the ultimate Power is the incomprehensible, the inscrutable, the Unknowable. And it can be so only because it is something foreign to mind. Nor must we overlook a further logical consequence, viz., that of regarding the human mind as having merely phenomenal existence—existence, i. e., only as phenomenon—and as therefore possessing no truly individual and abiding life, but rather as being destined to dissolve and perish.

In its inception, indeed, Christianity unquestionably presented its peculiar view of the world in pictorial rather than in reflective form. But in doing so it fixed upon a form for the expression of its fundamental conception which involved in itself the announcement of the unity and even the identity in nature of the worshiper and the object of his worship.

Nor was this without actual genetic relation with the past. Hovering vaguely, but with ever-increasing insistance, in the consciousness of the Hebrew prophets was the conception of Jahveh, their God, as deliverer, as redeemer of his people. And this deliverance came more and more to be conceived as inner and spiritual in nature. The true worshiper of Jahveh was to be delivered from his sins—even from his inner tendencies to wrong-doing—not merely from the outward consequences of his sins.

It was this vague but always deepening premonition, constituting the true ethical core of the Religion of Israel, upon which the Founder of Christianity seized as being all-essential and which he interpreted into universal form. And the figurative form which above all others he chose as best serving to set forth with richest suggestiveness this relationship between Divinity and Humanity was that of the Fatherhood of God and the Sonship of Man. He felt the eternal godhood within himself, and accordingly declared : "I and my Father are one;" and also : "Before Abraham was I am." The man Jesus, the "historical Christ," the Christ of time, felt within himself the universal, eternal Christ. He also beheld the same eternal godhood, the same universal, eternal Christ, in his followers—in those of like mind with himself—and accordingly he said to them : "After this manner, therefore, pray *ye* : '*Our* Father, . .'"

Divine Fatherhood necessarily implies divine Sonship. And this again was directly interpreted into full measure of explicit meaning. "God is a Spirit," —a Mind, a thoroughly self-conscious being—"and they who worship him must worship him in spirit and in truth,"—with honest intent and self-regulated will.

God is Mind.   Man is mind. And true worship consists in that divine-human activity which brings the
worshiper as mind, as spirit, into ever-increasing degree of practical adjustment on his part to the eternal
Type of Mind as once for all perfectly, and therefore
changelessly, realized in the one eternal Person.

And here we come upon the imaginary difficulty of
an "infinite Personality." Literally imaginary. For
it is due solely to the mistake of attempting to do
through the power of the imagination what can really
be done only through the ·power of thought.   It is
not the body that constitutes·the personality of man.
Man *as mind—that* is the real person.   And the less
adequately developed he is as person—as mind—the
less complex must be the bodily form in which he
expresses himself as person ; and conversely the more
adequately developed the individual mind as real
personal nature, the more complex must be its outward embodiment.   The mere physical organism of
man is by no means man's whole embodiment. Every
implement, from pruning-hook to printing-press, from
battle-flag to Bible, all are but further embodiments
of man as mind, as person.   Extend the conception
of Personality to its ultimate degree of infinitude, and
nothing less than infinite extension filled with infinitely manifold forms of infinitely multifarious characteristics can be conceived as sufficient for its embodiment.   Only an actual polytheist can conceive

divinity as finding its adequate expression in a single form, whether the form be that of cloud, or of river, or of tree, or of serpent, or of man.

But thus if the whole material universe is to be conceived as simply the utterance—the simple, literal self-expression or self-manifestation of Divinity as infinite Person—as absolute Mind—then it follows that to mind the universe presents no mystery wholly insoluble by mind. Nay, in such religion, worship itself, as was but just now said, consists precisely in that divine-human activity which brings the worshiper as mind into ever-increasing degree of practical adjustment on his part to the eternal Type of Mind as once for all perfectly, and therefore changelessly, realized in the eternal Person. And this self-adjustment of the individual, created mind to the eternal, absolute Mind, necessarily implies its never-ending growth in power to intellectually comprehend the eternal Person in his modes of self-manifestation in and through the forms and forces constituting the infinitely extended Universe as well as in and through the workings of the mind itself in its own non-extended modes.

Thus to the Christian Faith, in its fundamental character, there is nothing that is ultimately incomprehensible or wholly inscrutable, no hopeless background consisting in a phantasmal, mystery-crammed "Unknowable." On the contrary in its essence the Christian religion assumes the actual world to be the product of Mind and therefore wholly knowable by mind. So far, therefore, from forbidding science, or discouraging science, this religion logically demands the fullest development of science. And if the Christian Church, in one or another form, has seemed from time to time to discourage, and even actually to stand menacingly in the way of, science ; this is only because the fear of polytheism on the one side has driven those in authority—those therefore who felt the deepest sense of responsibility—to interpret the spirit of Christianity in the narrow monistic sense on the other side and thus to establish an "orthodoxy" from which all movement, all life was excluded, and which thus turned out to be itself a deadly heresy from the point of view of the central, vital doctrine of the true Christian Religion. And it is just because the Christian Religion has always in the outcome triumphed over the Christian Church, just because the inner vital Spirit has actually, though only little by little, moulded the outer form into the growing Spirit's appropriate organism instead of allowing it to harden into a rigid, changeless, external form constituting a fatal restriction upon the further unfolding of the spiritual life—it is just because of this that Christianity has come to be adopted by those races which are most active and progressive intellectually and morally, and adopted as just that religion which not only best satisfies their immediate spiritual needs, but which also in that fact, best serves to stimulate them to still further effort toward genuine spiritual development.

But thus it is evident that in the Christian Religion, rightly interpreted, Science and Revelation are but complementary terms. Science is the self-definition of the human mind as intelligence with reference to the modes of self-manifestation on the part of the divine Mind. Revelation is just this self-manifestation of the divine Mind as absolute Person to the human mind as progressively unfolding Person. It is divine stimulation leading to normal self-activity on the part of man, the end whereof is man's own self-realization. Nor can this be conceived—i. e., really thought—save as a wholly rational process. In other words, in accordance with the central conception of the Christian Faith, Revelation can have real meaning only as the normal interrelation between the divine Intelligence and individual human intelligence. The Christian Religion involves the serene assurance that the World—that is, the Universe—as the expression of the absolute, divine Mind, is rational through and through, and thus necessarily implies the endless progressive development of individual man as a rational being capable of progressively comprehending thewhole .

Thus the attempt to comprehend the World and to account for the origin of man in strictly scientific fashion—an attempt leading in modern times to such magnificent results—is by no means in conflict with, but rather is it wholly in the true spirit of, the Christian Religion. It is precisely this religion, and this alone, that gives the real clew to and also unequivocally affirms the infinite worth and destiny of man. And modern science confirms this affirmation in the very fact of the splendid achievements crowning the efforts of man as mind to comprehend the world in its total compass. The total conception of the evolution of man is but the obverse aspect of the total conception of the self-unfolding of God.

It is, indeed, as already pointed out, only through such evolutional process that man, even in his physiological character, can really be *thought* as arising, however easily one may *imagine* him to have arisen in some other way.

But in this very process, let us repeat, purpose is clearly manifest throughout, binding the whole process into one and showing it to be, what the Christian Religion has in truth always insisted, simply the expression of one conscious, creative Power knowing the end from the beginning, and unswervingly working from the beginning, throughout the process, to the end. On the other hand it is just this primordial factor of a conscious, purposing, creative Power which, in its haste, the current evolutional theory altogether ignores, or else, in its false modesty, simply consigns to the limbo of the Unknowable. For which reason the evolution theory, as currently advocated, falls to pieces of its own weight as refusing to allow for any really original, initiative, organically self-unfolding Power, excluding which the process itself becomes wholly unthinkable.[1]

Besides, as mind, man is himself a conscious, self-defining, self-unfolding power including original, initiative impulse. And nothing could be more illogical than the attempt to derive a being of such character from elements in which that character is conspicuously lacking and through a process from which that character is wholly excluded. In fact, Darwin himself everywhere assumes the teleological principle, though his teleology is that of the agnostic who, while recognizing purpose in the forms and forces of nature, is so modest as not to lift his eyes sufficiently to see the great purposing Power without which the "purposiveness" of nature is too far removed from anything substantial even to deserve being described as "shadowy."

On the other hand, let this great purposing Power

---

[1] There is something really pathetic in Mr. Spencer's solemn adoption of the term "persistence," in place of the term, "conservation," (of "Force") as a means of getting rid of any shadow of suggestion of a "conserver"—as if persistence, in its last analysis, must not prove to be essentially nothing else than infinite, self-directed self-conservation. (Cf. foot-note to heading of Chapter II, Part II, of his *First Principles of Philosophy.* N. Y. Ed. p. 185).

be once frankly recognized in its character of self-defining, self-unfolding Energy or primal, creative Mind, and at once the evolution of man becomes comprehensible. For whatever the forms and whatever the process through which he has come to be, in his animal nature, the primal Cause is seen to be adequate to the final cause or end of his being. And at the same time, let us repeat, it is clear that whatever the ancestry through which he may be said to have derived his special qualities of mind and body, yet it is from his primal Ancestor, the eternal Mind, that he has derived his fundamental nature as mind. Not otherwise than upon the basis of divine Ancestry can the descent of man be accounted for in truly scientific way. Nor can too great emphasis be put upon this fundamental truth. And thus the doctrine' of the divine Sonship as applied to man is found, on careful reflection, to be something more than a mere figure of speech. Rather in its essence the expression is justified by the strictest scientific analysis.

We say that man is the creature of instinct, of inherited tendencies. And it is so. It is so also, as we noticed at the outset, that for the individual his instincts are predetermined qualities. Hence as an instinctive being man is, as was noticed, predestined. Nay, as inheriting from innumerable divergent lines, he is at birth predestined to endlessly divergent action. That is, he is foredoomed to endless self-contradiction. He is predestined to sleep and to wake physiologically. He is equally predestined to the sleep of psychical indifference. But he is also predestined to the waking of inquiry. Predestined to credulity and predestined to doubt. Born a bundle of contradictions. Born also with a primal unity of nature which cannot but awake sooner or later in the form of an irrepressible sense of the necessity of practically unifying the multiform contradictions of his rudimentary existence and of reconciling its inherent contradictions.

And this again is the divine instinct of reason within him. It is, in truth, the secret of all his marvelous premonitions—premonitions leading to his ceaseless struggle toward a higher stage of being. It is the secret of his inborn sense of the perfection of Truth and of Beauty and of Goodness. And every tremor of dissatisfaction with what now is, together with its complement of deepened longing for richer degrees of life is but a further stage in the awaking of the God-consciousness within him.

Man is the Son of God and therefore "thinks it no robbery to make himself equal with God." He is heir to all things because his central inheritance is that of infinite Personality. And as this is true of each and every man, then with the primal Person, and with every man who has clear sense of the full significance of divine Personality, there can in the very nature of the case be "no distinguishing of persons." Each has infinite worth and should show forth infinite dignity, while each should receive from each the reverence due to a being thus divinely constituted. Thus all are equal, for all have the same divine Ancestry, and hence the same divine nature, to fulfil which requires endless existence on the part of each individual member of the race. So that, as we may notice by the way, individual immortality is of necessity involved in this conception of man.

It is this, too, that constitutes the true basis for asserting the common brotherhood of Man. In their very nature all men are equal. And the religion that assumes the infinite worth of each and every human soul could not consistently do otherwise than address each with the solemn warning: "Call no man master!" for in so doing he must abdicate his own rank as citizen-king in the Republic of God; just as, on the other hand, he who demands to be called "master" proves by that fact his own utter ignorance of true Personality—that central characteristic constituting the essential significance of every human life, and hence necessarily and forever condemning alike the despot and whoever submits to despotism.

Polytheism reduces the gods to the level of man. Christianity lifts man as man to a divine level as showing him to be of equal nature with God. And in doing so it presents a final and absolute standard of Right. That standard is based not in the will of one or another of a multitude of capricious divinities; nor in the inscrutable determinations of an irresistible and wholly arbitrary Power; but in the essential nature of Reason itself. In such religion the essential, central claim on the part of each is that of fullest, freest conditions, positive and negative, tending toward his own self-realization as a rational or divinely constituted being. And because this is an equal right on the part of each as toward all others it necessarily implies an equal and corresponding obligation on the part of each toward every other to aid in the common work tending toward perfect self-unfolding on the part of all.

Thus in proclaiming the doctrine of the divine descent of man, implying the essential divinity of human nature, Christianity announces the typical oneness of the race, the common brotherhood of man, and also the infinite worth and dignity of each individual member of the race. And precisely in so doing it sets forth the one sufficient ground of a truly rational and vital Ethics as pointing to self-realization on the part of man as a rationally constituted being through his own social-individual self-discipline and self-activity. Thus the human race is gathered into, or rather it is recognized as normally constituting, one divine Family. And the principle of relationship within the Family is no longer that of fear, no longer that of mere resignation, but that of mutual recognition, mutual comprehension, mutual esteem. In a word it is the *Religion of love.* The Christian Religion is the one religion of the world having for its care the principle of Personality consciously held and adequately comprehended. It is therefore the one religion of the world which from its very nature demands of each and every member of the race moral conduct of the highest order and upon purely rational grounds.

Even in polytheistic religions the divine instinct of reason in man has often developed the sense of the divine Sonship of man.[1] But for the most part in these religions this foreshadowing of the truth as to the relationship between humanity and divinity was of so crude a character that men gained little and the gods lost much in dignity through the grossly imagined forms embodying what were at best but vague guesses at the truth. Indeed it was not the divinity of humanity that was apprehended so much as the divinity in lower measure on the part of individual men of

---

[1] The familiar line: "For we are also his offspring," which appears in Acts xvii, 28, Paul is represented as quoting in his address to the Athenians, and as explicitly referring it to "certain of their own poets." The line has been found in the Stoic Cleanthes who flourished about 270 B. C. Two centuries earlier, indeed, the thought was already a familiar one to the Greeks. In "The Suppliants" of Æschylos (cf. Plumptre's translation), the Chorus, as the prophetic medium through which the poet expresses his highest notions of the divine World declare:

long past ages. Such men were, in fact, the heroes of a past that never was, heroes who could be believed in only by a people whose imaginings had never yet been brought to the test of critical examination. Before that test all such imaginings could not but fade into mere spectral form, leaving faith without substantial ground for its continuance and reducing the standard of morality to individual caprice.[2] On the other hand the more rigidly the essential conceptions of the Christian Religion are examined the more are they found to satisfy the demands of reason and to show that the fundamental basis of all morality is to be sought in the inmost nature of man himself as the ceaselessly advancing, forever reappearing Son of God. On this basis "Right" is whatever tends to the enriching of the essential life of man considered

---

"And so the whole land shouts with one accord,
'Lo, a race sprung from him, the Lord of life,
   In very deed Zeus-born !'
*   *   *   *   *   *
He is our Father, author of our life,
The King whose right hand worketh all his will,
Our line's great author, in his counsels deep,
   Recording things of old,
Directing all his plans, the great work-master Zeus."
Meanwhile Cleanthes, like Æschylos, was still a pantheist, though even the latter is not without indications of a higher and more spiritual faith, as at least the following lines attributed to him would go to prove :
"The air is Zeus, Zeus the Earth, and Zeus the heaven,
Zeus all that is, *and what transcends them all.*"

[2] As the Greeks lost faith in their gods their philosophy took the form of reckless sophistry and their ethics developed into the grossest hedonism.

as divine in nature and hence as destined to endless and endlessly intensifying conscious existence. "Wrong" is whatever tends to impoverish the essential life of man so regarded. The standard is not capricious and arbitrary, but fixed as the laws of eternally self-consistent Reason.

And as for the simple monistic form of faith of which Mohammedanism presents the most conspicuous example, the fact that, as a faith, it must logically suppress all tendencies leading toward a higher culture, could not but reduce the morality of its votaries even to a lower level than that of the more advanced polytheistic faiths—a conclusion already indicated on a preceding page, and of which practical illustration is presented by the Turks of to-day in contrast with the ancient Greeks and Romans.

Such monistic faith is in fact nothing else than a transition form which proves to be a simple and utter negation in which gods and men alike are annulled as individual existences—a spiritual night in which dawning Personality seems wholly quenched.

On the other hand the Christian Religion in its essential character not only represents the highest degree of the human spirit thus far attained ; but also its central doctrine of the spirituality of God and the divine Sonship of Man already involves in itself the highest conceivable ethical principle—the principle which demands the ceaseless self-unfolding of man as Mind, and hence of man as the divine Son, into ever richer degrees of realized likeness with God as the one divine Father—the one eternally perfect Mind.

IX.

ETERNITY.

A THREAD IN THE WEAVING OF A LIFE.

I.

Among my earliest recollections are those of the pictures of hell which I saw from Sunday to Sunday in a country church. They were drawn with wide-sweeping gestures by the frenzied preacher, and colored by the wails of the devout in the congregation. The pictures were balanced by the favorite hymns emphasizing the endless bliss of that place—

> "Where congregations ne'er break up
> And Sabbaths have no end,"

Especially was I impressed with the conception :

> "When we've been there ten thousand years,
>   Bright shining as the sun,
> We've no less days to sing God's praise
> Than when we first begun."

The drawl of the singing only served to intensify the significance of the lines to me, and each repetition filled me with a deeper awe and terror.

Out of what chaos of childish talk I can not say, but in some way there developed one day between a

playmate and myself the question : How far is it to
the end of the world ? Where my playmate went I
have no recollection. But I know that I ran eagerly
to my mother for the answer I doubted not she would
give. She was repeating my question, as a mother
will, when my father chanced to pass through the
room. He understood from the tone that the question was mine ; and, without stopping, he said in an
abrupt, half-bantering manner, ''The world has no
end.'' The same vague terror thrilled me as when
listening to the voices of the congregation wailing
out the hymns declaring the endless life of the saved.
I was repelled by it and soon lost myself in the usual
physical life of childhood. This I now infer from the
fact that memory shows no record for long afterward.

At the age of nine or ten years the idea of endless
duration flashed upon me with perfect clearness. And
the terror I experienced was beyond expression. I
had just gone into a very small ''house'' which I had
been building and which was barely large enough
for me to turn in. I had just seated myself with the
satisfaction of achievement when all the nebulous impressions of former years suddenly assumed perfect
order, and I felt that my existence must be endless.
It seemed as if all the world were crumbling in upon
me and crushing me. I hurried out of the cramped
place and ran again to my mother. I asked her
whether it was really true that I must live always if

I went to heaven. She seemed startled by the question, but answered as Puritan mother must, and asked quietly if I did not want to live always. I was too full of terror to answer, and only asked whether I must live always if I went to the *"other* place." The same stern Puritan faith answered unhesitatingly that those who go there must also live always. There was no subtilizing, no attempt to turn me away from the theme, to her so solemn, to me so dreadful. She went on about her work while I sat on the floor and sobbed out my despair. At that moment the prospect of endless existence, even though it be in heaven, was to me a very present hell. I had not yet heard of the "soul-sleeper's" doctrine with its annihilation of the wicked; and when I did hear of the doctrine, it was with such strong condemnation on the part of those in whose wisdom I had unshaken confidence that it seemed to me one of the surest of all the ways mapped out to *Sheol*.

Just as I reached the age of twelve years, my parents—pioneers in spirit—moved to a Western prairie. The summer proved a somewhat severe trial to my health. One day, while lying on a cot, my mother near me, I suddenly felt myself caught up to a height immeasureable, beyond all visible objects, and while I called out an agonized "good-bye" to my mother, I felt myself bound to a huge iron wheel that rolled without the slightest jar and with tremendous velocity along a thin, perfectly straight line of fire stretched through otherwise empty space. I knew that I must go in this way to the end of the line, and I knew that the line was endless. It was but a moment, and yet in that moment I felt the doom of an eternity with nothing but the iron wheel and the track of fire, and my soul destined to yearn endlessly for all that it held dear. When I was quiet again my mother spoke gently to me, moistened my lips and brow, smoothed back my hair and presently I fell asleep. But for long afterward the vision would recur to me at times and awaken unspeakable terror. And with it my terror at the thought of endless existence became more intense. It was only long after its occurrence that I realized how truly the vision symbolized the state of a "lost" soul, which can have become "lost" only by breaking connection with all that is good and worthy and enduring, and must therefore be whirled through eternity on whatever fiery track the iron wheel of its destiny may chance to roll.

II.

In school I found reminders of the same contradiction that met me elsewhere. In a text-book of arithmetic I found time defined as a "measured portion of duration." The definition seemed unquestionable, and yet from it I could only gather the impression that time must be understood to be just a measured portion of the measureless. And yet this dreadful ''measureless'' I was myself destined to measure. In my thought it was indeed a hopeless contradiction. Yet I doubted not of the fact. I felt myself bound to accept the impossible as the real.

Again, geography unfolded the same contradictions. Here it was, indeed, not endless duration, but boundless extension. I had chanced to be so taught the facts of geography that, instead of being nothing more than mere words, they seemed substantial realities which I could clearly picture to myself as existing there side by side in space. Especially, I had received a vivid impression of the solar system, with the immense orbits of its members.

By degrees this became assimilated in my consciousness ; and occasion soon came—as in such cases ''occasion'' must always come—to crystallize the vague impression into form. It was on a summer evening. I was following the cows homeward along a path in a ravine, and looking up now and then at the sky. As the twilight deepened a star gleamed out through the blue depths. Suddenly, and for the first time in my life, I felt vividly—vividly enough for the feeling to become a clearly defined thought—that, in looking at a star, I was looking at an immeasurably distant world. And the blue vault ! In the same instant that had vanished. I knew I was looking into the *depths*, not at the "floor of heaven." With this there was a sudden sense of giddiness, as if the foundations of the world had that moment been wrenched away, and it and I and all were falling swiftly—whither?

It was the definite beginning of my mental reconstitution, though I was then far enough from being aware of it.

III.

Years after, on the march and in battle—for I was just old enough to be accepted among the first volunteers in the late war—I saw how impossible it is to adjust a greatly enlarged and highly complex human world to the pattern provided by the simple primitive life of the ancient Hebrews. It was as if the friction of this great struggle had set my Puritan faith aglow, raising it to the point of fusion and plasticity. I had seen men in blue and men in gray lying where the demonic tempest had left them, with eyes strained widely open as if the unspeakable mystery of eternity had that moment for the first time dawned upon them. And these men—what had their lives been? What were their lives now? What were their lives eternally *to be?*

I had left school to take part in this struggle. And the experience of the struggle only intensified the problem of which I had begun to seek the solution in school. Thus it was that when the struggle ended I was again in school, seeking what help the school might give.

And yet, in school my teachers seemed concerned with little else than syntax and mathematical symbols. So that, when I asked them to help me construe a soul or to find the *locus* of my own existence, they repeated a text of Scripture and referred me to the conventional co-ordinates.

Evidently, then, I must look for help elsewhere. And I was like a beginner in astronomy, who must grope about in the night, through an instrument which he little understands the use of, to find the true polar star. Guides to reading I had none. I went often to the book-stand, and found little else than the usual trivialities.

A fellow-student talked admiringly of Dr. Holland's *Bitter-sweet*—think of it !—as solving the problem of evil. I read, and found nothing but bitter. If evil was to be accounted for as a necessary instrumentality in the development of good, then "evil" is not evil, but good. It was substantially the argument of the country preacher, that "If Adam had not sinned there would have been no occasion for the coming of the Redeemer, and hence man could never have known the extent of the divine love to man." (Though in this the country preacher was not without shining examples, such as Anselm.) Dr. McCosh's *Divine Government* fell into my hands. Surely this would tell me the thing I longed to know. In reality, the argument became focused for me into something like this: the things we know in part are to be explained by the things we don't know at all.

At least, these two books served as an irritant. If the received dogmas drove reason into such self-stulti-fications as these, then there must be something radically wrong with the received dogmas. For reason can only be reason by being self-consistent. And man is man only in the possession and use of reason.

While my school-days continued I heard scarcely a reference to the modern English school of thinkers. If Spencer or Darwin were mentioned at all, it was with a condescending smile or with an expression of horror — much as economists of the schools now refer to Henry George or to Karl Marx. Of German philosophy, not a word. It was while teaching a winter term of school in the country that I fell upon Agassiz's papers on the Glacial Epoch, as they appeared in the *Atlantic Monthly*. At the same time, in the school library of the district, I found Carlyle's *Heroes and Hero-Worship*. Here were two streams of vitality; and they proved a substantial relief from the sermons of a good man who came to the neighborhood once a month to make plain to the people the way of truth, and who labored zealously for two hours one Sunday to show his congregation that all storms with their destructive character were due solely to the vicious Prince of the Power of the Air.

Happily, school-days come to an end ; and when I had once realized that I was no longer to answer the call of a professor and report upon tasks assigned, I found my way to what seemed a favorable location for work, and began seeking everywhere for light—in magazines and reviews, and especially through the shelves of a library which a Western senator had been wise and generous enough to establish in the town.

Carlyle's *Sartor Resartus* proved somewhat puzzling at first, with its Titan extravaganza ; though out of it all I at length gathered the significant conception that all objects appealing to the senses are, in truth, nothing else than the transitory forms, the mere wrappage of spirit, or mind. Body, that which occupies space, is nothing more than a suit of clothes, or raw material for such, which mind puts on and off, wears out and flings to the rag-heap.

It was well for me that that conception took shape when it did, and that it was reinforced in a subtle way through the influence of Max Muller's *Science of Language*, which I read with intense delight. It was well to have this clear impression of the power of mind over materiality take shape then ; for I soon came under the spell of Spencer and Darwin and Huxley, whose works so constantly emphasize and so admirably present the aspects of truth unfolded in the material world as to tend inevitably toward a one-sided, materialistic view of the world on the part of the young and eager inquirer.

The *First Principles* of Mr. Spencer was of special value to me. Its statements of the antinomies, or seeming contradictions in thought, were at once a stimulus and a means of classification. In it I found wide and systematic formulation of the contradictions I had so long felt. And the more clearly those contradictions came to be formulated, the less endurable I felt them to be. And if the "reconciliation" offered in the *First Principles* proved to be by no means a satisfying one to me, yet only so much the more did it bring me to feel the absolute need of finding a perfect reconciliation.

Indeed, hope of reconciliation seemed to beckon along the lines of investigation presented in the positive portion of the *First Principles*. The discussion of the Indestructibility of Matter, the Continuity of Motion and the Persistence of Force all pointed to a working Unit, which was, indeed, not related to any other than itself. In that sense it did indeed seem to be "unconditioned." And yet just from that fact it must itself include all conditions, all relations. Nay, it must not merely include them as a vessel includes its contents. As the *persistent Unit* it must include all conditions and relations in the sense of unfolding them within itself as the modes of its own existence.

And, indeed, this conception has already become measurably explicit in the language of science. For what had previously been spoken of as "forces" are now classed as merely modes of that one Force which persists.

And this persistent Force could not be conceived save as having ever persisted—save as ever continuing to persist. The "forces" were measurable. And yet they were only modes of the one persistent Force which was *measureless*. And so I seemed bound to my iron wheel again with the doom of measuring the measureless renewed. And this feeling was rendered increasingly vivid by the disclosures of geology with the accompanying evidences of the continuity of life in the development of our world.

Most impressive of all, in this respect, was the ac. count which Mr. Spencer gives of the Nebular Hypothesis. Time expanded to my mind until it seemed indeed to vanish into eternity—a mere measured portion of Duration. Spencer and Lyell and Darwin and Huxley—what a magnificent, what an appalling, revelation they had formulated! And so much the more appalling as it seemed clashing ruinously with the other long implicitly trusted divine Revelation. No wonder that in the midst of all this poor Hugh Miller, struggling desperately through seas of doubt in search of the Golden Fleece of Truth, should be caught and crushed by such Symplegades!

Crossing a brook one day, I looked down at the bare strata of limestone. Crinoids were visible at every break in the rock. Just a glimpse between the edges of the leaves of how old a book! And with his hammer, aided by the occasional crowbar and explosive of the railway builder, the scientist has been for a little while working his way into this huge volume! How fragmentary, even at the best, his work must still be! Nay, the book itself, bound in the "everlasting hills," has gathered its meaning through myriads of ages, and, according to the estimate of science, must sooner or later be dashed into nebula again, all its rich, slowly gathered significance blotted out forever. And as I stood there I thought how men, in their pygmy presumption, move about over the rugged binding of this huge volume and construct their books, fondly imagining that these works of theirs shall last forever!

All this was leading up to a conception of which I was then, indeed, altogether unaware. The conception suddenly assumed definite formulation one evening while I was reading, in a history of philosophy, the theory of Averroes. This Arab interpreter of Aristotle had caught eagerly at the idea of unity and continuity unfolded in the work of the Greek, and had interpreted that idea in the Oriental sense. The Divinity is all. There is but one "active Intellect." Whatever of reality there is in man is but an emanation from God, and must be re-absorbed into the Divine substance. The Mohammedan, looking into the pages of Aristotle, arrived at the same pantheistic conclusion as did the Brahman looking into the swiftly changing manifestations of the world about him.

Could it be that this was the truth which science, in these latter times, was also unfolding in its discoveries as to the continuity of motion and the persistence of Force? For the moment I could not resist the conclusion that such was the case. And I experienced an inexpressible sense of relief at the thought that, though I might be a passing mode of the Eternal, yet I was, after all, not the embodiment of that dreadful contradiction which my early training had led me to suppose myself to be. The Divine is doubtless eternal. But all ''else'' is transitory. There is one Force that persists. All ''else'' is but a passing mode of that Force. Or, as Mr. Edwin Arnold has since expressed it, ''The gods but live ; only Brahm endures ''

V.

For a time I rested in this feeling.   But for a time only ; for I soon discovered that it was no more than a feeling. When I began to examine it more closely I discovered that it could not stand the test of analysis. It might be true enough that all physically constituted units were destined to dissolution. It might well be that an "atom"—an absolutely indivisible unit—is here wholly unthinkable as a reality. But there seemed to be characteristics in man that could not be accounted for on any theory of the merely "physical basis of life." So that, after all, the central problem of my life was not solved ; and the former sense of needed solution was renewed and redoubled in urgency.

So far I had trusted mainly to the English school of thinkers for guidance. There now fell into my hands the first numbers of the *Journal of Speculative Philosophy*, with its translations from and interpre·tations of the works of leading German thinkers.

I had, indeed, found reference in Mr. Spencer's *First Principles* to the philosophy of Kant. But these references were only incidental, and by way of accepting the "antinomies"—the alleged imbecilities of reason. But what had Kant really said of positive import ? In the *Journal* I found frequent and highly appreciative references to his *Critique of Pure Reason.*

In company with others,[1] I set about the study of this book, and found in it for the first time ground that became firmer the more I examined it. A critical study of the nature of thought itself and of the

---

[1] This group was the "*Kant Club*," of St. Louis, under the leadership of Dr. Wm. T. Harris. Several winters were spent in studying, first, Kant's *Critique of Purc Reason;* afterward, Hegel's *Logic.*

necessary conditions of the exercise of thought—that proved to be the really indispensable preliminary to all really systematic thinkiug. I began to discover with the aid of Kant that the "relativity of knowledge," to which the English school of thinkers were so entirely pledged, was an ambiguous and therefore misleading phrase. Very commonly the phrase was used to mean the relativity that is of necessity involved *in* knowledge. So far the meaning was legitimate enough. Doubtless there can be no knowledge that excludes relation. Especially and primarily there can be no knowledge save as involving the relation of a knowing subject to a known object. Subject and object are unquestionably correlative terms. But, then, when I think of my own act of knowing, and analyze the act into its correlative phases of act-of-knowing on the one hand and object-known on the other, I have already made my very act-of-knowing an *object* of my own knowledge. I can not know the correlatives of subject and object as such without making *each* an *object* of my thinking. The thinking unit thinks of itself as a thinking unit. That is, the subject, or thinking unit, necessarily becomes an object to itself. And this is expressed in the term *consciousness*, and is doubly emphasized in the term *self-consciousness*.

Whence there is to be noted this distinction : that, on the one hand, in the experience of the individual, the relativity exhibited between subject and object does indeed often present the object as a unit separate and apart from the subject; but that, on the other hand, in all self-examination the relativity subsists wholly within the knowing subject, which in all such acts proves to be its own object. And this is necessarily *implied* in every possible act of knowing.

It thus turns out that the fundamental relation in knowing is the relation of the subject to itself; it is self-relation And, while relativity is necessarily involved *in thought*, there is no real justification for saying that thought, as such, is involved in relation. Indeed, to insist upon the *absolute relativity* of thought is to insist that thought is related to something wholly different from thought. And the relativist himself is ready enough to insist that one can really know nothing else than his own mental states.

But he also insists that these states are still subject to something beyond us which we neither do nor can know. And so all our knowledge is built up of "experiences;" and, as we can never transcend "experience," it is evident that all our "ideas" must be accounted for as relative. as dependent, as experimentally derived. Thus it is that our idea of space is said to be derived from our experience of resistance, and our idea of time from our feeling of difference or change.

But Kant puts all this on a wholly different basis.

The question is not how we come to have the idea of space and of time.   Doubtless those ideas *are* derived from our experiences; and yet it is also beyond doubt that our "ideas," of whatever type, constitute the very core of all our "experiences."   But the essential question is: given the ideas of space and time, critically to examine them and discover the degree of their validity on the one hand and, on the other hand, to find their precise relation to those facts of our consciousness which have reference to space and time.   Could I perceive a tree or a bird or a star otherwise than as in space?   The question brings its own answer.   And the significant conclusion follows that space is a necessary condition of all my perceptions of external objects.   It is only by analysis that I become aware of this fact ; but the fact itself is unquestionably present as a factor in every possible perception of such object.   From which it follows that space is a necessary condition or mode of my perceptions, and in that respect is subjective—is a relation that subsists in my consciousness.

But it is just as unquestionable that space is a necessary condition or relation of the objects perceived. They are at such and such distance from one another and from me.   And since I can not perceive objects otherwise than as in these relations, then space is a necessary relation of object to object, and is therefore objective no less than subjective.   So that when one comes and says that, according to Kant's interpretation, "The head is not so much in space as space is in the head," there is strong temptation to comment : Very likely—at least for the one so reading Kant. In the same way, time, as the necessary condition of our perceptions of change, is at once condition of the perceptions and of the changes perceived, and hence is at once both subjective and objective.

But also since space can not be conceived as objectively anything more than the necessary negative condition of all outer limitation, it is impossible to conceive of it as itself in any way limited. Any boundary we may assume *for* space is at once seen to be merely an assumed boundary *within* space. It is true that I can not *imagine* space as unlimited, but neither can I *think* space as limited. I can not *imagine* time as unlimited, but neither can I *think* time as anything else than a measured phase of duration. When I attempt to measure space or time I am hopelessly baffled. They can not be conceived in the sense of imagining them. One can only conceive them in the sense of thinking them. One can not imagine the infinite, though he may think it; just as one can not really think a centaur, though he may imagine it.

It is just this failure to distinguish with perfect precision between thinking and imagining that seemed to me a fatal defect in Mr. Spencer's work—following, as he did, only too closely in this respect Sir W. Hamilton and Mr. Mansel ; the refusal to recognize which distinction had enabled the latter to "refute" German philosophy.   With each of these writers the term "conception" is constantly used as equivalent to "pictorial representation."   The "inconceivable" is with them "the unimaginable" *or* "unthinkable." And it is evidently by this confusion of terms that Mr. Spencer was led to his "Unknowable."

VI.

With the help of Kant, this at length became clear to me.   And, as it did so, I began to realize that I had made a further step in clarifying my own mind concerning the problem that had all along pressed upon me with such force.   Space and time were two undeniable modes of existence, both subjective and objective.   And I had now come to recognize that they can not be other than infinite.   They were in a twofold sense, then, modes of my own existence. They were modes of my subjective or spiritual existence, and also modes of my objective or bodily existence.   Doubtless they are *in themselves* only mere blank forms ; but they are infinite forms, which somehow I seem destined, after all, to realize in my own existence.   For, as it is impossible to conceive a boundary to space beyond which there is not still other space, and as it is impossible to conceive a limit

to time beyond which there is not still other time, so
I began to discover that there is no conceivable boundary for intelligence beyond which intelligence may
not pass.

I noted, too, that when considered in respect of
their infinite divisibility, space and time are manifestly modes of finite existence ; whereas, considered
with respect to their boundless extension, they are as
manifestly modes of infinite existence And infinite
existence—what could that be but the total of all
Reality organically unfolded into every possible phase
of finite existence expressive of every possible mode
of an infinite Power ! And for myself—I could only
be a mode of that infinitely developed Power, though
also, it appeared, a mode destined to infinite development.

Evidently, too, that Power could be no other than
the ultimate Unit which Mr. Spencer names the
"Unknowable." And yet, "unknowable" though it
be, Mr. Spencer refers to it as having an "established
order."[1] He calls it the "Unknowable Power,"[2] and
yet, almost in the same breath, speaks of it as "manifesting itself."[3] Nay, he is also able to discover "the
existence of knowable likenesses and differences
among the manifestations of that Power" as well as
"a resulting segregation of the manifestations into
those of subject and object."[4]

------

[1] *First Principles*, (New York ed.), p. 117. [2] Op. Cit.,
p. 157. [3] Op. Cit., p. 154 and elsewhere. [4] Op. Cit., p. 157.

True, he claims that these are in the main no more than "postulates." But he also claims to have "shown that, though by the relativity of our thought we are eternally debarred from knowing or conceiving Absolute Being, yet that this very *relativity* of our thought necessitates that vague consciousness of Absolute Being which no mental effort can suppress.."[1] So that, after all, Absolute Being does prove to be relative to the relative. "No mental effort can suppress" that fact.

And yet, though there are "knowable likenesses and differences among the manifestations of that [ultimate] Power," the Absolute is declared to have "neither *relation* nor its elements—difference and likeness."[2] It is the "Unconditioned." Yet this unconditioned or "non-relative" is "an actual existence." And nothing could be more certain than this. For by the very conditions of thought "an indefinite [doubtless he means : imperfectly defined] consciousness of Absolute Being is necessitated."[3] Nor is this all. For "asserting the persistence of Force is but another mode of asserting an Unconditional Reality, without beginning or end."[4] So that "the phenomena of evolution have to be deduced from the Persistence of Force,"[5] while the "universally co-

<hr>

[1] Op Cit., p. 163. [2] Op Cit., p. 162. [3] Op. Cit., p. 190. [4] Op. Cit., p. 189. [5] Op. Cit., p. 398. It is of no little importance to note that while, as Mr. Spencer says, the phenomena of evolution have to be *deduced* from the Persistence of Force, *our knowledge* of the latter is attained necessarily through *induction* from the former.

existent forces of attraction and repulsion are indeed
the complementary aspects of that absolutely persistent Force which is the ultimate datum of consciousness.''[1]

Surely, I thought, though the Absolute may be in
some sense the Unknowable, it seems far enough
from being absolutely unknowable in the pages of
Mr. Spencer or elsewhere. And I was especially impressed with the fact that this ultimate Unit is absolutely *known* to be "without beginning or end." I
could not but regard the conception of the Persistence
of Force as being perfectly valid; and yet in Mr.
Spencer's exposition it only served to further intensify in my mind the idea of eternity as boundless
Past and boundless Future, while the Present seemed
only a phantom rushing from infinity to infinity.

VII.

I supplemented my study of Kant by a prolonged
effort to thread the mazes of the Hegelian dialectic—
the most elaborate, as it is the most rigidly consistent,
of all the attempts that have been made to arrange
the fundamental categories of thought in the order of
their complexity and at the same time to show the
necessity of their sequence. And yet, however un-
expectedly, it was in the work of a poet that I found

---

[1] Op. Cit., p 514.

the immediate clew by which to reconcile the contradiction that had so long perplexed and distressed me.
Schiller had been an eager and appreciative student
of Kant, and with the poet's gift he had seized upon
the most concrete human aspects of Kant's philosophy   Kant had declared in the introduction to his
Critique of Pure Reason that the ultimate, transcen-
dently significant problems for human intelligence
are God, Freedom and Immortality. Schiller took
up these conceptions and based upon them his theory
of the Beautiful. He assumed that there is but one
ideal or type of personality. Different persons are
but different conscious units, struggling in various
ways towards the realization of that type. The perfect realization of that type is the perfect Person, ''the
absolute subject'' or God.[1]

Thus, freedom for the individual is to be attained
only through the realization of this Divine type for
and in the individual's own life. And because the
type is infinite its realization must involve infinite
duration, or immortality. That is the way leading
man to God. And because the Divine activity is
without external resistance it is forever unwearied.
And this is the absolute perfection of play—the unrestricted and therefore unwearied accomplishment of
results that must thus be faultless, and hence prove

---

[1] See Schiller's *Æsthetical Letters*, xi. to xv. inclusive.

the ceaseless occasion of divine joy. And in struggling towards the fulfillment of this divine type in his own life individual man participates unceasingly in the Divine life, progressively attains freedom, approximates the Divine, and realizes immortality.

VIII.

All this Schiller more or less plainly intimates. And now with this clew the doctrine of evolution presented to my mind a new and far richer significance than it had previously done. A distinction that I had not as yet been able to formulate clearly now became perfectly plain. The distinction was this : The term "unconditioned" can only mean that the ultimate Power or Cause is all-inclusive, and therefore unconditioned, in this sense only : that there is nothing whatever beyond it to impose conditions upon it ; while, on the other hand, and for that very reason, all conditioned existences must be involved *in* Absolute Being as modes *of* it. And since the Ultimate Power as Absolute Being can not change, there must unquestionably be an "established order" in its "manifestations." In other words, the ultimate, all-inclusive Power is perfect in its activity ; its activity is in accordance with an absolutely perfect, unalterable Method.

But by this established order or method the ultimate Power gives rise to conditioned being—unfolds an infinite series of concretely realized conditions within itself—and thus proves to be indeed, in one respect, the Unconditioned ; but also, and not less truly, it proves in another sense to be the absolutely *self*-condition. And, this distinction once clearly seized, others followed as necessary corollaries.

IX.

Thus, since in its modes of activity it manifests itself, and since we may become increasingly aware of the character and complexity of these modes, then it seems impossible to reject the conclusion that while the ultimate Power, or Force, or Energy,[1] as being absolute, self-limited, self-sufficing, and therefore perfect or infinite, is ''unknowable'' in the sense that no created mind can ever acquire an exhaustive, detailed knowledge of it, yet in the very fact that it ''manifests itself'' in accordance with a ''fixed order'' or changeless method, the ultimate Power proves to be progressively *knowable* to the created mind. And the extent to which it is knowable by such mind can only find its ultimate limit in the ultimate limit of mental growth on the part of a created thinking unit.

------

[1] Physicists now insist, significantly enough, on the use of the term ''Energy'' where the term ''Force'' was formerly used, as if feeling that the ultimate Power must be spontaneous and personal.

Nor is this all. For Absolute Being, or the all-comprising Energy, can not but be wholly and ceaselessly active. Ceasing to act is ceasing to exist; and ceasing to act in any degree is ceasing to exist in just that degree. But that something should become nothing is "unthinkable." The idea of the absolute persistence of Energy is, let us repeat, precisely the same as that of "an unconditioned reality without beginning or end." In fact, the persistence of energy is an "ultimate truth given in our mental constitution;"[1] whence I could not but conclude that causation, or creation—that is, the self-unfolding of Absolute Being—is an eternally self-equal fact; and I recalled, with a new comprehension of their significance, the phrases I had so often heard repeated in childhood and youth, declaring the Divinity to be "without variableness or shadow of turning," as being "yesterday, to-day, and forever the same," as being the "high and lofty One who inhabiteth Eternity."

Still further, I could not but think that Absolute Being. "manifesting itself" in accordance with a "fixed order" or method, must, in that very fact, be perfectly aware of itself in both its method and its manifestations. By no mental effort could I suppress the conviction that assumed shape in my mind, to the

---

[1] Spencer's *First Principles*, p. 191.

effect that the ultimate Energy, so unfailingly perfect in the method of its activity and self-manifestation, must, in its perfect self-guidance, be a perfect Intelligence.

X.

And here the objection of "anthropomorphism" seemed to find its answer. Men have conceived the Divine to be embodied in trees and rivers and clouds and serpents and fire and planets and sun and stars, as well as in human form. Was there no germ of truth in all that? I reflected that a thought is not complete until it receives expression, outer manifestation, explicit form or embodiment. It also occurred to me that the more complex the thought is, by so much the more must the expression or embodiment of it be complex. And, when I considered that the total thought of the Absolute Being must be infinitely complex, I saw that only the infinite totality of forms and relations could give adequate embodiment or expression to that thought. So that men have not been wholly wrong in supposing there is something divine in the various forms of the world about them. Their error has consisted rather in assuming that some one form sufficed as an embodiment of the Divine. Nay, even here, they blindly sought after the fuller truth by assuming that each form was an embodied god. They felt that something divine was expressed in

every form, and they could not interpret this impression in any higher sense than that there were as many
gods as forms. Nay, I can not but think that the
ancient Egyptians felt this great truth and groped
about for its expression in their strange commingling
of forms as representative of Divinity.

But the identifying of the divine with the human
form was an immense advance over all previous
stages ; for the recognition of the quality of intelligence as a divine quality was thus insured. What
remained to be accomplished was that man should so
far clarify his own intelligence as to recognize the
fact of the infinite complexity of the divine Thought,
and thus to learn that not any single form or group of
forms can embody more than a single phase of that
Thought ; that, in fact, nothing less than the absolute total of Existence in all its infinitely varied forms
could be adequate as a means to the perfect utterance
of the perfect Intelligence.

XI.

Thus, while in one respect Absolute Being would
seem to be changelessly perfect as the ultimate Cause
forever manifested in all particular forms of existence,
such forms being themselves the ''effect'' or modes of
Absolute Being, in another respect it would seem to
be also absolutely conscious of itself in all its modes.

So that one can not avoid the conclusion, on the one hand, that there is no *reality* which is not a manifestation of Absolute Being ; and, on the other hand, that there is no minutest phase of reality which Absolute Being as Intelligence does not perfectly think or know. It is in this sense that "what is rational is actual, and what is actual is rational."[1]

And now because the same Absolute Being manifests itself and knows itself perfectly in its own manifestation, it seems impossible to avoid this further conclusion : that what the primal Energy, or First Cause, is *absolutely*, just that is what Man proves to be *relatively;* that is, a Being who is knowing-subject and known-object in perfect fusion. Thus, if man once thought of the divinities as having a human nature, his final discovery is that man himself is, in reality, possessed of the divine nature. And this is but the thought of primitive man unfolded into maturity.

It is thus that I was brought to what seemed to me the real solution of the problem of eternity in its concrete significance. Reference has already been made to the fact that space in its character of relation between bodies, and time in its character of relation between events, seem to be modes of existence both infinite and finite ; and, from the point of view now

---

[1] Hegel *Philosophie des Rechts*, Dritte Auflage, S. 17.

reached, they may be said to be the negative modes in which absolute Being unfolds itself in finite and thereforechanging forms. Apart from these finite forms there would then be no relation of coexistence, and apart from the changes occurring in those forms there would be no relation of succession ; that is, there would be neither space nor time in any other sense than that in which mere blank ''nothing'' can be said to have an existence.

Absolute Being, then, is not in space and time in the sense of being subject to them ; for they are but modes of the existence of Absolute Being. And, if Absolute Being can not be conceived apart from its modes, so neither can these modes be conceived apart from Absolute Being. Nor is it to be forgotten that the highest—that is, more adequate—modes of Intelligence are wholly independent of space and time.

And, further, since Absolute Being is unchangingly perfect, it is evident that it could never have been either more or less in its total Reality than it now is, and that it can never become other than it is ; for that is a necessary corollary from the persistence of Energy. And, as time is a condition of the changing, then Absolute Being as unchanging can not be conditioned by time. On the contrary, since all finite, changing things are but modes of Absolute Being, it is evident that time, as nothing more than a condition of the changing, is but a subordinate and vanishing

phase of the total creative Process.   For example,
much of what is still future to the child is already
past to the youth ; and the to-morrow of youth is the
yesterday of old age.   Past, present and future are all
merged into to-day by the coexistence of generations.
So the northern and southern hemispheres of our
planet are measurably complementary to one another
in seasons as well as in geometric form.   Summer
and winter, autumn and spring, are perpetual, when
we consider the earth as a whole.   And so in total
space there appear to be innumerable nebulæ realizing
serially all stages of advancement toward solar systems, and innumerable solar systems realizing serially
all possible stages of progress from the nebulous state
to the state of collapse into nebulæ again.   So that
every possible stage of evolution, from the most diffuse and simple to the most tense and complex, including organisms of every grade—nay, including
every grade of human development—we may legitimately conclude to be *present perpetually* in the total
range of the divine creative process.

And so I came to recognize that all conceivable
duration must be merged in the changeless NOW of
Absolute Being.   That is the *concrete Eternity*.[1]

---

[1] Cf. Spinoza, *Ethices*, Pars I. Def. VIII.   Per aeternitatem
intelligo ipsam existentiam, quatenus ex sola rei aeternae
definitione necessario sequi concipitur.

EXPLICATIO.—*Talis enim existentia, ut aeterna veritas,
sicut rei essentia concipitur, proptereaque per durationem aut
tempus explicari non potest, tametsi duratio principio et fine
carere concipiatur.*

And the recognition of this truth brought with it a sense of great peace and rest, for now I have no longer to think of the past or of the future of the Universe. I have only to think of the absolute, actual Totality of Existence—the infinitely rich *present*, in which past and future are absolutely merged. It is this Totality which endures, and apart from which eternity, which is but the mere form of the enduring, could have no meaning. God is fulfilled eternity, needing not to look beyond himself, but resting ever in the contemplation of his own infinite fullness and perfection. The divine Energy, self-active, self-sufficing, self-ordering, self-unfolding, rests ever in the unmixed joy of its eternal self-conservation.

XII.

And now, when I recur again to the ideas of space and time, it appears to me that the proper terms are : Space and Duration. These, as already remarked, are nothing else than modes of existence. On the one hand, as infinitely extended, they are modes of infinite existence. On the other hand, as infinitely divisible, they are modes of finite existence. And finite existence itself is but the multiform mode of infinite existence. Infinite existence is the continuous, or universal. Finite existence is the discrete, or particular. Continuous and discrete, universal and particular, are but complementary phases of the same absolute Totality.   Infinite existence is the power of which finite existences are the modes.

I observe, too, that, since this absolute, self-knowing Power is forever completely unfolded in its modes, and since these modes are thus the self-manifestation of the Power, then, since the modes are knowable, the Power itself must also be thus far knowable. And this conviction became only the clearer the more I dwelt upon the relation between the Power and its modes. Looking out at the stars on a specially clear night, I noted the differences in their brilliancy, and along with this the varying appearance of vacancy or of fullness in different parts of the heavens. At the same time, I recalled the fact that the apparent nearness or remoteness of any two stars to each other is no proof of their real proximity, but only of the fact that a line drawn through them and the earth approximates a straight line ; and it occurred to me that, though vast spaces seem blank even to the eye aided by the finest telescope, yet, if I were possessed of unlimited power to receive impressions of light, then I should see vast numbers of stars now wholly invisible from the earth. Nay, I should doubtless see them in such numbers as to fill the whole field of vision with light of varying degrees of intensity ; and not only so, but with such delicacy of visual power I could so far distinguish between degrees of light as to judge of the relative nearness or remoteness of the stars, and so behold what would appear to be a solid, shining dome broken into infinitely complex arches, with the farthest stars for keystones and the nearest stars for pendants. And this magnificent vision would be perpetually varying, not merely because of the swift movement of the sphere from which my observations must necessarily be taken, but also because of the perpetual movement of every single element in the fluid-solid dome.

But thus also there would be presented an absolute limit to the field of my direct perception ; and yet, assuredly, I could not then, any more than now, resist the conviction that beyond this limit space still extends infinitely, and that Absolute being is just as actual in every part of that space as in the part thus roofed in by stars to me. And now I reflect that, though my direct *perception* would thus be limited, yet to that higher mode of vision, consisting of Reason, the innumerable spheres that give significance to infinite space are in truth nothing else than prismatic lenses, through which the radiance of the Divine Thought is focused, and yet also dispersed into its myriad forms of beauty. Thus they prove to be the means, not of limiting, but rather of extending vision in its most adequate modes. So that, while in one respect the ultimate Power is ''unknowable,'' yet in a higher sense what prove to be impassable limits to the less adequate modes of knowledge prove also to

be veritable means to the further extension of knowledge in its more adequate modes ; whence the ultimate Power is seen to be absolutely knowable. For
to think truly is but to trace the "fixed order" or
method of the ultimate Power as that Power manifests itself in the universe. In a word, to think truly
is to trace out progressively the eternal thought of
God.

XIII.

And thus once more do I find that in the very fact of
my being as a thinking unit I am possessed of a divine
nature. My chief, my sole, mission is to think the
divine thought with ever-increasing adequacy and
clearness, and to conform my life thereto. That is
living the divine life. That is the progressive realization of immortality. That is to bring freedom into
increasingly rich reality in my own existence. And
it *is* the realization of immortality, because as a thinking unit I belong to the same type of being as the ultimate, self-knowing Power ; and since I can conceive
of no absolute limit to the possible development of
that type within my own individual life, but rather
can only regard myself as being possessed of an infinite nature, which *as mine* it is my own natural destiny to fulfil, then' clearly I can not cease to exist as
an individual. For the perfect fulfillment of this in-

finite typical nature on my part can be accomplished in no less than infinite duration.

But I also note that while my progressive development involves time as a mode of my existence, yet the more adequately I realize the divine nature in my own individuality, by so much the more truly do I become superior to the limitations of time, and thus experience some semblance of the divine repose and peace of Eternity.

The way leading man to God then is not a mere path amid the stars through boundless space. It is rather the "way of the Spirit," the method by which the divine ideal or Type is to become progressively unfolded into reality in the individual soul. It is the way of escape from the vacuity of mere initial existence, the way out of the primitive Eden, with its walls and its gates and its insoluble contradictions, the way out of the uncertainties, the anxieties, the weariness and the terrors of Time into the clear assurance, the self-poised maturity, the invigorating self-activity, the divine repose and joy of Eternity. The way by which man approaches the Divine is the way by which man becomes divine.

And so I came at length to see that the one possible way for me to escape from the contradictions of endless time—the infinitely stretched out eternity—consists in the gradual expansion of my life so as more and more to fulfill the form of the infinitely present, concrete Eternity, whose essence is the Divine Life—God in me and I in God.